PRAISE FOR

Behind The Hedge

“I just finished reading *Behind the Hedge* in one sitting and was
captured by the powerf
should be required cau
teachers, and everyone

“This is my 20th ye
I just finished readi
years ago?! If only I
a magnificent accou
interaction with boa
ordered 3 more cop
and to my staff until
book. Thanks for w

“This is a fascinatin
good-intentioned p
tragic ending keeps y
member of an edu
of any non-profit o
pitfalls that can so e
a practicing attorney
have presented this

"This book truly captures the depth of pain and hurt I felt from being unceremoniously kicked out of a treatment center for women I helped found. It doesn't happen only in private schools!"

Arlyn Rudolph
Palm Springs, CA

"I loved reading *Behind the Hedge* and have talked about it with a number of people. Your book felt very real to me."

Deanne Benson
Head of School
Lesley Ellis School, MA

"Among other things, *Behind the Hedge* should be required reading for all heads of schools and boards of trustees. It is a reminder of the importance of understanding the subtleties of school leadership."

Matthew Hanly
Head of School
Oregon Episcopal School, OR

"As a retired school teacher, this book was a real page-turner for me. Having taught in both private and public schools, I have seen enough of the truly rewarding aspect of teaching, as well as the politics and personality conflicts that can be involved, to really appreciate the traumatizing situation explored here. Every school teacher and, especially, every school administrator would gain from reading this book."

Marion B. Eriksen
Delta, CO

Behind the Hedge

2nd Edition

Behind the Hedge

2nd Edition

a corruption of time, talent & treasure

Stanley Cummings

ISBN: Hardcover 978-1-4363-3120-3
Softcover 978-1-4363-3119-7

This book was printed in the United States of America.

To order additional copies of this book, contact:
Xlibris Corporation
1-888-795-4274
www.Xlibris.com
Orders@Xlibris.com
39814
10 9 8 7 6 5 4 3

♠

Dedication

Mom and Dad

whose commitment of time,
talent and treasure was without limits

Introduction

In my second year as a trustee on the board of Florence Bruce Seminary, I watched with my colleagues while Dr. Tom Whitman, head of school for less than ten months, defended himself. I was shaken to the core by what I heard. Led to believe by a single communication from our executive committee that he had somehow critically failed in his responsibilities, I was unprepared for his blow-by-blow description of events.

In the aftermath, I saw the impact of a violent act perpetrated by the board of trustees on a fine leader and his wife, along with a small cadre of administrators and faculty. The anguish, humiliation, and confusion they experienced were palpable to many of us.

The impact on Florence Bruce Seminary was even more devastating. Tom, his wife and the others did grieve for a while, but in time they established new connections and went on with their lives. The changes I saw in the people who remained, however, convinced me that something truly horrible had taken place that powerfully impacted the lives of principals and bystanders alike. Many left. Others continued to struggle with the consequences of what had taken place, while a community that once esteemed a Florence Bruce education sent too many of its daughters off to other classrooms.

Ten million American citizens serve on the boards of 860,000 nonprofit organizations that offer services spanning a diverse spectrum of missions: from schools, universities and churches to food banks, environmental advocacy groups and health care. Organizations classified by the IRS designation 501(c)3 are central to modern American society. Mostly they complement the private and public sectors by balancing the harsher side of government and big business, thereby creating a caring, compassionate environment and safeguarding the values of American society and of the American tradition.

The members of these boards are volunteers elected or appointed by their fellows to ensure that the mission of the organization is carried out. Serving on the board of a nonprofit organization can yield great personal satisfaction. It is an opportunity to contribute time, talent, and oftentimes treasure to a meaningful cause. It is also a responsibility that demands teamwork, attention and, especially, accountability.

The men and women who volunteer to serve on the boards of these organizations are entrusted with a great responsibility. That responsibility occasionally overwhelms those called to discharge it. Effective boards and board members add significant value to their organizations, while ineffective boards drain organizational energy and may do real harm to the people and the organizations they purport to serve.

This is the story of one such nonprofit board of which I was a member. It is a story that needs to be read, digested and internalized by those ten million of us who, like me, serve their communities as directors on nonprofit boards. Unfortunately, stories similar to this one play themselves out again and again, not only in private schools such as Florence Bruce Seminary, but in the many nonprofit organizations of every opinion, creed and denomination that shoulder the hard work of making our lives more human. If this recitation saves just one of these from the anguish of a similar fate, it will have been worth the effort.

Acknowledgments

Work in nonprofit organizations has been my professional calling for thirty-five years. Always, it seems, I have served at the bidding of a board of directors—five different organizations, including two that specialized in outdoor education, one private school, and one advocating environmental causes. At the same time, I have served on the boards of more than two-dozen nonprofit organizations, guiding a chief executive and being guided by him or her as we set out together to fulfill the mission.

In all this time, I have shared leadership responsibilities with about two hundred directors, including the very best as well as the very worst. The best of them guided and shaped the organizations we served for the better. The worst of them guided also, but not in ways that bestowed a benefit. Their names are better left unspoken, but for those whose "time, talent and treasure" served in positive ways to improve the lives of their fellow citizens through the organizations they commanded, I offer acknowledgment.

To Claud Sympson, a quintessential gentleman, a personal mentor, and a saint whose charm and grace impacted all who knew him—every board should have one like him; Charlie Houston, an old man who, in my youth, taught me passion for the mission; Bill Steel and Ralph Sabin, young men whose friendship was priceless during perilous times; Anne Schneider, who had a vision and made it real; Alice Culver, whose commitment was deeper than the ocean she loved; Robert Gerard and Tim MacMahon, both stalwart givers who made their presence felt; Judy Curreri, her intelligence crackled and her principles were of the highest order; Paul Hamilton, for all his flaws, he was a giant; Dennis Eversole and Terry Noonan, big men who wielded their influence with an unassuming demeanor; John Dravinski, who returned my favor a hundred fold and more; Tom Knapp, who brought enthusiasm and money and leveraged it; Bob McKnight, who committed himself and then his company; Lew Overholt, for whom time and talent were strengths; and Harold Kaufman, who taught me how to laugh and to absorb the slings and arrows.

To Rex Bates, Peter Morkill, Helena Lankton, Ron Leighton, the Rt. Rev. Vincent P. Warner, Betsy Greenman, Loren Anderson, Shirley Bushnell, Chuck Granoski, Laure Nichols and Steve Robinson, who all stood with me when I needed them most.

To Dick Ribble, who was a richer man than he thought and to Brad Cheney and John Connelly—no one knew the game better than they.

To Martha Curwin, Sylvia Sommers, Kari Rainer and Maxine Strom—their selfless and unassuming devotion to the mission of service was beyond compare.

No acknowledgment would be complete without mention of my wife Sigrid. The writing of a book is no walk in the woods, no casual stroll to the grocery store. It is a time-consuming, energy-depleting, head-banging, soul-wrenching exercise fraught with frustration, doubt and long periods of self-induced despair and isolation—she shared its torment with me or I would not have finished.

To my sister Cappy, who was always the better writer, and to my brother Bruce, who read my first draft and convinced me in his enthusiasm that I had something to say. To my daughter Tarla, who is the wind beneath my wings, and to my daughter Jennifer, of whom I am so very proud. Like her Dad, she perseveres no matter the obstacles. This book is really for them.

I also owe a debt of gratitude to my first edition editor Joe Lubow and to my second edition editor Shelly Randall, who did their best to tame my fractured phrasing, and to Margaret Loos, who designed the cover and turned my manuscript into a *book.*

S. Cummings

CHAPTER I

Best of Intentions

♠

Change is not a threat. It's an opportunity.[1]

Her stride made it clear she was not a woman to be trifled with. She covered the last fifty yards to her late-model Volvo and quickly unlocked the driver's-side door with her key. She didn't even carry the electronic doorlock in her purse. A metal key was solid in her hand. Its mechanical connection to the lock and the door was direct—uncomplicated—and she liked that.

Phyllis Killam was a woman who enjoyed being in charge. Now in her late forties and taking on a mature woman's cylindrical shape, she seemed larger than her five-foot, five-inch frame standing on one-inch heels. Her brown hair, its flecks of gray dyed to their original color, was held back away from her face in a controlled wave. She wore a brown business suit with a skirt that came to just below the knee and a matching blazer over a white oxford cloth shirt. While other women of her size and weight might begin showing their age with shorter, rocking steps, Phyllis still demonstrated an athletic grace that came from a youth spent in active sports, and she strode

---

[1] Drucker, Peter F. *Managing the Non-Profit Organization: Principles and Practices.* New York: HarperCollins Publishers, 1992, p. 11.

forward with purpose, taking each step as far as her skirt would comfortably allow.

She had a ready laugh and a distinctive, though not unpleasant, voice with just a hint of Southern influence. It stood out in a crowded room and commanded attention; interruptions would clearly not be tolerated. It moved through a sentence deliberately, enunciating each word, and when it reached a period it stopped and stepped back as if to say, "Okay, now I'm finished and you can talk."

Phyllis laid her purse and board meeting notes on the passenger seat and turned the key in the ignition. The engine came to life with a soft purr, and she pulled into traffic for the commute home suffused with feelings of fulfillment and of a job well done. She was nearing the end of her two-year tenure as president of the board of trustees of Florence Bruce Seminary, a boarding school for girls in the suburbs of historic Portsmouth, New Hampshire, and she had much to be proud of.

It had not been an easy tenure. John Sanford, just past 60 and headmaster of Florence Bruce, was retiring, which meant a search had to be carried out to find his replacement. The process had been long and difficult. Moreover, John's retirement was not entirely voluntary and had required delicate orchestration; that had been her first task. A search firm had then been hired to assist in finding a new head, a search committee had been appointed to review candidates for the position, and the tedious and lengthy process had culminated in two days of on-site interviews with each of the three finalists.

Now it was over, except for the celebrating. The board's choice for a new head had been approved minutes before, and the search committee head was likely making the call at this very minute to confirm his acceptance. It crossed her mind that perhaps she should be concerned that he might refuse, but she dismissed the thought. Phyllis considered herself to be a good judge of people, and she knew this one would not turn them down.

Dr. Thomas R. Whitman had not been her first choice, but the female candidate she preferred, a headmistress from a nearby school, interviewed so poorly there was little Phyllis could do. And the third finalist, a male with a too-obviously-bored wife, was stiff and formal—not at all suited to the warm, nurturing, friendly environment of Florence Bruce Seminary.

Tom Whitman was a good choice to lead the seminary, and his wife would be a wonderful addition to the school. Although Tom was older than Phyllis by almost a decade, he didn't look it, and he had a youthful naïvety about him . . . that appealed to her. She still had more than six months until her term was officially over, so there would be more opportunities to interact with him in her official role. It was something she looked forward to.

Her mind began a replay of her years with John Sanford. This was her sixth year on the board and it was John's eighteenth year as headmaster. Her twin girls were now in eighth grade and her older daughter was a sophomore. She had been asked to join the board two years after her family moved to town and enrolled the twins in Kindergarten.

Phyllis and her husband Andrew were both lawyers: she an on-again, off-again corporate litigator and Andrew Watson (for professional purposes, they both kept their own names) a district attorney. She herself was the product of an all-girls independent school and felt fortunate to have ready access to a similar school for her children. When John Sanford had asked Phyllis to serve on the board, that had been the start of a long and rewarding relationship for them both.[2]

John was there to console her when her mother took ill, and they spent many more hours in his office talking about life, kids and elderly parents than they did discussing school business. John was wonderfully attentive. She wasn't at all attracted to him romantically, but their relationship was about as close as it could be without being sexual. Andrew, her husband, was a good man and she certainly loved him, but he was also distant and often consumed by his work. John was caring, gentle and accessible. The school became the family's home; when Phyllis wasn't at work, she and her children were at Florence Bruce.

Three years ago, when John's wife Joan had begun showing signs of the cancer that would eventually claim her life, he had come to Phyllis

---

[2] John also recruited me to join the board. Most nonprofit heads take an active role in the selection of new trustees or directors. With a dynamic and positive relationship between them so critical to the organization, a personal connection between a trustee and head is to be encouraged.

for advice. The early diagnosis was inconclusive, and she urged him to get a second opinion—even made the call for him when he wavered out of fear of what it might foretell. When the cancer diagnosis was confirmed, she comforted him as the tears poured out.

As the disease progressed, Joan was confined to the Ahlborn House, a stately, brick two-story provided by the school for its headmaster. Phyllis lobbied the board to spend $26,000 to reimburse John for the experimental chemotherapy treatments not covered by the school's insurance. The motion passed.

When Joan fell ill, Phyllis had insisted that John get help running the school. His health had been declining for several years—he had suffered a mild heart attack a year earlier—and this was interfering with his ability to keep up with the job. The solution was to hire an assistant to free John from the more mundane chores demanded of a headmaster. That, too, had been Phyllis' idea. Although not yet board president, she wielded considerable influence over her peers. She had hoped the new assistant head, Roland Guyotte, would be able to deflect some of the criticism that was beginning to surface over John's absences.

The criticism was not overt, ever. After all, John had done marvelous things for the school, and both he and Joan were family. Now, in their time of need, the least that could be done was to be as supportive as possible, even if that meant overlooking some things. But the culture of solidarity could not stop a feeling of unease creeping over Florence Bruce Seminary that some truly important things were being neglected. John was away from the school far too much—sometimes for days at a time, sometimes for only a few hours, but at critical instances. He needed to care for Joan; he needed to attend conferences where he was chairing a committee or serving on a board; he needed time for himself. Even when John was present, his mental energies often seemed to be directed elsewhere.

Then Phyllis was elected by her peers to lead the board of trustees. It wasn't so much that she was elected as anointed. John had asked her to do it. It was her turn to do it. Everyone expected her to do it. When the nominating committee finished its report recommending that she be elected, the outgoing chair simply handed her the gavel, to a round of applause. Someone suggested they really ought to vote, but no one else saw any point to it, so no vote was taken, and the minutes reported her election was unanimous.

As president of the board, she also chaired the executive committee, which met between regular board meetings and was comprised of the board's officers—five in all—as well as the headmaster as a non-voting member. It was at an early meeting of this committee that Phyllis began to see clearly what was to become her mission. The proposal on the table was a recommendation to launch a capital campaign—the Campaign for Florence Bruce—to raise $7 million for construction of a new wing. John was at his best, laughing uproariously at his own jokes, cajoling recalcitrant trustees, backslapping as he circled the table while leading the discussion.

The committee was tackling some serious issues. A previous capital campaign to fund the same new construction had ended badly two years earlier. While the target was reached, pressing needs for a new roof on the existing building, a structural retrofit to meet building codes, and a sprinkler system had drained away most of the funds. The executive committee knew there were still disgruntled contributors who would be reluctant to contribute again until the circumstances of the earlier campaign were better understood. The school's accounting system was a mishmash of overlapping funds and accounts that no one seemed to be able to make much sense of. There was not even a clear understanding of how much money remained in the bank from the previous campaign. Finally, the design for the new wing had not been revisited for over five years and questions arose as to whether the costs originally projected, even updated for inflation, were still accurate.

Throughout the debate, John remained undaunted and steadfastly upbeat, and no one on the committee mounted a challenge, even a mild one. He didn't have all the answers, but the school needed to go forward. Anyone could see that. Disgruntled contributors were discounted—there would always be a few unhappy patrons. And besides, that was being addressed by a new hire in the development department whose job description included donor relations.

Phyllis was bothered mostly by John's dismissal of the accounting issues. She had an astute mind and had been around long enough to know the system. She knew it was hopelessly confused. But John's main point was not to be denied. Hadn't they always paid the bills and ended each year in the black? He blustered his way through the same explanation of the various funds and accounts that she had heard before. His manner, if not his words, left the distinct impression that if you did not now understand the explanation, numbers must not be your strong suit. But Phyllis was not fooled. She knew he was all bluff. Even for his faults she loved him and lent him her support.

The recommendation to launch the capital campaign passed, but Phyllis realized deep in her soul that John's house of cards would eventually fall, and she vowed she would not let her friend go down with it. In the ensuing weeks, she met with John almost daily. Sometimes it was only to express empathy for his suffering; sometimes it was to discuss her children's progress. Occasionally, she interjected questions about the future and John's plans for it. He had none, and the subject never stuck.

Joan's illness ultimately would be fatal, of that she was sure, but John was not ready to consider, much less accept, that conclusion. Instead she suggested that he needed more time to devote to caring for Joan and attending to his own needs. He was resistant. But slowly and almost imperceptibly over a period of months, she crafted a scenario by which John might be guided to depart Florence Bruce financially secure and with his dignity intact.

That July, the board announced that Florence Bruce Seminary had ended the fiscal year with a $61,000 surplus in the operating fund. At the next board meeting, Phyllis recommended they give John a $50,000 bonus. She had already shopped the idea around to the various members of the executive committee. Joan's illness was costing the couple dearly, she explained to them. Even though the school provided excellent health benefits, there was now the need for daily home care and specialized services that exceeded what insurance would cover. Phyllis often came back to the notion that the bonus would come from "surplus." They didn't know they had it until after the year was over—and they wouldn't miss it if they gave it to him. Her *coup de grace* to potential naysayers emanated from her compassion for the man. "It's the least we can do," she scornfully implored, "for a member of our family who has done so much for all of us." As if to do otherwise would be, at best, uncharitable.

In the end, Phyllis prevailed with the executive committee. There were questions about whether a cash bonus to John was the "best" use for the money. Another question arose about the legality of it, but a quick call to the school's attorney confirmed that the board could do pretty much what it wanted. Finally, there was a troubling question about how the funds might otherwise be used for the benefit of the students. No one came forward with a compelling educational use for the money, and the questioner abandoned the question.

Once she was sure she had consensus from the executive committee, Phyllis called the rest of the board to tell them what she wanted to do. They would take a vote at the September board meeting, she explained, but it was to be a *pro forma* vote. "The action," she said, "is already approved."[3]

On the day of the board meeting, she orchestrated John's presence in the room when the motion was made and the vote taken. She made a short speech that focused on their confidence in his leadership and their appreciation for his guidance. John was taken completely by surprise and afterwards, in private, they embraced, and she could feel him shaking with the intensity of his gratitude.

In the months that followed, she continued to question John gently about his future. One day, she threw the word "retirement" into her patter to test his reaction. A shadow seemed to flicker momentarily, but Phyllis couldn't tell if he was reacting to what she had said or if she was just looking too hard. She needed to probe deeper.

She invited him to join her for lunch at the Gables, an upscale restaurant on historic Market Square. When they were seated, Phyllis ordered a glass of chardonnay and invited him to join her. John hesitated briefly—he would be returning to the office afterwards—before accepting. There was the usual chitchat about kids and Joan. They discussed the capital campaign, which was getting ready to kick off its leadership phase. Problems existed in public relations and a prized math teacher was leaving after the holidays.

When she thought the timing was right, Phyllis launched into a story about her father who had retired the previous year from his own medical practice in an urban hospital. She effused over his newfound happiness in life, she praised him for his foresight and timing, and she made a point of telling John that her father had wisely chosen retirement at a high point in his career and before new restrictions kicked in that would have reduced his pension.

---

[3] Like the others, I voted in favor of the bonus. I recall thinking that it was a lot of money when Phyllis called, but since she said that it was already approved, I didn't dwell on it.

"Have you thought about when you might retire?" She dropped the bomb casually so as not to spook the intended target.

"No, not really. I suppose I should start thinking about it in a couple more years."

She was actually surprised by the response, even though she knew him well enough to have anticipated the answer. John was sixty years old, an age at which most men have carefully crafted their retirement and are eagerly anticipating its arrival. For John, however, Florence Bruce Seminary was his life. Physically, emotionally, spiritually, the school was how he identified himself. It nurtured him as he nurtured it. He could no more imagine leaving the school as he could imagine disowning the daughter who had graduated from it four years earlier.

Phyllis knew this and went on to paint in the scenario. "You'd want to protect yourself financially, of course," she began. "At least a year's salary." She knew that preparations for retirement and replacement of a venerated headmaster like John Sanford were extremely complex; John knew it, too. So she questioned, but let him provide the answers.

"How far ahead of actual retirement does a headmaster make the announcement?" Answer: About eighteen months.

"How does a school go about replacing a head?" Answer: It forms a committee and hires a consultant to assist.

"Where does the replacement come from?" Answer: A national search is conducted.

The conversation ended, but Phyllis knew she had planted the seed. A few days later, she watered it. It was the last day of school before the Thanksgiving recess. She saw John holding court in the hallway with a group of fourth-grade students, teasing them by mispronouncing their names and pretending he didn't know them. They loved it, and she marveled at the ease with which he handled people of all ages.

Approaching the group from the side, she said, "It's a sign he's getting older. Memory, you know, is the first thing to go." They giggled. Turning to John, she chided, "Do you need any help remembering who they are?" And when she had his attention, she whispered, "I need to talk to you confidentially."

An hour later they were in his office with the door closed. "You know, John, I've been thinking," Phyllis began. "I have one term left as president of the board, and then I'll have to step down. I'll also be termed out and will be off the board. After our conversation over lunch, I'm worried about you. You don't have that many years left before retirement, and you need to think about the transition and securing yourself financially. I can help now, but after I leave you can't be sure that others will be thinking along the same lines."

She paused to test his reaction. John didn't comment, but he was clearly listening, so she went on, "Here's what I think. You should be sure you retire with eighteen months of full salary and benefits. That will give you plenty of time to think about what you want to do next. If you think retirement is on the horizon, this might be the time to begin setting things in motion. After all, even if you announced now, you'd have another year after this one when you would still be headmaster, and I'd still be on the board to help you."

John and Phyllis had known each other a long time, and their relationship was as remarkable for its depth as for its length in years. John knew what his friend was proposing, and he knew that she was right. Eighteen months of full salary and benefits, in addition to the substantial pension he had accumulated, was more than generous—even in the private school arena, which was known for taking care of its leadership.[4] He knew that he would be hard-pressed to craft such a deal once Phyllis left. At a deeper level, certainly below that of real consciousness, John also knew that he was nearing the end. While he absolutely refused any notion that he was not operating at the top of his game, he could not escape the simple actuarial mathematics of old age.

The seed had been sown and watered and now began to take root. In April, as Phyllis' first year as president was coming to an end, John Sanford publicly announced his retirement effective the end of the following academic year. That kicked off a furious round

---

[4] John's compensation package included an annual salary of $125,000, a matching pension plan, a house (including all utilities and maintenance), a car, gas, memberships in two private clubs, and an unlimited expense account. The value of this package was more than double that of the compensation of next-highest paid employee at Florence Bruce. While not exorbitant by independent school standards, it far exceeded the compensation for chief executives in most nonprofit service organizations of comparable size.

of interviewing before school let out in June to find a consultant. Markham Nunlist, representing a prestigious Boston search firm, was retained. Committee work continued into the fall to review applicant files. It all culminated today in the selection of Dr. Tom Whitman as the next headmaster of Florence Bruce Seminary.

As Phyllis pulled into her garage, she gave herself a mental pat on the back. She had orchestrated every important aspect of the events leading up to this day. She had quieted the criticism and redirected its energy. As a result, the school was alive with anticipation. But, most of all, she had saved her friend, and it was this last acknowledgment that filled up her heart and brimmed her eyes with tears.

Phyllis checked the clock. It was almost 6:00 PM. She called up the stairs to see who was at home. Andrew would be out, she knew. The twins answered. Their sister Jennifer was at choir practice and wouldn't be home until late. She picked up the phone to order Chinese delivered for three: kung pow chicken, sizzling rice soup, mushu pork and teriyaki beef sticks—the twins' favorite. There would be some left over if the others came home hungry.

CHAPTER II

The School

♠

> The school's mission lives daily in the life of the school—within and beyond its walls . . . . Trustees need to be ever vigilant in their role as keepers of the mission.[1]

At the latitude of Portsmouth, in the Granite State of New Hampshire, it is quite dark by 6:00 PM in the middle of November. While a delivery boy from the Szechwan Palace searched the darkening gloom for the Killam house, the double doors at Florence Bruce Seminary opened, and the first half-dozen of what would soon grow to about sixty adolescent girls, laughing and giggling, poured through the opening into Kittery Dining Hall. Half were in pajamas, since no one would be allowed to leave the building for the rest of the evening. For all but the seniors and a few honors students, an obligatory two-hour study hall would follow dinner. Therefore, comfort was the overriding consideration.

The menu tacked to the bulletin board indicated the oft-disparaged "yellow" meal of chicken nuggets, French fries and corn. Most would

---

[1] DeKuyper, Mary Hundley. *Trustee Handbook: A Guide to Effective Governance for Independent School Boards*. Washington, DC: National Association of Independent Schools, 1998, p. 33.

take generous helpings, but a few would bypass the main serving line and head straight to the salad bar for tofu and salad fixings. While there were a few vegans sprinkled among the students and faculty, veganism was more often a topic of conversation than commitment to a way of life.

Food was served cafeteria-style. The line, never more than eight girls in length, grew at its origin with newly arriving students as those carrying trays with full plates left at the other end. Within fifteen minutes, service was done except for a steady stream of traffic back and forth from the condiment tray, the drink machine or the salad bar. Students were dispersed around the room in groups of five and six, seldom pushing the tables of ten to their capacity.

The mix of students was unusual for any school. About one-third were of Asian descent: Chinese, Thai, Japanese, and Korean predominated. Of course, the majority were Caucasian. The rest presented a mélange of skin tones ranging through many shades of brown to near-black due to three residents of African heritage. These diners were the Florence Bruce boarders, girls who lived at the school and by whose presence the Seminary achieved the enviable qualities of being a home as much as a school. Except for a group of about a half-dozen Asian students who struggled with the language and ate and kept together, the others mixed well and enjoyed each other's company.

There were no boys. This was, after all, an all-girls school and had been so for over two hundred years. This fact was evident to anyone accustomed to seeing large numbers of young women content in their own company. Dress was casual to the extreme. Very few sported any makeup at all. Hair was freshly washed, wispy, tousled and mostly uncombed and unbrushed with nary a sign anywhere of curlers, creating an appearance consistent with a relaxed, unpretentious group of young women simply being themselves.

At a table near the door sat a group of faculty or, more precisely, resident advisors who lived in the dorms with the students and provided round-the-clock supervision. Several of them were also members of the teaching faculty. Buster Jolley, a fifth-grade teacher, was there with his wife Cornelia, known only as Corny, and their ten-year-old daughter Colleen, who also attended the school. Corny had been a boarder, Class of '78 and was currently the drama coach. She had spent more than half her life within the confines of the old seminary.

It was not at all unusual to find individuals and families crossing more than one, and sometimes several, of the school's four major constituencies: students, parents, alumnae and faculty. Many parents were also alums, and the chain would go back through several generations. A fair number of the faculty had attended the school as youngsters. Now their daughters were enrolled.

Also sitting at the faculty table were Ellen Stein, a coach and chair of the history department, and Leigh Davis, a solid, substantial, outgoing woman whom the girls adored. Leigh, too, was an alumna but worked outside the school, trading evening duties in return for her on-campus housing. Leigh was rumored to be gay, but if so inclined, she was careful to keep it private. There had never been an indication of anything untoward in her behavior.

Lesbianism, or rather the assumption of lesbianism, was something the school often battled. It was rumored that Florence Bruce Seminary was a haven for lesbians, which was not helped by two students of that persuasion who had attended a couple of years earlier and been observed walking the neighborhood in romantic oblivion. But the students of Florence Bruce were, in truth, probably no more or less atypical in their sexual orientation than students at co-ed schools.

The steady hum of voices filled the hall. Hardly had the meal service ended when Leigh interrupted conversation. "Ladies, may I have your attention? This evening Mr. Jolley and Ms. Stein will be your floor proctors. Please be good to them, and I'm sure they will be good to you." Around the room, a halfhearted ripple of laughter followed her remark.

"I'm sure none of you need to be reminded that there will be a study hall in the library tonight beginning at 7:00. Attendance will be taken, so unless you received 'honors' last semester, be there!"

Leigh finished her comments with an announcement of some changes in the schedule for the next day and another concerning a drive to raise money for library books. Each girl was required to sell at least five tubs of cookie dough. From the gross receipts, half went to the supplier of the uncooked confection while the library got the other half. With limited access to sympathetic markets or a means for distribution, the boarding girls appealed to their far-away parents for help. The cookie dough thus purchased stacked up in dorm rooms, never leaving campus. What the students didn't consume, give away or wisely discard was swept out six months later with the year's detritus by the summer cleaning staff.

Following Leigh's announcements, an astute freshman raised her hand. "Is it okay if we just donate the money the library would get from the cookie dough and not have to sell any?"

Leigh's gentle reprimand about school spirit and team building was correctly interpreted as "No."

A junior announced a meeting of the student council, and dinner was over. Within minutes Kittery Hall was empty. It was 6:30 PM. Dinner had lasted one-half hour from start to finish.

Florence Bruce Seminary sits on a bluff overlooking the picturesque Piscataqua River at the edge of the Heights, an upscale neighborhood in the seaport city of Portsmouth, New Hampshire. Founded in 1784 by Guy Victor Bruce in the Episcopal tradition and named for his daughter, the school embraces 450 students ranging from barely five to eighteen years of age. Upper School, which includes all the boarders, begins in the ninth grade. Middle School includes sixth, seventh and eighth. Lower School encompasses Kindergarten through fifth grade.

Kittery Hall, where the girls ate, was constructed in the 1920s and provides 160 seats. Even when all the boarders are present, dinners seem sparsely attended—except when the dinners are formal and the entire Upper School—boarders and day students alike—are required to attend. These events occur about four times a year and are announced well in advance.

In the early years, almost all dinners were served according to prescribed rules of dress and conduct, but these, as well as many other features of the school, have been "modernized." Still, formal dinners are eagerly anticipated for their pageantry—Florence Bruce Seminary cherishes pageantry—and because the quality of the food is appreciably improved from the usual fare.

During John Sanford's tenure, formal dinners began in the Bainbridge Room, where faculty and seniors gathered for wine (for the former) and sparkling cider (for the latter). The dress code for the male faculty required coats and ties. Ladies wore cocktail dresses while students put on their best uniforms.

John was at his best at these occasions. He was never without a joke or a story. He had been at the school so long that he could play back the years like the keys on a piano—dancing about, picking out remembrances, touching on events or people and adding conversational tidbits that only a headmaster would be privy to. He was usually the center of these pre-dinner gatherings. Veterans of the school knew how to prompt him for the best stories and then interject at just the right time with their own variations to enhance the overall effect. A newcomer could not help but be impressed by the sense of camaraderie that infused these gatherings.

Promptly at 6:00 PM, Mrs. Clayworth, director of house, would signal that the meal was ready. John would erupt in a huge guffaw, throw his arms around his ample middle and announce in his booming baritone to the gathered throng, "Food's hot!" Much to Mrs. Clayworth's dismay, no formal dinner was ever truly formal when John Sanford was in residence. Mrs. Clayworth was English only by marriage, but she had adopted her husband's British accent, and sometime in her past—a former reincarnation as hand servant to the Queen was a credible explanation—Mrs. Clayworth had embraced and absorbed into her soul the characteristics of English gentry. Erect, impeccably groomed and proper to the extreme, Mrs. Clayworth was John's antithesis.

Students followed faculty by class, and faculty followed the headmaster into Kittery Hall. Sixteen circular tables set for ten filled the long rectangular room, and at the far end the head table stood in a slightly recessed alcove of its own. Colorful, holiday-themed centerpieces festooned the tables and often overflowed onto the walls, serving tables and window ledges. Mrs. Clayworth and her staff took great pride in these events and always extended themselves with fresh creativity, much to the delight of those who participated.

John led the way to the tables, taking his accustomed place at the head table while attendant faculty distributed themselves around the room in their assigned seats. Well before the dinner, a seating chart was hung outside the great double doors, containing the names of all who were expected. The posting of this document was greeted with some excitement as friends looked for each other's names and the names of favorite faculty to whose table they hoped to be assigned. There was also some degree of trepidation accompanying this posting, because sooner or later every girl was placed at the head table where she might find herself forced to relive some past indiscretion. John's memory was prodigious, and embellishment came as naturally to him as eating itself.

Kittery Hall was a perfect setting for these dinners. Stout beams buttressed at the sides with thick timbers carried the weight of the high ceiling. Six squared columns, fluted on the corners with handcrafted scrolls and ornate moldings, arose at intervals around the room, adding their load-bearing capability. Wainscoting, inset with trefoil flowers, extended around the perimeter of the room, interspersed here and there with a door or an ancient steam radiator that hissed and banged throughout the winter months. Above the wainscoting, an abundance of tall, leaded-glass windows looked out onto pastoral scenes, the specifics of which depended upon the season and the viewer's orientation: fresh-mown grass in spring and summer or a blanket of newly fallen snow in winter. The arched, colonnaded Copeland Commons was visible from the head table, while another window offered views of a lofty American elm planted by a pioneering alumna and a grove of poplar trees, through which the white lines of a manicured soccer field could be glimpsed.

Kittery Hall was a favorite gathering place that epitomized the very soul of Florence Bruce Seminary. More than one young lady fantasized a romantic wedding in Hanley Chapel and a reception in the tradition-bound elegance of Kittery Hall—a fantasy that was realized more often than not as, weekend after weekend, former students (and sometimes the children of former students) returned with family and friends to take their wedding vows. No event in Kittery Hall so inflamed these dreamy fantasies as much as a formal dinner followed by a two-hour required study hall in the steamy bosom of the library.

Even John was aware of the impact of these formal dinners and did his best to dignify the proceedings—although not without considerable effort. Students and faculty stood by their chairs until John properly graced the affair with well-chosen words from Episcopal liturgy. He did not deviate from expectations at these occasions, understanding that to do otherwise might imperil the latitude extended to him for the free expression of his boisterous nature.

Following grace, the assembled body seated itself and two servers from each table, whose time in the rotation had arrived, scooted off to the kitchen to receive the food, which was served family-style. Platters of food were passed counter-clockwise, received in the left hand for dishing out a personal portion and passed through the right hand to the next person. Tables were set with two of everything and a third spoon or fork at the top of the plate, depending upon the requirements for dessert. No one ate until the headmaster lifted his fork—the signal for the meal to begin. No one left the dining room without being excused.

Following dinner, the headmaster invited the assembly outside Kittery Hall to the reception area, where the kitchen staff served coffee and tea in demitasse cups with little demitasse spoons. One or two students were picked to entertain on these occasions, and after a spirited violin or piano rendition from the works of the masters, the girls dispersed to the library for study hall or to the waiting cars of parents for the ride home.

CHAPTER III

Formal Introductions

♠

Board members who help to create a spirit of joy and enthusiasm are a gift to any team.[1]

As Phyllis strode up the brick walkway to the school, she happened to glance up at the large granite block framed by red brick over the doorway. "Florence Bruce Seminary, 1784" was engraved deeply into the granite lintel. Smaller granite blocks, tightly fitted, formed an arch below the name. Block letters with ornamental serifs spelled out, "TRUTH WITHOUT FEAR." At one time, the words must have stood out in bold proclamation, but now the blocks and their letters were obscured by the passage of time—a blurring of lines and corners overlaid with a patina of mottled color.

The sun was shining brightly between intermittent, puffy clouds, and the sidewalks were glistening from a fresh passing rain. The air was cold and crisp. Fall was well along, with winter beckoning. A smattering of leaves, golden and brown with some dark reds mixed in clung to branches and stood stark against the skyline like lonely sentinels. Their fallen companions that had not been scooped up

---

[1] Lakey, Berit M. *Nonprofit Governance: Steering Your Organization with Authority and Accountability*. Washington, DC: BoardSource, 2000, p. 35.

and discarded lay in semi-compressed piles in corners and along the gutters where the wind couldn't dislodge them.

Phyllis pulled open the heavy outer doors underneath the arches and passed into a covered portico. Ascending a short stairway, she stepped into the lobby and a whirlwind of activity. Students were everywhere, scurrying in and out of the seven doorways and corridors that converged on the lobby, or hurrying up and down the grand staircase that spilled into the center of the room, split left and right, and continued down to the floor below. The excitement of anticipation around her was palpable. Two students, her daughter's classmates, greeted her instantly. "Hi, Ms. Killam," they chorused, with smiles as wide as boulevards.

She put an arm around each in a welcoming embrace, inquiring, "Are you keeping Jennifer out of trouble?"

They giggled and responded emphatically, "No."

Phyllis continued up the stairway, nodding and smiling, acknowledging students as she went. At the top of the stairs she made a hard right, then turned another corner and felt the adolescent cacophony fall away. She bid a hearty welcome to Jackie Jennings, John Sanford's gatekeeper, and swept into the headmaster's office.

Moments later, Tom and Allison Whitman, the emotion of the moment tumbling about them, entered Florence Bruce Seminary. Their last visit, a month earlier, was intense and focused on winning approval. That goal had been achieved, and today they were back for the announcement and for Tom to formally accept the mantle of leadership. News of his appointment had been withheld from the community—at least nominally so. But the buzz was out, and the older students and faculty congratulated themselves on making a superior choice from the three finalists presented to them.

Tom and Allison had arrived in Portsmouth the evening before. Their cross-country flight to Boston originated from their home in La Jolla, California, a bedroom community north of San Diego, where Tom had recently culminated a successful tenure as president of the renowned San Diego Maritime Institute.

With the drive north from Logan International Airport, it was almost midnight before they had settled into the cozy environs of a bed and breakfast a few blocks from the school. Rising at 7:00 AM, they partook of a sumptuous breakfast prepared by their overly attentive hosts and spent a leisurely morning luxuriating in the forthcoming possibilities while trying to prepare themselves for any eventuality the ensuing hours might present. In the interviews a month earlier, dozens of faces had passed before them in dizzying succession. Could they remember them all? Allison's penchant lay in matching face to name; Tom counted on memorizing names and associated facts. Together, they made a potent team.

At mid-morning, fighting off a touch of jet lag, the couple left the bed and breakfast for the short walk to the school with Tom's acceptance speech carefully tucked into a breast pocket. An on-again, off-again rain during the night had convinced the desert dwellers that raincoats and umbrellas were prudent choices, but now a brilliant sunshine made them feel overdressed and self-conscious. A nip in the air, not yet penetrated by the sun's warmth, showed itself in their exhalations.

A charming neighborhood greeted them. Most of the homes were small, bungalow-like, and individual in appearance. Many were freshly painted from a lively palette of colors. Here and there were older, much larger homes; some were partially hidden by a mature landscape grown thick, barely contained in some and neat and trimmed in others. The homes sported a mix of architecture with combinations of wood, brick, and stone construction.

This neighborhood contrasted with the one they had left behind in Southern California, with its veneer of differences behind mountains of sameness. Both were caring neighborhoods with an aura of means about them, but here, houses had been built one at a time as need, location and owner coalesced. There was no single builder, and no community association stalked the streets to force compliance to an arbitrary norm. Tom caught Allison by the arm as she tripped on the edge of a sidewalk heaved up by the mass of an encroaching tree root, squeezing her hand as she righted herself.

Rounding a final corner, they were struck once again by the full impact of the school's physical beauty. Florence Bruce Seminary was exactly as they imagined it would be six months earlier, before any awareness of this particular school and its need for a new leader. The images they cherished were drawn from browsing the catalogs of schools from other eastern states—Virginia, Maryland, Connecticut, Massachusetts—places known for ivy-covered brick, redolent of history and tradition. Tom had applied to several of these schools, too, but it was with Florence Bruce that destiny lay, and they were eager for the challenge.

Cresting the short stairway into the same lobby Phyllis so recently had vacated, Tom and Allison were met with a far different reaction. Conversations stopped momentarily, not all at once but in fits and starts as eyes caught sight of them, hesitated in recognition, then were quickly averted as their owners refocused on nearby companions. Words were exchanged in hushed tones.

Caroline entered the lobby. Caroline Odum, a member of the search committee, had been Tom's mentor through the selection process. It was her call that informed him the search committee was interested, her phone interview and advocacy that propelled his candidacy forward past other worthy contenders, and her hospitality that welcomed them into the Florence Bruce community.

Caroline ushered them efficiently past the knots of curious students to the Bainbridge Room, where a handful of board members were gathered in welcome. Tom and Allison knew them well—not only faces but names of spouses, their vocations and special interests, even the names and ages of their children. All had been carefully researched and memorized to overcome the inadequacy of short-term memory and to enhance first impressions. It worked, and Tom had been their unanimous choice to lead the school forward.

Tom recognized Dr. Warren Hudson, chairman of the search committee, parent of a freshman and president of the University of New Hampshire in Durham, talking to Saugus Wetherby, another parent with four young girls, all of whom were firmly ensconced in the Lower School. Saugus was a plant manager with the Portsmouth Navy Yard and an outspoken advocate for a Florence Bruce education. Kay Johnson, Class of '62 and president of the Alumnae Association, was there.

Archie Devlin, a parent, vice-president of the board and heir apparent to Phyllis Killam, broke off his conversation when he saw them enter and, grabbing a hand in each of his, welcomed them. "I am *so* glad you're here," he said slowly in a conspiratorial whisper, emphasizing the words and leaning in slightly from the waist.

John and Phyllis swept into the room, eliciting a round of affable banter. Glasses of sparkling cider followed, along with a few nibbles from a bounty of fruit, cheeses and a delectable quiche hors d'oeuvre prepared by Mrs. Clayworth's capable staff.

* * *

As the hour for the announcement approached, Caroline led Tom and Allison outside and through a side door into Bishop Matthew B. Hanley Chapel, where they were seated in the front pew. There was no time for conversation. The main doors opened, and the discreet murmur of four hundred voices warned seconds earlier to keep silent broke through the quiet of the sanctuary. Feet shuffled forward, bumping, scraping; knees and rumps knocked against wood as the pews filled. The murmur grew louder as more students filed in to take their places with those already seated. Tom and Allison, directed to face forward to avoid recognition, sat unmoving and braced themselves for whatever was to follow, feeling through osmosis the excitement tinged with hope and anticipation surrounding their presence in the room.

John and Phyllis were the last to enter and took their seats beside the new headmaster. Organ music swelled, and the assembly stood as one. An honor guard led by the crucifer and followed by flags—the Stars and Stripes, the New Hampshire state flag, the flag of the Episcopal Church and the school flag—paraded smartly up the aisle. A short prayer asking the Lord's blessing on this special day followed the "Pledge of Allegiance."

John Sanford was introduced, as he must have been a thousand times before, and he stood to receive the enthusiastic cheers and applause of his constituents. But as he ascended the stairs of the chancellery to speak, his step was heavier than usual and his shoulders seemed to sag with age and fatigue.

His speech was uncustomarily short, delivered in solemn tones and completely devoid of its usual lightheartedness. "It is an honor for me to be here this morning. Please welcome Ms. Killam, esteemed president of the Florence Bruce Seminary Board of Trustees."

Enthusiastic applause followed their headmaster's bidding, with just-audible cheers from the sophomore and seventh-grade sections where Phyllis' daughters held sway. She took the podium. "At the end of last year," she began, "your headmaster, Mr. Sanford, announced he would retire following eighteen years of service to this school and its students. The board of trustees has carried out a search over many months to find a replacement. Many of you were involved in that search.

"Today, I am extremely pleased to be able to announce to you that our search is complete. Please join me in welcoming the new headmaster of Florence Bruce Seminary, Dr. Tom Whitman and his wife Allison."

The couple stood, turned and faced the congregation. As one, the entire 450-strong student body of Florence Bruce Seminary leaped to its feet in an explosion of clapping and cheering. Tom and Allison were stunned. Nothing on earth could have prepared them for such an outpouring of enthusiasm at their presence. It was an overwhelming barrage of scenery and sound. Just a few feet away, legions of six—and seven-year-old girls, with eyes wide and trusting, were laughing, clapping and shouting in youthful exuberance. A sea of smiling, shouting faces spread back over the floor of the chapel while faculty and parents, gathered around the periphery, added their huzzahs to the tumult.

As the pews receded, the children grew older, and faces matured. But the welcome and the sense of trust they exuded extended all the way to the top of the balcony where the senior class—all of whom would graduate before Tom's time came to lead them—joined in unabashed celebration. Allison felt her heart, under normal circumstances well-contained and protected, burst from her chest, reach around and embrace the room. It was to remain there, exposed, vulnerable, and unprotected.[2]

"I am *so very* happy to be here!" Tom began with heartfelt passion after mounting the podium.

"One week ago today, I awoke for the first time with the realization that I was to be the head of Florence Bruce Seminary. Mrs. Whitman and I had returned to our home in Southern California late the previous night from a two-day round of on-campus interviews that included many of you. We boarded our plane knowing that, at that very moment, the search committee was reviewing the reports from those with whom we had met and would be determining its recommendation to the board of trustees within hours."

---

[2]The electricity surrounding this celebratory event was extraordinary. The enthusiastic and unabashed outpouring from a faculty and student body that had been virtually leaderless for two years as a result of John's inattention was one of unmitigated relief. Standing at the side of the chapel, I could see Tom, whose emotions rarely showed, struggling to maintain control. I do believe the moment cemented his determination to "take the bullet" for them when the time came.

Tom spoke in strong tones from his prepared text. His hand shook slightly from the impact of his recent greeting and from the significance of the occasion. He could hear his voice waver and hoped it did not show. Tom was an acceptable speaker, but this was not the kind of occasion that would bring forth his best. Careful preparation had been the hallmark of his career, and in circumstances where so much was unknown, adequate preparation was impossible. He was reading more than speaking now, and he knew his voice carried a slightly detached quality signifying a mind not entirely engaged with the words. He hoped the words themselves would be sufficient to convey his sincerity and commitment to this school and to the people before him.

"As Mrs. Whitman and I flew back to California, we dared not talk about the future. I had already been offered a position in New York, and there was another one pending in Massachusetts. But we had fallen in love with Florence Bruce Seminary, and we both knew that this is where we wanted to be."

Tom looked up, attempting eye contact, but his poor eyesight prevented it. Lasik surgery had corrected one eye for close-up work, and one eye for distance. It was not the best of situations, but he was able to function without glasses most of the time. Unfortunately, neither eye operated at one hundred percent, so now, the difficulty of seeing his text required concentration and left little opportunity for seeking connection with his audience.

"During my two days here, students from each of the three divisions interviewed me. I met with faculty, staff, parents, administrators and alumnae. Mrs. Whitman had the opportunity to visit several of your classrooms, and we attended an awards luncheon—the one time during my visit here that I had a chance to relax and watch, undisturbed, the flow of life at Florence Bruce. What spirit, I thought, what a cross section of ages, shapes, sizes and cultural backgrounds! This is an exciting place with so many opportunities to learn and so much to learn.

"Our visit ended in a meeting with the search committee. Everyone had been so kind and considerate, and yet the questions had been tough. How will you take advantage of diversity at Florence Bruce? Are your religious beliefs compatible with the Episcopalian tradition? What is your opinion of athletics, and how will you help our teams to win?

"You all asked so many difficult questions. Had my answers been good enough? Would I be the one honored to lead Florence Bruce into the twenty-first century? As we boarded the plane for home, we didn't know the answer, but we knew that the opportunity we wanted most was here at Florence Bruce Seminary.

"Getting off the plane, my cell phone showed that a message had been left while we were in the air. The message was from the head of the search committee, Dr. Warren Hudson. I called him back from our car on the way home. He said the committee's choice was unanimous: you wanted me as your next head of school.[3] We were overjoyed. We went to bed that night knowing that a new life for us had begun."

Tom glanced up and managed a smile, noting the slightly blurry faces in front of him were smiling back and nodding.

"Many of you are eager to hear me describe my vision for Florence Bruce, and how I will address the questions that await resolution. In the short time that I have been acquainted with the school, I have learned a great deal, but not nearly enough. I will want to take a period of time to listen carefully to be sure I understand the questions and to ascertain what has already been accomplished in reaching resolution and implementation.

"As a matter of fact, you already have a vision. It's been put in place by a remarkable man who has given and continues to give his time and energy to this school. During his years here, every aspect of the school has been improved and strengthened. You are financially strong and have a substantial endowment because of him. He brought the Alumnae Association together and made it a force for good. He strengthened faculty resources and improved student aid and admissions—recognizing that faculty and student well-being are the pillars of academic excellence. This man is, of course, John Sanford."

---

[3] Although the final vote was unanimous, the decision did not come easily. One of the candidates was a personal friend to several of the trustees. Despite her poor showing during interviews, the fact that she was female and already acquainted with the school almost carried the day. My admiration for Warren Hudson grew as I watched him assuage hardened feelings to bring about a unanimous vote after it became clear that the majority favored Tom Whitman.

Tom stepped back from the podium and approached John, who was seated behind him in the chancellery. Taking his arm, Tom pulled him to his feet. John's bewildered look turned to unaffected delight as Tom held his hand aloft, and the audience's response again crescendoed in cheers and clapping. A look of quiet acceptance infused with gratitude crossed John's face as Tom moved to return him to his seat.

"Mr. Sanford, I salute you, and I salute your accomplishments," said Tom with conviction, showing the semblance of a military salute. Again there were cheers, and as they quieted, Tom continued:

"Over the years, Florence Bruce has established a shared vision for a college-preparatory independent school whose citizens interact with civility toward one another and toward others. It is a school that values excellence and welcomes diversity. It is a school that guides students to be responsible citizens embracing a goal of life-long learning as self-educating, independent people. It is a good vision and one that I will seek to advance."

Tom took a deep breath and held it for a moment before continuing.

"I accept the honor of being your new head, because I believe that Florence Bruce Seminary is poised to continue building on its exceptional record of achievement. And I want to do all that I can to enhance the work that you have already accomplished and that you wish to begin.

"Thank you so very much."

He stepped away from the podium, bowed slightly from the waist and stepped down to his seat.

It was over—more clapping, less enthusiastic this time as young listeners tired. Those who were paying attention were left to ponder the character of the man they had chosen to lead them. He had spoken freely of his feelings and opened himself—unafraid—to their examination. This was a man who would not shrink from a challenge or seek protection if the going got rough.

Organ music filled the room. The collective body sang as one, "Hail to thee, our Alma Mater . . ." The cross and flags paraded out of Hanley Chapel, followed by the students. Tom and Allison lingered in the company of Caroline, John and Phyllis. Congratulatory handshakes and warm greetings from faculty and students trailed them across the lawn. As they were about to part ways—Tom and Allison to return to their home in California, Florence Bruce Seminary to complete the academic year—Phyllis pulled them aside.

"About the car," she said. "I think you should get a Volvo S80 like mine."

The contract Tom signed with the school included a personal automobile. Phyllis had arranged for John Sanford to buy the car provided him on favorable terms, so a new car needed to be purchased. Tom had suggested a Honda Accord would be suitable, but Phyllis was proposing a car that cost almost twice as much.

Tom was puzzled by Phyllis' largesse, and his thrifty nature balked at the extravagance. At the same time, he felt a shiver of anticipation imagining himself, for the first time in a life dedicated to service, actually "owning" a luxury automobile.

"If you think that would be best. It's certainly a fine car, but is it necessary?"

"You're going to be driving a lot of those elderly alums, and you'll be asking them for a lot of money. They need to feel safe."

"Well, thank you very much," said Tom in gratitude, as if Phyllis were spending her own money. "I simply can't thank you enough for all you've done. Allison and I will be forever in your debt."

They parted company and Phyllis drove home satisfied with herself. She was looking forward to this new headmaster. He had a youthful appeal and an exuberance that she would enjoy. The relationship, she thought, was off to a fine start.

CHAPTER IV

Enchantment

♠

Because hiring a head is the most important act the board of a school can do, it is an act that should be done carefully, procedurally, and not too frequently.[1]

When Tom assumed the presidency of the fledgling San Diego Maritime Institute, it boasted a staff of three and an annual budget of $80,000. Its board, however, was dynamic and emboldened by a recent upgrade from an all-volunteer to a professional staff. They articulated an audacious vision: build a world-class educational program and facilities to match it. It was audacious because the institute's beginnings were humble and the distance to be traveled great.

Tom embraced the challenge. His success at the main campus in San Diego led to creation of a satellite campus in San Francisco, another one in Los Angeles, and then one in Honolulu. The institute's unique immersion-style educational programs attracted adherents from many parts of the country. A capital campaign was launched to

---

[1] DeKuyper, Mary Hundley. *Trustee Handbook: A Guide to Effective Governance for Independent School Boards*. Washington, DC: National Association of Independent Schools, 1998, p. 116.

raise $18 million, and the idea for a new kind of "museum" began to take shape: instead of exhibits of *things*, this museum would exhibit the most creative teachers in the finest imaginable settings teaching students. It was to be a museum to exhibit exemplary *teaching*.

In the early years, while Tom was struggling to make payroll, his and Allison's second daughter Kimberly was born. Soccer games, coaching, PTA, Girl Scouts, band practices and all that goes into raising a family consumed the Whitmans for years. The children were educated in public schools as their parents had been. When Tom and Allison made the decision to leave California, Jayna had already graduated from high school and Kimberly was a senior.

The timing was right in many ways. The dream that had driven Tom nearly every waking moment for two decades was now at the point of realization. The institute's finances were sound; its management experienced. Tom had given what he had to give, and it was time to move on, both for his own sake and that of the organization.

Tom had grown up in Massachusetts, Allison in Michigan. Neither felt entirely at home in the semi-deserts of Southern California, although they had a good home, financial security and warm friendships extending back many years. Their roots were deeper than most, but not deep enough. Allison made no attempt to hide her eagerness to leave. Heat and congestion clashed with her Scandinavian blood. The endless similarity of Southern California's housing developments and the constant stream of newcomers left her disconnected, searching for solid foundation.

The time finally came when Jayna and Kimberly were on their way to independent living and the Maritime Institute was poised to fulfill its promise. Tom was fifty-six years old and wanted to challenge himself one more time before he retired.

He and Allison took stock of their talents and assets as they pondered their future. They were good conversationalists, accomplished dancers, interesting, established and respectable—sought after for social engagements and comfortable in groups of different cultural and socio-economic makeup. They could be an effective team when circumstances demanded, and were adept at working a room, prospecting for donors or seeking critical political support. Working together as partners in this manner also strengthened their marriage. With the children gone, they looked forward to having more time together and putting that time to a meaningful purpose.

In time, the prospect of Tom leading an independent school took hold. Spouses of school heads were always encouraged to play a supportive role. If they chose, the role could be far-reaching. Allison preferred and excelled in a supportive role. In addition, her attraction to learning and achievement in an academic environment was almost spiritual. Tom deeply valued their close relationship. He also knew, practically speaking, that his lovely and endearing wife was the greatest single asset he brought to a new position, and he advertised that fact freely.

They began investigating the process by which the heads of independent schools are selected. For nearly all schools, it begins with the selection of a specialized consultant to conduct a search. Nationally, only a dozen firms, most of which employ several individual consultants, conduct the searches.

They invested in two trips to the East Coast, crisscrossing states from North Carolina to Maine, inveigling meetings with consultants to gain advice and increase their own visibility. They visited schools engaged in the process of seeking new leadership to gauge their own marketability and assess the characteristics of schools that would meet their personal needs.

It would not be easy. Competition was fierce, with the better schools attracting dozens of candidates. Many had been following career paths up through the ranks for decades as they sought the apex of their chosen profession. Some candidates were already heads of schools in quest of a better assignment, while others were one rung down on the administrative ladder reaching for that final pinnacle of achievement.

Neither Tom nor Allison had any direct experience with the independent-school environment. Both had attended public schools, and Tom's early teaching experience—three years teaching biology in Connecticut—was in a public high school. Tom had attended an Ivy League college and held a graduate degree from Stanford University which gave him a foothold, perhaps, but the degrees by themselves were not sufficient to gain the credibility he needed.

Tom began marketing himself as a "non-traditional" candidate. While he could not claim experience within an independent school, he had a solid record of accomplishment with the Maritime Institute and extensive and well-documented experience with nonprofit organizations, with boards of trustees, with budgeting and finance, with promotion, legal issues, fundraising, and personnel management. There would be a risk in hiring him, but there was always a risk in choosing a new leader. Could he convince a school to give him a chance?

As Tom and Allison pored over catalogues and websites and expanded their number of school inspections, a picture emerged of the kind of place they were seeking. Tom had enjoyed the intimacy of teaching and wanted a school small enough for him to know all the students by name and to develop personal relationships with parents and alumni. For too many years, his contacts with students had been limited to a few hours—or at most, two or three days—before visiting students left the institute to return to homes and school.

For both Tom and Allison, the temporality of a Southern California existence left them longing for a community with history, traditions and permanence. Tom believed that values were best inculcated and fixed within the context of a history. Current generations, he preached, drew substance and meaning from playing out their roles in the epochal tableau of time, depending upon the past for context and contributing content to future generations. Ever so attractive were independent schools founded a hundred or more years ago, and these were relatively common along the eastern seaboard.

They set their sights to the east for another reason: both wanted to live by the ocean. Also desirable was a temperate climate—cooler and wetter than California, with distinct seasonal changes. With all this in mind, they focused their search on the East Coast states north of the Carolinas.

In the spring, eighteen months prior to his introduction to the Florence Bruce community, Tom explained his intentions to the San Diego Maritime Institute's board of trustees. Arrangements were made for him to stay on through the following spring, allowing both parties time to conduct a search—Tom for a new position and the institute for a new president. A month later, his decision was made public. By September, job announcements began appearing from schools looking for new heads for the following July, and Tom assembled the documentation for his applications.

His résumé and vita, filed unused for twenty years, required a significant update. References needed to be approached for consent. College transcripts sent for. A "personal statement of educational philosophy" constructed. Most difficult of all, individualized cover letters had to be crafted for each application. These letters, responding to criteria defining the school's desired leader, needed to extol the "match" between Tom, as a prospective candidate, and the school seeking leadership.

Tom was well past middle age. Many professional men in his age group were either already retired or impatiently approaching a fixed date for hanging up their cleats. Tom's chosen profession as head of school, however, rewarded wisdom and a record of successful achievement, both of which are best gained slowly over time. He was still in his prime, but age could soon tip the balance. Tom enjoyed his work, and he had at least ten good years left while his energy and stamina remained high. After that, who knew?

While Tom hoped his next assignment would be his last, Allison depended upon it. Without seeking change, Tom accepted it when it came—even thrived on it. He had left family and friends in the east to come west for graduate work. There had been several early job changes, relocations and a failed marriage—difficult at the time, but Tom could appreciate the personal growth that accompanied change and was not threatened when it loomed ahead.

Allison longed for stability and permanence. Nearly overwhelmed by the turmoil of growing up with an emotionally abusive mother, she too had experienced a failed marriage and rescued herself through therapy and determined hard work. Her marriage to Tom brought some welcomed relief but not the permanence she longed for. On her horizon, there loomed another move—away from Southern California—and she would not be at peace until that came to pass.

So they each approached the search and the subsequent change in their lives together with a sense of excitement and anticipation—Tom, as the next reasonable step in a life of many reasonable steps, and Allison, as salvation for a soul aching to sink its roots into nurturing soil. Tom recognized that truth lay in the axiom that change itself is the only thing that never changes—and can easily come when least expected. For Allison, if change came after this move, it would not be welcome. Her roots would go deep. This difference between them would find voice in the events to follow.

By the end of September, Tom had a score of applications pending. Telephone interviews and a few site visits quickly reduced the field to three schools: one in New York, one in Massachusetts and Florence Bruce Seminary. In October, Tom and Allison made the first of two visits to Portsmouth for interviews: the first while Tom was in a field of eight candidates and the second after the field had been pared to three.

For the first visit, Tom and Allison flew into Boston's Logan Airport and arrived the evening before Tom's interview. The school paid for his flight, but Allison's visit was on their dime. They were going to be partners in this effort even if it cost them.

In a hotel suite next to the airport, Tom met with the search committee for his interview. Dr. Warren Hudson was chair of the committee and a highly respected educator. His knowledge of board governance[2] and his skill in negotiating difficult issues would make him a valuable asset later. Caroline Odum, the parent of a student at the school, was there. Caroline and Tom had bonded during the telephone interview, but this was their first face-to-face meeting. When introduced they greeted each other with obvious warmth and affection. Phyllis Killam, board president, Archie Devlin, president-elect, Kay Johnson, a school alum, and 5th grade teacher Buster Jolley—these would become familiar names, but here he was meeting them for the first time.

They sat at a long table in a windowless room. Tom was positioned at the head of the table with the door behind him; the others were arrayed around its perimeter. There was a generous space between him and the nearest interviewer, making for an intimidating configuration.

Across the table sat Keegan O'Connor, whom Tom would learn identified himself as African-American despite his father's Irish surname, a self-employed engineering consultant and husband of a Florence Bruce alumna. It was a relatively distant association that set him apart from the others, whose connections with the school tended to be more intimate. A young man with a perpetual smile and a ready quip, Keegan tapped out notes on his portable laptop as the meeting progressed. After introductions and Tom's initial statement summarizing his background and interest in the school, the first question came from Keegan.

---

[2] Governance deals with the legitimate distribution of authority throughout an organization. It was the distribution of authority between the board at Florence Bruce Seminary and its executive committee that would haunt Tom's tenure at the school.

"You may have realized," he said, chuckling, "that Florence Bruce is an all-girls school, and you're of the wrong gender. How will you relate to an all-female environment?"

The question was not unanticipated. "Well," said Tom, "I raised two daughters and no sons, so I have some idea of what it means to be in an all-female environment." He was glad Kimberly and Jayna weren't represented at the interview. They were both very independent girls prone to speaking their minds and dubious of his new career choice. He doubted their presence would bring him any additional benefit.

"So you don't anticipate any surprises then?"

"In fact, surprises are the one thing I do anticipate. But joking aside, I believe single-sex education has proven itself, and I'm very supportive. In the 1970s, single-sex education got a bad name, and many schools were forced to go co-ed. Those that hung on, however, have been vindicated and are again thriving."

"Why?" Keegan pressed. "Obviously, there aren't the distractions of the opposite sex, but what are the advantages? Is there any proof that single-sex education is better?"

"Yes, there is evidence for both sexes. Girls from single-sex schools display more leadership qualities and are quicker to respond to leadership opportunities. They are more confident, have stronger self-images and test higher than their peers from co-ed schools in math and science."

"Good answer," said Keegan. "You sound like an advocate. Apparently, those girls of yours didn't discourage you somewhere along the way, did they?"

Tom laughed and nodded in affirmation. *This guy would be fun to work with.*

The next question came from Archie Devlin. "Tom, Florence Bruce is a community. The school is very caring and nurturing of its people. If you are selected, how will your administration support the culture of Florence Bruce?"

Archie Devlin was vice-president of the board of trustees, in line for the presidency, and Tom had already picked him out for special attention. Archie was a relatively young man, probably in his mid-forties. He had been a pediatrician but retired from active practice when his wife died of breast cancer eight years before. He had two daughters, both of whom attended Florence Bruce.

As he looked across the table at Archie, Tom saw a slender man, trim and athletic. He was fashionably dressed and immaculately groomed. A bold print tie, which could only have been bought to go with its matching cerulean shirt, set off a tanned, handsome face topped with a mane of black, wavy hair flecked with gray and combed back off the forehead.

The face was thin and angular, and Tom was struck by its expression of earnest concern. Archie leaned into the table when he spoke. His forehead creased with the intensity of his caring; his eyebrows drew together, and two vertical lines appeared just above his nose. As Tom replied, the fervor of Archie's expression only deepened. His head was tilted with his right ear slightly forward as if striving to hear. *Here is a doctor with a remarkable bedside manner. It's too bad he retired.*

Tom was unsure of what to do with the question. "One of the things that initially attracted me to independent-school leadership was the sense of community. Allison and I have always appreciated a close-knit community environment and look forward to immersing ourselves in that community wherever we find ourselves."

Archie's expression didn't change. Tom knew his answer was missing its mark, so he shifted gears and went for a more direct approach. "The style of leadership I have developed over the years is that of a player-coach. I know that I am only as effective as the team. I am prepared to throw a block as quickly as I am to catch a pass or to cheer from the sidelines. I recognize that the decision-making process is sometimes more important than the end product, and I value the input of others. I am sensitive to the needs and feelings of others and maintain a warm and friendly work place." Tom ticked off the points on his fingers under the table.

It was a pat response that satisfied a variety of questions, and he found frequent use for it in interviews. He had used it so often, in fact, that he had to work so as not to make it appear memorized. It was, however, a good and true answer to the question. Tom had always cared a great deal about the people who worked for him. He consistently sought consensus in a collaborative environment of give and take. He was careful to nurture talent. He encouraged efforts to improve skills, and he was sensitive within reason to needs for family and personal time.

Archie still didn't respond, and Tom thought he seemed satisfied. At least Archie didn't choose to press this issue. If Tom had been more discriminating, however, he would have seen that Archie was more bewildered than satisfied. His lack of leadership experience left him unsure of what to expect from such a question.

The grilling lasted about an hour. When it was over, Warren walked him down to the lobby of the hotel where Allison was waiting. He greeted her warmly. "Tom was very complimentary of you today. I especially appreciated what he had to say about your working together as partners. My wife and I enjoy the same relationship at the university."

Allison nodded appreciatively.

At that moment, Saugus Wetherby burst through the doors of the hotel. He was over six feet tall and weighed about three hundred pounds—a big man with a hearty laugh, a booming voice and a generous heart. Saugus was an engineer, and he saw things with an engineer's self-centered intensity and lack of nuance: yes or no, black or white, up or down. Saugus listened, but he often missed the meaning, as Tom would come to find out.

Saugus was an inveterate Florence Bruce booster in addition to being a trustee and had been commandeered to take Tom and Allison on a tour of the school. They clambered into his Land Rover, Tom in the passenger's seat and Allison in the rear, for the hour-and-a-half ride north to Portsmouth. They occupied the time with bits and pieces of personal histories, punctuated by Saugus' occasional outbursts about how much he "loved that school." His four girls, all under the age of eleven, were students in the Lower School, and Saugus' enthusiasm for the teachers and the curriculum was boundless.

They approached Portsmouth on I-95 and exited onto old Route 1 into the heart of the small, industrial port city. An ancient drawbridge—the kind that lifts the entire middle section of the roadway into the air when a vessel passes—took them over the river, and they turned left onto Newcastle, paralleling the waterfront. Saugus praised the new construction evident on both sides of the road—museums, condominiums, theaters, public transportation. Portsmouth was experiencing a renaissance from a recent grimy, ignominious past, insisted Saugus.

They passed through the city, back under the freeway and up a hill into the winding streets of a suburban neighborhood. Tom and Allison had been unable to gather much information about the school's campus in their research. They knew it was about ten acres in size. The original buildings had burned once or twice and were rebuilt in 1908. They had no strong visual references, however, and were eager to see Florence Bruce Seminary for themselves.

The website, normally a source of photos and good information about a school, was abysmal—one of the worst Tom had seen. He had been sent a portfolio with a number of school publications, but in addition to some dubious writing and editing, these lacked consistency and failed to give the reader a comprehensive feel for the school. Florence Bruce "viewbooks"—promotional brochures for the divisions—were better executed, but even these, while containing generic photos of brick, lush lawns and happy children, provided no map or overview of the campus.

Saugus drove them through a neighborhood of single-family homes, all well maintained, with a few, larger and older than the rest, set back amid spacious lawns and manicured landscaping. Fall had arrived, and broadleafed deciduous trees—chestnut, maple and oak—were blazing with brilliant reds and golds. Leaves fell about them as they drove, like snowflakes in a snow globe. Down a long sloping hill, around a corner and . . . there it was.

Tom stopped breathing on the intake. For a long moment, he couldn't speak. Before his eyes lay the embodiment of a New England boarding school—a massive (or so it seemed), three-story expanse of rich, red brick and slate roof constructed in the Tudor style. Dormers, porticos, balconies, and protruding extensions engaged the eye and enhanced the architectural interest. A neatly trimmed, English boxwood hedge perfectly framed the front of the school building. A maple showed brilliant red against the dark green of numerous rhododendrons. The magnificence of the building and environs was unmistakable and compelling.

Tom and Allison exchanged glances. If they had been anything less than fully committed to the search effort, this was the turning point. Florence Bruce Seminary now held their undivided attention.

School was not in session, closed for a long weekend, and even the boarders were gone when they arrived. Saugus' master key allowed them to wander the buildings undisturbed. Two new wings had been added to the original construction a generation ago to accommodate a growing student body. There were other renovations, among them Kittery Dining Hall, which extended the building to the rear and created a nearly enclosed commons. Hanley Chapel was positioned at the north end of the campus. Bowers Theater and the school gym, also of brick but more modern in design, were at the south end, partially hidden behind a knoll.

As they toured, Saugus kept up a running commentary. It was easy to lose one's bearings in the warren of passageways, doors and rooms, and before long Tom was hopelessly lost. It didn't matter. He looked for ways to subtly work into the conversation his enthusiasm for the school, but was overpowered by Saugus' exuberant boosterisms: "I just love this school," "My kids love this school," "Florence Bruce is our home away from home."

On the way out, Saugus pointed across the street to the Ahlborn House, remarking that the school provided this home for the headmaster. Allison longed to go inside. But it was occupied, and she knew that would not be possible. Still, from the outside, she noted it had possibilities. With brick construction like its confederate across the street, the Ahlborn House featured an attractive entrance and several large windows. A little too boxy, she thought, and the landscaping—mostly ancient, craggy rhododendrons well past their flowering peak and scraggly, overgrown junipers—would have to go.

Back at the airport hotel, they bid Saugus their goodbyes, thanking him profusely for his generous hospitality and the tour.

"Saugus, you've been absolutely wonderful," Tom said as they parted. "I hope we get to come back in the next round, just so we can see you again." It was a veiled attempt to test the waters.

"Well, I hope you do, too," responded Saugus. "You know how I love this school, and there isn't anything I wouldn't do to help out. If I can be of assistance on your next visit, just let me know."

It was more than enough to bolster Tom's optimism. *Too bad Saugus isn't on the search committee.*

Tom and Allison caught the plane to return to San Diego to begin the waiting. Within the week, Caroline Odum called, bubbling over with the good news. Tom was one of three finalists, and they wanted him to return in four weeks for a longer stay when school was in session to meet faculty and students. This time they would host Allison. Tom confirmed the dates and wrote them in his calendar.

The intervening days were a whirlwind of activity. Back home, the capital campaign for a new maritime center was advancing well, and Tom hoped to cap the fundraising effort before his tenure was officially over. In the middle of it all, they were invited to New York for an interview that Tom was able to combine with another interview for a position in Massachusetts. Both meetings went well. In New York, Tom was offered the job at the end of the interview, and he and Allison spent the evening in a hotel anguishing over the "bird in hand or the one in the bush." Taking a chance, Tom requested a two-week extension before giving his reply. It was granted, but he knew he was off to a bad start. If Florence Bruce turned him down, he would have some ground to make up in New York. No one likes to be second choice, or to embrace a leader who otherwise wished to be somewhere else.

CHAPTER V

Courtship

♠

As a leader, you are visible, incredibly visible. And you have expectations to fulfill.[1]

Allison checked the Internet for coastal New England weather news. Overcast with rain and possible snow flurries was the forecast, so they added raincoats and umbrellas to the packing list.

They would arrive for their second interview at Florence Bruce Seminary on Wednesday evening and stay through Friday. Tom was sent a full schedule of conferences and meetings with the school's various constituencies: students, faculty, parents and alumnae. Allison would join him for a reception and dinner with the board of trustees at the end of their stay. Otherwise, her schedule included classroom visits, and on Thursday she would join Phyllis Killam for lunch.

Strong, accomplished and well-educated women intimidated Allison, and she hoped, for Tom's sake, that she could pull off scrutiny by the board president. Growing up in a dysfunctional family and with a mediocre education, Allison felt ill-prepared in some ways for her role as the wife of the head of a prestigious college-preparatory

---

[1] Drucker, Peter F. *Managing the Non-Profit Organization: Principles and Practices*. New York: HarperCollins Publishers, 1992, p. 19.

school. Her innate acting skills served her well in the cocktail-party environment where, for short intervals, she could portray a woman of self-assured confidence, but could she sustain that image over a lengthy one-on-one luncheon?

Tom and Allison didn't arrive at the bed and breakfast in Portsmouth until 11:00 PM, and it was after midnight before they retired. Tom's first interview wasn't until 9:00 AM, so there was time to sleep in and enjoy an enormous, cholesterol-laden breakfast that would have jumpstarted a toad.

They dressed for the day, since it would be well after dinner before they returned. Donning their raincoats, they stepped out the door to an icy fog that shielded a rising sun behind muslin-like layers. Shivering, Allison opened the umbrella, and Tom moved close to her for protection, but the umbrella was too small for them both, so Tom stepped away. The air was thick with the frosty mixture, but it was coming from all directions, defying gravity as it hung in the air. Allison put the umbrella away and covered her head with the hood of her coat for the short walk to the school.

Their visit began with a tour of the campus, duplicating the route Saugus had followed a month earlier, except that the halls were now full of commotion. Navigating the oncoming traffic, they found themselves the subjects of cautious scrutiny and intense curiosity—a fishbowl effect that was about to become permanent.

Tom was led to a classroom where seven or eight upper-school girls awaited his arrival. All were in the required Florence Bruce Seminary uniform of plaid skirt, navy-blue knee socks or tights, white blouse and colored neck scarf. Tom had memorized their names from a list he had been provided and managed to match class year and in some cases a fact or two he had picked up from school publications.

As each girl introduced herself, Tom nodded. When Susan Lair announced herself, he said, "Susan, I saw your photo in the *Seminary Log*. Congratulations on your orchestra appointment." Susan seemed delighted by the acknowledgment. Later on, he would make an opportunity to talk to her further about her accomplishments as a flautist and share with her his daughter Jayna's interest in the same instrument.

After introductions were over, the questions began. Carlye Nelson, an attractive young woman with jet-black hair set off handsomely by the green of her scarf, opened with, "Dr. Whitman, why do you want to be headmaster?"

"Teaching is my calling," said Tom. "I come from a family of teachers and missionaries. My grandfather on my mother's side worked to define a role for science in the national curriculum at the turn of the century. My mother was a teacher and instilled in me a love for the elegant communication of an idea that, for me, often surpasses the beauty of the idea itself." He stopped. Tom knew he hadn't directly answered the question but purposely left room for a follow-up. It didn't come.

"Are you for or against uniforms?" It was Jennifer, Phyllis' oldest daughter.

"In principle, I'm in favor of uniforms." Tom was taking a chance, but the risk was minimal. Did Jennifer ask the question because she chafed at wearing a uniform? Would his answer alienate her? Perhaps, but he needed to be supportive. Uniforms were the policy at Florence Bruce. In actuality, it was a topic he cared little about. He had been permissive with his own daughters, preferring they experiment with clothes rather than with other things he considered far more dangerous.

"Uniforms accomplish several things. Some of you come from very wealthy families; some of you don't. A uniform eliminates any vestige of superficial and unfair competition between girls. It seems to me that uniforms are also quick and easy, so you can spend your time thinking about your studies rather than worrying about what you're going to wear the next day. Am I right?" Tom ended with a question, hoping to prompt a dialogue.

Jennifer allowed as how what he said might be true. They were on a tight schedule, however, and everyone in the room needed a turn. Tom found the rapid change of topics—a new one with every question—a bit disconcerting. He needed time to get his mind around a subject and much preferred the give-and-take of a discussion.

A bell rang, and the last girl could only ask her question. There was no time for an answer, but she seemed content at that.

Next, he found himself with a group of middle-school girls. Again, he managed to connect with two of them during introductions based on his memorization of certain facts gleaned from school publications. Archie's daughter Meghan was in this group. He was struck by her shyness and had to ask for her question, delivered in an inaudible whisper, to be repeated.

The most challenging question he was to be asked all day came from tiny Maureen Brenner. With an irrepressible energy, eyes as wide and bright as dinner plates, she asked, "What character trait—do you—consider most important for—your job?" She twisted from one side of the seat to the other and crossed and uncrossed her legs twice before getting it all out.

It was the only question he would be asked all day that caught Tom off guard. It was the only question he had not anticipated and for which he did not have a prepared answer.

Fortunately, a reply bubbled to the surface as Tom searched his mental databanks. It was unconsidered, and that made him uncomfortable, but he went with it anyway. "Integrity! I believe 'integrity' is the most important quality for a person in any job. Integrity is doing what you say you will do, whether it's a big thing or a small thing. Integrity is being honest with yourself and with others. Your integrity is a measure of your character."

As if on cue, Monique Fontembleau, the middle-school teacher moderating the discussion, grabbed a flashcard from her desk. It contained the one word, INTEGRITY. "Remember our 'value word' for this week?" she asked the children. "We've been trying to define it. Who can tell me what Dr. Whitman just said?"

A brief discussion followed before they moved on to the next question. *That's a good teacher*, thought Tom. She had seized upon a "teachable moment" and used it to advantage. Tom made a mental note to pay her a compliment when he saw her next.

Tom's next meeting was in the library with faculty and key administrators. He expected it to be difficult and had carefully memorized names and what facts—mostly names of children and spouses—he could distill from his meager sources. There were ten in the room when he entered. Once again, he tried to connect with individuals during the introductions, but the setting was more formal this time and he was not given the opportunity.

He was asked the usual questions: adjustment to an all-girls school, relevance of his professional experience to the independent-school environment, and the like. When it was Everett Laurie's turn, Tom mentally reviewed what he knew about the man. Everett was director of the Middle and Lower Schools. He had been at Florence Bruce for twenty-five years, starting as an English teacher and rising through the ranks. His wife's name was Claire, and their daughter Pamela was in the second grade. Tom thought Everett somewhat owlish, with close-cropped hair and round glasses on a round face. He was in a state of constant, nervous agitation and had been fidgeting with a pencil while the questioning made its way around the circle.

"What do you see as the role of evaluation in education?"

It was a huge question with many spokes. Evaluation of what? Students? Faculty? Curriculum? The headmaster? Tom began cautiously, "Education is about student achievement. The role of evaluation is to provide guidance as we all work toward that goal. What did you have in mind with the question?"

"Oh, nothing in particular. You answered the question."

Tom was astonished. Apparently, it had been a throwaway question, and he had provided a throwaway answer. Everett had opened the door to one of the great debates in education—and closed it again.[2]

Ruth Gladstone, director of development, was more persistent. "What is your vision for Florence Bruce Seminary, and what do you see for its future?"

"I've been acquainted with the school only a short time, and it would be imprudent of me to assume I have enough information at this point to articulate a vision. If I am selected as your new head of school, I will want to take a period of time to listen carefully to you and to the school's other primary constituencies to be sure I first understand the underlying issues."

"Haven't you seen anything you'd want to change?" Ruth invited.

Tom hesitated. Against his better judgment, he said, "I hope I'm not offending anyone here, but your website needs a lot of work. With so much information now available on the Internet, prospective students and parents are probably going to make their first judgment of Florence Bruce based upon what they see on your website. Frankly, it's not very good."

It was a gamble for Tom to offer a criticism from so tenuous a position, but from the nods of agreement around the room, he guessed he had struck a chord. *If there are stakeholders in the current website, they must be keeping it to themselves.* He was wrong.

[2] It was an evaluation that would ultimately prove to be Tom's downfall. Everett was not the only one who was vague on the concept.

The next question came from one of those stakeholders. Deanne Bakker, the director of public relations, was a tall, raw-boned woman, well muscled, Tom thought. At age thirty-five, Deanne was strikingly handsome. A statuesque brunette with straight hair framing her face, she was dark-complexioned with a strong nose, high cheekbones and a mouth that did not laugh easily. Tom observed a poised woman who seemed to exude self-confidence.

"Florence Bruce is a close community," she said. "How will you fit in and support that community?"

This question again, thought Tom. "I have a strong sense of community. Growing up in a small New England town taught me the importance of relationships and the need to support the infrastructure upon which those relationships are built. I have an extensive record of community service even apart from what I've done as a career."

The website was Deanne's assignment, and her voice took on an edge now as she retaliated for Tom's indiscretion. "But this is a school, not a town. We are all very close. To most of us, Florence Bruce is our family."

"I understand that," said Tom, all but oblivious to the undercurrent of animosity. "My family is grown. My girls are out on their own and demand very little of my time. Allison and I are looking for a new community, a new home. If it turns out to be Florence Bruce Seminary, I can assure you that our focus, our time and our hearts will be here."

"How will you support the rest of us?"

"We are all on the same team," said Tom. "I support you; you support me. We have one goal together: to provide our students with the very finest education possible. My job is to make sure you have what you need to do the very best job you can to help reach that goal."

The questioning moved on, but Tom's thoughts lingered on Deanne. *This is a woman to be watched.* She was intelligent with an aura of power about her that piqued his interest. And, as director of public relations, Deanne Bakker was sure to be an important member of his team. Public relations, marketing, and promotions had all been key to his success at the Maritime Institute, and he knew they would have significant play in a strategy for addressing issues confronting him here.

Deanne was on alert. She didn't like what she heard, irrespective of the derogatory comment about her work. This guy was way too intense, too business-like. Her life revolved around alliances and friendships, and Tom didn't seem to possess any of John Sanford's soft, forgiving edges.

Deanne was the product of alcoholic parents and an abusive father. She was fighting substance abuse problems herself. Her poise and apparent self-confidence hid unplumbed depths of insecurity. As a young child, Deanne had learned that an aggressive offense was the best defense, and it was now a part of who she was—as ingrained as the natural brown of her hair. Her input to the search committee would not support this candidate.

They broke for lunch. While Tom was meeting with a group of alumnae in the Bainbridge Room, Allison was waiting for Phyllis Killam in the lobby under a regal, seemingly larger-than-life portrait of Florence Bruce. Allison had arrived early. She had dressed conservatively—black suit, turtleneck sweater and flat shoes. But under the outward poise, she was scared.

Allison could perform well as long as Tom was near, but this time she was on her own. Their future depended upon her act, or so she assumed, and she was playing a charade. Allison compared her lower-middle class background against wealth she could only imagine; her crowded, inferior public school against this independent school of opportunity; her nondescript undergraduate education against advanced degrees at prominent universities. She wanted to be like them, to fit in.

Phyllis arrived as expected, punctual and friendly, and blew through the door with a hearty greeting. "I've made reservations at one of my favorite restaurants on Newcastle." She named the restaurant, a popular waterfront eatery, and asked, "Have you been there?"

"Yes, we have," said Allison, relieved to have the right answer to the opening question. "Saugus Wetherby recommended it when we were here the last time. We thoroughly enjoyed it."

After both ordering the lobster bisque and house salad, their conversation began in earnest. Phyllis dominated the early going, much to Allison's relief. She described the school and some of its recent history. She talked about children, the Portsmouth community and its renaissance, and the law firm where she was a partner.

Phyllis was genteel and gracious as befitting her Southern heritage. She came from a wealthy Virginia family, attended a prestigious private school, and received her law degree from Duke University.

Of course the discussion eventually led to Allison's background as a social worker, and Phyllis' empathy was genuine when Allison spoke of her dreadful internship at a welfare office. She related how she had been thrown into a position requiring her to call on neglectful trailer-park moms with the intent of turning them into more caring and nurturing parents. "It was absurd," said Allison, "to assume these mothers would trust me, a twenty-one-year-old college student with no concept of the conditions in which they lived."

Phyllis agreed and added that it was not uncommon in her experience for lower-echelon employees to be poorly trained for the jobs expected of them. Allison's degree in social work and her commitment to community service seemed to register with Phyllis—as if, Allison thought, it made up for other deficiencies in her background. In reality, it was Allison's unabashed eagerness to be a contributing participant in the Florence Bruce family that caught Phyllis' attention. She was feeling beneficent and wanted to reach out and embrace this fragile woman, whose enthusiasm so touched her heart. Allison's meager background only contributed to this desire.

Allison was a little surprised, following lunch, when Phyllis announced, "Now I'll show you around Portsmouth. If you're going to consider living here, you need to see it from all angles, both the good and the bad." It was more than could be expected from a lawyer with a busy practice, and Allison was appreciative.

Riding through Portsmouth's downtown area, Allison was impressed with the prevalent early nineteenth-century architecture and the town's emphasis on historic preservation. She had often felt herself floundering in the newness of Southern California and had fantasized about living in a community with historical character and charm. She envisioned life in the stately Ahlborn House as the fulfillment of a dream.

At tour's end, Phyllis dropped Allison in front of the school with a quick goodbye. The time had run longer than she had thought, and there were appointments to keep. But as she drove back to her office, she was pleased as she imagined herself in the role of mentor and guide to this seemingly younger woman—in reality, older by two years than she.

Allison returned to the lobby to receive her next assignments: a visit to a Kindergarten classroom and then an upper-school religion class. In a moment of reflection before being hustled away, she felt the lunch had gone better than expected. Allison had shown she was up to the task of representing her husband and, more importantly, the school.

Following his lunch with the alumnae and a meeting with the director of Upper School, Tom and Allison met in Kittery Dining Hall for a reception, which preceded dinner in the Bainbridge Room with the board of trustees. The reception was a blur of faces, hand shaking and welcoming chitchat, remarkable only for a brief exchange with a curly-haired moppet Tom guessed to be about twelve.

Standing on the edge of a crowd of adults surrounding him, she appeared to have something she wanted to say. Detaching himself from the group, he bent toward her. "Hi there, did you have something you want to ask me?"

"Yes, I do. I want to know how you feel about athletics." The youngster had not hesitated and now stood ramrod straight with a determined set to her mouth.

"Well," said Tom, taking the question under consideration. "I have always felt that athletics are an important part of a well-rounded curriculum. We need to educate not just the mind but also the body."

Sensing from her quizzical expression that he was missing the point, Tom tried to find it. "What did you have in mind when you asked me that?"

"I just want to know what you're going to do to help our teams win. I'm tired of always losing."

"What sports do you play?"

"Soccer and basketball."

"Those are great sports, I used to coach my daughter's soccer team. Now I certainly can't guarantee you'll win if I become your new headmaster, but I can guarantee that I'll come to some of your games and cheer as loud as I can. Do you think that will help?"

"I guess it will help some." Her mouth relaxed and turned upward slightly at the corners as Tom continued.

"I do think athletics are very important. I will encourage every student at Florence Bruce to participate and support the sports teams. Maybe if we can generate some spirit, it will make you more competitive, and you'll win more often." He reached out and took her hand in his. "That was a good question. Thanks for asking."

As the crowd began to thin, Tom was asked if he would like to make any remarks.

It was an opportunity not to be refused. He introduced Allison, commenting on their unique partnership and intent to work as a team should *they* be selected (a veiled self-promotion for a "two-for-the-price-of-one" value sale). He commented on the extraordinary hospitality they had enjoyed, and he told a story. Tom liked stories and told them with gusto, reaching for the audience as he spoke.

"My mother was a biology teacher. She introduced me to the natural world at a very young age, and to this day, as my family will tell you, I am never so happy as when I'm messing about in a tide pool at the seashore or turning over an old log to see what lives underneath.

"One day—oh, I guess I was about five years old—I was out playing with a group of my friends, all boys, and we found a snake. We managed to pick it up by the tip of its tail, and using sticks to keep its head away we took it indoors to my mom, who said to us, 'Oh, you've found a little garter snake.' She held the snake by its head and showed us how its jaw could unhinge to eat things bigger than its own body. She showed us how its tongue came out to 'sniff' the air and how its belly scales overlapped to help it crawl over the ground. My friends were most impressed, and I was pretty puffed up for a few days.

"There was also a little girl about my age who lived in our neighborhood. A couple of days after finding the snake, we were playing together and found a large toad. Now my mother had already taught me about toads, so I picked it up and showed my little girlfriend that it wasn't really slimy. I showed her how its eyes could go down into its head and how it breathed with its throat instead of its chest.

"She was very attentive, and we decided to show the toad to her mother. She was in the kitchen sweeping, and my little friend walked in holding the toad in her outstretched hand. Her mother's reaction was not at all what we expected. Instead of bending down and cooing over what we had found, as my mom would have done, her mother swung her broom, knocking the toad out of my friend's hand, and swept it right out the door, screaming all the while, 'Don't you *ever* bring one of those things into this house again. Don't you know you'll get warts? How could you do something so stupid?'

"Then, to my absolute horror, the woman grabbed my little friend, took a bar of soap, and stuck it in her mouth, twisting it back and forth while yelling, 'Don't you *ever* do anything like that again.' Of course, my friend was crying and I was scared to death and ran out the door. From that day forward, I was never able to talk to that little girl again, because I felt so badly about the trouble I had caused.

"Of course, I didn't become an educator because of that single incident, but I have often thought about it throughout my career. And I am guided by its lesson: people driven by fear do things that range from the ridiculous to the horrific. Fear is brought on by ignorance. As educators, we bring knowledge to our students, and knowledge drives away ignorance.

"That is what Florence Bruce Seminary is all about—driving away ignorance. Allison and I hope we are selected to join you in that quest."

It was an appreciative group that dispersed that evening from Kittery Hall. Tom and Allison were ushered into the Bainbridge Room by Caroline Odum, where the camaraderie continued through dinner with the full board of trustees.[3] Tom recognized about half of the two-dozen or so men and women seated around the long table, but names and faces had, by this time, blurred together. A round of introductions didn't arouse any new recollections from those he had memorized until they came to the unmistakable starched, white collar of the Right Reverend William P. Moseley, bishop of the Diocese of Boston and *de facto* member of the board of trustees.

Florence Bruce Seminary was an Episcopal school. Tom was a committed Unitarian. He was sensitive to the conflicts that religious differences could generate and was careful to examine how Florence Bruce defined its relationship to the Episcopal Church. The question had been skirted in his interviews with the search committee, but he knew it was coming now.

---

[3] Informal reports coming to me from people who had met with Tom were very positive, and I was already confident that we had found our next head of school.

Dinner conversation was informal, but once the coffee was served, things got down to business. The first questions were soft tosses previously asked by members of the search committee—questions to which he had already responded and reiterated now to bring the remainder of the board up to speed.

After about twenty minutes, Bishop Moseley, who had not spoken previously, cleared his throat and resettled himself in his chair. The assembled trustees respectfully waited for him to speak. "Tell me, Dr. Whitman, how compatible do you see yourself being with the Episcopal traditions of this school?"

There was a hint of mirth in the barely audible expiration of breath from several of those present. It was a question that had been, by unspoken agreement, left for Bishop Moseley to pose. Now it was on the table.

"As you probably know, I'm a Unitarian, and I have been concerned about that compatibility as well," Tom began. "I took the time to carefully review a statement recently approved by you, the board of trustees, concerning spiritual life at Florence Bruce. This statement says the school is 'committed to helping students find the ways and means to access and understand their spirituality.' It talks about honoring diverse backgrounds and traditions and respecting the dignity of each person. It says you view Hanley Chapel as a 'celebratory vessel' for new and old traditions, both secular and sacred. You encourage everyone in the community to cultivate their spiritual lives.

"A Unitarian might easily have written this statement, with its broad goals of personal spirituality and non-dogmatic teachings. So, in summary, I find my beliefs absolutely compatible with what has been expressed; and if selected to lead Florence Bruce, I will join in the spiritual life of the school with unbridled enthusiasm."

Warren Hudson, who was guiding the discussion, allowed a moment for these words to be digested before he said, "Well, Bishop, does he pass?"

"Yes, that was an acceptable answer; he'll do fine."

The rest of the evening was uneventful, and Tom and Allison retired feeling optimistic about their performance.

As he drove home, the Rt. Rev. William P. Moseley mulled over what he had seen and heard. *That's a good one. He has passion and conviction, and there's no question that his spirituality is intact.*

He would be good for that school. They need someone to grab hold and provide some leadership.

Tom awoke early the next morning for a 7:30 AM breakfast meeting with John Sanford in the headmaster's office. Leaving Allison at the bed and breakfast, he arrived at Florence Bruce precisely at the appointed hour. Tom had not met John, except to shake hands during the reception the day before, so he was looking forward to spending some time with the man who had been in charge for almost two decades.

Arriving in the lobby, Tom saw no one else around. Faculty and staff wouldn't start arriving for another fifteen minutes. He climbed the broad staircase to the second floor and took a sharp right turn down a winding hall to John's office. The light was on, so he walked cautiously up to the open door. There was no need to knock. The creaking and groaning of the ancient wooden floor announced his arrival more effectively than a motorcycle escort. John was seated behind his desk at the far end of the room—a surprisingly long distance away.

"Come in! Come in!" he urged, rising from his desk with some effort as Tom stepped inside the door.

The office itself began a string of startling revelations for Tom. It was huge, probably forty feet on each side. Tom had occupied a score of offices during his professional lifetime, the largest being less than one-fifth the size of this one. The view, from what he could briefly take in, was stupendous. Since John's office was over Kittery Dining Hall, it enjoyed the same panorama on three sides with the added benefit of having a higher vantage point. Straight ahead, across the expanse of office floor, was John's desk, and behind the desk, a view of the broad Piscataqua River just emerging in the early morning light. The school commons with views of the lower- and middle-school wings lay to the left, and, to the right, Bowers Theater was hidden partially behind a giant elm tree. To Tom's eyes, the room was palatial. Heretofore, his occupancy of such an office would have been unimaginable.

On an ornately carved, wooden serving table to the left of John's desk, Mrs. Clayworth's kitchen staff was laying out breakfast as the two men met to shake hands. Out of the corner of his eye, Tom was amazed to see eggs benedict on the serving tray.

John greeted him with warmth and enthusiasm, or so it seemed to Tom. In reality it pegged a notch or two below John's normal ebullient manner. Retirement had seemed a long way off when Phyllis first proposed it almost a year earlier, but it was feeling a lot closer now that his potential successor was in view. John was also disappointed that things weren't going quite the way he had hoped. One of the three finalists was an old friend—a woman, recently stepped down from another nearby private school, who also had lost a spouse. They had much in common, and John had urged her to apply for his position when it opened. She had interviewed the previous week and, despite his coaching, she had not done well.

John steered Tom over to the breakfast table, where there was enough food for ten people. Tom asked if someone else was joining them, but John indicated no, it would be just the two of them. Tom took a plate and began helping himself. In addition to the eggs benedict, he was greeted by a plethora of fruit, rolls of several varieties, oatmeal and hot coffee or tea served from a sterling silver tea set. John declined any food himself, not even a cup of coffee, which put Tom at somewhat of a disadvantage, he thought—to be eating while his host abstained.

They sat at a conference table set into the corner of the room opposite from John's desk, and, amid the small talk, Tom had a chance to take a measure of the man. John seemed taller than his five feet, eleven inches. He was a heavyset man anyway, but a large belly made him seem even bigger. His shirt buttons, straining against an expanding girth, left little lens-shaped bulges between them, and his necktie, a poor match for the shirt, showed an end just a few inches from the knot, which had been tied to allow sufficient length for the rest to reach the beltline.

Here was a man who needed a wife to tidy him up. Tom made a point of selecting his clothes the night before so Allison could give them a once-over, and his picks seldom survived intact. He felt a sense of pity for John—and kinship. There, but for the grace of God . . . . Like Garrison Keillor's "bachelor farmers" of Lake Woebegone, Tom would have been hard-pressed to present respectably without a woman's watchful eye to guide him.

John was saying, "This school pretty much runs itself. We've got a good faculty, good parents. Oh, there might be a few things that need attention from time to time, but all in all, it's a good school."

"Do you see any challenges ahead?" The documents produced by the search consultant proclaimed a number of significant issues that John's benign description didn't address.

"Yes. There's an accreditation review scheduled for next year that will have to be attended to. We get them every six years. We were due this year, but I requested an extension to give the new head the opportunity to participate."

Not having any experience with an accreditation review, Tom asked, "What's the schedule?"

"You can begin with the self-study in the fall or wait until spring, which is what I would recommend, but the process must be started before the end of next academic year. Six months after the self-study is complete, you'll have a visiting team from other schools here for a few days. Their job is to be sure you're doing what you say you are."

Tom was encouraged by John's use of the familiar second person, which seemed to assume he already had the job. Nevertheless, he had prepared a list and began ticking items off. "I understand you're in a capital campaign. How's that going?"

"Well, we want to build a new wing to expand the Middle School." John gestured out the window toward the Piscataqua. "It's been on the drawing boards for several years. We started a campaign several years ago, but we had to use the money for a new roof, sprinkler system and other stuff. Never did get the wing built, so we've got a new campaign going."

"I understand the figure is about $7 million. How's that coming?"

"We just started. I think we're a little over $2.8 million right now."

Tom did have experience with capital campaigns, having just finished raising several millions for the Maritime Institute. "That's not a bad start. How far do you expect to be by the end of this academic year?"

"Oh, I expect we'll be at about $5 million and ready for the public phase of the campaign to begin," said John confidently.

Tom hoped he was right. He would be at an extreme disadvantage starting in the middle of a campaign. It would take time for him to cultivate relationships with lead gift donors to the point where he could ask them for money.

"I understand you are somewhat short of full enrollment in some areas," said Tom continuing down his list. "How much of a problem is that?"

"Oh, we're pretty close most of the time. There's a little attrition between the eighth and ninth grades when girls decide whether they want to spend their high-school years in an all-girl or a co-ed environment. It's a year-to-year thing. Depends on what the 'alpha' girl does." John went on to explain his theory that every class has an alpha girl who takes the majority of the class with her, whatever she decides to do. "Sometimes, we're better off when the alpha girls leave. They can be pretty disruptive, if they don't want to be here."

The discussion went on for over an hour. They covered strategic plans (the school had none), public relations (John admitted there were some problems with the quality of publications), and finance (a new CFO, hired this year, was getting the books in order). Tom was surprised at John's relaxed, almost lackadaisical attitude about what Tom saw as fairly serious issues. Tom didn't see them as unsolvable or even especially difficult to solve, but they would require his serious attention. In Tom's experience, an organization lived and died on enrollment and financial issues. He probed deeper, but John not only didn't profess to know the numbers, he also wasn't too concerned about not knowing them.

When they had parted, John walked slowly back to his desk. His sense of unease was growing. He was concerned about this fellow "fitting in." Florence Bruce was a cozy little enclave, and this guy would shake it up, of that he was sure. Most worrisome, he didn't know what he was going to tell his friend when she called that night to ask about her chances. He had looked forward to being the first to break the good news of her appointment. Now, he wasn't so sure.

For Tom and Allison, the morning disappeared in a haze of further interviews and classroom visits. There was an informal pass through the Kittery lunch line, and a few bites of food between interruptions from well-wishers and expressions of welcome from those they had not yet met. At 1:00 PM, they made their goodbyes and hurried off to catch a plane back to California.

Late that afternoon, the search committee gathered to consider the three candidates. Buster Jolley, reporting for his faculty colleagues, was solidly behind Tom; the parent and alumna groups were also generally supportive of him. As debate waxed and waned around the table, Phyllis was uncharacteristically silent. She was not comfortable in so open a forum, and Warren Hudson's democratic running of the meeting empowered everyone to express an opinion.

Finally she spoke. "We've had a male headmaster for almost two decades. I think it's time we had a female head. After all, this is a girls' school."

Phyllis' statement had the ring of finality to it, and an uncomfortable silence hung in the room when she finished. Warren waited a moment. "Well, how do the rest of you feel?"

"I feel simply that we should select the best candidate." The speaker was Monique Fontembleau, who along with Buster Jolley was one of two faculty members on the search committee.

Emboldened, Keegan O'Connor added, "I'm sorry our female candidate didn't do better. I know she is a friend to a number of people at Florence Bruce." Keegan glanced at Phyllis, who flushed slightly at the attention. "The fact of the matter is that she seemed unimpressive, especially when compared to Tom Whitman." A number of heads around the table nodded in agreement.

Phyllis' bias was not for a female head for this all-girls school, but for the known over the unknown. There was something about Tom that made her uneasy. He was too confident of himself and brash, perhaps; but that wasn't it either. His questions, or maybe his manner of asking them, were so direct and penetrating. For heaven's sake, he was just a candidate. Somehow, she expected him to be—what? More compliant? More acquiescent? Certainly more appreciative of what Florence Bruce and she, Phyllis, could do for him.

She found it difficult to articulate her feelings. In the end, she voted with the group to unanimously recommend Dr. Thomas R. Whitman to the executive committee for appointment to become the next headmaster of Florence Bruce Seminary.[4]

---

[4] It is worth noting that it was the executive committee that approved Tom's appointment and informed him of his hire. The board of trustees would meet in November to formally approve the appointment, but their consideration was *pro forma*. To my knowledge, none of my colleagues on the board realized at the time that our responsibility to appoint the head had been effectively abrogated and assumed by the executive committee.

The executive committee gathered later that evening to make the final decision. Now, chairing the meeting, Phyllis once again pressed her case for a female head. Although several agreed with her, the recommendation of the search committee and Warren Hudson's presence were too strong to oppose, and the final vote was unanimous for the second time.

Landing in San Diego, Tom switched on his cell phone as soon as the seatbelt lights went off. There was a message from Warren Hudson. As they cleared the airport, with Allison driving, Tom returned the call and received the news. That night and for the next few days, the Whitmans celebrated their success while notifying family and friends. Their search had been a long one and not without its risks. Tom had boldly announced his intentions and the curtain was inexorably closing on his tenure at the Maritime Institute. Would they find another position by the time it closed for good? They had, and the worry was over. He and Allison were headed for a new life.

CHAPTER VI

Pedigree Check

♠

Good schools have a sense of mission that kids and adults can all articulate. They have an identity. They have a character, a quality that's their own, that feels quite sturdy.[1]

Florence Bruce Seminary was the result of an unusual confluence of landscape, people and politics. Unlike settlements to the south founded by religious zealots escaping British rule, the original New Hampshire towns, on land granted by the British Council of New England and wrested from the Indians, were essentially plantations designed to make money. With no gold, coal or spices to speak of and with fewer furs than hoped for, the seacoast settlers turned to what was indeed plentiful. Farming and salt production were possible, but fish and timber were the true cash crops. By the early 1700s, there were fifty working sawmills in the state and the tiny Isle of Shoals, nearly unpopulated today, was home to fifteen hundred fishermen.

The Portsmouth elite, united under the Anglican Church of England in the heart of a Puritan world, controlled a deep-water

[1] Lightfoot, Sara Lawrence. *The Good High School: Portraits of Character and Culture.* New York: Basic Books, 1985, p. 15.

harbor that rivaled all but Boston's, sixty miles to the south. Successful families began carving out new turf of their own along the five-fingered tributaries of the Piscataqua. One of these was headed by Guy Victor Bruce, an enterprising Scot, financier and self-promoter, who arrived in the summer of 1734, with mostly other people's money in his pocket.

Hugely impressed by the seemingly inexhaustible supplies of timber lining the river's tributaries and the already booming level of enterprise, Guy purchased a shipyard turning out gundalows—flat-bottomed scows that cruised the upper reaches of the rivers—and began expanding it to include a hierarchy of sloops, frigates, shallops and wherries. His first transoceanic cargo, a shipment of spars from the huge white-pine forests of the interior, was sent to London consigned to his backers. It sold at huge profit, and more investment money poured in.

Guy brought his wife and two brothers from Scotland to join him and increased his investments to include another shipyard and three sawmills. His wife bore four sons, who followed him into business, and then, finally, a daughter upon whom he lavished attention until she died of the contagion at the age of eighteen.

In recognition of his service to the Crown, Guy Victor Bruce was appointed royal governor of New Hampshire, a post he held for nearly twenty-five years until the colonial kettle began to boil. As a loyal British subject, Governor Bruce sided with the Tories until the fortunes of war turned in favor of the colonists. As the war ended, fearful of being branded a traitor, he stepped down from his post and endowed a number of public works to keep his name continually and favorably in the public consciousness. A public waterworks, a fire department, a lovely stone church and a school for young women were all founded under the Bruce name.

The school he named after his beloved daughter Florence, who had passed away some years earlier. Construction of Florence Bruce Seminary was overseen by Bishop Matthew B. Hanley, newly appointed first Episcopal Bishop to New England,[2] who envisioned

---

[2] The Episcopal Church is part of the worldwide Anglican Communion. It arrived on American shores as the Church of England, brought along by the early colonists and settlers. Following the War of Independence, it adopted the name of the Protestant Episcopal Church in the United States.

it as an "opportunity to make possible a Christian education for the rising generation of daughters who should lay a firm foundation for building a great land and meet wealth with simplicity, poverty with dignity, and face life with great strength." Whether the governor felt a hint of civic pride as his philanthropies took form and grew is not known. He died in 1783 and never saw any of them completed.

Florence Bruce Seminary was built on twelve acres situated along a curve of land overlooking the Piscataqua River with a commanding view of the inner harbor. It was completed in 1784 and graduated its first class—a total of eight young women—four years later. The original building was made of wood and burned to the ground twenty-two years later. A succession of structures followed, continually renovated, expanded and rebuilt until 1908, when the whole edifice was removed except for the stone-fortified Matthew B. Hanley Chapel.

The new building that arose on the site was declared a city treasure even before its first occupants arrived, and its stature grew as the years passed and generations of students grew from girls to women within its walls.

Each season had its own allure. In summer, the seminary brick caught the early morning sunlight and, glowing red-gold, stretched and crowed its splendor before settling into quiet repose—the residents having dispersed to other pursuits. With their return in September, the campus sprang awake, and before too long the deciduous petticoats surrounding her lower extremities burst forth in glorious fall color. In winter, the building took on a somber, dignified hue, often sporting a mantle of white under gray, overcast skies, its solid brick construction radiating strength and confidence. In the early evening darkness, lights burned in a score of frost-scored windows, and one could imagine the occupants rising to Bishop Hanley's manifesto with the determination and fortitude of Anglican pioneers.

The seminary's rectangular footprint was set in an east-west orientation lengthwise along the street, which gave it the appearance of being larger than it really was. As the student body grew to accommodate the region's burgeoning population, new wings, add-ons and renovations would quadruple the size of the original building while leaving a street-facing facade that appeared to change very little.

The building consisted of four floors—three above grade, one below. The upper two, apart from the headmaster's office, were dormitories for the resident girls and their faculty advisors. Classrooms occupied the ground floor, in addition to Kittery Dining Hall, the Bainbridge Room and some administrative offices. The basement floor was reserved entirely for classrooms. Below ground level, they lacked any visual access to the world outside except toward the rear of the building where the ground sloped away and classrooms with windows, cherished by students and teachers alike, welcomed in the light.

As the years went by, each graduating class sought to improve the landscaping as a remembrance of their youthful tenure. Rhododendron was a favorite, and soon the campus was offset everywhere with the plant's dark-green colors that, for a brief period in the spring, exploded in shades of pink and red blossoms. Other classes added a flowering dogwood here, a Japanese maple or a lilac there. When examined carefully, there was little pattern to it all; but the eye of the young ladies and their advisors was good, and the whole was most pleasing.

A broad, flat lawn separated the building from the street, and close to the street grew a formidable hedge of English boxwood, broken only in the center by a wide, brick walkway bordered by cobblestone that ran straight to an archway. Inside the archway was a pair of worn, oaken doors set with tiny panes of beveled glass, making a clear view in or out impossible.

When originally planted, the boxwood hedge—its delicate, oval leaves a shade paler than the brilliant emerald green of the lawn—reached barely to the waist, with space between the bushes for a body to pass between. The hedge was meant to serve as a decorative border, a delineation between street and academic campus. This was, however, the same boxwood that could stall a tank and nearly halted the Allied advance out of Normandy. Slowly, imperceptibly, as a succession of headmasters and headmistresses passed through the halls, graduating class after class, the hedge grew. Gardeners going about their rounds periodically clipped new growth, but failed to notice the persistent shrubbery was gaining on them.

An innovative form slowly gains acceptance and is incorporated into the body whole. In the beginning, it serves a recognized need. Over time, however, innovation becomes tradition, and the connection to the need is obscured. Critical examination is not brought to bear. The form gains adherents from those who recognize it as familiar and falsely identify it as integral to the body.

Such was the case with the boxwood hedge of Florence Bruce Seminary. The decades came and went, and no one thought to contain the expanding vegetation. At first, the boxwood branches reached out and grabbed each other in a firm embrace, making passage between them impossible. The faculty and administration were relieved. Shortcutting through the hedge was unseemly and to be discouraged in any case. A student chasing an errant ball simply muttered a ladylike "Oh, bother" as she trudged around the perimeter.

All the while, the boxwood grew taller. When it reached the top of a man's head, those responsible for deportment applauded its protection from outside distractions, and no one could imagine Florence Bruce Seminary without its enclosing hedge of boxwood. Eventually, the school was all but obscured, despite its four stories, from those passing on the street, and the street, along with its views of the world outside, were hidden to those so assiduously pursuing their studies behind the hedge.

The founding of Florence Bruce Seminary occurred during a period of unprecedented growth and expansion for the small city. The board of trustees assembled by Bishop Hanley was an ebullient group with high hopes for their foundling school. As the colonies in the eighteenth century became more settled and prosperous, American life took on an increasing vigor, autonomy and cosmopolitanism. America was coalescing as a society of its own making, not merely an offshoot of Europe's. One of the byproducts of that process, along with a general rise in the standard of living, was a new consciousness about social standing. Americans living in a frontier society had prided themselves on being unsophisticated and unlettered; now they began to worry about respectability.

Portsmouth, however, was not London, and what might be suitable in the latter was not necessarily suitable in the former. The finishing schools of Europe were not convincingly the best preparation for the daughters of the pioneers, whom the bishop expected to "meet wealth with simplicity, poverty with dignity, and face life with great strength." The early years were marked by strict discipline, a code of rigid deportment, and extreme formality, which, for lack of alternatives, attracted a fair share of tuition-paying scholars.

Years passed, but the standards of refinement and of carefully cultivated behavior did not much change. Entering the twentieth century, Florence Bruce girls still followed the unyielding customs of the latter half of the nineteenth. Voluminous black bloomers and constricting blouses and middies attended such athletic activities as were available. One elderly alum who attended the school in these years was quick to defend any notion of laxity, "Let no modern Miss misjudge and infer that we Seminary girls wore extreme décolleté. Let it be known that your grandmothers wore dress skirts, over the colored underskirts, reaching to the floor, and basques with high neck collars, boned, if you please!"[3]

Latin, Greek and religion were required classes along with scholastic-lite versions of mathematics, science and English grammar. Many of the classes, however, tended toward fluff and folderol. "Decoration on china and plush velvet," reads the entry in an early course catalogue. Instruction in music was commonplace and very popular.

It was an age when roles were rigid and one did not disturb the comportment of others. Behavior was strictly regulated. At midday, the girls lined up in twos, youngest first, and were marched to the dining room. A stern teacher presided at each end of the long tables, with the pupils arranged along the sides. Fare alternated between honey and hot rolls on Tuesdays and Thursdays, cocoa and crackers on Mondays and Wednesdays, and fish on Fridays. Grace was said, and the girls proceeded to their meal. There was no talking. No one left the table until all were finished and formally excused.

For day students, relief came at the end of classes when they were escorted to their homes, but for the boarders, there was little respite. "It is a strange thing," wrote one alumna, "that in most people's minds, a girl in boarding school must divest herself of any romping or noisy proclivities and assume the virtue of sedateness if she have it not. At the old Seminary, if she did not, she brought down upon her head all the criticism of a scandalized neighborhood."

Another student memoir written in those days reads, "As I had no mother, my father told me I was to go through to graduation. That meant twelve years. After five years, I'd count to myself, 'Seven more

[3] This quote as well as others in this chapter are credited to a hand-published manuscript, *Annie Wright, The Biography of a School* by Henry Martin, circa 1983.

years.' After eight years, 'Only four more.' It was the only world I knew except summer holidays with an aunt and classmates. I admit it was very lonely, and I often cried in my bed at night."

The English boxwood hedge, at first simply a decorative and symbolic barrier between the world outside and the young charges inside, eventually grew into something far more formidable. Tall, opaque and physically impenetrable, the hedge was a constant, foreboding reminder—especially to the boarding students—of the prison that confined them. "Behind the hedge," as it was used in those years, connoted not some benign planting of green shrubbery, but a real intellectual, emotional and physical obstacle to the greater mysteries of life on the outside.

Despite the feelings of isolation it instilled in some, Florence Bruce Seminary continued to grow in numbers and increase in popularity. Then came, alas, the lean years of the Great Depression. While the public schools raised their standards and modernized their equipment, Florence Bruce was slow to respond to the changing times. The numbers of boarders, as well as day pupils, dropped steadily.

By 1931, Florence Bruce Seminary was in danger of failing. Enrollment was waning. An entire wing of dorm rooms for boarders was abandoned, and day pupils were going elsewhere for a more practical education. The morale of the teachers was eroding, not only because academic programs had been weakened, but also in some part because of the economic depression. Financial problems besieged the institution.

In desperation, the board of trustees recruited Cynthia Wright, then headmistress of a prominent Episcopal school in New York. She came to Portsmouth not to further her already stellar reputation, but as a missionary called to duty by her rector to salvage an outpost of Christianity. Certainly, she did not come for economic gain. Her contract contained the dire provision that "if the school does not survive the year, all conditions of this contract are null and void."

Some thought Miss Wright austere and unbending. She was very tall, almost statuesque, and carried about her the aura of a "modern woman" when a more genteel, ladylike style replaced the boyish, flapper look of the twenties. Former students recall her imposing figure in skirts with layers and ruffles, full with pleats or gathers, falling almost to the ankle. Her necklines, beneath squared shoulders, also received dramatic attention, often with wide scallop-edged or ruffled collars.

Her talents, in addition to her personage, were prodigious. She shored up the school's finances by introducing philanthropy into the boardroom and recruiting trustees who would support the school with their pocketbooks. Within five years the enormous debts were wiped out with enough left over to start a small endowment.

She is credited with doubling the enrollment with what can only be described as an acute sense of the power of advertising. In road trips to Greenfield, Bennington, Lewiston and other prospering Northeast communities, she spoke to members of the International Order of Odd Fellows, the Elks and chambers of commerce. Miss Wright's extolling of the benefits of a fine upbringing and good schooling for girls was persuasive, and she herself a compelling argument.

Because of her deep devotion to the Church and her astute perception of its interrelationship with the school, she was able to understand and mediate the sometimes-conflicting interests of the several boards and bishops with whom she had to work. In those years, the girls were required to start each day with chapel services. A bell was rung, and students assembled in the library to don white veils before entering the sanctuary. Miss Wright ordered several rows of pews in the front cut down so younger students could see better, and restructured the teaching of religion.

Cynthia Wright, however, was first and foremost an educator. She had attended Smith College and was determined that her alma mater be blessed with a graduate from Florence Bruce Seminary, if she had anything to say about it. She began by attracting a strong and talented faculty and insisting upon academic excellence above all else. She strengthened the curriculum and integrated courses so that study in one supported the expectations of the other. By the end of her tenure in 1949, the seminary had been accorded national respect as her graduates enrolled in ever-greater numbers in prestigious eastern colleges—including Smith.

Miss Wright endeared herself to parents because her commitment to strict discipline was seated within a warm, homelike atmosphere of companionship and personal concern for the girls. Behind the hedge, she provided an esprit and élan that was refreshing, but it did not outlast her.

* * *

Following Cynthia Wright's retirement, Florence Bruce again experienced a long, slow decline into mediocrity marked by a procession of school headmasters remarkable for their ordinary leadership, short tenures or both. During this period, there was dissension among the trustees, particularly over all-female exclusivity. Portsmouth had no comparable institution for boys. For those trustees with sons as well as daughters, the situation was untenable, and they grew increasingly restive. Admitting boys into the Lower School was begun as an experiment, but it faltered for lack of a genuine commitment to their presence.

When the experiment was finally abandoned, the board split in two, with half its members leaving to open a new school for boys a few miles to the south in Brentwood. After a few years, stressed by economic pressures, the all-boys school became co-ed and began to attract some of the more gifted young ladies of the community, along with their financially robust parents. With its market share of qualified local applicants diminishing, Florence Bruce was compelled to enroll students of questionable ability—including a few who had outlived their welcomes at other institutions.

It was in this climate that John Sanford was appointed headmaster. John was a graduate of Choate Rosemary Hall and Princeton University with a successful record of teaching and administration in another independent school when he came to Florence Bruce. He was smart, young and charismatic—a people person. He was also a good fundraiser and an excellent judge of character.

John eased a few aging faculty into retirement and brought in new, younger teachers to invigorate the curriculum. He went on the stump, targeting alumnae and parents with means. With his good-humored arm twisting, he raised enough money to increase faculty salaries and build a new wing for the Lower School as well as a new theater and gymnasium, while adding substantially to the endowment. He made himself known on the conference circuit, attending four to six meetings annually where he impressed his colleagues with a gregarious, outgoing manner and a willingness to serve on committees and panels. Once again, the reputation of Florence Bruce Seminary among its peers began to rise.

John began making changes by ordering removal of the boxwood hedge, which by this time had grown to nearly ten feet tall. It was as if a light had gone on. The red brick of the building glowed with greater luster, the grass seemed greener, and patrons blinked in the sunlight as they exited the double doors underneath the lintel.

Soon afterwards, a reporter for a national journal of architecture was to write: "No school in the country can excel the aura that emanates from the very building that is Florence Bruce Seminary. Its imposing presence speaks of academe. There is grandeur without elegance. There is rituality without formality, ceremony without conventionality. Through the entry under the hallowed pediment carved with the enduring motto 'Truth Without Fear' there is a strong sense of permanence."

Of course, a hue and cry was raised among some of the older alumnae over the loss of their legendary hedge, so John replanted it with knee-high nursery starts which, along with his good-natured rebukes and assurances that all would be well, put them at ease. It was a scenario that would play itself out over and again as John set about making changes—some intentional and some that just seemed to happen, and increasingly it was the latter. Yet always, the results were the same: voices raised in objection were mollified and criticism deftly turned aside.

Observance of many traditions and rules began to change during John Sanford's tenure. The changes were small, subtle at first, but the overall impact on the school became more obvious as time went on. John was never one for formality, if it could be avoided. As he grew older, more entrenched and more comfortable in his mandate, he didn't interfere as parents, faculty and students molded traditions or bent rules to circumstances. Entropy, the oft-quoted idiom of science implying that systems tend to chaos if not supplied with a constant input of energy, seemed to be at work as apathy and indifference expanded without an articulation of vision to contain it.

To be sure, many of the changes were beneficial and resulted in a school more in tune with contemporary thinking. Most were, at worst, harmless. The privilege of seniors' exclusive use of the main staircase was suspended. (It was inconvenient for the other girls to use alternate routes.) The wearing of veils in chapel was abandoned. (It was about time.) The number of formal dinners was reduced. (They were time-consuming and expensive.) The overall effect, however, was a gradual loss of structure and discipline and the rise of a casual, more relaxed culture far different from the ordered formality and rigorous expectations under Cynthia Wright.

Was John's leadership better or worse? Did students learn more or learn less? Both had their supporters and their detractors, but there is no research, no standard by which to judge one over the other. That Florence Bruce flourished under different styles of leadership and different cultures during its long history is all that can be said with certainty.[4]

Some changes occurring during John's tenure were to have greater consequences than others. Standardized uniforms fell into a near hopeless state as the responsible faculty committee gave in to a never-ending stream of parent and student requests for clothes for hot weather and clothes for cold weather; clothes for young bodies, clothes for adolescent bodies; clothes for thin shapes and clothes for bulkier shapes; and so on.

John's financial acumen, never strong to begin with, began to show its weakness as accounting needs became more complex. Ill-advised by his business manager, who was fiercely loyal to him but otherwise inept, John gradually lost the ability to accurately predict financial outcomes. In response, his modus operandi devolved into three objectives: 1) keep board expectations as low as possible; 2) raise as much cash as feasible through tuition and contributions; and 3) save money as opportunity presented itself. It was, under the circumstances, an effective although blunt strategy and kept the school in the black year after year. The only drawback, and not a serious one at that, seemed to be that the annual outcome was always in doubt until months after the close of the year, when accounts were reconciled more or less.

Over time, John's fundraising success, and that of his predecessors, had left dozens of accounts scattered hither and thither. Individual donors had set these up according to their own whims, and they might

---

[4] I received a copy of *A History of Florence Bruce Seminary* upon election to the board of trustees and found it fascinating reading. The contrast between administrations, that of Cynthia Wright and that of John Sanford, is remarkable. Historical perspective is liberating. Our deeply emotional attachment to John's style and the culture it engendered as being the "Florence Bruce way" was ill placed; it was only John's way.

include Florence Bruce Seminary as only one of several charitable entities to receive monies. Each account contained unique provisions regarding who was to receive funds and under what conditions. Florence Bruce had no direct control over these funds, but failure to comply with the provisions—often requiring no more than a timely request—meant the funds might go unclaimed, possibly even irretrievably so.

Several times each year, John and the accountant were surprised by the arrival of checks, often for substantial amounts, from donor funds largely forgotten. Fortunately, in those cases at least, the trustees of the funds did not forget Florence Bruce.

In the early 1990s, John was at his peak, seeking to secure for himself a legacy of unsurpassed achievement. A capital campaign of some $6 million was launched to build a new wing linking the main building with a previously built wing. It would fulfill his grand vision for the completed seminary campus by creating an enclosed central courtyard and allowing for an increase in enrollment to five hundred students—a number that John considered optimal.

It was a splendid campaign. The city's best architect was called in, along with a reputable contractor, to ensure that the new wing met the exacting standards of the existing buildings. Artistic renderings gave substance to John's vision. The board, through a small number of wealthy constituents, raised a substantial amount in lead gifts. All was going well, and permits were sought to begin construction.

Only then was it discovered, unfortunately—for the project at least—building codes for schools had changed over the years to better protect the small charges inside. The city's building inspector told John he would have to install a sprinkler system throughout the existing building. It was a big-ticket item, but John convinced the trustees it could be accomplished within the existing capital campaign. There would be savings later, he insisted, and the work was begun. The next challenge was structural reinforcement of the old brick walls. That, too, he argued, could be done with monies that were already being raised without breaking the budget. Actually, John had no idea if it could be done. He was not a planner. He was the visionary, a promoter and raconteur—and his schemes had always worked out in the end.

Finally, the permits were granted and a date was set for groundbreaking. The capital campaign, now only a few hundred thousand dollars short of its goal, moved into the final public phase. Parents were recruited for what dollars they could spare over the substantial tuitions they were already paying. Appeal letters went out to alumnae. Classes collected pennies, and there were bake sales, auctions and a car wash; everyone pitched in to help reach the goal.

Workmen probing for starting points confirmed the next surprise, but the evidence had been there for several years. Everyone knew there were leaks. Catch buckets covered sections of the attic floor, now off-limits for dorms and given over to storage. The roof, they were told, was rotten and endangered the integrity of the entire building.

"Fortunately," John, ever the optimist, announced, "we have the money to cover it." Already one-third of the campaign goal had been spent on the sprinklers and structural reinforcement; the new roof consumed most of the remainder of the funds raised. John did his best to put a positive spin on events. The new wing would have to wait, but it would get built, he promised. Together they had accomplished a worthy project, and the school was now prepared for the next millennium. Still, there was grumbling, and a bad taste remained with some large donors who had been promised that their names would grace prominent features of the new wing.

In the beginning, John's talents far outweighed his failings; the school was well served and thrived. Then he suffered a mild heart attack followed a year later by the diagnosis that Joan, his wife, was ill with breast cancer. A radical mastectomy was followed by chemotherapy. At first she seemed to recover, but the cancer came back—gradually at first, a few bad days in between many days of normalcy. But, over time, the number of bad days grew, and John's world began to come apart.

His habitual pre-occupation with responsibilities at Florence Bruce diminished. Soon, John found himself forgetting about the school, sometimes for two or three days at a time; then it would come back to him in a confused rush. Luckily, he had a good faculty and administrators to pick up the slack, and a board of trustees that loved and supported him.

Fearing for her friend, Phyllis Killam convinced him to hire an assistant. John, however, was never one to delegate. He liked control and kept his hands tightly on the reins. The assistant head, Roland Guyotte, a competent manager in his own right, was consigned to routine chores—things John didn't want to be bothered with. There was no real empowerment, and John insisted on holding court over every issue, large or small, that came through his office.

Therein lay a strategy, as members of the faculty soon came to realize. As long as the issue didn't appear on John's radar, those lower in the ranks could make their own decisions, and frequently did—always, however, with a degree of trepidation. With John's increasingly frequent absences, his radar could be avoided by flying just low enough. Of course, if the decision resulted in an aggrieved party, John's open door eventually allowed for an appeal. It was not uncommon for the headmaster to overturn the decision of an underling if it suited him. Fear of being overruled kept significant issues off the official calendar, and subordinates busied themselves with the day-to-day running of the school from within the comfort of a self-defined, narrow sphere of influence.

As he grew more distant and removed, John's prodigious people talents, once used to cajole and inveigle a consensus in advancement of the school, came to be used to obfuscate and conceal his lack of attention. Board meetings were dominated by feel-good committee reports and gabby presentations from John. Little real business was conducted at these meetings. The primary role, the hard work, of an effective board of trustees—that of keeping the mission and serving as fiduciary of the school—was all but ignored.

Valiantly, even while Joan's cancer was nearing its conclusion, John convinced the trustees to launch another capital campaign to make good on his promise to donors to complete the new wing, but it was dogged by miscalculations from the previous campaign. Expenses and revenues could not be reconciled. Despite the fact that the goal had been reached, the former campaign had been branded a failure, and a crisis of confidence hung in the air as the fundraising began.

All these issues were festering the day Phyllis came to talk to John about retirement. It was the sense that his tenure was building, albeit slowly, to an unfortunate climax that prompted Phyllis to act when she did. Once John's decision to retire was made public, tensions subsided. John was now a lame-duck headmaster. Concerns were put on hold, issues filed away, grievances buried, and old wounds bound with duct tape to wait it out and see what the future held.

While Florence Bruce was otherwise occupied with internal affairs, the rise of the dot-com industry created a mini-boom throughout the country. Independent schools in neighboring Maine, Vermont and Massachusetts took advantage of good economic times to vault themselves into the upper echelon. Their enrollments grew and program offerings expanded; some schools started waiting lists that added favorably to their local reputation; and the ratio of admits to acceptances in several of these schools increased dramatically. Florence Bruce, however, already claiming a rarefied position among the elite at the beginning of the decade, was distracted, and opportunities were lost. Although still considered in the top ranks, Florence Bruce was now at the bottom of that tier and struggling to keep up. This was the unenviable situation Tom would inherit.

CHAPTER VII

Relationship Building

♠

The new leader of a non-profit doesn't have much time to establish himself or herself. Maybe a year.[1]

Winter passed. In April, Tom and Allison began packing in earnest. Tom's assignment at Florence Bruce didn't formally start until July, but they were impatient to begin. With no direct experience in independent-school leadership, Tom was eager for time to acclimatize and wanted to meet with faculty and school leaders before summer vacations dispersed them. Allison wanted to participate in the extensive remodel, beginning in late June, of the Ahlborn House, where they would be living.

Plans were made to move into rental housing early in May and into their permanent residence as soon as the remodel was complete.

Seth Ahlborn was a major financier of the Boston and Maine Railroad at the turn of the twentieth century and had become wealthy with the sale of land grants the government provided the railroad consortium. Seth's two daughters and one granddaughter attended Florence Bruce. A trust fund that he established on behalf of the

---

[1] Drucker, Peter F. *Managing the Non-Profit Organization: Principles and Practices*. New York: HarperCollins Publishers, 1992, p. 18.

school funded a new wing and purchased the home across the street now used as a residence by the headmaster.

The Ahlborn House was built in 1932 and sometime later acquired by Florence Bruce. It was constructed of brick in the same Tudor style as the school. Visitors ascended a stepped walkway curving up from the sidewalk and entered a covered brick portico open at the sides.

Once inside the door, the guest was presented with three choices. To the left was a spacious living room reaching all the way to the back of the house, with a large bay window facing the street and another looking out the back onto a fenced-in courtyard. A conspicuous fireplace graced the center of the room.

To the right of the door was a dining room leading into a small kitchen, a breakfast nook and the laundry room. These were awkwardly configured. The kitchen, which serviced the nook through a pass-through window, was cramped, while the laundry room was too big. Floor linoleum was cracked and peeling. Paint was yellowing and stained with all manner of spills and splatters. None of the appliances was salvageable.

The third choice was up a stairway leading to the second floor. There were four bedrooms and a bathroom, accessible from a broad landing that bent back upon itself at the top of the stairs. The spacious master bedroom lay at the end of the landing, overlooking the street, and featured a duplicate of the large bay windows in the living room. This window lay partially hidden behind a huge pine growing in the front yard that afforded a peek-a-boo look through its branches at the comings and goings at Florence Bruce.

For someone with a little creativity and modest amounts of cash, the Ahlborn House had potential. Solid construction, built-in alcoves, curving junctures between walls and ceilings, widespread paneling with crafted moldings, unique stylings, and here and there a leaded window all contributed to a building with classic, old-world feel. The school had budgeted $60,000 for a remodel, and Allison wanted to contribute to the decisions that would determine how the money was spent. Entertaining guests in their home would be a significant part of her support of her husband's work. It was critical to her that she be able to reflect a proper tone and style during Tom's tenure at the school. The décor of the Ahlborn House needed to be just the way she wanted it.

With most of their furniture consigned to a moving company, the couple began their passage into a new life with a romantically adventurous drive cross-country. They stopped along the way at small motels and camped out one night east of Amarillo after detouring onto one of the numerous ranch roads that crisscross that part of Texas. Laying sleeping bags on the desert sage beside their VW van, they counted shooting stars and waxed philosophical on the benefits of calculated risk-taking.

On the fifth day, they left I-40 at Knoxville to head north through Virginia, Pennsylvania and New York. Driving on to Providence, Rhode Island, they spent their last night on the road at the home of an old college friend, sipping a chardonnay late into the evening, reliving past exploits and ruminating on the future, kids, politics, and getting older. Optimism ran rampant. They would be in Portsmouth the next day.

They entered the outskirts of the city late in the afternoon. Allison had arranged for a temporary apartment at the western end of town, past the Seminary and near Memorial Bridge. They spent the next two days moving in, stocking the refrigerator and exploring the neighborhood. This would be home base for the next two months during renovation of the Ahlborn House.

The apartment was about two miles from Prescott Park, an expansive area of beautiful and well-kept gardens with access to biking and hiking trails. It was an asset of immense value, and many long summer days that year found the Whitmans enjoying another garden bloom, exploring trails or biking through the side streets.

Tom often took longer bike rides. Looping through Prescott Park, he emerged into a neighborhood of older, compact two-story homes. Past the homes, the road curved to the right, following a steep embankment that presented an unobstructed view of the harbor to the left. The route took him through a tunnel near an abandoned fish-processing plant to the waterfront along Newcastle, a two-mile stretch of roadway bordering the water and paralleling the tracks of the Boston and Maine Railroad. He followed a meandering pedestrian walkway set with postage-stamp parks recently reclaimed from the blight of too many years of unbridled commercial development. Now waterfront restaurants looked out on forests of decaying pilings that punched through the water's surface everywhere, silent reminders of shipyards and warehouses that had once peppered the shoreline.

Tom cycled over an old drawbridge and passed a wetlands restoration project at the site of the last of the sawmills, closed for good in the mid-1930s. He turned right and ascended a small hill onto a bike path that took him past loading docks for military transports and a pair of cranes for handling large shipping containers. The bike path continued straight into the city center on the upper reaches of State Street, the main thoroughfare through old Portsmouth.

From the city center, he zigged and zagged up side streets to Highland Avenue, which, after a pedal of about three miles, returned him to the apartment. He was to make the fifteen-mile round trip on his bike many times. Even after moving into the Ahlborn House, until the cold and darkness of winter grounded him, Tom would pick up the route near the school on Newcastle and complete the loop. Since college, he had used bicycle riding and jogging to keep fit and to reduce the tensions of his work. It was a cure that had worked well in the past and would become essential to his survival once the school year began.

School was still in session for two more weeks after the Whitmans' arrival in Portsmouth, and before everyone dispersed on summer vacations, Tom arranged a number of appointments with key administrators, beginning with John Sanford. Renovation of the Ahlborn House was to begin as soon as John moved out at the end of the month, and Allison was looking forward to reviewing the plans with Steve Harrison, a trustee assigned to oversee the project on behalf of the board.

Steve was a gregarious fellow. His specialty was buying raw land, generating entitlements and selling at a profit. He had minimal experience with actual construction, but what he did possess was more than any other trustee had, so he got the assignment. Steve and Allison had spoken several times by phone. They had taken an instant liking to one another, and she was looking forward to meeting him in person.

On the appointed day, Tom and Allison drove to Florence Bruce together. In the next few hours there was much to learn and absorb as their new future began to reveal itself. They kissed at the car before entering the building to go their separate ways. The anticipation of sharing a lively conversation over dinner that evening was delicious.

Tom headed straight for John's office. It was later in the day than his last visit, so he didn't expect a repeat of the eggs benedict. John's door was open, and Tom saw that he was on the phone, so he stepped into the adjoining office to chat with Jackie Jennings. Jackie was John's executive assistant and had been in the position through two headmasters before John. She must have started young, thought Tom to himself; she doesn't look that old—maybe late forties, he concluded.

He greeted her affectionately. Tom knew his relationship with his executive assistant would be second in importance only to his relationship to the president of the board. Jackie was small, slight—birdlike. A sparrow, he thought, but later changed his mind to a house wren—converted by her short, quick movements and difficult-to-get-a-word-in-edgewise chatter.

Jackie was very close to John, and her anxiety over the pending change in leadership showed. "I hear you moved into an apartment by the old Memorial Bridge. Is it by those new Goldpointe Apartments? I live right near there myself. I'm on Second Street, just two blocks down from the Seven-Eleven and the Chevron station on Highland Avenue. I've lived there with my son Chad for about two years now, and before that I lived—"

"You live near the bridge, too?" Tom broke in amicably. "It's such a beautiful area, and the commute to Florence Bruce is so easy."

John finished his phone call and came out to greet him. They chatted briefly with Jackie about the weather, whose constantly changing nature made it a useful subject for innocuous conversation whenever the situation demanded. John was in a good humor and, once he had pulled Tom into his office, offered coffee from the silver serving set on the conference table. "Give me a minute. I want to get my thoughts down while they're still fresh in my mind."

John picked up a pocket tape recorder from his desk. Seating himself at the conference table across from Tom, he leaned his bulk back in the chair until it squeaked in protest. Putting one hand behind his head in a contemplative pose and holding the tape recorder to his mouth, he began to dictate.

"Jackie, please address this letter to the Nelsons. They're a new family with a child in fourth grade, I think. You can get their address from Admissions. 'Dear Mr. and Mrs. Nelson . . .'"

Tom was stunned. He would have been no more astonished to see John pull out a slide rule to do a math computation. He hadn't seen anyone give dictation since he sat at the foot of his father's desk as a little boy. He had always been amazed at his father's ability to talk off-the-cuff into the machine in the clear, precise sentences of a lawyer, but that had been a long time ago. For most of his thirty-year career, Tom had prepared his own letters. He could type about as fast as he could think and, from the beginning, eschewed the cycle of dictating, transcribing, rereading and retyping for its inordinate waste of time and cost. Now he used the latest word-processing technology and expected his assistant to be able to proof his letters, mail-merge them with addresses from a database, print envelope and letter together, and deliver them to his desk for signature.

The contents of the letter had something to do with a parental complaint about the foreign-language curriculum. John's formula was a common one that Tom also used. Reword the complaint to indicate it had been heard; provide assurance that everything possible is being done to solve it; thank the complainer for bringing the matter up. Tom listened for a fourth element, the next step—a promise to follow up in some manner. He didn't hear it.

When the dictation of the letter was finished, John gave a shout for Jackie and she flitted in the door with a little laugh and a bright smile. She took the tape recorder and had the letter back for John to sign before their meeting was finished.

The two men spent some time getting reacquainted. They talked about the schedule of activities for the next two weeks through to graduation. It would be busy. An awards assembly was scheduled for the lower and middle divisions. There was a special dinner being held in John's honor, and receptions for alumnae and parents around graduation. When John invited his participation in these events, Tom declined, much to John's inner relief. "You need time to say goodbye, and I don't want to get in the way of that," Tom said. With the exception of a few scheduled work sessions, he intended to stay out of the way until his tenure officially began on July 1.

The conversation turned to the faculty. John offered to provide a synopsis of his opinions and evaluation of each faculty member, which Tom gratefully accepted. John's insights would be invaluable. It was important, he knew, to make his own judgments, but at the same time, he felt confident in his ability to avoid being prejudiced by what John might say. And so they started, Tom taking notes while John picked names at random. After reviewing four or five, Tom, fearing they might miss some, opened to an alphabetized list of faculty he kept in his notebook and checked off the names as John brought them up.

The Florence Bruce faculty and administrators were, for the most part, a fine group of educators. Some were outstanding. There was a husband-and-wife team, who, with no children of their own, had adopted the school. Both were excellent teachers in their own right, and although they didn't live on campus, they coached athletic teams and never turned down a request for extra duties. John also rambled on about Buster Jolley and Monique Fontembleau, whom Tom knew as faculty representatives on the search committee. They were, John indicated, highly respected and superb teachers. Buster was one of only three male teachers in the Lower School. Monique was a Latin and French teacher for the Middle School.

Tom had met about one-third of the faculty while interviewing and had memorized the bare facts of their assignments—what grades or classes they taught, how long they had been at the school, and other odds and ends. For the most part, he simply scratched a few notes beside each name as John talked. He was listening for certain things. If John's evaluation was wholly positive, he marked a star or a double star next to the name. But he was also listening for the weaknesses, problem faculty who might require special attention on his part. There were only a few.

Two departments were engaged in internecine bickering that was more nuisance than anything else, according to John. The athletic department and the music department both contained individuals who couldn't seem to get along with each other. John was vague as to the causes, but they seemed to extend back several years.

Another problem involved a male middle-school teacher, Miguel Barrera. Mr. Barrera was Hispanic, a handsome and charismatic teacher who continually challenged his students—not an easy accomplishment when dealing with a room full of pre-teen girls trying to prove they're all grown up. But Mr. Barrera was accused of stepping over the edge at times and had drawn considerable criticism from parents this last year—some issue involving a computer that displayed a pornographic website during class, according to John, and another unseemly incident where girls were observed braiding his ponytail. "This is a good teacher," said John. "It would be too bad if we lost him. Middle school is the most difficult age to teach, and it's nearly impossible to find teachers who can do it well, not to mention that we have only three teachers of color as it is."

"It looks like he may need to be protected from himself."

"Yes, you're right, if it hasn't gone too far already. This was a difficult year for him." John glanced at the list Tom was keeping. "I see we skipped over Deanne Bakker. I need to talk to you about her. Can I get you some more coffee?"

"No, thanks. I allot myself one cup in the morning. After that, I start to bounce off the walls." Tom checked his list. Deanne was the director of public relations. He remembered her well from her questioning during his interview as someone he would want to get on his administrative team. "What about her?"

"I'm worried about that one," said John, acknowledging ownership. John usually avoided identifying problems as belonging to Tom, but there was no mistake in Tom's mind that he would be the one responsible for solving them.

"Yes, I've already met her. To tell the truth, I was impressed."

"She does make a good impression," admitted John, "but she also has a lot of problems. She's had difficulty getting her assignments out, and she doesn't get along with folks in the development department."

Tom recalled the work of Deanne's he was familiar with. He had been very critical of *Voyager*, the school magazine, and he thought the latest issue of the newsletter, *Seminary Log,* was a mishmash of unrelated material and poorly written—the worst piece, however, being John's "Message from the Headmaster." *Was this Deanne's fault or John's?*

John was vague under Tom's questioning. "What is the performance issue really? Is it just that she can't meet deadlines?"

"Deanne's an alcoholic. I think she's been drinking since she came here, but I only began noticing it this year."

"What did you notice?"

"It was on her breath, and one of the custodians found a bottle she left in her trash. I think she was drinking here at the school. I sent her into rehab and would have let her go, but I didn't want to risk a liability suit—you know, with alcoholism being considered a disease and all, you can't fire someone for that reason alone."

"Whew," said Tom, letting out a long, muffled whistle. He had sure missed that one. He was going to add that he thought drinking on the job was a dismissible offence but decided against it.

"One more thing. She and Archie Devlin are dating."

An epithet, inappropriate under these circumstances, almost slipped out, but Tom caught himself in time. "How long have they been dating?" Archie Devlin was next in line to be president of the board. Tom had known supervisors who dated people they supervised, and he had experienced firsthand the problems that could generate—but a board member dating an employee, and the president of the board at that, he had never heard of before.

"It started around the winter holidays."

"Will it last?"

"I don't know," said John. "She's pretty needy. Archie lost his wife about eight years ago, and, to my knowledge, he hasn't dated anyone for any length of time since, which is a little odd in itself. I think she's bringing out the 'protector' in him. My guess is that it will pass eventually. They really don't have much in common."

Tom drew a circle around "Deanne Bakker" in his note pad. He went back and added a circle around "Miguel Barrera," too, and John's run-down continued. A dozen or so names later, John cleared his throat, and a look of concern crossed his face—signals that Tom had come to recognize by then.

"Everett Laurie has been around here a long time . . ."

Tom remembered Everett. He was director of the Lower and Middle Schools. During the interviews, Everett had asked Tom his opinion on evaluation, but the discussion never went anywhere. Tom remembered him as a bit of an odd-looking fellow, nervous, fidgety. He walked slightly pitched forward, as if he had to take his next step to keep from falling over—the kind of guy you'd think must have been one of those geeky nerds in high school, the one who always got picked on.

"He's a good administrator," said John, "but not much of a leader. There have been issues in the Middle School that Everett just hasn't been able to control. You know—parent complaints, faculty stretching the limits, things like that. You're going to have to make a change there at some point." His conclusion acknowledged that this problem, in fact, belonged to Tom to solve.

That was it. Tom didn't know what to ask to shed more light on Everett's failings. There were just too many unknowns. What were the specifics of the issues? What were the parents complaining about? They had already talked about Miguel Barrera's forays into the quicksand of gender propriety. Did other faculty issues exist that they hadn't discussed?

John continued with bits and pieces of Everett's history at the school and mentioned his wife Clare and little girl Pamela—details that never stuck with Tom anyway. Tom's memory required scaffolding on which to build. He didn't have enough background information on Everett to fit the pieces to. He circled Everett Laurie's name in his notebook and waited for John to go on to the next name.

As they parted about an hour later, John said, "You know, Tom, you've landed yourself a good assignment. The school will pretty much run itself. Just take some time settling in; get used to things." Tom acknowledged John's comment, but he was wary, not at all sure it was an assessment he could trust—at least the part about the school "running itself."

"You've done a great job here," said Tom, mindful of the need for a compliment to fill the space. "I'll e-mail the item I spoke to you about for the board-meeting agenda." Markham Nunlist, the consultant hired to conduct the search that resulted in Tom's appointment, had recommended a transition committee be formed to assist the new head in his first year. Tom wanted the board to charge the search committee with the task without delay.

"That will be fine," John replied. "Jackie takes care of all my e-mails, so she'll get back to you on it."

As Tom headed off to the business office, he ruminated on John's parting comment. *Jackie takes care of all his e-mail?* He pondered the point. *How does that work?* In Tom's experience, e-mail was another form of conversation. Having someone else "take care" of it would be like using a translator who didn't necessarily understand your language. He wasn't far from the truth.

Nancy Wolf was the director of financial operations. Tom had spoken with her briefly at a reception during the interviews, and they developed an instant liking for one another. She was all business and he appreciated that, especially from someone in her position. This was Nancy's first year at Florence Bruce. Although the financial health of the school was never in question, reporting systems were in dismal shape. Nancy was having a difficult year trying to wring order out of the chaos she found when she arrived. Tom wanted to talk to her about the Volvo Phyllis had promised.

He was ushered through an outer office to an inner office and finally to the cubby that Nancy occupied. They shook hands warmly. "So this is where you hang out. Who are you hiding from? We don't have any disgruntled creditors, do we?"

She laughed. "This is the only place I can get any work done. How are things going with you? Are you settling in?"

"Sort of. We've moved into an apartment out by Memorial Bridge, but I'm going to stay pretty scarce for the next few weeks. You know, let John say his goodbyes—do what he needs to do. I don't want to get in the way of that.

"What I want to talk to you about is the car the school provides its head. Allison and I sold our second car before we left California, and we need to get another vehicle. I know the intent is to lease or buy a car. Can we make that happen soon? Allison and I would be happy to pay a few weeks' prorated rental until my contract kicks in."

Nancy said she didn't anticipate a problem and added, "I prefer to purchase, since we don't get any of the tax benefits from leasing, but I'd need to see the terms first."

"Well," said Tom, hesitating. "Phyllis is thinking of a Volvo S80. It's a forty-thousand dollar car. To me, that kind of expense doesn't make sense, but Phyllis seems to think it's what we should do. I'm just not sure of expectations here."

Tom was conflicted. Without actually expressing disapproval of the decision, he felt compelled to demonstrate to Nancy that it was not something he would do if it was left up to him. His response had a dual message: 1) I am fiscally conservative, and 2) I'm not responsible for this decision. But if pressed, he could justify the expensive car. After all, a new Volvo would be wonderful, and maybe Phyllis was right—he would be driving around a lot of wealthy, elderly alumnae who would appreciate such a vehicle.

Nancy's sentiments reflected his own. "It seems expensive to me, too," she said in the deprecating way a mother would tell her daughter that she disapproved of her getting her ears pierced, but wasn't going to say "no." She advised Tom to work out the details with a dealership, and she would make a determination on the lease or buy option. Tom thanked her, and they set another date when they could meet to review next year's budget—the one Tom would be responsible for.

Steve Harrison was waiting for Allison in the school lobby when she walked in. He must have recognized her from one of their interviews, because he walked straight over without any introduction and said, "Hi, kiddo, are you sure you really want to do this?"

She laughed. He was exactly as she had imagined him—tall and rugged, with an absolutely winning smile. "Of course I want to do this. It's really nice to meet you. I've been so looking forward to getting started on the remodel."

Steve invited Allison to join him for a trip to a nearby Lowe's showroom. Pleased with her choice of casual clothing for the day's adventure, Allison hopped into the passenger seat of his well-used Ford pick-up. As they drove, Steve described the challenges ahead. The Ahlborn House had received little attention since John had moved into it eighteen years earlier. The kitchen needed a complete overhaul, and the hardwood floors were badly stained and mottled throughout the house. The floors were already scheduled for stripping. The challenge before them lay primarily in the kitchen.

Somewhat familiar with the need, Allison had been perusing kitchen designs in books and magazines and had even attended a product demonstration in March. She had developed a good idea of the options available in furnishings and appliances. The next two hours were spent looking at countertops (granite was best, but would the budget support it?) and cabinetry (they both liked the cherry as being in keeping with the trim molding and some existing built-in cabinets). While driving back to the school, Allison commented, "You know, Steve, it's really uncanny how much we agree on things."

"Yup, in my business we call it 'simpatico,'" said Steve with a laugh. He had enjoyed her company. This project was going to eat up a bit of his time, and he was glad for the opportunity to do it in the presence of a good-looking, personable woman.

On their next meeting, Steve obtained John's permission to inspect the Ahlborn House and arranged for the architect to join them. They all agreed that eliminating the dividing cabinetry from between the kitchen and dinette area was desirable. It was also apparent that removing the small wall between the kitchen and laundry room would create a much more livable space, provided it did not involve a load-bearing wall. (The architect said she would check into it.)

Allison continually expressed the desire for a kitchen to accommodate the extensive entertaining she anticipated. A second sink, a 1,400-BTU stovetop and ample refrigerator with freezer space all became part of her plan, along with a double oven, warming drawer and microwave. Since she envisioned the entire downstairs becoming a showplace for visitors, the kitchen linoleum—all three layers of it!—was unacceptable. As she talked, Steve was captured by her vision of making the house an historic extension of the school. It had always been just a house. Despite being on the board for five years, he had never been in the house until assigned the remodeling project.

Steve had never felt that his open, freewheeling style was a fit for the overly correct, stodgy, and cautious-to-the-point-of-inaction expectations for his position on the board. Until now, a meaningful contribution had eluded him. He was simply marking time for one more year until his term on the board ended. Now he was fired up, sure at last that he was in a position to make a meaningful contribution.

When John moved out, the contractors moved in, and the "fun" began. Steve came by at least twice each week to meet with Allison and review the progress. It wasn't until the kitchen was stripped to the wall studs that Allison was struck with an unanticipated dilemma. The project was coming in on budget, but what about the designer elements: window treatments, carpeting, furnishings and the like? Of course, the couple had some furniture, but most was of insufficient quality. Florence Bruce had some antique furniture in storage, but it was old and needed restoration. Allison planned to use inheritance money from an aunt to fulfill one of her lifelong dreams—the purchase of a baby grand piano—but the disconnect between her vision for the Ahlborn House and the resources available to make it happen was widening. She decided to take her concerns to Steve.

After his first meeting with Nancy Wolf, Tom and Allison met with the Volvo dealer, who happened to be a Florence Bruce parent, and picked out the car they wanted. Armed with the specs and the financial information for this extravagance, Tom's parsimonious nature again needed reassurance.

Allison had no such qualms. "You're head of a prestigious private school now," she said. "You deserve a nice car." He noticed she'd said "deserve." At another time, she'd said he'd "earned" it, and added, in support of Phyllis' claim, that Florence Bruce "expected" its head of school to have a nice car.

Still, Tom's Puritan heritage demanded prudence. The guilt was real but so was his acute awareness of perceptions. Would parents feel pride of ownership when the head appeared driving a new Volvo, or would they look askance wondering if this was the best use of their tuition dollars?[2]

Tom called Phyllis. "I need to go over the research I've done on the new car," he said without preamble, relating his conversation with Nancy and the details of the negotiations with the dealership.

Caught off guard by Tom's speedy arrival at the point of his call, Phyllis responded by repeating the argument she had made earlier. "You have a lot of elderly alumnae, Tom, who need to feel safe."

"What about the board?" asked Tom, trying to ensure his bases were covered. "This is a sizeable expense. Do we need to get approval?"

Phyllis hesitated for just a moment. "No, I'm going to make this call myself. Besides, it's in your contract, and the board approved your contract."

It may be in my contract, but it doesn't say it has to be a Volvo.

"If you hear any complaints, you have them call me. I'll tell them it's just none of their business. There are too many people around here who think they have a right to complain about everything."[3]

"Okay," said Tom. "I very much appreciate your support on this. It's so refreshing in my experience to have a board president stand up and take a position. I'll take the paperwork to Nancy, and we'll figure it out from here."

The call ended. Tom was pleased with the exchange. Despite his misgivings about the car, his compliment to Phyllis was genuine, and

---

[2] Tom's instincts were correct. When the time came to choose sides, however, it would be certain faculty, rather than parents, who would criticize the vehicle purchase as an extravagant excess.

[3] This was typical of how things were done at Florence Bruce. A $40,000 decision is not one that any trustee, even the president of the board, should make unilaterally. Tom's failure to recognize that real power at the school was vested in just a few individuals, rather than in the board itself, would prove to be his undoing.

a neat little piece of business had been concluded—his first success, and the curtain had not yet even opened.

Phyllis wasn't so sure. She had poured herself a cup of tea when Tom called, expecting to settle in for a chat, but the call was over before she got the bag out of the cup. Sure, he had thanked her, but it felt cursory. She was a little unsettled as she poured the tea into the sink and went upstairs to check on the children's homework.

Two days later, Tom and Allison drove back to the apartment in a brand new, 4-door, metallic platinum-green S80 Volvo with seat warmers, a sun-roof, a 4-CD in-dash sound system with 200-watt amplifier, and Dolby Pro-Logic premium speakers for alumnae with hearing loss.

The meetings continued, as every other day or so Tom stopped by the school for a scheduled appointment. One morning, Nancy invited him to attend a meeting of parents to review proposed changes in the school's uniform standards. John had asked her and Everett Laurie to head a committee to look into a number of uniform issues. The committee met several times, conducted a survey of parents and faculty, and engaged students to explore the community's wishes. Nancy and Everett had reviewed the survey results and devised eight recommendations for implementation.

One recommendation reduced the color options for sweatshirts that could be worn over the standard uniform, so the school would not have to carry so many colors in stock. Another recommendation removed the Florence Bruce Seminary **FBS** monogram from the breast pocket of the jumpers worn by the little girls who thought it was "scratchy," and had it sewn into the collar.

The meeting was held in the Bainbridge Room with about thirty parents present—a good turnout, thought Tom, inasmuch as it was 10:00 AM. The meeting began well, with everyone expressing relief at finally being able to get the "uniform issue" off the table. Nancy presented the financial data, including the savings to the school from being able to keep a reduced inventory. Everett reviewed results of the survey and the committee's recommendations, listing them carefully on a flip chart.

When the presentations were over, the discussion started—cautiously at first, as one parent after another expressed a reservation with this or that recommendation. Everett moderated the meeting, listening carefully at first but becoming increasingly agitated as the list of reservations grew. Parents were by no means in agreement. For every reservation, there was a counter-argument that the recommendation did not go far enough.

Tom thought a number of good suggestions were made, but they were soon again lost, as first Everett and then Nancy were distracted from the thoughtfulness of the comments by their defensive posturing. Everett paced back and forth, twirling a marker, and stopped every few moments to push his glasses back up on his nose. He was prone to interrupt as soon as a speaker's position was identified, without listening for the nuance. It seemed he thought if he talked fast enough, said the same things enough times, or held the floor long enough, he would prevail.

Tom saw missed opportunities for consensus building, but thought better of entering the discussion. When asked for his opinion, he demurred, saying he still had too much to learn to form an opinion as yet.

The dialogue continued without anything being resolved for—what seemed to Tom—far too long. No one seemed to get really angry except, perhaps, for a thin-lipped young mother who talked in clipped, precise sentences. No one agreed, everyone had their say, and on it went in this manner until the participants began to drift away as boredom set in or other duties called. By noon, after two hours of discussion, attendees were down to a handful and the meeting dissolved.

Tom drew Everett and Nancy into a huddle to commiserate. Opposition to the recommendations had obviously surprised both of them. The logic of the survey, they all knew, had led reasonably to their conclusions. Everett said he thought he could make a few changes, but both he and Nancy were loath to consider significant alternatives to the ones they had presented. Tom agreed that significant changes were not what was needed.

"It isn't that your recommendations are wrong," advised Tom, "but you are going to need to build a consensus, if this is going to work. Otherwise, you'll continue to have complaints, and you'll be accused of not listening. Why not ask the Parents' Association to approve the recommendations so you can use them as a buffer?"

"We don't have time," said Everett. "School is ending, and we've got to get the uniform guidelines printed up for next year. The Parents' Association won't meet again until September."

"You need their blessing. These issues have been out there for a long time. Can't you wait?"

"We've already signed a contract with the supplier," Nancy cut in.

"Before you got approvals?"

"We don't need approvals. John already gave us the assignment. There isn't any other approval necessary," Everett replied.

"Then what was the purpose of the meeting?" asked Tom. "These parents all think you assembled them here for input. They provided it, and will be very upset if you don't make any changes. They'll think you didn't listen."

"You heard them," said Everett. "Half wanted to tighten the recommendations and half wanted us to loosen them. All things considered, we're about in the middle."

"That's right, you are in the middle. It won't matter what you do. At least half are going to complain no matter what. That's why you need the formal backing of the Parents' Association. Then you can say, 'we listened, but the consensus was otherwise.' You take the onus off yourselves, and put it on the PA."

Tom's argument was unpersuasive. Everett made two minor changes to the eight recommendations, and the resulting uniform code was published in the handbooks prepared for each division for the opening of school in the fall.

In addition to John, Nancy and Everett, Tom requested meetings with the rest of the administrative team: Craig Gowdy, director of admissions; Ruth Gladstone, director of development; Deanne Bakker, director of public relations; and Peg Scott, director of the Upper School. With one exception, Tom approached these as fact-finding meetings with open agendas, and conversations frequently continued in an exchange of e-mails as he struggled to understand the Florence Bruce organization and culture.

In Peg's office, they discussed the Florence Bruce approach to college admittance. Later, Peg sent him an article from the *Wall Street Journal* on the subject and Tom e-mailed his reply:

> That article is really eye opening—kind of scary actually. The pressures to get students admitted into the elite colleges can be intense, and it isn't always in the best

> interest of the student. I like your focus on finding the 'right' college for our graduates.

The director of maintenance and security gave Tom a thorough tour of the building, from its spanking new roof to the basement-level classrooms. Mrs. Clayworth, whose culinary acumen he had already encountered, enthralled him with her intimate insider's knowledge of the school's history and buried treasures—antiques and a variety of art objects hidden away from "sticky fingers" as she put it, indicating that her concern was not student digits but those of their elders. There was a lot to digest, but this was Tom's game. He relished the play—absorbing details and reveling in the fit of the pieces.

CHAPTER VIII

Due Diligence

♠

Trustees lose patience and interest when the board does not deal with the most crucial questions facing the institution.[1]

Tom's meeting with Deanne Bakker was different from the others. Deanne, he had learned, was responsible for the school website, and criticism of the site during his interview was not likely to have put him in her favor. Tom also was mindful of what John had told him about her problem with alcohol and her vaguely defined performance issues. So, determined to push his way into the thicket, he sent her an e-mail:

> Dear Deanne,
>
> I didn't have much of an opportunity to introduce myself when we met back in November, so I'd like to find some time for us to get better acquainted before school ends. Do you have time for lunch on Friday? Best, Tom W.

---

[1] Chait, Richard P., Thomas P. Holland and Barbara E. Taylor. *The Effective Board of Trustees*. New York: MacMillan Publishing Company, 1991, p. 115.

Tom strode into Deanne's office at 11:45 AM on Friday as they had agreed. "Hey, Deanne, que pasa?" he greeted her, grinning widely and extending his hand. She rose warily and took it. He was surprised at how large her hand was—big enough to completely encircle his own. "Ready to go?"

"Should I bring something to take notes with?"

"No, this is casual. There will be plenty of time for notes later."

Deanne was on guard. The hairs on the back of her neck tingled while her response mode alternated between "fight" and "flight." There were too many unknowns in this encounter. She knew unknowns to be capricious and unpredictable, and they were always at the forefront of her experience, it seemed: an alcoholic father who could be loving and caring and then lash out with a fierce backhand; frequent encounters with social services and their unrelenting bureaucracies where nurturing was a job and follow-through problematic; and an array of relatives as needy as she.

Her identity as director of public relations in a prestigious private school was testament to her determination, ingenuity and fortitude. Deanne worked hard to put herself through college. With almost no funds of her own, she relied on a succession of strategically planned male relationships to stay solvent. While any suggestion that she sold her services would have been vehemently denied, Deanne was well aware that her looks were often decisive in achieving her goals, and she cultivated the asset with careful grooming and a daily workout.

Graduating cum laude, Deanne had left no stone unturned in pursuit of that distinction and was justifiably proud of the accomplishment. Grades were just as often a matter of negotiation as of careful study and preparation. No grade, if it mattered, went unchallenged, and campus tales of her skill and aggressiveness circulated among faculty with grudging admiration.

After college, a loveless relationship ended with divorce and custody of a daughter whom she adored. Deanne's fiercely passionate mothering was driven by her determination to protect her offspring from the same abuses she had known. She relished her position at Florence Bruce, which she obtained following a well-placed recommendation to John by an ex-boyfriend. It was, after all, a substantial promotion from her former employment as account representative in a large advertising agency. And it enabled her to enroll her now 10-year-old daughter at the Seminary at a substantial discount.

A tinge of the wonderment of it all crept into her voice as she related to Tom how she came to Florence Bruce, leaving out, of course, the part about the ex-boyfriend. He had taken her to a small, cupboard restaurant on Market Square where they could talk in quiet. Tom did most of the talking, telling stories of his background, his kids and what brought him to Portsmouth.

Deanne was beginning to relax. She wasn't used to sharing her background with strangers, but this fellow didn't seem dangerous. "I should tell you," she said, thinking it time to establish herself in the pecking order, "that Archie Devlin and I are seeing each other."

Tom, protecting his source, allowed as how he thought that might be the case when he saw the two of them together during a reception, but he missed the intent of the message Deanne was sending him. She was alerting him to her powerful connections, not opening up her heart. It did not occur to Tom that a romantic relationship might exist for any purpose other than love and mutual attraction. He was well aware that Deanne's relationship with Archie was cause for caution, and if he determined it was not in the best interests of Florence Bruce Seminary, he would not be deterred from taking action. Archie, he assumed—naively as it turned out—would also want what was best for the school, whatever that might be. Tom was sure good communication would enable the three of them to come to a reasonable solution.

When the food came, Tom let Deanne start eating while he continued to pursue his agenda. Leaning in to the table, he affected his best conspiratorial style. "Deanne, in my visits around the country, I have repeatedly been impressed by the importance of a website in marketing a school. I'd like to enlist your help in making the Florence Bruce site as good as it can be."

She stopped chewing to look at him, her fork poised above her plate.

"In today's world, we have to assume that every new student admitted to Florence Bruce will, at some point during the decision-making process, consult the website. Whether it's a determining factor in their decision to apply and enroll here is conjecture, but that is almost beside the point. The website, for most students, will be one of their first points of contact, and it needs to present as favorable a picture as possible."

Still no response from Deanne, but she was now on full alert.

"I'd like to make the website a priority project this summer and be positioned to launch a new site in the fall." Tom paused, taking a mouthful to fill the anticipated silence that followed.

When it was clear it was her turn to speak, Deanne said without expression, "There's no money in the budget."

"I notice that it was in your budget for last year, and didn't get spent. Wasn't it carried over?"

"No, it was in last year's budget, but John took it out this year."

"Well, as head of school, I have some discretionary authority, so I'll find the money. Will you help me get it done?"

"But it's not in my budget," Deanne repeated, hoping to deflect whatever Tom was driving at.

"I understand that. I'll find the money somewhere else. The website is a public relations department responsibility, isn't it? I'd like you to lead the effort to update it. Will you help me?"

"What do you want me to do?"

"We'll need to do a lot of the work ourselves, but we'll use a consultant to actually create the site. And we'll need a committee from the school to represent stakeholders." Tom stopped again, hoping Deanne would pick up the ball. She didn't.

"Can you do some research and put together a list of consultants who do websites?"

"I guess so."

"Now, who do you think should be on the committee?" It was like killing warts. Every time he came up with a name or a suggestion, Deanne had an objection. She volunteered nothing. Acceptance, when it was given, was given grudgingly but, finally, they had agreement. Tom would contact people to invite their participation. Deanne would arrange a first meeting, at which time she would also have a list of consultants. Tom reassured her at regular intervals that he wouldn't leave her hanging, that he would work side-by-side with her, that she would still be in charge, etc.

When lunch was over, Tom congratulated himself on a nice piece of work. He would open school in the fall with a dramatically improved website—a hard-not-to-notice accomplishment—and was now positioned to monitor the thorniest of the three personnel issues fingered by John. Life was good.

Deanne also indulged in a bout of self-congratulations. She had maintained the space around her fortress. Options were open, commitments minimal. She was publicly attached to the next president of the board, arguably the most powerful man in the school. Life wasn't too bad.

After graduation, the school emptied as if a warm Chinook wind was blowing out of the attic, sweeping old cobwebs and the detritus from a year's worth of living and learning before it. Dorm windows were opened and curtains billowed forth, while the occupants shouted out greetings to parents and siblings below. Girls tumbled out the doors with luggage in tow, laughing gaily in anticipation of vacation with families, only to dissolve into rivers of tears as departure from friends became imminent. In a few hours it was over, leaving behind only the cleaning staff, one of whom dispensed with her push broom in favor of a garden rake when the piles of trash became unmanageable.

Tom was anxious to begin his assignment. His commitment to stay removed to give John the space he needed to say his goodbyes was increasingly difficult to observe as his task list grew. Now, with students and most of the faculty gone, he had more freedom to move around, although he studiously avoided the school whenever possible and John's office absolutely. By entering that room, Tom was afraid his "appraiser's eye" would betray his eagerness—an unnecessary affront, certainly, to a man facing the end of his career.

Tom's appointment did not formally start for two more weeks, during which time the annual meeting of the board of trustees was scheduled. It was to be John's last board meeting,[2] and Tom was invited to sit in and observe the protocols—an opportunity he eagerly anticipated.

On the appointed day, Tom arrived ten minutes early and stepped out into a nearly empty parking lot under a stunningly blue sky. He was too early, but better to misjudge and be that than to intrude on a meeting already underway. Dressed in a new suit and trim from his daily workouts, he walked with studied self-confidence along a walkway lined with variegated petunias and breathed an air thick with the scent of lilac. Stepping briskly up the steps, Tom glanced

---

[2] John was more subdued than usual. It was difficult for him and it was difficult for those of us on the board as we tried to convey proper respect for a former leader and, at the same time, congratulations for a new one.

at the lintel over the door. His jaw set in resolve as he entered the building.

The slightly musty smell of old wood and tradition greeted him. In the center of the lobby was a table with a large bouquet of flowers, their sweet perfume mingling with the other aromas of the room. It registered a flicker of admiration in recognition of Mrs. Clayworth's handiwork.

Only half the lights were lit in the eight small sconces, two on each wall. None of the recessed ceiling lights high overhead were on, and the four wrought-iron drop lights cast a pale, gloomy light over the dark wood, high ceiling and recesses of the room. The dreariness of the place was accented by the absence of any of its usual youthful gaiety. Tom made a note to check into the lighting. Energy conservation was a noble goal, if that was indeed the cause, but this dim lobby held the first impression of the school for most visitors when they entered, and it contrasted sharply with the dazzling, sun-dappled exterior.

He caught sight of the large, full-length portrait of Florence Bruce. She smiled demurely down at him with a look that he found difficult to interpret. "Benevolent" was the word that came to mind as he hurried by.

Tom had formed a mental map of the seven separate egresses from this lobby—a space about the size of a normal living room. He turned confidently to the left into a hallway leading to the library. At the doorway, he ran into Jackie.

"Hi, Jackie, everything all set for the meeting?"

"Oh, yes, I had the maintenance crew bring down the board notebooks last night so they were already here when I came in this morning. I needed to do some copying for John. That would have gone faster, but the copier got stuck and I had to remove all the paper—"

"How many are you expecting?"

"We should have almost everyone here. There were three who didn't respond to my e-mails, but John said he expected Kay Johnson to come. She's been sick. I think she might be over it by now."

Tom saw Archie Devlin round the corner and greeted him warmly as he approached. Then Phyllis Killam appeared, and Tom, taking Jackie by the elbow, steered her into the library. "We better clear the hallway. It looks like we're starting to attract a crowd."

In the library, a half-dozen or so long tables with white linen tablecloths were set end-to-end, with another table set crosswise at each end in an exaggerated capital "I." At each of the seats, about thirty in all, was a place card and a large three-ring white binder. These, he learned, were the board notebooks, which contained documents for the business at hand and a record of previous board deliberations. They were not allowed to leave the school, ostensibly because trustees were notoriously lax about bringing them to meetings.[3]

In addition to the board notebook and place cards, there was a crystal water glass, napkin and writing tablet at each place. On a table set for refreshments were coffee and tea in silver pots and bottles of sparkling water poking out of a bowl of crushed ice. Fresh fruit and an array of cheeses and crackers, along with a dessert tray with an abundance of sweets greeted the arriving trustees.

Tom was inundated with well-wishers, since each trustee felt obliged upon arrival to welcome him, which left no opportunity for a meaningful conversation with any one of them. At ten minutes past the hour, Phyllis called for everyone to take seats, and the meeting commenced.

It was a fluid meeting that moved on and off the printed agenda, making it difficult for Tom to keep his place. Frequent citation of documents in the board notebook left him floundering to find the references, while most of the trustees referred to their notebooks rarely if at all. On the occasion when review of a particular document was necessary, there was an awkward moment while trustees flipped through the notebooks and someone held the desired page aloft for visual reference.

One item of intense interest to Tom was the election of new trustees and appointment of the executive committee. It was over in less than five minutes. The chair of the nominating committee was Reveta Bowler, an older alum with a penchant for interrupting

[3] My own questioning of the utility of these notebooks, which we were never allowed to bring home to review, fell on deaf ears. Agendas, minutes, committee reports, financial data and other relevant documents were entered into the books prior to the meetings rather than being sent to us ahead of time, so there was no opportunity to adequately prepare.

whatever was going on when a thought crossed her mind, which fortunately didn't happen all that often. She referred to a list of candidates for the various positions buried somewhere in the board notebook and proceeded to read off the names. Tom was still struggling to find the list when someone called for the vote, and it was done. To Tom's surprise, no request was made for nominations from the floor.[4]

As in most organizations with large boards, Florence Bruce Seminary granted authority for making many of the business decisions to an executive committee made up of the officers and a few trustees. These were the people Tom would interact with between board meetings, and he reviewed what he knew about them while carefully writing their names from his memory of Reveta's narrative.

Archie Devlin was president, as expected. Tom looked forward to working with Archie, who seemed eager to collaborate and open to new ideas. Vice-president was Geoffrey Bellingham. Tom had only met him briefly. He had a daughter who would be a senior next year and was himself a research scientist—something to do with anthropology, Tom thought. Secretary of the board was Saugus Wetherby—a great choice, in his opinion.

Bodie Bickerstaff, whom Tom was meeting for the first time, was elected treasurer. She was a businesswoman and owned an automobile dealership. Loud, opinionated and always ready to mix it up, Bodie had a reputation as devil's advocate; there was never an idea she couldn't find fault with—an assessment Tom had already formed in the short time the meeting had been underway.

The seven-member executive committee was rounded out by Warren Hudson, chair of the search committee and for whom Tom had developed an immense admiration; Keegan O'Connor, whom Tom knew would be a fun guy to have around; and Phyllis Killam.

---

[4] "When the [nominating] committee makes its report . . . the president asks if there are any other nominations, which may be made from the floor . . . . When the nominations are completed the assembly proceeds to the election." Robert's Rules of Order Section 66: Nominations and Elections. Lapses in accepted protocols were routine at Florence Bruce board meetings, and I have regretted my own acquiescence as contributory to the unfortunate events that were to unfold.

Most of the meeting was consumed with committee reports, which were either immensely informative or laboriously repetitive, depending, not unexpectedly, upon the skills of the reporter. Phyllis led the discussion, but she and John maintained an on-again, off-again banter interspersed with humorous asides and occasional stories, so the effect on the whole was somewhat entertaining.

The business of the meeting was conducted here and there as it appeared to fit. At a seemingly random point in the meeting, Jackie was sent to fetch Deanne Bakker and a middle-school science teacher whose assignment had been to create a crisis-management plan for the school. Tom stole a look at Archie, who, leaning back in his chair, beamed benevolently.

"I'd like to turn the report over to Matt to make the presentation" was the extent of Deanne's contribution, other than to distribute to each trustee an inch-thick, bound report. Her associate Matt proceeded to make a very competent presentation.

Appearances were impressive. John assured the board that money was available to implement the crisis-management plan, and it was approved. The need for and basic design of these plans had been around for a long time, and if he'd thought about it, Tom might have assumed the school already had such a plan in place. The fact that they did not was fortunately now remedied. Still, Tom thought, implementation of the plan would fall to his watch.

Other than election of the executive committee, the item that most concerned Tom was the realignment of the search committee to act as an ad hoc transition committee during his first year. Tom wasn't sure of the charge for this committee, but its formation was recommended by a number of sources including Markham Nunlist, the consultant who had guided the search process.

Meeting minutes would state the committee was formed to create an "entry plan" for Tom's first year. An important side task would be handling the new head's evaluation—another recommendation in the Nunlist report. In any case, the item was approved. Sadly for Tom, Geoffrey Bellingham was appointed chair when Warren Hudson, who had served as chair during the head search, could not make the time commitment.

At a break in the meeting, Phyllis managed to corner Tom apart from the others. As he approached her to extend a greeting, a slight shift in her stance adroitly blocked interruptions from would-be well-wishers. "Tom, I'm hearing some good things. It seems like you're already making a mark."

"Well, I don't know what you've heard. I'm just trying to get a head start. There's an incredible amount to learn. Florence Bruce is a complex organization, and I'm going to have to come up to speed pretty quickly."

"Have you figured out what you're going to tackle first?"

"No, not really. I do want to see if we can't make some progress on getting a new website up—the existing site needs a lot of work. But other than that, I'm still learning"

"You're going to need to deal with some personnel issues soon," said Phyllis. "The Middle School has had a difficult year. Some faculty members have come under a lot of fire. And there have been a number of other problems, but Everett hasn't been able to deal with them effectively. He's just not the kind of leader middle-schoolers need."

After John had expressed a similar concern, Tom had watched Everett more closely. The head of Middle and Lower Schools seemed to be a by-the-book kind of guy—perhaps not as situational as the middle-school environment often demanded. "I've heard there have been some difficulties. It's something that's certainly on my radar."

Phyllis changed the subject, her point made. With two of her own children in the Middle School, she knew firsthand there were problems. Her twins—tough, articulate, popular with their classmates—excelled, but other children more delicate in their constitution had not fared as well, and their ever-watchful parents were outspoken. Phyllis was not one to coddle—not by a long shot—and these parents did not receive much satisfaction from her. Still, they had managed to generate a groundswell of complaint, against which she had done her utmost to protect John. In her opinion, Everett was at the root of the problem. Everett and John virtually began their tenure together at Florence Bruce, and she knew that John didn't have the heart to force Everett out. She expected the new guy would.

Before he made it back to his seat for the continuation of the meeting, Tom was spun around by the shoulder and came face to face with Steve Harrison. "I'm having a lot of fun with your wife," he laughed.

Tom laughed, too. He knew Allison was enjoying Steve's company. Nightly, she regaled him with stories of their adventures together planning the Ahlborn House renovations. Steve was too open, his personality too exposed for Tom to suppose he had any other intentions in mind.

"You know, Tom, I envy you. You've got a great job. This school is like a ship. You know, one of those giant freighters on the open ocean. Your course is set. You've got momentum. You couldn't stop it if you wanted to. All you've got to do is sit back and tweak the steering every now and then to stay on course." Steve shook his head at the wonderment of it all.

Tom was too astonished at Steve's simplistic interpretation of the road ahead to muster a coherent reply. Instead, he muttered something like, "Yeah, it's a great job all right." His to-do list was growing geometrically, and he didn't even know the half of it yet.

Later that evening, Tom continued to ponder what a proper metaphor might be for his new job. His career at the San Diego Maritime Institute eventually provided the right image. It was, he thought, a great tall ship making its way through a turbulent sea, buffeted by waves, driven by the currents and at the mercy of the winds for any progress at all. Instead of a freighter's standard crew of hardly a dozen men, this ship required a crew of nearly a hundred sailors, each highly skilled and coordinated as a team. Small course corrections might be made from time to time without much effort, but large ones required everyone working together in a closely choreographed dance. And, since the ship could not sail directly into the wind, the best course was not always a straight line but rather a zigzagging combination of tacks and jibes that kept the ship moving in the general direction. He dozed off with a white bone in his teeth.[5]

[5] A tall ship under a press of sail creates a substantial, continuously breaking bow wave. Such a ship, sailors would say, has a "white bone in her teeth."

CHAPTER IX

Engagement

♠

The mission should appear on all documents, on the phone, and in the conference room. *Live* with the mission.[1]

July 1st was a Sunday. Tom awoke before dawn full of anticipation for the day ahead. He lay in bed with Allison, his hand on the curve of her hip, waiting until the first rays of sunlight streaming in the cracks around the drawn shade drove him out of bed. It was to be his first day on the job at Florence Bruce—the first day he'd had a steady paycheck since leaving the San Diego Maritime Institute almost four months before. Most importantly, today he would occupy his office.

The couple had plenty of time to eat a leisurely breakfast and read the morning paper before packing up the car with a few odds and ends and heading off to the school together. The blossoms had long ago fallen from the rhododendrons, but the annuals—petunias, pansies and geraniums—were in full bloom as Tom and Allison walked from the parking lot to the main entrance.

---

[1] Carver, John. *Boards That Make a Difference: a New Design for Leadership in Nonprofit and Public Organizations.* San Francisco: Jossey-Bass Publishers, 1990, p. 66.

Turning right up the walkway, they faced a full frontal view of Florence Bruce Seminary. Tom felt his knees go weak from the weight of what he was about to begin—four-hundred-fifty students; one-hundred-twenty faculty, administrators and staff; along with countless parents and alumnae, all with more than two hundred years of tradition behind them. The burden of the chain of history had now shifted to his shoulders. It was a daunting realization and yet, at the same time, thrilling beyond anything he had known. The magnificent edifice before him seemed to reach out, extending its embrace. He waved the electronic key fob in front of the sensor and the door unlatched.

At 10:00 AM Sunday morning, no one else was in the building, at least no one they could see. Tom and Allison ascended the main staircase, passed the portrait of Florence Bruce, and turned right at the top of the stairs down the narrow hallway to the headmaster's office. The ancient wooden floor creaked in protest under their step. If anyone had been in residence, it would have been impossible to keep their presence a secret. Tom felt on his ring for the key he had been given only two days earlier, inserted it into the lock and opened the door.

They felt like intruders in someone else's domain—like Goldilocks entering the home of the three bears. His office was big, even bigger than Tom remembered. Allison's mouth dropped open in astonishment; it was her first visit. Rather plain as rooms go, it more than made up for that deficiency by its sheer size and its stupendous views of the campus and the flow of water traffic in the nearby Piscataqua River.

Opposite the door, against the far wall and to the left, was John's desk, now cleared of its accessories, leaving behind only footprints in the dust. Tom approached this penultimate symbol of authority, gingerly running his hands over the smooth top and feeling the plush leather of the chair. He came around and stood behind the desk, both hands on its surface, and surveyed his realm. After a moment, he closed his eyes, feeling the mantle of leadership descending upon his shoulders, and allowed himself to sink back into the chair behind him. His whoop of laughter startled Allison as he collapsed into its interior.

"Well, that's the first thing we'll change," he said as he arose. He slid the chair, fitted for John's huge bulk, out from behind the desk and replaced it with a smaller chair from the conference table at the opposite end of the room.

In addition to the desk and an attached credenza for a computer terminal, the room held a conference table with seating for eight and a serving table for coffee—and occasionally, as Tom already knew, eggs benedict. A sofa, two chairs and a coffee table occupied another corner of the room, while a filing cabinet, a bookshelf nearly devoid of books and a side table were positioned around the room against the walls. A pair of square, load-bearing columns in the middle of the room held up a low, uneven ceiling that sagged at its joints.

As Tom set about assembling his own laptop computer, which the school's technology guru had already outfitted with a wireless connectivity card, Allison busied herself straightening up the room, disposing of odd scraps of paper and examining the few artifacts John had left behind. "You know," she said, "this room could sure use a coat of paint." The walls were a kind of cream color. The exact shade could no longer be determined, as age and dirt had varied the tint, depending upon where in the room one looked. The paint was peeling in places and cracks showed through where pieces of drywall had been fitted together when the room was built or last remodeled.

"And another thing . . ."

Tom looked up. His focus on the computer setup had been total, but with connectivity achieved to his satisfaction, he returned to the world at hand. "What's that, honey?"

"I think you should switch the desk with the conference table," she said in her best I-know-what-I'm-saying tone of voice.

"Why would you do that?"

"It's too exposed opposite the door. Everyone can look in and see what you're doing. If your desk was here by the wall, you'd have privacy and be able to look out across the room. Besides, when you have meetings at the conference table, it would be over there next to the windows where everyone can enjoy the view."

"Perhaps you're right. I've got other things on my mind right now, though. Maybe later." But within a week, the furniture was rearranged. And before the summer ended, the wall cracks were filled and his office was painted a rich caramel color.

After a second trip to bring over a few family photographs and to hang his diplomas, they celebrated with two drinks each and dinner out at the Kittery Lobster Barn, talking long into the evening about Allison's plans for the Ahlborn House and reflecting on the various tasks ahead of them.

* * *

It was summertime, a time for relaxation and rejuvenation of body and spirit. Minds worked at half-speed. Inertia followed every project as if attached to a pair of leg irons. Tom had been around schools before. He knew this to be true and was not surprised. Still, adjusting to the rhythm of summer within the culture of Florence Bruce would take some effort, especially in his energized state.

Tom was at the office by 7:30 AM, as would be his routine for the rest of the year. He would leave the office at 4:30 PM whenever he could for a 45-minute run or a bike ride before dinner. He and Allison would eat dinner while watching the evening news, following which he would retire to his desk to catch up on paperwork; sometimes he would return to school for an evening activity. When school was in session, most weekends would be consumed as well: speech preparation, meetings, sporting events, field trips with students, drama productions. The list seemed endless. This first year, Tom would take no sick days or personal days—although he seldom got sick, maybe three or four times in a twenty-five-year career. He would take three vacation days so that he and Allison could join Caroline Odum and her husband on a cruise to Penobscott Bay, and three more in the spring to visit his daughters in California. It was a grueling schedule, and it would tax his stamina to its capacity and more before it was over.

Monday morning, after hanging up his coat on the rack in the corner and reminding himself to bring a hanger, he turned on his computer and watched its lights blink awake. While it was booting up, he dropped down two floors to the kitchen. Hot coffee was already brewed and ready on a hotplate, but no one was in sight. He poured a cup and returned to his office, busying himself by responding to e-mails, setting up a few personal files in a lower drawer and making lists of things he would need.

Jackie arrived at 8:05 AM. He heard her coming. Even her slight frame and buoyant cheerfulness were too much for the aging floorboards, and they creaked in feigned protest. His door was open and she bounded in. "Welcome to Florence Bruce Seminary," she chirped, setting a bouquet of flowers and a wrapped package on his desk. "It looks like the big day for you has finally arrived."

Tom stood up and gave her an impulsive hug, thanking her for the gifts. The package turned out to be an artificial apple about the size of a grapefruit, and it instantly became a permanent fixture on his desk. They chatted a bit about weather, summer vacations and faculty. Jackie was an inveterate gossip.

"Miguel Barrera might get married this summer," she offered after a convoluted description of her psoriasis that Tom could have done without.

"Really, I heard he was quite the ladies' man." Tom, thinking the conversation had already gone on too long, was looking for a way to end it.

"Oh, he is. He's had a couple of flings," Jackie replied conspiratorially, lowering her voice and naming two of the more comely females on the faculty. "And there were even some parents, but I heard he's met someone now."

Tom looked at Jackie intently but didn't break in, so she went on. "You know he has a lot of people mad at him. They say he's the reason why the Middle School is so bad."

"I'm surprised. John seemed to think Miguel is a good teacher."

"Yes, he is a good teacher. Did you know he directs the middle-school play every year?"

Jackie was able to adapt effortlessly to the prejudices of her listener, but it was too late. Her casual criticism of the school and its faculty ran contrary to Tom's own feelings of loyalty to the institution entrusting him with its leadership.

Mildly troubled by what this might portend for his own relationship with her, but with much already on his mind, he chose to ignore Jackie's ramblings and focus on the business ahead. Time was already set aside this morning to begin working out expectations and protocols for the business side of their relationship.

Tom expected it to be a close one. At the San Diego Maritime Institute, his executive assistant Penny had been at his side for thirteen years, and no one else, Allison included, knew his personal habits and working style as well as she did. Penny was an extension of Tom; they were joined at the hip. Her loyalty to him was unquestioned. He trusted her with the most confidential knowledge of the organization and the most intimate details of his working relationships. He kept nothing hidden, and her value to him increased exponentially with her ability to second-guess his needs. He hoped to find in Jackie a similar confidant and aide-de-camp.

Once they settled in together at the conference table, Tom leaned close, imploring, "Jackie, my relationship with you will be as important as any other relationship in the school, as important, even, as my relationship with Archie Devlin. You will know things that I won't be able to share with anyone else. I will need to trust you completely and be able to count on you keeping what I say confidential."

She seemed surprised by his blunt admission. "Oh, you can count on me. My lips are sealed once I leave this office. You can't believe how much gossip goes on around this school, but I've never been one to gossip. I know how much it can get you in trouble, and I listen but stay quiet. Last year, there was a big brouhaha about some information that leaked out about the candidates, you know, for your job. Some of the board members thought I did it, but it wasn't me." Jackie's eyes grew moist from the memory.

Tom let her go, interrupting from time to time to be sure he got the gist of the story. It wasn't anything that appeared to be of particular concern, but he was not convinced she did as much "listening" as she claimed. Finally, he decided enough was enough. "Tell me what you did for John. I want to know how he ran things and what he expected from you. I saw him give you a tape for transcribing when I was here for a meeting—did he do that often? How did he handle correspondence?"

"That's how he did all his correspondence. He dictated his speeches and all his work, or else he wrote it out longhand for me to type."

"Didn't he know how to type?"

"He typed kind of with two fingers, you know. He had big hands, and I'm not sure they fit on a keyboard. Anyway, I hardly ever saw him type."

"What about a computer?" Tom asked, somewhat aghast. "There was one on his desk. How did he use it if he couldn't type?"

"He didn't use it much. It didn't even work most of the time. He had all his e-mails sent to me, and if I thought it was important, I'd print out a copy for him. If he wanted to reply, he'd write it or dictate it, and I'd send it from my terminal."

Tom was floored, and his astonishment compounded when Jackie told him that John didn't use the Internet either. Aside from a poor website, the Florence Bruce technology program was first class. Wireless technology allowed access to the school server and the Internet from anywhere on campus. A laptop program began in the sixth grade and continued all the way through to graduation. Every classroom from Kindergarten on up contained computer stations, and many of the teachers had received specialized computer training. How did all this come about when the headmaster was so ignorant of the technology?

"It was mostly the director of the technology department," Jackie told him. "He was always making appointments with John to tell him about this or that project, and John mostly went along even when the tab got pretty high." Tom had met the director and already congratulated him on the school's advanced programs. Jackie confirmed his initial assessment.

"Jackie, you will find I work a little differently than John did. I do most of my own correspondence, except when I'll ask you to create a letter from scratch. I prefer to e-mail my letters to you for proofing and preparation of the envelope. Do you have a database of school addresses to work from?"

"I use the school directory."

"Where does the information in the directory come from? What happens if it changes during the year?"

"The directories are published in the fall. I keep the information for the board directory in a Word document and change it when I need to."

"A Word document? What about John's special contacts? What about donors and parents or school alumnae? How do you keep track of them?"

Jackie seemed nonplussed at Tom's concern and rapid-fire questions. "Yes, I kept a Word document of John's contacts and checked with the admissions department or the development department on the others."

Since so many of the school's constituencies overlapped, Tom knew that a simple address change would need to be recorded in several different places. Errors and duplications were inevitable. "Who develops mailing lists when school publications are sent?"

"I think the public relations department takes care of that."

"How can you be sure the trustees or any of John's special contacts get mailings of school publications?"

Jackie hedged, but added helpfully, "If anyone calls to say they didn't get one, I just put it in a separate envelope and mail it to them."

That explained why Tom, despite two separate calls since January, had been unable to get the *Seminary Log* mailed to him as a matter of course—no system existed for getting him on the mailing list. And if he couldn't get one, how could anyone else?[2]

Getting all the constituencies into one umbrella database would be a major undertaking, but there was no other way to avoid duplication, make corrections that stuck, and ensure everyone in the community was accounted for. That would have to come later. For now, he looked for a less complicated solution. "Jackie, I'm going to install a simple database so you won't have to keep Word document lists. Do you know Access?" he asked, naming the Microsoft application in which a database can be easily written.

"No, I'm afraid I don't, but I'd love to learn. Do you know where I can find any classes?"

They talked for a while about options for improving her skills. Tom was impressed with Jackie's enthusiasm and apparent willingness to jump into a new endeavor. For the next two hours, he grilled her on all manner of topics. How did she help John prepare for board meetings? What was the report structure like? Who reported directly to John? Did she have a copy of the school calendar? How often did board committees meet? Which committees had been most active over the past year? He probed her knowledge of personalities, naming individual trustees and faculty members, and compared her responses to the ones John had given him.

Jackie was sharp, her knowledge of the school encyclopedic, and she seemed willing to adjust to his peculiarities in style. She had some skill deficiencies, but those could be overcome. Her tendency to fill any void with gossip and chitchat was an annoyance that Tom thought could be controlled, since she didn't seem to mind when he interrupted her mid-sentence.

That afternoon, Tom unwrapped a large mounted poster imprinted with the Florence Bruce mission statement and headed to the Bainbridge

[2] Conversely, my problem was duplicate publications. It was not uncommon for me to receive two or even three copies of a school publication, and, try as I might, I could never remedy the situation. In my experience, however, this is not unusual. I belong to a number of nonprofit organizations where my participation as a donor, trustee or some other member group leaves me on different, unreconciled lists within the same organization.

Room. The previous week he had addressed a memo to all school employees inviting them to join him for a meeting to get acquainted. Many administrators and most of the faculty were on vacation or otherwise pre-disposed, but it was the gesture that mattered, and he would engage whomever showed up.

About fifteen people were in the room when he arrived. Another fifteen would drift in and out over the next hour as the conversation flowed. Most of the participants he recognized, but there were a few he didn't.

A round of introductions gave way to questions. "What do you want to be called?"

"I prefer the familiar. After all, we are colleagues here. Call me Tom, except when there are students around and then please refer to me as Dr. Whitman."

"You use the term 'head of school.' John Sanford was 'headmaster.' Do you prefer one over the other?"

"Either one will do, but I prefer 'head of school.' The term 'headmaster' is a bit old-fashioned. It refers to a time when there were master teachers and the principal of the school was the head of the master teachers, or 'headmaster.'"

After thirty minutes of give-and-take, Tom stood and propped his poster with the school's mission statement on a chair where everyone in the room could view it. "I want to draw your attention to something I feel is very important for us to keep in the forefront of our thinking this year," he said.

"All school mission statements have elements in common. This one, however, embodies the thoughts, feelings, dreams and aspirations of a group of people deeply committed to Florence Bruce Seminary, people who worked very hard to communicate to those of us who now hold the future of the school in our hands." Tom lifted the poster from the chair and walked with it around the room to emphasize his point. "During the coming year, I will display this poster of the mission statement at various meetings and events. My goal is to encourage all of us to appreciate its meaning and use it for guidance as we go about our work."

Tom's analysis of the Florence Bruce mission statement when he first encountered it was positive. It articulated three components he considered praiseworthy: service to self (happiness/success), service to the state (good citizens) and service to God (spiritual vigor). This was a school whose trustees had put serious thought into its mission.

After the meeting Tom posted his notes via e-mail to every employee. So positive was the response that he pledged to hold a "town meeting" every week during the summer and was true to his word. At a subsequent gathering, he asked, "What can we do to improve the first impressions of the people who come to visit?"

"What do you mean by 'first impressions'?"

"First impressions may determine whether a highly qualified student chooses to enroll or whether a prospective donor makes a contribution. First impressions will enhance or detract from a school's reputation and often set a pattern for classroom behavior."

Suggestions were not long in coming:

"Upgrade the telephone system, so calls are answered promptly and routed to the right person."

"Get more light in the lobby and maybe a sign or some form of greeting for first-time visitors."

"Replant the garden out by the street. All the plants have died, and there's nothing there but weeds now."

"Proofread the publications, especially the *Seminary Log,* to get rid of typos and grammatical errors."

These were all good, doable ideas. Tom added them to a list that began, "redo the website," and set in motion plans to address each one before the opening of school in the fall.

Allison was doing dishes and Tom was reading the paper when the phone rang. It was Archie. "Got any plans for tomorrow? Deanne and I are going to rustle up a barbeque with the kids and some friends, and then walk down to Newcastle to watch the fireworks. Want to join us?"

It sounded like fun. Archie lived a few blocks from the school in an antebellum-style mini-mansion that he had bought several years ago when it became too small for Phyllis Killam's growing family. Tom and Allison knocked on the door at 4:00 PM. Deanne Bakker was in the kitchen chopping vegetables and looking very domestic. Archie greeted them in his overly solicitous manner: bending forward, taking their hands in his, and saying how so very pleased he was they could join him.

A few family members and friends were scattered around the house while their kids romped out of one room and into another. Tom and Allison engaged in small talk with the guests and enjoyed a typical American Fourth.

As the sky began to darken, which at this latitude and time of year was well after 9:00 PM, folding chairs and blankets were gathered for the short walk to the waterfront, where the fireworks display was set to be launched from a barge anchored offshore. The streets filled with parked cars and were closed off one after the other. People streamed down the hill, spilling off the sidewalks into the streets. A band struck up "The Star Spangled Banner." When the music reached "the rockets' red glare," a bright flash rent the sky, followed by an enormous bang.

After the display, Allison and Tom walked home together hand-in-hand. "That relationship looks pretty solid to me," said Allison quietly.

"You mean Archie and Deanne," Tom said, nodding agreement as he spoke. It had looked pretty solid to him, too.

"Yeah, that could be trouble down the road. If she's an alcoholic like John said, you'll have a problem on your hands, because Archie won't see it."

"Well, John didn't exactly say she was an alcoholic. Besides, I'm working with her, and we seem to be making progress."

A week into his tenure, Jackie asked Tom if he wanted to distribute a policy regarding "summer hours." She said it as if she thought he should.

"What are summer hours?"

Jackie said John always posted a memorandum before school let out in June stating that summer hours were from 8:30 in the morning until 4:00 in the afternoon, meaning that faculty and staff didn't need to arrive for work before 8:30 AM and could leave at 4:00 PM.

"Why didn't John issue the memorandum already?"

"John said it was up to you to do it."

Summer hours were not part of Tom's lexicon, so he demurred, saying he would take the matter under advisement.

"Nancy, tell me about this 'summer hours' thing." Tom plopped into a chair in the corner of Nancy Wolf's cramped office in the finance department, drawing up his knees so his feet didn't encounter hers.

"It's a private-school deal," she said. "Full-time, non-faculty employees are supposed to work a twelve-month year just like everyone else, but in the summer, without much going on, many schools have summer hours and cut back on the eight-hour workday. The problem is that some departments—mine for instance—have a heavy summer workload. I've told my people they can't have summer hours. I need them here with me. We're buried, and it will take us most of the summer to dig ourselves out."

"I don't get it. Doesn't every department have projects that have been put on hold during the school year? It seems to me there should be a lot of work to do in the summer."

"To be honest, you'd think so. Some do, but most don't. It's kind of up to the department head. Maintenance and the kitchen staff are pretty busy; most of them are hourly anyway. John used to disappear during the whole month of July, and things would kind of fall apart. Some people you'll see in here on a regular basis, and some you won't."

"How do you know when someone's on vacation or just not coming in?"

"Oh, don't get me started." Nancy rolled her eyes. "Before I came there were no records of vacation-time use. Everyone just kept their own. When I asked for an accounting, I got these staggering numbers of accumulated vacation days from some employees. I instituted a policy that put a limit on the number of vacations days that any one person could accumulate. I gave everyone to the end of this summer to use up whatever they had. Gosh, you should have seen all the complaints, but I stuck it out. Now, I require people to fill out a form for their vacation time."

"You mean up until this year there were no official records of vacation time accumulated or used?"

"That's right."

"Geez, we could get killed if the labor relations folks[3] decided to do an investigation." He pondered the implications for a moment and then added, "Didn't the audits take into account unused vacation time?"

"No, not before I got here."

---

[3] The New Hampshire Department of Labor investigates and remedies employer/employee relations under the Federal Fair Labor Standards Act. The NHDL seldom investigates unless an employee files a complaint. Tom's experience came in California where enforcement can be rigorous and the consequences to an employer devastating. New Hampshire, however, takes a more benign view.

"That means our assets are probably overstated," said Tom, looking up at the ceiling, mentally calculating.

"You're right, but it's not that bad. I've pretty much got a handle on it now. The audit for this past year will show unused vacation time as a liability."

Tom continued his inquiries on summer hours through the rest of the week, receiving varying opinions on the subject. Peg Scott, director of the Upper School, had a different twist. "I work my tail off during the school year," she said, which he knew to be true. "There isn't any sacrifice I won't make to get my job done, but when summer is here, I don't expect to be held to an eight-hour day in the office. I come in most days, but this is a time for thinking, catching up on my reading and maybe doing a little writing. I can do that at home or at the beach as easily as I can do it in the office." Then, with a touch of vehemence, she added, "I'm a professional, and I expect to be treated like one."

She was right. Tom knew Peg to be one of the hardest working people in the school and someone to be trusted. Except for a couple of meetings during the summer when he needed her input, he didn't care what she did with her days. She was as capable of getting her work done outside the office as inside the office.

"Here's what I've decided about summer hours," he told Jackie a few days later. "I'm not going to declare them. We'll issue a memo that says, in effect, we're all professionals here. If there's work to be done, we need to do whatever is necessary to get it done. If the work is done, then there's no point staying here. It seems to me that's the reality anyway."

"What about me? What should I do?" Jackie's anxiety was evident.

"You can come in at 8:30 AM. If your work is done by 4:00 PM, then you can go home like anyone else."[4]

---

[4] Jackie, unlike the school's other administrative assistants, was classified as an "exempt" employee, which meant she was considered by law to be a "professional," as were the school's teachers and administrators. For her, Tom's statement to her accurately reflected the professional attitude—as long as the work is completed to the best of one's ability, the time it takes to do it or when it is done is immaterial. The IRS, however, would likely have disagreed with the classification for Jackie, as her work assignment did not warrant the exempt status.

Unbeknownst to Tom, his memo was an affront to a school culture where everyone watched, everyone compared, and standards were set to fit the lowest common denominator. Nancy's attention and dedication to her workload were rare. Craig Gowdy better fit the mold. Despite three years of stagnant enrollments, the director of admissions and his assistant mentally vacationed with the students each summer, occupying their offices only as required. For them, as for others in the school, official permission for their neglect came in the form of "summer hours."

Tom's refusal to provide that permission angered some. "We've always had summer hours." "We work hard and deserve a break." "He just got here; how does *he* know what we do?" The grumbling was not substantial, and few were around to hear it, but that would change.

"Do you have plans for vacation this summer?" asked Tom, directing the question to Jackie, who had just entered his office with an armload of filing.

"Yes, I do. With you just starting and all, I thought you'd probably need me; but I do plan to take a week in July and a week in August."

"That will be fine," said Tom, opening his calendar. Together they picked the weeks for Jackie's vacation, and Tom asked her to complete the proper forms for submission to the business office. Jackie had never filled them out before, so he showed her how.

CHAPTER X

The Journey Begins

♠

Dreaming is not only permissible for leaders, it is obligatory.[1]

Deanne walked into her office at 9:30 AM after delivering Lexi to her summer school class on the floor below and lingering for a while to confab with the other parents who were dropping off their children. She found the routine relaxing. That she arrived at her office an hour after her colleagues had already collected their coffee and were hard at work didn't seem to be a problem.

Nevertheless, this morning she was ill at ease. Her website committee was meeting for the first time, and she didn't know what to expect.

The group of faculty assigned to the task assembled with great anticipation. Though not openly expressed, it was a commonly held opinion that the present website was beyond redemption. Moreover, those attending looked forward to seeing their new leader in action.

It was five minutes past the hour, and eyes were beginning to stray to the clock on the wall when Tom turned to Deanne. "Would you like to begin?"

---

[1] Carver, John. *Boards That Make a Difference: a New Design for Leadership in Nonprofit and Public Organizations.* San Francisco: Jossey-Bass Publishers, 1990, p. 29.

"You called the meeting."

"I thought you might like to lead it."

Deanne was trapped. Her preparations had been minimal. She thought fleetingly of leaving the room, but that was out of the question. A counterattack was not possible in so public an arena. Lapsing into a childhood strategy, she curved her lips into a smile, and in a soft, little-girl voice pitched half an octave higher than normal, said, "Well, I have this list of consultants that could help us."

There was a moment of uncomfortable silence while the committee looked at the three names printed on the sheet that Deanne had handed them before Tom spoke again. "Do you have any information on any of these consultants?"

"No, you didn't ask me to do that."

The words, though delivered in the same soft, singsong monotone, felt like ice. Her eyes flashed a smoldering hatred.

Where did that come from? Tom looked around, but the others in the room seemed oblivious. *Am I the only one who noticed?* Deanne's voice also puzzled him. Why had it switched so suddenly from authority and strength to a little girl's falsetto?

Tom had no choice but to take the reins of the meeting. Deanne's anger seemed spent, and she sat passively, responding only when spoken to. It ended with a discussion of the website's stakeholders. Tom asserted that everyone in the school was a stakeholder whose lives would be affected by the work they were about to begin. The new site design would result in web pages that would need to be researched and then filled with text and photos. Committee members were assigned sections of the design and asked to seek creative input from faculty whose job responsibilities provided expertise.

Work on the website continued throughout the summer. Deanne did bring in qualification statements from the three consultants, and interviews were held. Despite Tom's encouragement to make a selection based on the committee's input, she demurred and insisted he decide.

Refinement of the design continued. Text and photos started to accumulate, and the designers went to work. "Let's make the site warm and friendly, like the school," encouraged Tom. He made room for a photo of himself and Allison with a personal statement welcoming visitors, and encouraged each faculty member to do the same. In the beginning, there was reluctance on the part of the faculty to include personal names and e-mail addresses, but gradually, over a period of months, one after another came around until every faculty member had uploaded a photo and a personal note on the website. Use statistics would show these to be the most popular pages on the site.

Deanne eventually caught the spirit. She created a splendid section called "Student Life," and Tom was effusive with his compliments. "News & Weather" was added, along with a search engine, daily menus and sports schedules. The Parents' Association took possession of its own section and personalized it. The admissions and development departments did likewise. The new Florence Bruce website was launched on schedule, in September, and kudos began arriving from parents and alumnae drawn to a site that was compelling in its architecture and downright fun to explore.

After the second meeting of the committee, however, when Deanne had again resisted a leadership role, Tom had taken her aside. "Deanne, I can see this is making you uncomfortable. I will lead the meetings from now on, but let's get together and reflect on what I'm doing from time to time. There's a skill involved in motivating people, making effective assignments and achieving consensus. It's a skill you need in your position, and I want to help you be more effective."

Deanne was angry later that evening when she recalled the conversation. *He was putting me down*, she said to herself, and poured her first drink—a vodka martini—in almost four months. Although Tom hadn't yelled or otherwise threatened her, and that was reassuring to a degree, she would avoid him whenever possible just to be on the safe side.

Archie was eager to get started on his new charter. He had recently quit a committee of the American Medical Association to allow more time for his responsibilities as president of the board at Florence Bruce Seminary. Archie was a pediatrician by training, but he no longer practiced. Although still in his forties, Archie had retired when his wife passed away to devote himself to raising his daughters—both of whom were enrolled at Florence Bruce. A small family trust allowed them to live a comfortable lifestyle despite the lack of earned income.

The passing of Archie's wife was indescribably traumatic. They were high-school sweethearts, best friends, and inseparable in marriage.

Archie was heartbroken when she died, despite the combined efforts of family and friends over many months to console him with their comfort and support. Archie was the center of concern whenever they gathered, and all around him felt his grief.

As the years passed, Archie became convinced that no woman could ever take the place of his deceased wife, and he resigned himself to live out the rest of his life as a single man. Why fate had chosen him to be so cruelly tortured, he could not comprehend. Having been given such bliss, to have it snatched away at the height of its promise was too much for him to bear.

One of his few consolations was Florence Bruce Seminary. Archie's own family lived on the other side of the country, and professional friendships dwindled as his involvement in the medical community grew less and less. Florence Bruce filled the void in his life, and he found himself spending more and more time there. His stature in the school community took on the aura of myth. He was a stoic father and grieving husband who had lost his wife to a cruel cancer.

More than a few dinner parties were arranged with Archie opposite a comely, sensitive young woman with the breeding carefully calculated to please a man of his cultured temperament. Often, a date followed and then another—dinner at a fine restaurant, a night out at the theater. By and large, these were all accomplished women, and as their personalities emerged and began to shape the relationship, Archie would retreat. They didn't look like his beloved, they didn't act like his beloved, and they didn't feel like his beloved. In time, Archie would return to his well-meaning hosts and sadly explain that it wasn't going to work out—he just wasn't ready yet—and the hosts would explain to the young woman that it wasn't her fault.

Deanne was different. Like many of the others, she first came to his attention at a dinner party hosted by friends. She had been employed at the school for some time, but she wasn't someone he encountered all that often. Deanne, however, wanted to meet him and arranged the opportunity through a mutual friend.

She was tall, handsome, even elegant, and Archie certainly was attracted to her. A succession of dates followed. She made no demands on him. Archie chose the topics and piloted the conversations; she reflected back only what she heard him say. Archie chose the place, the time and the dates of their assignations; she quietly acquiesced. Deanne didn't call him and she certainly didn't nag him. She was gentle with the children and brought a feminine presence into their lives. She was so very patient and empathetic when his wife's name came up, and she didn't comment on the photos of her that filled the house. Deanne had been to this place before, and she was very careful.

When Archie took her to bed, it was with some trepidation. He had not been able to drive his wife's image from his mind, and his attempts at intimacy had heretofore not met with much success. Deanne was very patient. When nothing happened on the first night, she wasn't in the least bit fazed, and they slept together until dawn. It took three times. When Archie reached his first climax with a woman since the passing of his wife, his gratitude was unconditional.

Gradually, Deanne began to reveal pieces of her own life. They needed no embellishment. Archie was smitten by the terrors she had known, and hours were spent commiserating in each other's arms. They were two victims of fate blown together in a hard, cruel world, and Archie pledged to her his unwavering support.

Archie's close friends—mostly other parents whose daughters shared a grade with one of his own—were happy to see them together. The few who knew Deanne at school remarked how different she seemed around Archie—more reserved and certainly more deferential than they were accustomed to seeing her.

It was mid-July when Tom entered the restaurant where he and Archie had planned their first formal meeting. Archie was already there. The two men greeted each other with genuine affection and spent the next two hours excitedly painting with broad strokes their future together. Archie had served on the board for three years, but was coming to the table with a clean slate. He was not part of the inner circle that had included Phyllis and John, so his knowledge of the details of school leadership was limited; whereas Tom had served on several boards and had definite ideas about their efficient running. Archie talked about forging a dynamic partnership between the board and the new head, and Tom added his endorsement.

Their mutual optimism and confidence fueled Archie's anticipation. His apprenticeship had run its course and he was eager to take the reins. He had admired Phyllis and John, and coveted their elevated stature in the community and the close relationship they enjoyed.

Until now Archie had been kept at a distance from all that, and now it was to be his.

Tom saw a school with more than its share of challenges—certainly more than he had seen when he signed on—and there were more, he knew, that had not yet surfaced. Tom was not intimidated, but meeting those challenges would certainly be less problematic if the board of trustees was in harmony with the direction he took. To that end, no relationship would be more significant than his relationship with Archie Devlin.

Their conversation was sprinkled with positive words, such as cooperation, teamwork and collaboration. They shared thoughts on the Campaign for Florence Bruce and the new construction it would fund. Tom described what he knew about the accreditation process that would commence in the fall. Archie asked Tom to help him assemble a list of members for the board's seven standing committees—appointments he would make at the September meeting.

The lunch was going well. Tom decided it was time to broach the topic of Archie's relationship with Deanne. "Archie, there's one subject I think we need to get out on the table. I feel a bit awkward about mentioning it, but it's your relationship with Deanne. Ordinarily, it would be no business of mine, except, of course, that she's an employee."

A sigh, deep and emotive, escaped Archie's lips. He knew this would be a worry. When he had first begun dating Deanne, Archie had sought "permission" from John, who had told him he did not see the relationship as an insurmountable problem so long as Archie kept in mind that he was wearing two hats.

To Tom, Archie said, "I know why you're concerned, and I am very mindful of the fact that I am wearing 'two hats.' When you and I speak, I am wearing my 'Florence Bruce hat.' You can be absolutely assured that what you say will be held in strictest confidence."

"Thank you for that," Tom replied. "I do expect to be sharing my thoughts with you on topics no one else in the school will know about. Confidentiality is important."

"You can count on me. Deanne talks to me occasionally about what is happening at school, but I know it can't work the other way around."

Confidentiality was a concern, but it was not at the top of Tom's list of worries.

"Archie, I need the public relations director to spearhead some of the issues we want to tackle this year, and I don't think Deanne is up to it right now. I expect to work closely with her; in fact, I've already started a dialogue with her on a new website design. I'm going to do my best to mentor her through the next few months, but it could get rough. If that happens, I'll need you to—"

"Oh, I understand," Archie interrupted. "My Florence Bruce hat is on now, and I won't say anything about what we've talked about."

Tom was just as sure he *didn't* understand. "There may be times, Archie, when you have on your 'family hat' and will have to guide Deanne through some difficult times. In my experience, you can't keep the hats separate. What you need to do is be judicious in how the information you gain while wearing one hat is used when you are wearing the other."

Tom had stretched the metaphor too thin, and Archie lost the thread of its meaning. Deanne had shared nothing as yet of her encounters with Tom, so Archie saw nothing to be particularly concerned about.

He gripped Tom's right shoulder as they left the restaurant. After two handshakes and a dozen expressions of goodwill, they parted. Tom was about to embrace him—benevolence filled his heart—but he thought better of it and stopped before his arms left his sides.

"Steve, I need your help," said Allison as they stood among the bare studs and exposed wiring in the kitchen of the Ahlborn House. "I'm just realizing, once we're finished with the remodeling, there will still be a lot of work needed to get this house looking the way we want it to."

Steve was admiring the deconstructed kitchen, imagining how it would look when the cabinetry was in. "What else do we need?" Walls, floors, bathrooms—Steve thought in big chunks and didn't consider that a transition might be needed between an empty house and a van full of household belongings. Nor did he yet fully appreciate Allison's emerging plan to utilize the house as an extension of the school.

"We tore up the carpeting when we redid the floors and we'll need to replace it with something. The drapes are old and falling apart; the window blinds are broken. We have furniture for personal use, but not of the kind or quality these front rooms will need if we're going to use them for entertaining.

"I'm going to buy a baby grand piano," Allison went on. "It's something I've always wanted, and it will look beautiful in the living room. I envision we can use it for school recitals, but that's all Tom and I will be able to contribute."

Allison's concerns were a little beyond Steve's own level of competence or interest, but he agreed to talk to Phyllis about it. Phyllis had been through a number of remodels and had no trouble understanding the problem. "The board approved $60,000 for the renovation; I guess we can go up another $10,000 for decorating," she said. There was no doubt the board would approve the addition, had Phyllis brought the matter to them for a decision. Therefore, in the interest of sparing the effort, she eliminated that unnecessary step.

Told she had another $10,000 to spend, Allison was elated, not knowing just what that would buy. As she was soon to discover: not very much.

Continuing her quest for interior decorations, in a locked storeroom across the street on the third floor of the school, Allison found an antique treasure trove—a dining room table with chairs and matching sideboard, assorted arm chairs, two settees, three end tables, lamps and several room-sized oriental rugs. She found historic artwork from the school, including a beautifully framed portrait of Guy Victor Bruce with his daughter Florence. At that moment, her inspiration to turn the Ahlborn House into a historic extension of the school took hold with an iron grip that would not be denied.

Using the oriental rugs as her basis and with the help of a designer knowledgeable about regional décor and the seasonal interplay of light, Allison chose colors for the rooms. She selected cornflower blue and dusty purple for the walls in the two guest rooms and ordered matching bedding. She chose a shade of beige for the "public" areas of the house and then left with Tom for a long weekend of cruising Penobscott Bay with the Odums. Twenty-four hours later, she was agonizing over her decision of "brown walls" and called the designer by cell phone from Eggemoggin Reach. He reassured her that they would be lovely, suggesting she think of the color as "warm camel."

Allison sketched floor plans to explore room arrangements with various pieces of the antique furniture. All of the upholstery was badly worn and stained, but the furniture's woodwork was beautiful and perfectly in keeping with the décor of the school. Among the array of plush fabrics for re-upholstering, she opted for rich colors and textures, which, of course, were reflected in a higher per-yard price. She was approaching the limit of her budget and the end was not yet in sight.

She was thrilled with the mock-roman swags, hung from iron rods and trimmed with luminescent fringe, chosen to adorn the windows in the living and dining rooms. The dated, blue carpet in the entry and up the stairs was replaced with a rose-embossed stair runner that allowed the rich grain of the wood to show, so she continued the pattern into the hallways. The costs were mounting and now exceeded the budget by almost $5,000.

Allison brought her concerns to Tom. "I've discussed all these improvements with Steve, and he thinks they're great," she said, referring to the furniture re-upholstering, swags and carpeting.

"That isn't the same as 'approving' them. Steve can't go back to the board again. Has he given any indication of where the money will come from?"

"I don't know anything about budgets. All I know is that we have to get this work done. We've spent so much money already. We're almost finished. If we don't complete the project, it will all have been wasted." Budgets and dollar amounts were not in the vocabulary she and Steve shared.

Tom did know about money, and making financial decisions on the fly was not his style. As head of school, he had places he could go to bury an expense if he needed to. John had done it all the time and even had a $30,000 line item in his budget labeled simply "discretionary." However, burying an expense—although certainly not in the same category as stealing—was not without risk. People could talk, and things could be misconstrued. He didn't know the players well enough to be sure they would go along.

His other concern was Allison. She was still unwilling to put a ceiling on the expenses. He feared her boundless enthusiasm for the project was blinding her from a comparison of the cost with the benefit. But he had been removed from the decision-making loop and elected to stay where he was. Allison was on her own.

Lacking leadership or even good guidance, and any formal process for reaching a decision, Allison made a fateful choice. She would make up the difference out of her small inheritance. Tom swallowed hard when she told him this. He knew the risks. On the other hand, he assumed, as did Allison, that there would be an opportunity to ask for reimbursement as part of a salary enhancement package later on. Before it was done, Allison's contribution to the renovation of the Ahlborn House would exceed $15,000.

August 3rd was moving day. Allison had made her remodeling decisions prior to actually living in the Ahlborn House and had had no opportunity to develop a "feel" for the space. Her anxiety didn't show, however, and on that day Tom set off for work for the last time from their temporary apartment, while Allison set about the task of unpacking a mountain of boxes at their new home.

The house was still in chaos. Carpets were being cleaned; there were rooms still to paint, window coverings to install, and the kitchen remodel was a work in progress. Still, they had a refrigerator, a stove and a bathroom that worked. It was better than camping.

With the boxes unpacked, Allison continued to decorate, adorning the house with silk plants and live plants in places where the light permitted it. She hung artwork and added school mementos and personal touches. Gradually, she grew more confident that her work adequately represented the school—and her husband.

By early September, the last of the furniture was delivered and the last painting, a portrait of the school done by an early art teacher, was hung. She and Tom planned to host a meeting and reception for the transition committee. These were all friends and would be appreciative first guests.

After that first, successful gathering, Allison would write to a friend, "This was the first time I saw the two public rooms in a completed state. I can breathe again. It's magnificent, and I feel so proud. Of course, I paid for some of it out of my own pocket, but at this moment it doesn't matter. Last night, I welcomed the people who chose my husband into 'my' home, and let them see their confidence in me was also well placed."

CHAPTER XI

Impediments

♠

The most important task of an organization's leader is to anticipate crisis. Perhaps not to avert it, but to anticipate it.[1]

While Tom and Allison were still moving furniture into the Ahlborn House, the transition committee met for the first time. It had been charged by the board to develop an "entry plan" for Tom's first year. No one was quite sure what an entry plan entailed, but all agreed one was needed.

Archie, feeling a bit full of himself and newly energized by his elevated ranking, looked forward to executing his first official function—installing the committee's new chairman. He could officiate this first meeting himself, however, by holding the installation at the end of the agenda. Tom, bemused at Archie's transparent eagerness, agreed, and the two worked up an agenda together. Prior to the meeting, Tom e-mailed Archie a bulleted draft with talking points appropriately highlighted.

It was a meeting of friends who, with the exception of Archie and Tom, had spent many long hours together during the selection process.

---

[1] Drucker, Peter F. *Managing the Non-Profit Organization: Principles and Practices*. New York: HarperCollins Publishers, 1992, p. 9.

Although some fatigue had naturally set in, they were all proud of their work and willing to contribute further to its success.

The committee's new task, according to the consultant's recommendations, was an evaluation of the school under the first year of Tom's leadership. The relevant passage was this: "The committee should make clear at the outset what the expectations are and what the criteria and procedure will be to measure progress in meeting the expectations. It ought to be a formal process, and it is essential that understandings are set and agreed to at the outset by and between the two parties—the board and the head."

The evaluation that emerged from the committee's discussion that day was to take two forms: one would evaluate the effectiveness of Tom's personal leadership style with a survey; the other would attempt to ascertain performance against a list of measurable goals or objectives. Both were to be formative in nature—meant to bring issues and concerns to the surface and to give the parties direction in addressing them. Warren Hudson, although unable to attend committee meetings due to his increased workload, agreed to meet with Tom to develop the survey—to be given to the board and a select group of faculty—so that it reflected Tom's personal style.

"We have to be careful here," advised Warren. "Ordinarily, a survey like this is submitted only to trustees. We have to remember that the hiring and firing of the head are the board's responsibilities, and the head's evaluation is ultimately the responsibility of the board." He went on to explain that, in times of change, differences of opinion will invariably arise as to the directions that change should take. Only the board has the perspective to negotiate the minefield laid by other school constituencies, such as faculty and parents, as each pursues an agenda affecting its own interests. "There will be winners, and there will be losers," Warren cautioned. "It will be the losers whose voices will be heard, and a board needs to protect its head from the loudest of these."

Tom was gratified that Warren agreed to the survey assignment. As president of a major university, he was the only trustee familiar with the evaluation of school leaders. Kay Johnson also agreed to help. Aside from representing the Alumnae Association on the transition committee, Kay was president of a community volunteer association and had accumulated considerable experience in the evaluation of nonprofit leadership.

When it came time to set goals, Tom addressed the group. "I've spoken privately with each of you, and you've all shared with me your concerns and your ideas for the future of Florence Bruce. Unfortunately, they aren't all the same, and you aren't the only ones who have been talking to me. I need your help in sorting out the key issues to address this year."

With Tom facilitating and taking notes on a flip chart, they set about articulating goals. As the walls filled with pages from the flip chart, Tom grew increasingly concerned over the growing shopping list. The items were not insignificant. At the top, not surprisingly, was the need to develop a long-term strategic plan.

Also, rising to the surface was faculty angst over unfairness in compensation and benefits and the manner in which assignments were administered. Parents objected to the way tuition increases were announced willy-nilly without justification or any increase in perceived benefits. School marketing was in shambles—a hodgepodge of unrelated bits and pieces without a consistent message. Board members were concerned that the three divisions—lower, middle and upper—were evolving into separate entities, each with a distinct character that, at times, overwhelmed its identity with the school. There was little agreement on the chapel program. Some thought it should approximate more closely the Episcopal liturgy, while others wanted it to be more inclusive of other faiths. Curriculum, accountability, capital campaign, and building program—all these and more wanted for immediate attention.

The magnitude of the torrent surprised Tom and even surpassed his earlier estimate of the things he would need to address. This certainly was not a "freighter" on the open ocean needing a few minor "course corrections," as Steve Harrison had described it. This was a school that would require a significant overhaul. There would, however, be time for that. Tom wanted to get his feet on the ground first. Experienced heads from other schools had advised him to "take a year off," to enjoy the honeymoon and get to know the school before making major changes. Would the transition committee let him do this?

Before the committee adjourned, Tom asked for advice regarding an "installation ceremony." It was common for institutions of higher learning and private schools with a religious tradition to "install" a new leader. Such a ceremony was meant to bring the community together in an affirmation of the relationship, somewhat akin to a marriage. While selection of a new leader was, in reality, made by the board, the leader's relationship was with the entire community. An installation ceremony helped generate a commitment by all parties to make the relationship work. It should be, Tom said, a cornerstone to the "entry plan."

The meeting was almost two hours old. Everyone was tired, and Tom was unable to glean anything useful either for or against an installation. Sentiments were generally in favor of it, but no one had any experience to bring to bear.

The next meeting of the committee was scheduled for September 13th at the Ahlborn House. Allison was eager to show off her creation, and the transition committee deserved a first look. Tom volunteered to consolidate the pile of flip chart sheets into a few manageable goals for them to review at that time.

Archie nominated Geoffrey Bellingham to replace Warren Hudson as chair of the committee. Geoffrey, in a professorial baritone that resonated authority, coughed and accepted. The meeting adjourned.

Jackie's voice came over the intercom. "Tom, I've got a former parent—a Mrs. Schantz—on the phone who would like to come in to see you."

"Do you know what it's about?"

"She won't tell me, she just says she and her friend have something they want to talk to you about."

"Okay, go ahead and schedule them."

A few moments later, Jackie's head peaked around the edge of the door at Tom's bidding. "You probably have a good idea as to why they want to see me. What can you tell me?"

Jackie came in and sat down. She told him Mrs. Schantz was a former tuition-paying parent who had pulled her child out of the sixth grade two years ago. There was trouble with one of the teachers, and a couple of students had left as a result.

"Who was the teacher?" asked Tom.

"Miguel Barrera."

"Ah. Do you know what it was about?"

"There was something about a movie Miguel showed in his film class and a book he had them read. Some of the kids got upset and told their parents. I know there were a lot of calls to John and some meetings, but I don't know what happened. Mr. Barrera gets quite a few complaints."

Jackie was uncharacteristically brief, and Tom gained no more useful information until Mrs. Schantz and her friend Sarah Thomas arrived for their scheduled appointment.

The two women didn't waste any time. "Dr. Whitman, I know you have a lot on your mind, and we're very pleased that you're here. We want to thank you for giving us the opportunity to talk to you. Our children are no longer enrolled here, but we care very much about Florence Bruce, and there are some things we think you should know about."

They were still standing where Tom greeted them at the door to his office. He ushered them to a couch and a pair of comfortable chairs arranged around a small table in the corner of the room. Offering them coffee, he poured and bid them continue.

"You have a teacher in the Middle School who should be fired. He's a danger to the girls he teaches and he's going to get the school in trouble."

"You mean Miguel Barrera," said Tom, now seated and beginning to take notes.

"Yes, I see you know about him already. My daughter was traumatized in his classroom, and I had to take her out of school. It took her a year to recover. Sarah here, the same thing happened to her daughter. She stayed in until the end of the term, but then Sarah pulled her daughter out, too. And we're not the only ones. You'll hear from other parents, if they dare to speak up."

"Can you be more specific? What happened exactly?"

"There's so much. I just don't know where to begin. Has anyone told you that he showed an X-rated film to his class? These are middle-school girls, mind you, and he's showing X-rated movies."

"He has pornography on his computer," chimed in Sarah.

"He plays favorites with the prettier girls," Mrs. Schantz went on. "You know, the ones who are . . . maturing—and he makes inappropriate comments to them. My daughter was one of them, and it made her very upset."

"He's single, you know, never been married," said Sarah.

Their accusations were ugly. John had told him about the pornography on Miguel's computer and something about girls braiding his ponytail (Tom hadn't noticed any ponytail, so he must have since cut it off). But what these women were suggesting, if true, would certainly be cause for alarm.

"Did you ever bring any of this up with Mr. Sanford?" he asked.

"Many times. He always seemed like he was listening, but nothing was ever done," said Mrs. Schantz. "Finally, I just gave up and took my daughter out of Florence Bruce. She's at Brentwood Academy and doing very well. We've never had any trouble there like we did here. Dr. Whitman, we want you to know that we've heard good things about you. They say you are here to make some changes, and we certainly hope that's true. Florence Bruce is a good school, but this man has got to go. He's a menace."

Mrs. Schantz concluded her diatribe with a thinly veiled threat. "We're both very active in this community, and it's a small community. We talk. We'll be watching what you do. We want to be able to support Florence Bruce again, but if you don't do something about this . . ." She looked at him fixedly as her voice trailed off.

Tom thanked the two ladies for their time. In a personal, handwritten note following up the conversation, he wrote, "Mrs. Schantz, thank you for bringing your concerns to my attention. I have learned to appreciate critical comment, especially when given in a reasoned and constructive manner, as the basic mechanism of change." It was a phrase Tom would use many times over the next few months.

The claims of these two former parents would have been easy to dismiss. Whatever may have happened, it was in the past, and their girls were no longer enrolled in the school. The facts, such as they were, were sketchy, with nothing that could be substantiated. Private-school parents are notoriously prone to irrational hysteria when it comes to the well-being of their children, and anything or nothing could have prompted these two to level the charges they did.

The claims would have been easy to dismiss except that they were to be repeated on several more occasions within the first few weeks of the opening of school. Even two faculty members, both women, shared their fears about Miguel.[2] Tom tried to reassure

---

[2] *Sex in the Forbidden Zone*, by Peter Rutter argues, "Men so often control access to a woman's future—and to her physical, psychological, spiritual, economic, or intellectual well-being—the mere presence of sexual innuendo from a man who has power over her can become a barrier to her development." Certainly, the various claims made against Miguel reinforced this theme and were accentuated by the all-girls environment. On the other hand, sexual-abuse scandals fill the media snaring innocent and guilty alike.

them that he was monitoring the situation. "I have quite a bit of first-hand information," he told them. "The difficulty is that much of it is conflicting and masked by the style of communication that was in place at the time between the school and parents. The 'truth' is so obscured at this point that I feel the need to see how it plays out with me here."

Other parents with students still in the Middle School made it a point to pay him a visit and voice their concerns. Among the more reasoned comments was this one: "I'm afraid that some of Mr. Barrera's alternative behavior and teaching methods may have tipped over the edge of what is ethically acceptable. If he hasn't gone over the edge, he is close enough to be ringing the alarm bells of more than a few parents."

Tom was a bit overwhelmed by all the accusations leveled at a teacher who was simultaneously acknowledged to be a charismatic and effective educator. Each of those who came forward was thanked with a handwritten note. To one parent, after her third visit, he wrote, "I inherited a situation involving a Florence Bruce faculty member and a group of current and former parents that is counterproductive to all that I would like to accomplish here. The details of the stories I hear are fuzzy and inconsistent, and often delivered second—or third-hand. I want to assure you that I am aware of these stories and that I am paying attention. I encourage you to contact me if you feel there is anything of an inappropriate nature happening at school during my tenure. At the same time, my request for you is that you listen with your own ears and heart, and question what you cannot verify for yourself. We will do this together."

A week after classes began in the September, Tom paid a visit to Miguel's classroom, where he found a boisterous group engaged in a question-and-answer session with their mentor. Miguel was quick—so quick that he often had two or three questions on the floor at any one time, tracking the responses and providing timely retorts. He teased, exhorting the girls to do better. He was flamboyant in a brightly colored tie and paisley slacks and stalked the room with exaggerated gestures, his face animated with the intensity of his efforts. Miguel was not a large man, but looked bigger than he was, with a rugged, muscular build and eyes set deeply in a craggy, slightly lopsided face—not particularly handsome so far as Tom could see, but what did he know?

Later in the period Tom was observing, Miguel took a seat in the back and encouraged one girl after another to the front of the class to give a report. A shy and reserved student received tender encouragement, while the outgoing and bold were robustly challenged. One intrepid pubescent pushed back verbally, and the repartee took on a mildly personal tone. The two people involved in the exchange clearly understood the communication, and yet Tom wondered what the wide-eyed girls around him thought they heard. At the end of the period, Tom asked Miguel to meet with him, and they chose a convenient time at the end of class on the following day.

When Miguel settled himself in Tom's office, he was already on the defensive, and his voice and bearing bespoke hostility.

"Miguel, I am not here to pass any judgment whatsoever on you. What I saw yesterday was a great teacher doing great work. That is not what this is about."

"Okay, so why am I here?"

"You're here because I need an open and honest dialogue with you. For weeks, there has been a virtual parade of people into my office with very strong opinions about you."

"I can imagine."

Tom went on to describe some of his encounters, being careful to add repeatedly that he was not passing judgment, but simply relaying what he had heard. "Miguel, you have strong supporters, but you also have your share of detractors. I want to help. John told me you were a good teacher, and from what I've seen, I think he was right. I want to help, but I can't do it without your assistance."

By the time Tom finished, Miguel's hostility had dissipated. "I don't know," he said. "I've been teaching for fifteen years, and last year was the toughest in my career. Maybe it's time I got out of this. There's just too much politics. I have no idea where half your stories came from. You know how middle-school kids exaggerate. They go home and tell their parents such and such happened. The parents read their own prejudices into it and get all worked up. Then they go talk to other parents . . ."

"I know that can happen," said Tom, "but you said 'only half.' That implies some basis for the other half of the stories. Can we see if we can eliminate or at least reduce that half while I see what I can do about the rumor mongering?"

Miguel was not quite ready to admit that anything needed moderating. The X-rated movie was an R-rated movie shown during an elective class on film. The computer porno, he recalled, was an e-mail attachment sent to him by some off-color associate. Nevertheless, Miguel grudgingly accepted Tom's offer to help and shook hands as he left.

Thinking back on his meetings with Miguel and the people who had come to complain about him, Tom pondered the source of it all. The culture of any school is often a reflection of the head, especially when that head has been in place for a long time. Florence Bruce Seminary was no exception. It embodied the person of John Sanford. Those around John adjusted to his style, which effected adjustments in those near them, and these spread like ripples emanating from a stone thrown into a pond, hitting the edges of the pond and bouncing back until they covered the surface of the water with their dance.

John did not like to deal with problems and often began by denying they existed at all. At times, he simply wasn't available to deal with them, or perhaps he excused himself when he saw them coming. The current outpouring of issues, concerns, and problems bombarding Tom at every juncture was nearly overwhelming, and would continue to be so. During the first meeting of the transition committee, it was as though a veil had been lifted and permission granted for the first time. It was finally okay to talk about things that needed fixing, and talk they did. John's school that needed a little "tweaking" now and then was a school that was badly frayed at the edges and whose seams would soon begin coming apart without some cutting and re-stitching.

Tom soon learned more than he wanted about John's modus operandi. If denying the existence of a problem didn't work, John's next tactic was to keep it from ever seeing the light of day. He listened to complaints but did nothing. He said he would get back to people, but didn't. If a problem could not be avoided, John dealt with it quietly himself or he enlisted the aid of a close confidant to help him. John's public persona was boisterous and friendly, but the real business of the school—sometimes the dirty business of the school—was done behind a screen, hidden from view of all but a very few.

Those around John abetted him. Phyllis Killam made sure no item of real substance ever made it to the board of trustees, or, if it did, she surrounded it in such a way that the outcome was assured before it reached the floor. On the everyday, operational level, a few members of the faculty and staff—Jackie among them—kept colleagues in line, and their loyalty was amply rewarded with budget perks and special privileges. Poor Everett Laurie, down in the lower and middle divisions, tried his best to follow his boss's lead. He was the first line of defense for many of the day-to-day troubles that arose, but he lacked John's skill. Everett tried to deny problems; he tried to bury them; but often they simply wouldn't go away and bubbled to the surface in John's office, for which the unfortunate Everett only earned John's censure.

Tom did not yet understand all of this, but it was not in *his* nature to bury problems. In fact, the opposite was true. Tom relished digging them up, bringing them to the surface, engaging them. He enjoyed communal decision-making and trusted in the outcome. When a tale surfaced in his office of a teacher's classroom transgressions, he would approach it far differently than did his predecessor. But the cultural paradigm Tom faced was truly a formidable enemy. It was firmly entrenched in the fabric of the school and would not go quietly. Tom chipped away, but when he got too close, it rose snarling to the surface looking for blood.

Ellen Stein sat on the sofa with a handkerchief, dabbing angrily as tears welled in her eyes. "You have no idea what this has been like. I feel like a criminal. I'm afraid to walk in the halls. I'm afraid to leave my room. I got an unlisted phone number, but he got it from somewhere and calls me every day, sometimes two or three times."

Ellen was reverently referred to as a "triple threat."[3] She lived at the school and was a resident advisor. She also chaired the history department and coached both varsity soccer and junior varsity basketball. She was well liked by faculty and students, and John had praised her contributions.

Ellen was also a school alumna, her parents were substantial contributors to the capital campaign, and she was married to the director of security Gene Stein. In this way, she was typical of many

---

[3] In the parlance of independent schools, a "triple threat" is that rare individual making significant contributions in academics (teacher), athletics (coach) and residential life (live-in advisor).

people associated with Florence Bruce in that her relationship with the school cut across several constituencies.

Now, her marriage was disintegrating—or rather, it had already disintegrated and was taking a nasty turn. She accused her husband (as they were not yet divorced) of harassing her. On a recent evening, by her account, Ellen had been confronted by Gene in the parking lot. An argument had ensued, witnessed by several people. During the argument, Gene had been loud and domineering, according to witnesses. He had accused her in graphic terms of being a lesbian, with people they both knew looking on. It hadn't helped that he was clearly drunk at the time.

"Tom, you've got to do something about him," Ellen demanded. "This is sexual harassment in the workplace. Do you know he keeps records of people who visit me and the license number of the cars they drive? I feel like a prisoner. I'm being watched in my own home."

"How do you know that?" said Tom.

"Because he tells me so when he calls. Sometimes all I hear is heavy breathing on the other end of the line. Sometimes he calls when I have a guest and even describes what they look like. He tells all our friends I'm a lesbian."

Tom promised he'd look into it, and the next day Gene and Nancy Wolf, his supervisor, arrived at Tom's bidding. "Gene, I think you know why I've asked you here. Do you want to tell me what's going on?"

Gene admitted to the incident in the parking lot, admitted he'd been drinking, admitted to the phone calls. He was not an articulate man, and his story came out in spurts that were preceded by a reddening of the face followed by a burst of grammatically fractured English. With more than enough pain and anger to go around on both sides, the story held nothing that Tom had not heard before. "Gene, you know I can't let this continue. This is a school. Even though it's summer, we have parents and kids around all the time. You and Ellen need to get some counseling and find a way to keep this between yourselves." Tom paused to rub his eyes and then asked, "What about Ellen's claim that you track the comings and goings of her guests?"

"That's my job—when school is closed, like in the evenings. My job is to keep the bad guys out. It's dark. My boys log every car in the parking lot and the streets near us. Most of the residents here let me know when guests are coming, but not Ellen."

"It's one thing to keep a record; it's something else again to be harassing someone."

"But she has the same woman visiting her all the time, and her car don't leave until morning. It ain't the same as a guest; she's living there. And it's not what you'd call a good relationship—to be going on in a school full of girls. I mean what are your parents going to think?"

Tom's mind darted off to the consequences of Gene's accusations before he yanked it back to the present. "If these things are going on and you think there is an impact on the school, shouldn't you be telling Nancy or me about it?"

"Yeah, I suppose so. Well, I'm tellin' you now."

"Do you have log books where all your records of cars and guests are kept?"

"Yeah."

"And it's complete? It has every car and every guest, not just Ellen's?"

"Yeah."

"Do you have a form or some way for dorm residents to inform you when they are expecting guests?"

"Nah, they just tell me."

Turning to Nancy, Tom asked, "Do we have any policy regarding reporting of guests or how long they can stay?"

"Not that I know of." Anticipating Tom's next question, she added, "There's also no formal approval process if a resident gets married and wants to add a spouse or a child to their household. There are no written guidelines that are consistently applied. The resident supervisor is the gatekeeper; they have to get past her, and that's it. They say, 'if she likes you, your problems are solved.'"

And if she doesn't like you? Tom let the unspoken question hang in the air. Turning to Gene, he said, "I want you to develop a form for residents to complete when they are expecting guests. Ellen probably isn't telling you because she's afraid to talk to you. You develop a form, and I'll make sure that everyone knows they need to fill it out in advance if they are expecting a guest. Will that work?"

"Yeah, I guess so."

"And another thing. I need for you to leave Ellen alone. You both have divorce lawyers. If you have a problem, let them work it out. You need to stay away from Ellen. The school should not get involved in this, but if there are any more of these public outbursts, I'm going to have to do something to stop it."

"What about Ellen's live-in roommate? What are you going to do about her?"

"You've done your job by reporting it. For one thing, we don't know if she's 'living' here or not. I might want to take a look at your logbooks, so you make sure they're up-to-date and accurate. Other than that, you just have to leave it up to me. That's my job,"

After Gene left, Tom turned again to Nancy, "This lack of written policies is going to catch us. It seems so much of what goes on around here is done with a handshake as a favor or payback for something."

"You've only seen the tip of the iceberg, Tom. There's very little in the way of documentation covering a lot of things around here. By the way, I want you to know this Gene/Ellen thing is not black and white. Ellen puts him down unmercifully—calls him dumb and stupid and makes fun of his speech in front of their friends. She knows just how far to push his buttons; she's just a lot more slick about it. Gene's a good man. He'd be tough to replace. He does a good job, and his people respect him. But you know the security and maintenance folks are at the bottom of the pecking order around here, and Ellen is on the top. She takes advantage of that every chance she gets."

Their unrelenting proximity to one another made further conflict inevitable. Gene continued his phone calls. Ellen again camped herself in Tom's office, angrily insisting Gene stop tracking the movements of her guests. Tom explained it was security's responsibility to document vehicles, but she was vociferously unpersuaded. Tom refused her request, but promised he'd talk to Gene again. And, again, Gene was warned.

A week later, Ellen obtained a restraining order, and her teary-eyed portrayal as the harassed victim gained her much sympathy throughout the school. Gene e-mailed Tom—and unfortunately copied Ellen—with logbook entries showing the frequency and duration of her female guest's visits. He never produced a form for residents to report expected guests, and Ellen took three days off from work due to "stress." A few days after her return, Ellen came to Tom's office with a phone receipt and a tape recording of a call from Gene in which she claimed he threatened her. The threat was unspecified—a vague "You'll be sorry you ever started this." But it was clearly a threat. Even more damning, the receipt showed the call was made to her apartment from a school phone at a time when Gene was on duty.

Gene admitted making the call. Not two months into his tenure and Tom had to fire his first employee. Ellen's guest stopped her overnight visits, while Ellen's evening absences from the residency increased.

Nancy's warning about the lack of documentation proved prophetic. Arriving at his desk one morning in August, Tom watched e-mails from the night before pop onto the screen. Clicking, responding, deleting his way down the list, he skipped over four or five to open the one with "HELP!" in the subject box. It was a lengthy e-mail from a local aerobics instructor who claimed John promised her use of the gym to teach classes. John did this, she said, because so many of her clients were Florence Bruce parents. The arrangement was six years old and had never created a problem, since her classes ordinarily were sufficiently early in the morning so as to not interfere with student classes.

This year, however, the Upper School was in the process of renovating its schedule, and PE courses had been planned for the early time slots. Peg Scott had e-mailed the aerobics instructor about the conflict. The instructor's meandering e-mail message swung from a pleading "I'm a single mother, and this is how I put food on the table for my children," to a threatening "If you do this, you'll have a dozen angry parents in your office."

Tom investigated. Yes, the practice had gone on for several years. No, there was nothing ever written down: no contract or letter of agreement. No, there was no payment being made to the school, although someone remembered there might have been at one time. Tom received two calls from parents who lobbied hard for continuation of the aerobics classes, citing the instructor's tearful tale of woe as the overriding reason. "We can't throw her out into the cold; she has nowhere else to go." "This isn't the way Florence Bruce does things. I'm active in this community, and you don't want me telling people this is how Florence Bruce treats people."

Tom sat at his desk staring at the large poster of the Florence Bruce mission statement. Where does it say, he wondered, mocking his own words, that we should be setting aside space for roving vendors to sell their services? In the end, he and Peg were able to adjust the PE course schedules to allow the aerobics classes to continue. Tom crafted a letter of agreement stipulating a term of one year and requiring renewal of the agreement on an annual basis. He also added a requirement for a small percentage of the fees collected to be paid to Florence Bruce.

Before the school bell would ring to announce the opening of school on September 6, two more handshake relationships came to light. In one, the school swim instructor was using the pool for private instruction. The other involved a quid pro quo with the Portsmouth City Parks District for free use of city fields for Florence Bruce soccer games. In return, the parks district got free use of the Florence Bruce gym for after-school basketball and volleyball leagues. Tom also crafted those arrangements into formal contracts.

On one of his now almost daily visits to Nancy's office, Tom was depressed. "I've already uncovered three of these ad hoc relationships, and I know more of them are out there. The school is assuming a huge liability risk, especially when the arrangements are with private individuals. Even when these people have insurance—and most don't—Florence Bruce is clearly the 'deep pocket.' If anything should happen, we'll take the brunt of it."

"I know," Nancy replied. "Not only that, but without written documentation, our negligence will be easier to prove. I agree this could be a disaster. No one has been factoring in the liability risks when these things are allowed to go on."

Tom stood to leave placing his hand on Nancy's shoulder. "You know, this is going to be a tough year. It'll be nice having a kindred spirit in residence."

CHAPTER XII

Communion

♠

To put it simply, the board sets the overall goals and policies and the staff implements them.[1]

The first day of school was but two days away. Faculty appeared as if from nowhere and scurried about ritually anointing classrooms for the arrival of new life. Shouts of greeting eager with anticipation dissolved into exchanged snippets of summer adventures or a hurried hallway conference. It was the season of rebirth, and the annual cycle of academic life at Florence Bruce Seminary was about to begin anew. A fresh breeze curled like smoke through the musty air that had pooled all summer in the stairways and corners of the old building. Rooms were charged—electric with subdued excitement.

An all-staff meeting was scheduled in the afternoon. Tom's anxiety built as the hours ticked away. This was the first real test of his appointment—the culmination of two years of study, travel and research to obtain the assignment, which was a ninety-degree turn from a twenty-year career managing the San Diego Maritime Institute.

---

[1] Hutton, Stan and Frances Phillips. *Nonprofit Kit for Dummies.* New York: Wiley Publishing, Inc., 2001, p. 77.

While the school had snoozed through a languid summer schedule, Tom had labored, delving deeper and deeper into the files. He had visited every corner of the building, crawling into places not even Jackie knew about. The development department had assiduously guided him to many of the more financially capable Florence Bruce families at what they called "roll-out" receptions and events. He had reviewed budgets and financial reports until he knew the business of the school better than anyone but Nancy. He had memorized names—oh, so many names. He knew the faculty and the board and had developed budding relationships with many of them.

None of this, however, felt real. A school is not a school until it is filled up, brimming with students and teachers. Facing the full faculty—not a few at a time as he had done in summer town-hall meetings, but all of them at once—would be the first real indicator he had arrived at his destination.

The script for the faculty meeting was unremarkable: opening comments, followed by department reports, followed by topics of interest and adjournment. It was the kind of meeting Tom could lead in his sleep. Other administrators and faculty would carry the ball; he only needed to call signals. Still, he would be judged. His opening remarks and his conduct at the meeting would tell many of them what they wanted to know—what kind of a man had been chosen to lead them?

The mentor who guided Tom as a science teacher his first year out of college, had once admonished, "Make the first day count. It will be your best opportunity all year to set a tone and communicate your expectations." Tom took the advice to heart and always endeavored to make his lesson plans for the first day of classes creative and exciting. As his career advanced from the classroom into administration, the advice served him well in other roles, and he worked hard to make first impressions communicate a message.

Finally the clock read ten to three. Shouldering an easel and his mission-statement poster, Tom paused at the door to Jackie's office. "Come on, it's show time."

"I'll be right along."

Kittery Hall was fragrant with the history of two hundred beginnings just like this one, and it was slowly filling with arriving faculty. Tom moved among them, engaging some in small talk, introducing himself to others; all the while gauging the temperature of things. The mood was quiet, reserved, a bit more formal than under his predecessor's watch.

Although never entirely comfortable in social situations where he was the focal point, Tom had learned to cope effectively and glided from person to person with purpose. Still, to those who might look closely, there was a shy awkwardness to his dance. He would never be as fluid or as comfortable or as in command of his audience as John Sanford could be. There were but a few who noticed. They pulled up their chairs around the periphery of the room to wait and watch. They had done well under John and would withhold judgment to see what advantage this new guy might be able to bring them.

"Good afternoon." Tom had taken off his coat, rolled up his shirtsleeves, and now stood in the sultry September sunshine that streamed through the tall windows, splashing across the tables and spilling onto the floor. Several in the audience shielded their eyes, and over their shoulders through the opposite windows Tom could see the old elm, a lacy, gray-green canopy against the rock-solid blue of a clear New Hampshire sky. He waited for the room to quiet.

"Good afternoon, I'd like to welcome all of you back to Florence Bruce Seminary to a new academic year, although I feel a bit awkward about doing it. You have all been here longer than I have—some of you have been here much longer." Laughter. "I'm not really sure who's welcoming whom here.

"A friend of mine," Tom continued, "a new head of school like myself, composed a rhyme about what it feels like to face this job for the first time. It's a feeling that's almost impossible to put into words, but my friend came pretty close and captured much of what I am feeling at this moment. To help you understand my perspective as your new head of school, I'd like to share his creation with you."

Tom cleared his throat. "It's in the form of a rap." Several in the room sat a little straighter.

Their new head tapped his foot on the floor and snapped his fingers on the up-beat, trying to establish a rhythm. "Chi . . . chi . . . chi'boom. Chi . . . chi . . . chi'boom," he chanted, deadpan.

What's this all-white, straight-up, Ivy League preppy doing?

Breaking off, Tom cleared his throat again, smiled and joked about getting into character. Then resuming the tapping and chanting, he struck his best approximation of an M.C. Hammer pose, and, in street-talk guttural, grunted, "Yo." Tittering laughter filled the pause.

Yo, I'm a new head
Yeah that's what I said
Gonna knock 'em dead
I'm the Big Cheese, #1, this is fun
I got plans, I'm the Man
This is great! I anticipate
That I can tempt fate
Be creative, educate
If I work smart, it's not rocket science
It's an art, and that's great
But wait!

Tom lost his rhythm and stopped momentarily. His audience was laughing and their sporadic clapping had put him off stride. Grinning hugely as he tapped his feet and bobbed his head in time, he got it back and continued:

Man, I don't know what to do
Got no clue
How to start to play my part
I'm the Big Cheese?
Oh please!
More like Cheese Whiz
I'm gonna be dead
I got angry parents
I'll be gored by the board
Oh Lord!
Me headmaster?
Could spell disaster.[2]

By the time Tom finished his performance, any formality that may once have existed was gone from the room and much good-natured laughter and ribbing followed.

---

[2] Credited to Tom Lovett, head of school, St. Johnsbury Academy, 2001.

When the hilarity of the moment subsided, Tom said he was looking forward to a long tenure with the Florence Bruce faculty—a tenure that would be at once satisfying and fulfilling, rich in its rewards and marked by success at every turn—both for him and for them. He concluded his remarks by saying, "My job is to make sure you are successful. Your fulfillment is my fulfillment; your successes will accrue to me as they also accrue to you."

An hour of department reports followed, which Tom managed with skills honed from long experience. Longwinded types were tactfully distracted, reports too brief were extended with careful questioning, and question-and-answer sessions were kept on point. Tom weighed in himself on occasion.

On Faculty Dress: "I'm told there is no code of dress for faculty here. My own opinion is that you are all professionals and are fully capable of dressing yourselves. I want you to keep in mind, however, that appearance, like almost everything else, is one of the arrows in your teacher's quiver. Your students will notice what you wear. Their impressions of you and of your expectations for them will be formed to some extent by how you look. When I see you in the halls, I will assume that you got up that morning, got dressed, looked at yourself in the mirror, and came to school intending to look the way I see you."

The Mission Statement: "This statement embodies the thoughts, feelings, dreams and aspirations of a group of people deeply committed to this school; people who worked very hard to communicate this to us. I urge you to study it. If you do, you will find that our mission is all about students. You and I are not even mentioned; neither are parents nor the alumnae. That means that every decision we make, every action we take, must benefit students first and foremost."

On Excellence: "Excellence is not a quality we can preserve by somehow keeping things the same. It requires constant adaptation to changing realities so that we stay in the forefront of new ways of teaching, new fields of knowledge, new discoveries and insights, and new developments in the larger world. To stand still in the hope of preserving excellence is ultimately to stand by and watch it dissolve."

The meeting ended at five minutes past the appointed hour, much to the surprise of those who were accustomed to long, indeterminate faculty meetings under John's tutelage. The room emptied quickly, since there remained much to be done before opening day.

"I guess you were right," said Corny Jolley to her husband Buster as they left Kittery Hall. "I've been worried Dr. Whitman wouldn't fit in, that he was too formal for Florence Bruce. This place can be pretty casual sometimes . . ." She trailed off, leaving the thought hanging in the air. "But when he started that rap, it was the funniest thing I've ever seen!"

Corny had been in and out of Florence Bruce Seminary since the age of fourteen, when her father first sent her off to board. It wasn't long after college that she and her husband returned as members of the faculty and had lived ever since at Florence Bruce as resident advisors.

Hands down, no one was as close to the pulse of the school as Corny Jolley. She was a drama coach with the irreverent, exaggerated demeanor sometimes affected by those who take the stage as a profession. At the same time, she was fragile, almost childlike in her manner, so that other faculty members viewed her as but one step removed from the student she had once been.

The faculty did not take Corny altogether seriously. She was, however, never far from the action, and she saw and heard things others might miss. She knew Florence Bruce could be a dangerous place for those who did not fit in or who lost favor, and she was afraid for this new headmaster. Her husband Buster had served on the search committee representing the faculty and had advocated on Tom's behalf. He was impressed with Tom's strength and no-nonsense approach. "You watch, Corny, Dr. Whitman is just what Florence Bruce needs. He'll get things back on track."

Tom was a likable guy to be sure, but Corny knew that would not be enough. He was so direct and up-front in what he said to them. He seemed to her stripped of armor and vulnerable—to what, she didn't know exactly. But he was changing the old ways of doing things, and there were still many invested in the past. She rejoiced at his presence and his new ideas, but she also worried about him and the future of her school.

Now she felt a little better. The faculty meeting had gone well; everyone was in high spirits, and Dr. Whitman had made them all laugh. She relaxed—for a while.

Convinced of the value of a first impression, Tom had done everything he could think of to make a good one for the opening day of school. Crossing the street from the Ahlborn House, he noted with satisfaction the fresh plantings in the streetside gardens. Not as much color as he would have liked, but it would do. Passing under the lintel and into the lobby, he was more pleased. All the illumination possible was being squeezed from the room's sconces, chandeliers and recessed ceiling lights. It was an awkward conglomeration of fixtures, to be sure, and the light was a little too yellow, but this was better than the morose gloominess he remembered from his first visit.

A large bouquet of flowers in a crystal vase adorned the lobby's center table, and beside the bouquet Mrs. Clayworth had erected a sign in a plain black frame that announced "Today's Activities," with the date stenciled boldly across the top. It was a small greeting, but a touch of welcome for those in an unfamiliar place and a useful tool for a returnee needing a quick overview or a reference check on a time or place.

Near the top of the sign was an announcement for the new Florence Bruce Seminary website. The project had been finished on time and posted two days beforehand for testing. Further down the page he saw: "9:00 AM Opening Day Chapel." His watch said 7:30 AM—only one-and-one-half hours before his next big test.

While Tom might have passed muster with the faculty, soon it would be time to form a connection with the students—all 450 of them at once, from Kindergarten tykes to the young sophisticates of the Upper School. With so wide a range, the challenge of his Opening Day speech lay in finding the means to address each in an age-appropriate manner. An insight, the flicker of an idea from his maritime past had thrown his preparations into overdrive. So pleased was he with the solution that his natural anxiety over the approaching presentation was nearly overridden by eagerness to perform it.

Tom took the stairs two at a time and approached the door of his office with key already in hand. Hardly breaking stride, he thrust the key in the lock, turned it and opened the door in one motion. Depositing his navy-blue blazer on a hanger, he straightened his official Florence Bruce Seminary tie, emblazoned with the school coat of arms, clicked his slumbering computer awake and retrieved his speech notes from his coat pocket. There was no e-mail that wouldn't wait, so pacing slowly back and forth across the room, he reviewed a section in his notes that had given him difficulty when he had rehearsed with Allison after breakfast.

At 7:50 AM, Tom retrieved his blazer and began a walkabout of the school. By now, his familiarity with the physical layout was well fixed. Several routes offered themselves to anywhere he wanted to go, although none were direct. Never, except on the north coast of Maine, has it been truer said that "You kaen't get to tha'ya from hea'ya." Florence Bruce Seminary was a maze of old-wing remodels and new-wing add-ons, so that most destinations required a roundabout route from his office.

As he passed into the lobby, he found that a stream of parents with youngsters in tow had already engulfed the entrance. He strode up to the nearest. "Hello, I'm Dr. Whitman, the new head of school here at Florence Bruce. Can I be of assistance?" And so it went for the next thirty minutes. Tom didn't know many of the answers, but he usually knew where to find them. Most of the parents were slightly awed to be greeted at the door by the head of school and fumbled for an appropriate response to his greeting. "Florence Bruce is a wonderful school, and I'm so happy to be here," sufficed as answer to most of the questions they thought to ask him. In turn, Tom asked the parents about their kids, grades, teachers, and siblings—factual questions they knew by heart and communicated his interest in them and their children.

There was, however, an unavoidable drawback to this first-day method of meeting the members of the Florence Bruce community. A lobby introduction was merely an exchange of vitals. It was all that time permitted. Nevertheless, it was an exchange that would repeat itself many hundreds of times over as the year progressed. Once a family's identifying personal information was communicated, recollection might be expected at the next meeting, and therein lay the drawback.

Retaining such information was a virtual impossibility, given the sheer numbers and the frequency of occurrence, for anyone not truly gifted in these things. Tom's questionable eyesight hindered recognition, and a miserable short-term memory for details compounded the problem. Fortunately, most of those on the other end of the two thousand or so introductions Tom was subjected to during the year would patiently bear up if he did not acknowledge them immediately upon a second meeting.

When a break came, Tom set off for the Lower School lobby where the scenario repeated itself. By 8:45 AM classes were underway, and parents were dispersing. Tom wound his way back upstairs to his office.

"Hey, Jackie," he exclaimed, and then shushed himself as she turned to show him she was on the phone. Mouthing the words, "Do not disturb," and pointing to himself, he entered his office, closed the door, again retrieved his notes, and took a series of deep breaths to calm himself for what lay ahead. Pacing slowly in a figure-eight pattern in the middle of the room, he reviewed one more time the speech he would make a few moments hence.

At 8:55 AM, Tom picked up the now-familiar easel and mission poster, tucked his notes in his jacket and headed for Bishop Matthew B. Hanley Chapel. In the Lower School, students were already lined up in twos and teachers moved among them tying shoes, straightening jumpers and wiping noses. He passed out of the building into the waning crispness of an early-fall morning and, feeling the sun on his face, inclined it slightly to absorb more of the radiant warmth. At the chapel, Tom conferred briefly with the school chaplain, found a glass of water that he hid under the dais, and checked the sound system. Moments later, the chapel doors opened.

His thoughts flashed back to that December day nine months earlier when he and Allison were first introduced to the Florence Bruce community in this very place. So profound the changes, so many adjustments, so much that was unexpected—he marveled at the twists and turns his life had taken to bring him to this point. Interrupted by the reverberating strains of the organ, his reverie dissipated quickly; the official opening of school was underway.

The Crucifer stepped out, then a parade of flags; the chaplain indicated his position beside her, and Tom joined the procession. At the top of the steps to the sanctuary, he hesitated while His presence was acknowledged by his companion and then turned left to take his seat behind the pulpit.

He tried to relax by concentrating on his breathing. This day was the culmination of a long journey, but it was also a new beginning. So much was at stake. Was he up to the expectations of those who had come to hear his welcome? He followed along in the program, ticking off the items until his turn came to speak.

Rising slowly, Tom took the few steps to the dais and retrieved the notes from his coat pocket along with the glasses he'd had specially made for this purpose. They were a recent purchase to provide an arms-length focal point. Used only in practice, this would be their first real test.

Laying his notes on the lectern, he adjusted his glasses and saw the words swing into sharper focus. Looking up, he surveyed his audience. The first rows of little girls stared up at him wide-eyed, mouths agape. Beyond them was an unfocused, indistinguishable sea of faces and the uniform greens, reds and blues of the official Bruce plaid. They were as quiet as 450 youngsters sitting on hard wooden pews could be.

"I can feel the electricity in the *air*!" he said, his voice rising at the end of the sentence.

"The opening of school is an exciting time, and I'm just as excited as all of you. In fact, I've been waiting all summer for you to come back."

Tom was talking to them, not reading from notes. He removed his glasses to better focus on his audience.

"Before Mr. Sanford left in June, we met in his office so that he could show me where things were and give me the keys. On my first day of work, I took the keys and opened the door to what was now *my* office. I stepped inside, admiring the splendid view and the mementos hanging on the walls. I went over and stood behind the big headmaster's desk and sat down in Mr. Sanford's big chair. Whump! My chin came to the top of the desk. I felt like Goldilocks when she sat in Papa Bear's big chair."

He smiled and swept his glance over the first rows, trying to establish eye contact with each youngster. His loud "whump" had gotten their attention.

"That was back in July. During the summer I met Mr. Burnett and the people who were painting, scraping, hammering and sawing, getting the school ready for you to come back. I met Mrs. Clayworth and the people who work in the kitchen. They were cleaning, polishing, and restocking the shelves to be ready for you. It's been a good summer with lots of things to do, but I've missed all of you."

Tom chose Mr. Burnett, who was head of maintenance, and Mrs. Clayworth, for specific recognition in his opening remarks. His message that all employees of the school, regardless of their assignment, were equally valued members of his team was to be continually reinforced in the months ahead and did not always sit well with the stratified, ingrained class-consciousness of the private school community.

Tom put on his glasses and straightened his notes. "I want to spend my time with you this morning talking about 'what Florence Bruce Seminary means to me,' and I want to do it using a metaphor. What is a metaphor? For those of you who haven't studied metaphors yet, a metaphor is a comparison of one thing with another thing when the other thing may stand as a symbol or representation of the first because they share similar characteristics. I can tell that's as clear as mud," he said with a chuckle, "so let me give you a few examples."

Another of his early mentor's maxims—"Don't talk about it, do it!"—was the inspiration for inserting a simple English lesson into the middle of his remarks. Florence Bruce was a school; a school is about teaching and learning. Tom hoped his example might also inspire a "teachable moment" for one of the listening faculty.

After illustrating the meaning of metaphor with several examples, Tom continued:

"Now let me tell you about my metaphor for Florence Bruce Seminary. I like to think of Florence Bruce as a great tall ship—one of those wondrous, winged vessels that for over two hundred years carried men and women across great expanses of ocean on voyages of discovery to learn about the world they lived in.

"In 1492, Columbus sailed aboard three tall ships: the *Niña, Pinta* and *Santa Maria*, to the New World. He didn't discover the Americas, because there were already native peoples living here who had discovered it before him. But what Columbus did discover, for himself and for his fellow Europeans, was that it was possible to cross the ocean and arrive at a huge land mass—two whole continents—filled with strange people, wondrous animals and beautiful places. Likewise, the native peoples of the Americas discovered that there was another great land across the ocean settled by people with technology and weapons that often overpowered their own.[3]

"Like Columbus, you and I are about to embark upon a voyage of discovery. We probably won't discover anything new this school

[3] Ellen Stein, who taught history in the Upper School, brought to my attention Tom's nod here in his speech to political correctness while he avoided, as is so often the case, denigrating the achievements of "dead white men." She was very complimentary of Tom at this point in time, and I never understood her "conversion" later in the school year.

year that someone else hasn't discovered before us. But it will be new to us, and it will be new to our fellow travelers; that's what makes it a voyage of discovery.

"Florence Bruce is our vessel of discovery. From our classrooms, we will voyage out and record our discoveries in our writings, homework papers, drawings, tests and performances on the athletic field or on the stage. These records will become the logbook of our voyage.

"There are other ways that Florence Bruce reminds me of a tall ship. These ships of bygone eras, with their graceful lines, ornamental figureheads and great billowing sails, were magnificently beautiful, just as the school building with its Tudor-style architecture and stylish interior spaces, was designed to impress with its beauty.

"The stout, red-brick exterior of our school is like the strong oak hull of a tall ship. Inside such a ship, it smells of damp wood, oakum and tar. You can feel the aura of history somewhat past its prime but still powerful in its effect upon the souls of the sailors the ship embraces. Florence Bruce has that aura, and it still exerts a powerful effect upon the souls of the students she graduates.

"The crew of a tall ship is like the faculty and students at Florence Bruce. We work in coordinated gangs, and the gangs work together as part of a greater team. If a storm appears on the horizon, the captain orders, 'All hands on deck,' and everyone scrambles to their assigned tasks. Just like at Florence Bruce, teamwork carries the day, and each one of you has an important role in the success of all."

Tom's tenure at the San Diego Maritime Institute had left him chockablock with material on maritime history and tall ships. He was talking from experience, having stood out himself a time or two from the cross-trees furling sail on a topsail yard.

"On a ship the crew is usually divided into two watches, but we have three. Lower-school students are the 'greenhands.' This is their first voyage. They don't know much about being sailors, and they often get seasick. Middle-school students are the common sailors. They've been on one or two voyages before. They think they know more than they really do, and they often get into trouble on shore leave." Knowing laughter could be heard from the parents present. "Our upper-school students are able-bodied sailors. They are the most experienced, and we count on them to mentor the rest.

"Many forces affect our little ship. As we make our way through a turbulent sea, we are buffeted by waves, driven by currents and at the mercy of the wind for any progress at all. Our parents are like the wind. The tuition they pay is the engine that drives us through the water. Our alumnae are like mighty currents, mostly hidden from view but exerting a great influence on the school."

Parents and alumnae present listened intently. They had come to the opening of school celebrations filled with hopeful anticipation, seeking justification for their optimism. Most of them sensed that their ship had been rudderless for some time, trusting in providence to keep its course. They craved strong leadership, and Tom was determined to not disappoint them.

"Our ship is about to sail," Tom said solemnly. He slowly folded his notes, put them in his pocket, and took a long drink of water from the glass at his side. No one dared to clap. Bending to the microphone and breaking the silence, Tom said sternly, "Ms. Scott and Mr. Laurie, report to the altar steps."

Removing his jacket and folding it over his chair, Tom strode to the center of the sanctuary. With his legs spread wide, he deliberately rolled the sleeves of his starched white shirt while fixing his audience with as malevolent a glare as he could muster. Every eye was on him as Peg and Everett made their way down the aisle.

Peg Scott and Everett Laurie were directors of their respective divisions and just a notch below Tom on the organization chart. Both had been briefed as to what would happen next, but nothing could truly have prepared them. Crossing his arms high on his chest, Tom puffed himself up as far as his 160 pounds on a 5-foot, 9-inch frame would allow. In as loud a voice as he could project and still maintain control, he bellowed, "Now, Ms. Scott, I see a good crew before me. There are some greenhands among them, but with a little hard work, sweat and discipline—Ms. Scott, don't forget the discipline—they'll be fine sailors, and they'll make us proud.

"Are you ready and willing to do whatever it takes to prepare this crew for the journey ahead?"

"Yes, sir."

Now Tom stretched for the edge where control could be questioned, and fairly roared, "Ms. Scott, this is *not* some namby-pamby private school; this is a sailing vessel, and I am the captain. When you wish to address me with an affirmative answer, you will say 'aye, sir' or 'aye, aye, sir.' *Is that understood*?"

His audience was stunned. Shock and horror were etched on the faces of the tykes in the front rows. Farther back, the faces wore looks of pure astonishment. No one could believe what was happening. With the hint of a tremor in her voice, Peg responded as directed. "Aye, aye, sir."

Tom's composure returned, and he continued in a moderated captain-of-the-fleet bellow, "Very well, Ms. Scott. Now, louder. I want your affirmation to ring from the yardarms."

Struggling to reach his volume, Peg pronounced the requested "Aye, aye, sir."

"Very good, Ms. Scott. Now, Mr. Laurie, are you ready to give me your best effort to turn this raggedy bunch of greenhands into salt-water sailors?"

Everett's surprise was only by a degree less than that of the audience, but he was a man accustomed to the vagaries of teenagers and did not shock easily. Eyes wide behind his glasses, he managed an appropriately lusty, "Aye, aye, sir."

"All right then, prepare to get underway. Weigh anchor, and cheerily now. Get this crew into the rigging, and loose the sails. I declare the 218th year of Florence Bruce Seminary to be open and in session. Flag bearers, lead the way."

CHAPTER XIII

Prenups

♠

Evaluations are based on mutually agreed-upon goals set in advance of the school year . . . . Ordinarily these evaluations are submitted, according to an agreed-upon format, only to trustees.[1]

The doorbell rang. Allison removed her apron and straightened her clothes. She was wearing a tailored black dress high in the neck, set off with diamond stud earrings and her grandmother's cameo broach—an accessory, she thought, befitting the antique furnishings of the Ahlborn House. It was a studied look she wanted to project—elegant but not pretentious, in charge but not controlling, gracious but not frivolous. No detail of the evening had been too insignificant to escape her attention. She flicked a speck from Tom's jacket and opened the door.

It was Archie Devlin. He was the picture of casual elegance in pressed, gray Tommy Hilfiger slacks, a knit-silk crew shirt under a tweed sports coat that nicely set off the distinguishing salt-and-pepper

[1] DeKuyper, Mary Hundley. *Trustee Handbook: A Guide to Effective Governance for Independent School Boards*. Washington, DC: National Association of Independent Schools, 1998, p. 117.

highlights in his hair. "Am I the first one?" he asked, seemingly embarrassed at his punctual arrival.

"Oh, you're exactly on time. Please come in."

"My dear, you are absolutely lovely. You're just wonderful to put up with all of us this evening." Archie stepped into the vestibule and kissed Allison lightly on the cheek. His voice was soft and flowed like warm chocolate drenched in exaggerated empathy. She laughed and gently pulled him out of the doorway to make way for the next arriving guest, whose form already loomed in the darkness just beyond the step.

Archie was the first member of the transition committee to arrive. Although not technically a member, his position as board president gave him *ex officio* status on each of Florence Bruce's seven standing and two ad hoc committees. For the next nine months, it would be a rare intrusion to cause Archie to miss a committee meeting. He was at the apex of the school hierarchy. In the small community of Florence Bruce Seminary, around which his life now revolved, Archie's stature was at an all-time high. For the first time in the eight years since his wife had passed away and his medical practice had been put aside, Archie was involved with something he truly cared about. He was determined to leave no stone unturned in fulfilling the responsibilities he assumed to be under the mantle of his leadership. The typical board president of an independent school might attend a smattering of committee meetings during the year, but if it would make a difference, Archie had resolved that he would do his best to attend them all.[2]

The rest of the transition committee arrived in rapid succession: Dr. Warren Hudson, Caroline Odum, Kay Johnson, Buster Jolley, Keegan O'Connor, Monique Fontembleau, Phyllis Killam and Geoffrey Bellingham. By now they were all well known to Tom and Allison, and it was entirely fitting they be the first invited to inspect the results of the Ahlborn House renovation. These were the people who had selected Tom as one of eight to be interviewed from a pool of seventy candidates, included him among three finalists to visit the

[2] A good leader charges his subordinates and then empowers them by stepping aside to let them do their work. Archie's assumption—that his participation at committee meetings would make a difference—was accurate, but not in the way he intended.

school, and recommended his appointment to the board of trustees. No other group was as strongly vested in Tom's success.

This evening was for Allison the consummation of all she had worked for. From the moment of her arrival in Portsmouth, she had spent hundreds of hours with Steve Harrison and a cadre of designers, contractors and vendors; even her sleep had been consumed in preparation for this unveiling. Conservative by nature and lacking inner reserves of self-confidence, Allison relished the safety of Tom's embrace and was not prone to expose herself to unforeseen hazards. This time, however, she had thrown caution to the wind and bared her soul and her wallet to the vagaries of public approval. The results were extraordinary.

The dining-room table, covered with her mother's linen, was festooned with delectable selections approved either by Martha Stewart or by one of dozens of sources Allison had consulted while preparing for her role as first lady to the head of school. A salmon mousse, shaped like its namesake and decorated with cucumber scales, pimiento-strip fins and a Spanish-olive eye, was much appreciated and would become a signature item at her parties. Archie's favorites were the mozzarella-basil-grape tomato cocktail skewers, and a collection of brightly colored, plastic toothpicks accumulated on his napkin. Mouth-watering lemon bars and candied ginger pecans, along with chocolate meringue and English matrimonial cookies, were carefully placed to add color, variety and interest to her table.

The kitchen, of course, was everyone's first tour choice, because everyone knew it was the area of the house that had received the most ambitious facelift. Exclamations of approval multiplied as Allison expounded upon initial impressions by pointing out the capacity she had built in for entertaining larger groups: warming oven, oversized refrigerator and freezer, capacious oven, commercial gas stove, and separate sink for washing vegetables. "It's so perfect, and functional, too," gushed their champion, Caroline Odum. From a more reserved Kay Johnson: "You made it modern, but look how it blends with the older aspects of the home"; while Monique Fontembleau proclaimed, "I just love the hardwood floors. *Est ce magnifique*? That awful linoleum was so depressing." The men, too, demonstrated their appreciation as they wandered the room and ran their fingers over the granite countertops, but their low mutterings were overshadowed by the enthusiasm of the women.

While most of the women headed upstairs with Allison to inspect the living quarters, the men, along with Phyllis Killam, filled their plates and stood around the table kibitzing about golf scores and business prospects. Tom struggled to keep up. Golf was a game he played only to be sociable, and his knowledge of community movers and shakers was still in its infancy. In due course, the tour returned and the party retired to the living room.

Lights from the school, twinkling among the swaying branches of a gnarled old pine, could be seen through the room's large bay window. An enormous oriental rug covered the center of the floor in front of the fireplace where a crackling fire greeted them. A couch and two chairs surrounded a marble-topped coffee table, creating a cozy center to the room. Around these were an American Federal mahogany settee, a gothic-style armchair with blue needlepoint dating from the late nineteenth century, and numerous other antiques that Allison had rescued and restored from the Florence Bruce attic collection.

A feeling of déjà vu swept over Tom as he watched Allison play the host. She suddenly reminded him of Jackie Kennedy on one of her televised White House tours: so poised, and yet around her a palpable aura of vulnerability. As Allison described the room's decorative pieces, she came to an acrylic painting of an early commencement celebration done by a former art teacher. She had found the painting in a corner, she said, gathering dust and cobwebs. Omitted from her comments was the fact that she had taken it to be professionally cleaned and set into a new $170 frame, which she paid for herself. The painting was the capstone to her vision for the Ahlborn House, said Allison, her features luminous in the glow of the fire.

Allison's soliloquy caught them all unawares, and each person in the room struggled to comprehend the full meaning of what they were witnessing. Even Tom, who never quite grasped Allison's vision until this moment, struggled along with them. She had created, as she had said she would, a showplace for entertaining guests of the school. Far beyond that, however, the Ahlborn House was now a repository for the rare and beautiful artifacts of Florence Bruce Seminary. In it, a cross-section of the school's history was carefully curated and put on display in such a way as to pay homage to and to honor a distinguished heritage. Allison brought style where before there was only the mundane; she brought dignity where before there was only the ordinary; excellence instead of the average; elegance instead of the commonplace.

This was the first of eighteen special events Allison would host for the school over the next six months. Following the gathering of the transition committee, she prepared a reception to show appreciation for the kitchen staff, which would later be responsible for catering some of the larger events. This was followed by a reception for the maintenance staff as a special "thank you" for completing the renovations on time. Leaders and faculty from each of the school's three divisions were invited. She served a formal dinner for six that included a scion of the wealthy ship-builders who succeeded Guy Victor Bruce. A gift to the capital campaign of $200,000 followed shortly thereafter.

Allison's Ahlborn House tour became the stuff of legend. Students trick-or-treated their way in on Halloween to see for themselves. Allison met them at the door as the ghost of Florence Bruce. Carolers arrived twice during December to be invited in for spiced cider around the fire. Tottering, silver-haired alums were steered up the winding walkway into the parlor to rekindle ancient memories of their sojourn at the seminary.

Allison was not prone to self-congratulation. It wasn't that she was a modest person, but rather that she was genuinely and appreciably insecure in her capabilities. Confidence that her accomplishments were worthy did not come easily, nor did she ever fully trust the praise of another. In her youth, compliments were few, and seldom did her achievements warrant praise or applause from those she loved. In fact, the opposite was often the case. Tributes from others brought her mother's attention—and jealousy. Accomplishment was put down. Excellence was demeaned. Allison learned early not to extend herself, because success was followed by nullification and humiliation.

Two years of therapy in her late twenties helped her overcome damage from an abusive mother and the dysfunctional family life that revolved around her. Although the residual from that life would be with her forever, since coming to Portsmouth she had not succumbed to the clamoring voices holding her back. She had erected no protective barriers. Florence Bruce had put its trust in her husband, and she would invest her trust in the school. All she could muster went into the effort. The Ahlborn House renovation was the best she could do, and it was better than she thought.

Following Allison's well-received presentation, Geoffrey Bellingham directed attention to the business at hand. Warren Hudson reported that he had met with Tom and Kay Johnson to craft a survey instrument to be used in Tom's evaluation in the spring. Respondents were to rank their opinions of the head of school from "strongly agree" to "strongly disagree" on such items as: "Communicates effectively and listens carefully," and "Demonstrates a deep commitment to the mission and future of Florence Bruce." The survey contained twenty-one items and left plenty of room for comments.

Warren cautioned, "Surveys can be very dangerous, and we need to be careful. This survey should be given only to the board and perhaps a select group of faculty. Above all, the results must be kept confidential."

"I understand the need for confidentiality in the results," said Caroline Odum, "but why not give it to everyone?"

"Because the board of trustees is in charge of the school. We're the ones who will be guiding Tom. Only our opinions will count."

"Okay, I understand that, but don't we want to hear from everyone?"

"That's where the danger lies," Warren said patiently. "We know there will be changes in the coming year. We want change to occur and are giving Tom a mandate to affect change. When there is a great deal of change going on, some people will not adjust well. Their evaluations of Tom will be negative, but they will be negative for the wrong reasons. They will be negative precisely because Tom is doing what we want him to do."[3]

Caroline still seemed perplexed. One eye seemed to wander, while the other fixed on Warren. "No more sugar cookies for you, Caroline," Keegan O'Connor piped in with good-humored exasperation, seeing her confusion. "We need to pay attention to those who are on the same wavelength as we are and not be confused by those who aren't."

"I wouldn't say it exactly that way," said Warren, "but that's the idea."

---

[3]This became a critical point later in Tom's tenure. John Littleford, the recognized national expert in heads' compensation and evaluation issues, states, "Only the most naïve of schools would involve faculty or other representatives outside of the board in the evaluation of the head of school."

Geoffrey Bellingham moved the meeting to the next item on the agenda, the articulation of goals. Tom rose to give his report and explain how he had grouped and consolidated the myriad items the transition committee had produced in its last session. Four overarching goals had emerged.

The first goal addressed concerns about the compensation and benefits package offered to the school's faculty and a perception that the system was biased. Tom traced the words with his finger as he read:

"Attract the best faculty/staff and retain the best by addressing fairness in compensation."

Another set of concerns surrounded the school's declining enrollment and its ineffectual marketing. Despite a recent nationwide surge in attendance at all-girls schools, enrollment at Florence Bruce remained flat. The second goal was:

"Advance the philosophy of Florence Bruce Seminary as a college-preparatory, all-girls school with three divisions by coordinating public relations, admissions, the building project and program."

Many, many issues at the school arose as a result of poor communications. Together, they filled half the flip chart pages from the last meeting. Tom encountered the problems even as he began his candidacy. Vehicles such as the website and *Seminary Log* were poorly done and simply didn't communicate anything of much value. John was a shoot-from-the-hip administrator who eschewed written strategy and lacked consistent policies. Procedures emanating from John's office dictated that problems were often ignored, hidden or otherwise kept from seeing the light of day. Thus, the third recommended goal was comprehensive if not altogether explicit:

"Improve communications both internally and among Florence Bruce constituencies, including alums, faculty/staff, parents and students, trustees, administrators, and the surrounding community."

Lastly, tuition for the year had just been raised by seven percent across the board. Although well above inflation level, the increase was not unjustified nor was the resultant tuition outside the norm for other private schools in the area. Nevertheless, this increase, along with increases of the past, had not been adequately "sold" to parents. Deep-seated anger and resentment lingered over the issue. The transition committee was determined not to let it happen again:

"Ensure that student tuitions and any future increases are justified on the basis of costs versus benefits to current and future students."

Here Tom stopped his recitation. "To tell you the truth, I'm feeling a bit overwhelmed. It's been recommended to me from several sources that I take a year to get to know the school before I try to affect significant changes. If you ask me to make progress on each of these goals, you are asking for a lot to happen very quickly."

"What about the capital campaign?" said Archie. "Several of us addressed the need to get on with the fundraising, and you haven't mentioned it." Archie was determined that his administration leave behind a worthy legacy, and he was aware that building a new wing was the best way to ensure it.

A nodding of heads and murmurs around the room signaled Archie was right. "Yes, I'm aware of that," Tom responded. "My recommendation is that we keep working on the capital campaign but not make it a top priority. I need time to get to know your donor base, and a capital campaign is extremely labor intensive for a head of school."

"But we can't let the campaign slip. The school has been working on this project for six years. We've got to make the campaign a priority."

"We've already had one failed campaign, and there's a lack of confidence out there in the community. We can't let up," agreed Keegan O'Connor.

"All right," Tom capitulated. He realized the truth of what they were saying, while at the same time recognizing the implicit danger of moving too fast on too many fronts. "How does this sound:

"'Advance the "Campaign for Florence Bruce" on the board-approved timeline'?"

The committee agreed on this language for a fifth goal, and again, Tom expressed caution. "This is a significant agenda you're giving me. I'm new, and I'm being asked to do both John's job and what Roland Guyotte did as assistant head. I'm going to need to move pretty fast to stay up with this agenda. If we don't seem to be moving fast enough, I'll expect your patience, and I'm going to need your help if this is going to work."[4]

---

[4] Pent-up frustrations from several years of neglect drove all of us to want to push ahead too fast. The anticipation of Tom's arrival, his raw energy, and the desire to "get going" made an active agenda seem self-evident and any other path irresponsibly cautious. It was to be a fatal mistake.

The committee assured Tom that he would have both and recommended approval of the five goals to the executive committee.

The final agenda item concerned an "event" to celebrate the appointment of the new head. Some in the community had expressed a need to reinforce the commitment that had been made, to demonstrate the authority invested in Tom by the board of trustees, and to provide Tom with a platform to share his developing ideas with school leaders.

It was late and the conversation wandered. Tom, again, suggested an "installation ceremony." He still didn't understand exactly what it meant, but conversations with colleagues around the country assured him it was important. The transition committee, happy for a way out and anxious to get home, agreed and passed along to the executive committee a recommendation that an installation of Dr. Tom Whitman be held in the month of November.

Promptly the next day, Tom called the Rt. Rev. William P. Moseley, bishop of the Diocese of Boston and trustee of Florence Bruce Seminary. "The transition committee is recommending that we do an installation as you suggested. Now, tell me again how an installation is different from what happened when my appointment was announced in front of the student body last December?"

"The announcement then was like telling people you are getting engaged. The installation is like the marriage ceremony itself; it's a promise before the community and before God pertaining to certain things. In a marriage, it's to 'love, honor' and such. In an installation, it's a promise between the leader and members of the institution to accept certain obligations relative to one another."

"What might those obligations be? Can you give me an example?"

"Well, it might be to work toward certain goals together. For example, you might promise to provide a good education while the students promise to study hard. The important thing, as in a marriage, is that the promise is reciprocal, made in front of the community and before God."

Obviously, the installation would take place in Hanley Chapel, and Tom asked if the bishop would officiate. He agreed, provided the ceremony was on November 11, as that was the only available date that month in his busy schedule.

* * *

Three days later, Tom met with Archie in their second weekly meeting since school had opened. Archie was in an ebullient mood. He was now visiting Florence Bruce at least two hours every day, sometimes to attend committee meetings, sometimes to visit classrooms and sometimes just to hang out and chat with faculty and parents who dropped by. His life felt full, and he was engaged in meaningful work.[5]

He and Deanne were seeing each other regularly. Whereas before they kept their relationship relatively quiet, now it was more open, and Deanne often spent the night with him. The three girls—his two and Deanne's one—got along famously, and for the first time since his wife passed away, Archie was feeling whole again.

The first gathering of the executive committee was a week away, and Archie's first meeting of the board of trustees as its president was the week following. On this day, most of his and Tom's time together was spent reviewing the agenda for these meetings.

In other business, Tom briefed Archie on the situation with Ellen Stein and his firing of Gene. There was also another incident. One of the receptionists had been caught red-handed stealing from petty cash. It was a small amount, but suspicions about the woman's trustworthiness went back more than a year. Tom said a conference with her was planned for the next day, and he anticipated he would be letting her go. Archie listened with rapt attention. Tom saw Archie's brow crease and his head tilt in pained expression, as if straining to catch every word.

Near the end of their meeting, Tom mentioned he had spoken with the bishop about the installation ceremony and related its purpose as it had been described to him. He said the only date the bishop was available to officiate was November 11.

---

[5] I was appalled when I heard how much time Archie was spending at the school. A board president needs to stay apart from the day-to-day activities of an organization and not get "underfoot." Archie was already beginning to act like he "ran" the school. His attendance at every committee meeting, where he often dominated the proceedings, was also marginalizing the chairs of these committees and interfering with the fresh flow of ideas.

"But that's Veterans Day; we can't hold it then."

"I wondered about that, too. But I checked with the calendar, and it turns out school is in session. Apparently, Florence Bruce doesn't take Veterans Day as a holiday."

Archie hesitated, but only for a moment. "Well, it should be a holiday. Everyone else takes it off, but that's beside the point anyway. I have to attend a tribute at the navy yard, and then I'm taking the girls to the parade. We can't hold it on Veterans Day."

"Archie, I'd love to have you participate, but I certainly understand that you've made commitments for that day. Perhaps Geoffrey Bellingham can fill in for you." A cloud passed over the table. It was fleeting, but it brought on an expression Tom had never seen before. Archie's body stiffened, although his head remained tilted and his aspect never changed. The lines and the creases were all in the same place they had been before, but his eyes narrowed just slightly and his skin tone darkened perceptibly—like an octopus under attack.

"I don't think holding the installation on Veterans Day is a good idea," was all Archie said.

Tom saw the expression but did not read its meaning. He knew Archie was upset, but incorrectly assumed his passion was for honoring those who had fought for their country, when in fact Archie's real concern lay in not wanting to be left out of such an important event. Tom checked with the bishop to ascertain that November 11 was the only date available. It was. He checked with his head of school list serve to see what other private schools did on Veterans Day. Three quarters of those he checked remained in session. In the end, Tom confirmed the date with the bishop's secretary and left a message for Archie that evening relating the results of his research, apologizing, and promising to make Veterans Day a holiday in next year's school calendar. It was a promise he kept, but Archie was not in the least bit mollified because Veterans Day *per se* was not his real concern. It was the first of several miscommunications between the two men, the consequences of which, in the end, would be catastrophic for both of them.

Facing the computer screen with his back to the open door, Tom heard the shuffling of little feet and muffled voices coming down the hallway to his office. The noise stopped at the doorway, but turning around, he saw no one there. Jackie was away on some errand, he remembered, so he got up and walked to the door. "Hey, what do we have here!" he exclaimed as three rambunctious ten-year-old girls in Bruce plaid jumpers poked their heads around the corner with wide-eyed curiosity. "Come in! Come in!

"Why you've come to pay me a visit. How nice! You know I don't get many visitors up here. What can I do for you?"

"We've come to give you an invitation," said one.

"An invitation for me? I'm thrilled! What's it for?"

"It's to the fifth-grade ice cream social this afternoon. Will you come?" said the speaker, while another youngster produced a hand-drawn invitation.

"Of course I'll come. I wouldn't miss it for all the world," said Tom, taking the invitation and examining it with exaggerated interest.

The third little girl had drifted off from the others and was looking at a large framed photograph hanging on the wall. It showed a new wing of Florence Bruce Seminary under construction at some time in the past, with the workmen in formal attire strategically posed around the construction site. Pointing to the photograph, she exclaimed, "That's my great-grandfather."

"What? What did you say about your grandfather?" he said, rising and walking over to the picture."

"That's him right there," she said, pointing to a tiny figure on the roof. "That's my great-grandfather. He fell off the roof and died."

Her story seemed improbable, yet it was not something a little girl would make up. Further questioning failed to provide any more clues, and Tom asked her to get a note from her mother to verify the story, thinking that would be the end of it. Yet the next day he received a note neatly written in a feminine hand. Yes, the story was true. The girl's great-grandfather had fallen to his death while working on the seminary roof. He was twenty-three and left behind two sons. One of the sons had married and produced a daughter who was the writer of the note. The little girl recognized the photo from a copy John had given the family some years earlier.

Tom was an opportunist, and when such an opportunity as this came knocking, he was not about to let it pass. Connecting with students was one of the most important and, at the same time, most difficult aspects of his job. Walkabouts, which he tried to do at least once a day but only succeeded half as often, were only so effective. In the first few weeks, he would stop students and invite introductions until about the fourth week, when a first-grade tyke he had stopped previously queried flatly, "You don't know who I am, do you?"

Tom, obviously forgetting the earlier meeting and embarrassed at being caught, had to admit that he didn't.

He pledged to the faculty that he would visit every classroom and was already ticking them off three or four a week. It was something he needed to do to bond with the teaching faculty, but simply sitting in a classroom watching wasn't of much help in becoming acquainted with the student body.

This was an opportunity, however, to connect in a meaningful way with a whole class. It was also another occasion to work one-on-one with Deanne Bakker while obtaining valuable publicity for the school. A three-in-one opportunity didn't come along often.

Good publicity is gold. Tom knew that no amount of clever advertising could take the place of a well-placed, interesting story with a creative photo or two. He had always eschewed paid advertising, opting instead to cultivate relationships with reporters and tempt them from time to time with a tantalizing lead. Already, he had sent a number of story ideas to Deanne without a response. He had brought in relevant newspaper stories about other schools, asking her to make contact with the reporters in the bylines and send them information about Florence Bruce. So far, these suggestions had been ignored.

Tom called Deanne into his office and pitched her the story. "Did you know we have a student here whose great-grandfather fell off the seminary roof and was killed while working on a construction crew? And, we have a great photo of him in life. I just know there is a reporter out there who would love to have this, if we present it right." He went on to tell her his plan to have a reception in his office for the student and her parents and the entire fifth grade, and to dedicate the photo in memory of the great-grandfather.

Deanne was instantly defensive. "What does this have to do with education?"

"It doesn't—at least not directly—but it will portray Florence Bruce to the community in a positive light and begin to combat the outsider's view of the school as being only for elite lesbians."

"Okay," Deanne shrugged in capitulation. "Do you want me to do a release?"

"No, releases are only good for standard, run-of-the-mill stuff. Reporters see hundreds of them a day. You need a relationship with the reporter. You've got to know what their interests are and show how the story will work for them. Who was that fellow who did the story when I was appointed? Bill Cogden. Wasn't that it?"

Reluctantly, she found the telephone number, and he placed the call. With Deanne listening, Tom spoke into the phone, "Hi, Bill, this is Tom Whitman, the fellow at Florence Bruce you did the story on last spring. Yeah, I'm the one. You know I just stumbled across this great story and I thought you might recommend someone I can pitch it to. Yeah—well, okay, we've got this kid here whose great-grandfather fell off the seminary roof and died back while he was working on a construction crew. We've found this wonderful historic photo of him on the roof. Oh, I'd guess about 1935. I'm going to do a little reception with the kid's classmates and dedicate the photo to him. So, *you* might be interested in the story? That's great. Sure, I can get you a copy of the photo . . ."

Tom hung up and made several more calls, finally sending a courier to deliver the photo for reproduction. At the appointed hour, the reporter as well as thirty youngsters from the two fifth-grade classes appeared at his office door. With great fanfare they were ushered in and invited to partake of Mrs. Clayworth's homemade cookies and punch. Tom seated the wide-eyed students on the floor and spun them a tale about the importance of history. He said that life was like a long, unbroken chain. Their moms and dads were carrying the chain now, but the students held in their hands the next links, and soon it would be their turn to bear the weight. Tom told them the story of the young man who had built the roof on their school and fallen to his death while working to shelter them. He described the links from father to son, from son to daughter, and from daughter to one of their classmates. He reminded them that the great-granddaughter was now benefiting from the good works of her ancestors, just as their children or their children's children might someday benefit from the good works they would perform.

Two weeks later, a front-page article with the eye-catching old photo of the seminary under construction appeared in the community section of the *Portsmouth Tribune,* headlined "Workman's legacy: Florence Bruce honors construction worker whose descendants attend Portsmouth school." Tom characterized it as a feel-good story about Florence Bruce, but it sent an important message: "If a construction worker's kid/descendent can attend Florence Bruce, it can't be too elitist." Tom chalked up a point for Goal #3: Improving communications.

Deanne seem nonplussed by the whole incident. Tom didn't want to embarrass her with a direct confrontation, but he was perplexed. *This is supposed to be her area of expertise, and she doesn't get it; she should be telling me how to get a story placed, not the other way around.* Still, the publicity plug had worked exactly the way he had said it would, and he hoped—in vain as it turned out—a lesson might be learned. For the remainder of Deanne's tenure at Florence Bruce, the school received no further publicity as a result of her efforts other than event announcements in the calendar sections.

CHAPTER XIV

Matrimony

♠

> The final and most dangerous pitfall in the process of choosing a head is to think that the wedding is the goal, when in fact it is the marriage . . . . Making the marriage work takes effort on everyone's part.[1]

The executive committee met monthly for lunch in Tom's office. The board of trustees, which assembled only quarterly, charged this committee of their peers with conducting the regular business of the school. Archie Devlin chaired the meetings, which also included Geoffrey Bellingham, Warren Hudson, Saugus Wetherby, Keegan O'Connor, Bodie Bickerstaff and Phyllis Killam.

The executive committee Tom inherited was very much the creation of John Sanford with two notable exceptions: Tom Whitman, not John, was now the head of school, and Archie Devlin, not Phyllis Killam, was president. These two changes at the top were significant ones and would require from the rest an adjustment of seemingly impossible proportions. With the notable exception of Warren Hudson, none

---

[1] DeKuyper, Mary Hundley. *Trustee Handbook: A Guide to Effective Governance for Independent School Boards*. Washington, DC: National Association of Independent Schools, 1998, p. 128.

of the others had ever served on a board of trustees or reported to one, so all they knew about best practices and effective governance, they had gained at the feet of John Sanford.

Where John was secretive and held important decisions close to the vest, Tom was open with information and encouraged a collaborative, democratic process. Where John relied on friendships and loyalties to achieve his ends, Tom trusted in facts and logical argument to win the day. The former head and president of the board knew each other well. John and Phyllis were close friends with a relationship that extended over many years, and they were intimately familiar with the important issues facing the school. Tom and Archie barely knew each other. They had no history of working together, and neither one carried an intimate knowledge of the school. Phyllis was a natural leader who commanded respect. Archie was a lightweight, a likeable guy with neither the attributes nor the hardheaded drive for leadership. Phyllis was smart, shrewd and strategic. Archie was naïve, reactive and narrow. The changes about to engulf the executive committee were profound ones.[2]

Lunch arrived on trays brought up by the dumbwaiter to Tom's office—chicken tortellini soup, ham-and-cheese croissant sandwiches, tossed green salad, assorted drinks and Mrs. Clayworth's chocolate-dipped strawberries. Good attendance at lunchtime committee meetings was no doubt due in some measure to the fine fare the school provided.

The meeting opened with Geoffrey Bellingham's report from the transition committee. Prof. Bellingham occupied the acclaimed Annenburg Professor of Anthropology Chair at Concord and Franklin University and was considered to be near genius level, with a Mensa IQ and ego to match. Iconoclastic and a loner by nature, Geoffrey was self-assured, arrogant and distrustful of authority. He served on several faculty committees and was known for his constant tilting at the university's administration.

---

[2] "How to" books on nonprofit governance recommend that a new chief executive and new board president not be brought in at the same time. A new school head benefits greatly from the advice and guidance of an experienced board president. Unfortunately, the issue was never considered prior to Tom's arrival.

Geoffrey gave his report in crisp, concise terms. He described the process by which his committee had established goals to guide Dr. Whitman over the next year. He announced that an installation ceremony was being planned for early November. He shared a copy of the survey reviewed by his committee and included the recommendation that the evaluative instrument used to measure Dr. Whitman's performance should go to the full board of trustees and a select group of individuals. "Dr. Whitman," he said, "and the executive committee should review the returned forms together and prepare a report to the full board."

Archie asked Tom for comment. Clearing his throat and taking a deep breath that showed his concern, Tom said he was worried about the number of tasks before him, especially the desire to keep the Campaign for Florence Bruce on track. Groundbreaking for the new wing was scheduled for May, and only $3.3 million of the $7 million campaign goal had been reached. To achieve the goal, he said, "I will need each of you to be active participants in the campaign. You'll need to make calls on prospects and follow up on them; you'll need to host cultivation events or, at least, participate in them; and above all, I need you to be unflinchingly enthusiastic about this project."

No sooner were the words out of his mouth when Bodie Bickerstaff exclaimed, "You've got as much money as you're going to get from me. We raised all that money last time and nothing happened. The wing never got built."

We've been over that, Bodie," Phyllis interjected, well acquainted with Bodie's outbursts. "The money had to go into infrastructure: sprinklers, a new roof—that sort of thing."

"How much money? We never did get a good accounting of how much we spent or how much is left."

"Now Bodie," Keegan O'Conner clucked, halting the tap-tapping on his laptop, "we told you how the money was spent, you just didn't like what you heard."

"I heard it; I just don't agree with this campaign thing. We've been raising money for years. I told them I'd help, but nobody calls me."

The conversation continued tit for tat. Nothing would mollify Bodie. She was, thought Tom, a classic piece of work. Known for playing the devil's advocate, it was not the advocate she usually played, but the fool. Bodie never stayed on the same subject for more than two sentences. Instead, she played off any counterargument by changing the focus of the conversation to another subject, which always retained some ephemeral connection to its former cousin. Most of her colleagues eventually learned to discourage her by simply not responding after one or two attempts.

All boards benefit from a member or two who will challenge conventional wisdom. Their value lies in helping to anticipate the unexpected and explore what might be. Bodie was given nominal credit for this role, but her value in the role was far from certain. She lacked any ability to defend her positions past a superficial plea for attention and, when cornered, simply repeated her point with mounting agitation. She could create an argument to support her position and, moments later, counter her own argument to support another position without realizing the incongruence. The origins of her opposition to subjects were usually lost in the obscurity of her thought processes. Since they might as well be derived from an unfortunate incident in childhood or a perceived slight suffered at the hands of a protagonist, her moral authority to foster opposition was bankrupt.

Bodie was thought of as being a good businesswoman, but the successful auto dealership she owned was an inheritance from her father and pretty much took care of itself. She also controlled a substantial family foundation, which tended to mute any criticism and was, in fact, largely responsible for her position on the Florence Bruce board of trustees. Term limits made this Bodie's last year as a trustee, and Tom would simply have to attempt to ride out her obstructionist's ways.

He was now forewarned. One member of the executive committee had stated unambiguously that she wasn't going to participate in the fundraising effort. Any thought of "unflinching enthusiasm" on her part was out of the question. He should have then and there insisted the capital campaign take a back seat to the other important work he was tasked with, but Tom lacked the critical circumspection to balance his energy and boundless optimism. There was no obstacle he was not confident of overcoming.

Before the meeting ended, he also made a plea to permit his "advisory team" to attend board meetings. "These are the people I count on for advice," he said. "I need them to hear from you firsthand and not have information filtered through my retelling." John's habit, born in a culture of secrecy, was to keep board meetings closed to all staff except when they were needed for a specific report; it was Tom's habit to include senior staff and thereby to empower the team needed to achieve the goals of the organization. It was agreed the item would appear on the agenda for consideration by the board.

In the lobby of Florence Bruce, Archie was helping Phyllis into her coat. "How often do you and Tom meet?" she asked in an offhand manner.

"Oh, we get together about once a week."

"Do you get together other than for meetings? Do you talk on the phone?"

"Tom calls me once in awhile if he has something on his mind. Why do you ask?"

"Well, I was just thinking," said Phyllis. "He hasn't called me in the two weeks since school started. I wonder what he's doing with his time."

"I dunno. He seems to be pretty busy."

Archie failed to catch her point. Phyllis was hurt. She missed the close relationship she had shared with John at the seat of the school's power. She had gone out of her way to initiate a relationship with Tom and Allison. She had gotten them a nice car and an additional ten thousand dollars for the Ahlborn House renovation, but neither one had contacted her. Oh, she had received a thank-you note from Allison, but it wasn't the same thing. She didn't feel her efforts were being reciprocated or fully acknowledged. Maybe the relationship was passed along with her job to Archie, but from what he said it didn't seem so. *Who is close to Tom? Who is he collaborating with? Who is he confiding in? If not Archie and if not me, than who?*

The following week the board of trustees met for the first time under Archie's leadership. With his blessing, Tom revamped the format used by John by bringing all business items to the front of the agenda and defining them with a careful delineation of the decision to be made, related background, and recommended action. Contrary to past practice, committee reports followed the business section to ensure sufficient time for the latter. The dominance of the "business" agenda baffled a few who regarded trustee meetings as "dialogues," but for the most part the change was appreciated.

As was customary in the first meeting of the year, Jackie distributed copies of the *Trustee Handbook: A Guide to Effective Governance for Independent School Boards.*[3]

Tom's request to permit his senior administrators to attend future meetings was met with consternation, the danger of a breach in confidentiality being the prevailing counterargument. However, most were persuaded by Warren Hudson's description of historical trends toward more openness on boards. He offered his own institution, which included faculty representation on the board, as an example. Someone suggested that improving communications at the school might begin at the top, and perhaps opening meetings to administrative staff would set a positive example. The suggestion to include a closed session in future agendas finally mitigated concerns over confidentiality.

In the end, Tom's call for more open, inclusive board meetings succeeded with two dissenting votes (Bodie Bickerstaff was one). He had prevailed in the first real test of his leadership. As the meeting adjourned, a trustee was heard to remark, "This is the most exciting meeting I've ever attended here. Imagine, a vote that wasn't unanimous. It's the first time I've seen that in my five years on the board."

Archie's manner of conducting the meeting was dreadful. He was compelled to comment on every agenda item and often engaged in the discussions to such an extent that he forgot his responsibility was to lead them. Tom prided himself on being able to count votes and looked to achieve consensus and a comfortable majority. Archie wanted unanimity on all counts, as was customary at Florence Bruce, but this meeting was not the norm. It had some meaty items. As a result, the proceedings dragged interminably despite a scheduled break. After the three-hour time limit had expired, those marking place on the agenda found they were only one-third of the way through. Extending the meeting by half an hour allowed for hurried completion of another third, but the remainder of the committee reports and all of the head's report were tabled.

---

[3] Mary Hundley DeKuyper, 1998. The book is published by the National Association of Independent Schools and is considered the preeminent source of information for the proper conduct of a school board. Each trustee was encouraged to read it. None did

Still, the meeting was considered a success and ended on a positive, upbeat note. Archie was elated, albeit somewhat chagrined that he had been unable to complete the agenda. He asked Tom to provide an agenda for the next meeting in December that included time limits delineating each item. *Archie may be inexperienced, but he seems teachable,* Tom decided.

The five goals recommended by the transition committee and approved by the executive committee received a full airing and a unanimous vote by the trustees. Tom was able to review each of them individually and explore the thought behind their articulation. When it was over, he reflected on what had been achieved. He had received a definitive green light to move ahead, but it was a full, active agenda the board had given him for his first year. When he compared notes with his peers, no other school head on Tom's list serve had nearly so ambitious a governing body.

* * *

Service of Celebration
Honoring the New Relationship
of
Florence Bruce Seminary
and
Dr. Tom Whitman

With the installation only weeks away, Tom made plans to address each of the divisions in preparation for the ceremony. He hoped to make the most of the opportunity to impart a lesson in values and ethics to the students. Typically, an installation is a high, formal affair to equal the expansive egos of invited alumni, community leaders and big-time donors. When the transition committee did not respond to this opportunity with sufficient enthusiasm, Tom took it upon himself to alter the classic configuration. He explained his rationale to the executive committee just prior to the ceremony.

"The opportunities for using the installation to educate our student body are really quite numerous, but I have settled on two. First, we will explore together what it means to make a promise. During the ceremony, I will be making them a promise—or rather, we will be making a promise together—to work toward a shared vision for the future of the school. Second, we will try to find out what it means to be inclusive, honoring all faiths and nationalities from within our Christian Episcopal tradition." Tom disclosed that he was consulting with Bishop Moseley, whose leadership was guiding the program.

Archie continued to grumble that November 11th was Veterans Day and the school should not be distracted from honoring the country's military. "The bottom line," Tom pleaded, "is this is the only day Bishop Moseley has available on his calendar." Archie was not pacified, and Tom could not understand his obstinance. He failed to realize, of course, that Archie's resistance had nothing to do with Veterans Day but rather with his own prior commitments, which prevented his participation in so meaningful a school event.

In the weeks prior to the "Service of Celebration" as it was called, Tom met in chapel separately with each of the three divisions. "A promise is like a guarantee, isn't it?" he asked, addressing the Lower School. "It's an extra guarantee that you will do what you say you will do. Have any of you ever made a promise?"

"Dr. Whitman, I promised not to hit my brother," ventured a third-grade student.

"I promised I'd do my homework after school," said another.

"Who did you make the promise to?"

"My mom."

"Have you ever made a promise to yourself?"

A half-dozen hands shot up, "I did," said one. "So did I," said another. "Me, too," came a chorus of eager voices.

"How about the rest of you? When you make a promise to yourself, do you keep it?"

"No . . . Yes . . . Sometimes," the responses came back.

"And what happens when you break promises to yourself? Are there any consequences? Does anyone get hurt?"

As Tom wandered the rows among his young charges, he poked and prodded their intellects, seeking articulation and demanding clarification. He challenged their outlooks on right and wrong. "What's the difference between a promise you make to yourself and a promise you make to someone else?" he asked. "Is one more important than the other? Is it 'lying' if you break a promise even to yourself? Is there a difference when you break a promise to a friend?" Every student knew of a time when someone had broken a promise, and there was no dearth of opinions to share.

"Can anyone give me an example of a promise you make in front of other people?"

Silence.

"Some of you made such a promise this morning."

A single hand was raised in response. "The 'Pledge of Allegiance'?"

"That's right!" Tom, inspired by this moment of insight, fairly shouted. "Every time you say the 'Pledge of Allegiance,' you are making a promise. What is it you say? 'I pledge allegiance to the flag of the United States of America . . .' The promise you are making is to our country—or the flag as the symbol of our country—and to all of us who are citizens of the United States. Sometimes we make a pledge to a group of people—not just to ourselves, not just to another person, but to a whole community. How important are these promises?"

At this point in the chapel session with the Middle School, a bright young lady pointed out that a traitor, whose pledge to his country was not kept, might cause a lot of people to be killed. Another suggested that a basketball player who broke a promise to come to practice might jeopardize the team.

"So promises we make to the whole community are very important," Tom emphasized. "If we break them, the consequences can affect everyone, not just ourselves. Now, there is another kind of promise that some people feel is more important than all the rest." Tom paused for effect. "What does it mean to make a promise with a hand on the Bible, as the president of the United States does when he takes the oath of office?"

During the upcoming Service of Celebration, Tom told the students, they would be making a promise together. Since it would be made in the chapel, if God were listening, He would know the promise had been made.

Later that evening, a group of upper-school girls sat in the dorms debating the merits of a promise made before God. "A promise is a promise," said one. "You should always keep a promise. The rest doesn't really matter."

"A promise I make to you dies when I die," said one young scholar, "But, since God is with us after death, a promise made to Him and the consequences of breaking that promise last forever."

"Is that the difference between getting married in a church and living together?"

"Do you have to be in church to make a promise to God?"

"No, you can pray anywhere, it's just better in a church."

"Why?"

"I'm an atheist," said another, "and I think you're all crazy. You can't talk to God; He doesn't answer prayers. You go through all this . . . stuff, and it means nothing."

The conversations blew on into the night and, the next day, spun off into little whirls around the breakfast table, in hallways and in classrooms. The answers weren't of so much importance as the questions that were being asked and considered.

On the morning of November 11th the entire student body gathered. The first students to process into the chapel carried the cross, representing the crucifixion of Christ, followed by the *Qur'an*, Islam's holy book, Jewish Sabbath candles, and an om, a symbol of the sound used in Hindu meditation. A Buddhist gong was used to mark the transition from one part of the ceremony to the next. The selection of these symbols from many faiths was recommended and encouraged by Bishop Moseley. *He's showing us a way to address our diversity,* marveled Tom, inwardly awed by the courage of this man of the cloth so boldly stepping from the mainstream to challenge his congregation.

Caroline Odum was one of only two trustees to attend. Credited with shaping the relationship of Florence Bruce Seminary to its Episcopal tradition, Caroline was pleased to witness the most significant statement of that relationship to unfold during her six-year tenure as a trustee. No one was present from the executive committee. That was unfortunate, for the true business of the school—the education of its young charges—was now unfolding at hyperspeed. The pomp and the majesty of the traditional Episcopal ceremony, juxtaposed with the incongruence of the symbolic imagery, left 450 young women and girls with singular memories.[4]

---

[4] I was chagrined to be the only other trustee in attendance. Education—at its core an accumulation of experience rather than of knowledge—is the only reason the institution ever existed at all. To further that educational mission is the fundamental, sacred purpose every Florence Bruce trustee embraces when they agree to serve at its altar. If it does not remain central and primary in the entirety of their actions and deliberations, a hallowed responsibility is abrogated.

After opening comments, a Thai student read from the *Dhammapada*. Another student read from the Hindu *Rig Veda,* followed by a selection from the *Old Testament*. A reading from the *Qur'an* preceded the final selection from the *Torah*. Tom thought the ecumenical sight truly remarkable.[5]

Tom's sister Kate, visiting from her home in New Mexico, was present to address the student body. "Her role is a critical one," Bishop Moseley had said in advising Tom to approve the travel expense. "You need to bring in someone from the outside who knows you well. Your sister will strengthen the relationship that has begun here by helping the congregation to connect the past with the present."

Kate, an educator herself, spoke of the need to trust the capabilities of young people by allowing them to take risks, and thereby learn from their mistakes. She reinforced her message with stories from Tom's childhood. She told of the time their father took a risk by leaving Tommy, as she called her brother, on the far side of a swollen stream to find his way across. Tommy did by finding a pathway over some rocks in the stream and gained confidence in himself by so doing. She told of the time her brother taught her how to "fly" by constructing a rope swing higher than any she had ever seen. Eventually Kate was convinced of the swing's safety, and because of the trust she placed in her brother's judgment, was thrilled to soar high enough to look inside the chimney of their own home. As she concluded her remarks, Kate stepped into the aisle to distribute little 2-inch by 2-inch laminated photos—four hundred and fifty of them—of her brother Tommy in Halloween cowboy garb.

The invisible veil between headmaster and student lifted another notch as Kate spoke. Tom was slowly emerging as "approachable"—as John had been—especially to Florence Bruce's younger students. As a carryover from his opening-day speech, youngsters commonly greeted him in the halls with, "Hi, Captain," to which he would gruffly respond, drawing giggles all-round, "Aye, mate, fair winds

---

[5] Liberal attitudes within much of the U.S. Episcopal clergy, as evidenced by Bishop Moseley's guidance of this service, have threatened to split the Church in recent years. I don't think any of my colleagues on the board, with the exception of Caroline Odum, ever appreciated—or took full advantage of—the contributions this man made to the education of our students.

today," or, to their obvious delight, "Avast ya swab, away to class with ya." Now, Cowboy Tommy would smile back at these students from refrigerators and bulletin boards. Bonds were being built and a common vocabulary fashioned from the bits and pieces of his life that he shared with them.

As the celebration continued, students, parents, alums and faculty presented Dr. Whitman with their hopes and dreams for Florence Bruce, given physical shape and symbolically represented in the form of patches to be sewn together into a quilt. Kay Johnson from the Alumnae Association presented "the gift of tradition," a patch with the seminary's shield. The Parents' Association shared its vision of "working together to make a difference" with a patch depicting the figures of students, parents and teachers. A lower-school student emphasized the importance of "play" when she said, "Recess is our most important class," and presented a patch showing the playground equipment she hoped he would purchase for them. Little Maureen Brenner, from the Middle School, presented a patch image from a kaleidoscope, applauding and celebrating the changes that students in that division undergo. Five upper-school girls, each from a different country, asked for continued support for the rich diversity of backgrounds, ethnicities, religions and cultures seen in their faces. Concluding these presentations, faculty presented a drawing of a Celtic knot, symbolizing the intertwined commitment shared by the head and the faculty to the school and to each other.

Tom was frankly overwhelmed by the outpouring of support. His eyes glistened, and he cleared his throat once and then again before he spoke:

"Since the start of school in September, I have attended classes in every division. I have met and conversed with faculty and staff, with students, and with parents and alums. I have burrowed into the recesses beneath the library, cooked in the kitchen and visited the boiler room. I have studied the curriculum, read the history and looked at the photographs hanging on the walls.

"I did these things so that I might understand what is at the core of this institution—the beating heart, as it were—of Florence Bruce Seminary. Today, here in this place, I think I have come close. Florence Bruce is about community and sharing. It's about being the best that you can be and helping others to be the best that they can be. It's about these things and so much more. It can't really be crafted into words; it has to be felt, and here today I felt it—perhaps you did as well."

The Rt. Rev. William P. Moseley bestowed the benediction:

"If you look back at the history of Florence Bruce, this is the first time the religious symbols shared have been Buddhist, Christian, Jewish, Hindu and Islamic. This is very important because we have in this community a world of many traditions, and part of your work and part of your headmaster's work is to learn about those different traditions."

Organ music swelled, and the procession moved smartly down the aisle. For Tom, it had been a wonderful and moving ceremony. His leadership had been affirmed. He was certain his school had taken an important step in embracing a unique position among independent schools everywhere—that of inclusiveness from within a Christian tradition. He was also convinced that the students, through their participation, gained significant ground in understanding something of their own spirituality.

Some among the faculty and leadership of the school, however, did not share fully in Tom's enthusiasm. Why? Who could possibly find fault with an event that provided so many benefits at so little cost? Archie continued directing disparaging comments toward the timing of the celebration. Couched in sympathetic language for another worthy cause, his antipathy grew from feelings of being left out. What about the others?

The answer to that question is obscured in the peculiarities of school culture—not all school cultures, but certainly the one prevalent in Florence Bruce at the time. There was, without doubt, some jealousy at work. Who did this upstart newcomer think he was, shining the spotlight on himself? Resentment simmered at so much attention being directed at any one member of the community. Standing too far out in front of the crowd was not looked upon favorably. Besides, Tom was brand new, without any of the scars sustained by others from years and years of contributions and sacrifices. Where was their share of the adulation?

What about me? The question always floated just below the surface, sufficiently buoyant to keep it from sinking. To speak the words would have been blasphemy. Service and community, first and foremost, were deeply espoused values. But everyone watched their colleagues intently and many kept score with a mental checklist: *Am I working harder? Is my assignment more difficult? Are others getting more vacation time? Is my compensation below that of my colleagues?*

In many cases, these questions were redundant—answered in the affirmative by the source, which was to be expected. It is natural in the human condition for one to feel, in some way or another, more deserving than is recompensed. Significantly, at Florence Bruce, evaluation of one's condition was based upon a comparison with colleagues rather than upon some inanimate standard.[6] Therefore, equal satisfaction was had from one receiving more or from a colleague receiving less. And so there was in the Florence Bruce culture a dynamic that found expression, as often as not, in a manner most destructive to the school and its citizens.

All of this notwithstanding, more than anything Tom's installation ceremony was met with fear—fear that the old and the comfortable were in jeopardy, fear that change was coming and the pace of it increasing, fear that old expectations were no longer relevant and that new ones could not be met. The chorus was barely a murmur now: a "harrumph" around the lunch table, an expression of disapproval, a comment couched in the language of concern and caring. All would feel the fear. For a few, only a few, the fear would grow to dominate their waking hours.

---

[6] A salary scale, which Florence Bruce lacked at the time, is an example of an "inanimate standard." Rather than comparing compensation to a written scale, therefore, employees of the school compared themselves with each other, setting up a debilitating competition.

CHAPTER XV

For Better or Worse

♠

Before asking anyone else to contribute to their organization, a board should look to themselves.[1]

As the cold, gray curtain of a New Hampshire winter descended on Florence Bruce, the community grit its collective teeth and braced itself. Tom and Allison forsook the warnings and welcomed the change from the endless sunshine and oppressive heat of Southern California. Investing in a wardrobe of fleece, flannel and tweed, they hunkered down most evenings in cozy comfort to read and work except when a school function called them out. Tom, to his surprise, found he was able to maintain a regular schedule of three-mile evening jogs along the waterfront. Gloves, watch cap, long underwear and a full sweat suit provided all the protection he needed.

Sometimes morose, frequently moody or melancholy, the temper of the Florence Bruce community changed little by little as winter set in. Those with opportunity and resources lit out for a brief respite over Christmas break for sunnier climes in Florida or the Caribbean. The rest fortified themselves as best they could and sought respite

---

[1] Duca, Diane. *Nonprofit Boards: A Practical Guide to Roles, Responsibilities, and Performance*. Phoenix, AZ: Oryx Press, 1986, p. 95.

from any source available. Family, friendships and a menu of activity served well enough for a constitution that was otherwise stable and healthy. For the less fortunate, a regimen of pills, alcohol and sometimes more nefarious substances were employed to relieve the monotonous drone of the weather.

Most of those involved would pooh-pooh the assertion that weather had anything to do with the events that began to unfold at Florence Bruce, but it would be imprudent to dismiss the possibility out of hand. So unusual—so extraordinary—was the behavior of some in the community toward their fellow members, so extraordinary that no other combination of factors could fully or rationally explain the spite and malice that was soon to manifest itself.

Allison, Tom and Ruth Gladstone crested Petersburg Pass cocooned from the pelting rain in the luxurious comfort of the school's spanking-new, platinum-green S80 Volvo and began the rapid decent down the western slope of the Berkshires to the Hudson River and Albany. The purpose of their trip—a four-hour drive each way—was a lunch date with Viola Albright, Class of 1928. Their commitment to this one alum was a significant one. Add up just the salary and benefits for one day for the two Florence Bruce employees, plus mileage and lunch, and it easily topped seven hundred and fifty dollars. It was rumored, however, that Viola had left a substantial—the exact amount was unknown—bequest to the school in her will, and this trip was an opportunity to reconnect her with her alma mater.

From November through March, Tom made several such trips. The longest was a three-day affair in Georgia, with a hop to West Palm Beach, Florida. The sole purpose of that trip was to become acquainted with two alumnae of reputed means and a record of charitable giving. An evening reception in Chicago and lunches in Boston, New York City and Baltimore were all arranged by Ruth Gladstone and her development department to jump-start Tom into the Campaign for Florence Bruce. Close to home, the number of lunches, meetings and gatherings at the school and the Ahlborn House and in the restaurants, country clubs and private homes of the immediately surrounding communities were too numerous to count. It was a significant commitment in both time and resources.

When the board of trustees directed Tom to keep the building program on schedule, no one had any concept of the toll it would exact. With one or two exceptions, this group of trustees individually and collectively had little or no experience raising money—and not the bake sale, dinner/dance/auction kind of spare change, but the real six- and seven-figure donations that are made over dinner at private clubs or in the quiet confines of five-star restaurants. Tom had raised that kind of money before, but then he did not have to contend with the baggage that attached itself to this campaign.

John brought Ruth on board when he decided to launch the Campaign for Florence Bruce, mindful of the former campaign disaster when funds were consumed without accomplishing the building objective. Ruth assembled her department from the ground up. Besides herself, it consisted of four people: a campaign director and assistant, an annual-fund director and an office manager. She chose them well, and the group functioned together as a smoothly synchronized team.

Raising substantial amounts of money year in and year out requires a carefully orchestrated process of cultivation of prospects and stewardship of donors. On average, it is said to take seven meetings, letters, calls, tours, event participations and the like, of increasing sophistication, to complete the process and bring the potential donor to the point when an "ask" can be made. When the time does finally arrive, those in the profession recognize the most effective ask is done peer to peer. Although professional fundraisers know how to make an ask, they do so only as a last resort, preferring to train and support trustees or other volunteers who can approach the prospect as equals.

In the long term, the single most important function of a development department is "stewardship," or the care and attention given to making sure the expectations of the donor are met in all respects—beginning with a timely thank you when the donation is received. Development professionals recognize that most of the money in any campaign is raised from those who have already given at least once, and they will go to almost any length to cement a relationship with a good donor. Such stewardship is effort well spent and ensures existing donors are receptive when the organization again comes knocking.

The Campaign for Florence Bruce suffered mightily from dual weaknesses. To begin with, the campaign that preceded it was perceived as a failure. Although Ruth's predecessor managed to reach the campaign goal, the school didn't complete or even start the building project touted by the campaign literature. But the real problem stemmed from an abysmal failure to properly steward donors to that campaign. Ruth spent much of her first two years at Florence Bruce installing an adequate database and ensuring records were brought up to date, and the rest of it apologizing to those donors who believed their concerns to be inadequately addressed or who simply felt downright mistreated.

The second weakness was a thoroughly inexperienced and untrained board of trustees that didn't understand the process and resisted the role they were required to play for the campaign to be successful. It is axiomatic, for example, that all members of a board that elects to enter into a capital campaign must become donors to demonstrate their own personal commitment. (If trustees don't find the case for the project sufficiently compelling to make a donation, who else will?) The amount of the gift is a secondary consideration; participation is paramount. In the eighteen months since the launch of the Campaign for Florence Bruce, two trustees remained who could not be persuaded to part with a gift of any size.[2]

The trio of travelers arrived in Albany and located Viola Albright's modest bungalow in a private retirement community on the outskirts. After a leisurely period spent getting acquainted and reliving a few of Viola's treasured memories from Florence Bruce, Tom drove the party to a quaint, colonial-style restaurant for lunch. It was crowded and noisy, but the food was excellent; by the time they ordered coffee, the lunch crowd had departed, leaving them alone to reminisce, laugh and enjoy each other's company. Tom was careful to allow his personality to reveal itself at these times and to actively explore his designs for the school while inviting comment and suggestions from his listener. The script was deliberate and carefully calculated to encourage bonds to form between people and with the school. Except in a few instances where the personalities simply did not

---

[2] I was responsible for soliciting gifts from trustees. Frustrated over the unwillingness of these two to participate and not wanting to burden the campaign, I contributed $25 each in their names—a deception that bothers me to this day.

mesh, it was an effective technique. Allison was usually at his side and mindful of the objective. They played well off one another and were a potent force in crowds large or small.

Three hours after meeting, Tom walked Viola to her doorstep and they parted, cheerfully vowing to reconvene in the spring at Florence Bruce. On the way home there was plenty of time to debrief with Ruth and add to the accumulated load of information on Viola Albright. Three months later, the dear old lady passed away suddenly of a heart attack, and the trustees of her estate called Tom to let him know that a check in the amount of $500,000 for the school's endowment would arrive soon.

Did the expensive trip over the mountains make any difference? In all probability, it did not, at least not with respect to receipt of the donation or its amount. Most likely those factors were predetermined before the meeting took place. As one effort among many, however, the meeting and its cumulative effect with all the others was of inestimable value in building a Florence Bruce contingent of supporters and demonstrating a lifetime of respect and caring for its members.

In the next few months, with consummate staff support from the development department, Tom—along with only two trustees and two volunteers—raised $1.4 million for the Campaign for Florence Bruce. This was a significant achievement for so small a group against a backdrop of carping and criticism from other trustees, most of whom, despite promises to the contrary, failed to even make a single phone call. Why this should be so is ultimately a mystery, but it is worth some degree of speculation to understand the dynamic that might bring about a state of affairs where those charged with the success of a campaign—any campaign—are the very ones most prone to stand in the way of its success.

It should be remembered that decisions at Florence Bruce, for a very long time, rested in the hands of a few individuals who orchestrated board meetings to achieve the desired results. Despite having voted unanimously to begin the Campaign for Florence Bruce with a goal of $7 million, few trustees were truly vested in the decision. When presented to the group for consideration, the outcome of the motion was already a forgone conclusion. Yes, there was discussion. Yes, there was dissension. Yes, there was an airing of past grievances. But none of it affected the outcome.

Those voting in the affirmative did so for a variety of reasons. Reason enough was ignorance of pertinent facts purposefully withheld. In addition, terms of office on the board of trustees generally extended six years. Therefore, many current trustees were in the middle of the fray as events conspired to turn the previous campaign sour. The memory of their own disappointment and frustration, along with the criticism they received from others as funds were diverted to new needs, was deeply embedded and prevented them from a genuine embrace of the current effort despite having voted in favor of pursuing it.

While receiving little support from the trustees, Tom and his staff, along with a handful of volunteers, waged an intense crusade to salvage a wavering campaign. In his final year at Florence Bruce, John Sanford had bent to the task and raised $3.4 million. Lacking John's intimate relationships with potential donors and with the top prospects already committed, Tom managed less than half that amount. The cost of this effort, however, was considerable. Tom's estimate of the time sacrificed to fundraising, to meet the goal set by the board and keep the building project on schedule, was about thirty percent of his overall time on the job.

The administrative structure Tom inherited from John was nominally built on a classic Japanese model for collaborative decision making. Three groups consisting of six to ten individuals, each culled from the various departments to achieve a different slant on any given issue, met regularly to deliberate the business of the school, set priorities, make decisions and implement the results. "Collaborative," however, is not descriptive of how decisions were made at Florence Bruce Seminary.

John's constitution made it impossible for him to invest others with any real power to control the outcome of important decisions. Problems he didn't want to deal with himself might be tossed into these groups for an interminable cycle of debate, delaying the outcome but effectively removing the problem from John's desk. If an issue managed to survive the deliberative process and emerge well articulated with a recommended course of action, it was, as often as not, sent back into committee for more debate on implementation and outcomes before any action might actually be taken.

Important decisions—those regarding finances or budgets, those regarding leadership and control of the school, and those affecting mission and direction—were never submitted to the collaborative process. These deliberations were held close-in among just a handful of individuals. While an important issue was being deliberated, it was hidden. When a decision was reached regarding such an issue, it, too, was hidden. Only when the results of a significant decision began to be felt, were those affected able to discern that something truly important had transpired.

The saga of the school's *Crisis Preparedness Plan* is illustrative of how the committee process at Florence Bruce worked—or didn't work—in practice. A written plan for managing an unexpected crisis is a requirement for accreditation in all schools, both public and private, and has been so for some time. The need for one at Florence Bruce first emerged in a report prepared by an accreditation team visiting the school six years prior to Tom's arrival on campus. The matter was relegated to the collaborative process, which in due course (about three years) resulted in a committee formed to create the needed plan. Progress was slow inasmuch as the committee chair changed every year, but finally (about three more years), a complete plan emerged and was submitted to the board of trustees, which dutifully acknowledged and approved it. Tom was a witness to the consummation of this process when he attended the end-of-the-year board meeting in June.

Settling in one evening to peruse the document before going to bed, Tom was jolted to the core and spent a restless night mulling over the consequences of what he had just read. The *Crisis Preparedness Plan* was certainly, as the title implied, a plan for dealing with a crisis, but it assumed a crisis of catastrophic proportions: a collapse of the school building accompanied by massive injuries and compromised public services. Probable causes of such a cataclysm were described as a nuclear attack, an earthquake in excess of magnitude 7.5, or a volcanic explosion—none of which offered a very high probability of occurrence, especially in the geologically stable Granite State. Omitted was any mention whatsoever of those events that happen with far more regularity and, while arguably less susceptible to loss of life, still fall within the definition of a crisis.

Within weeks of the opening of school, two calls to emergency 911 were placed by members of the Florence Bruce community in response to a perceived need for intervention. In one case, Tom was oblivious to the fact for an hour or more, and, in the other, several days passed before he heard that a student had collapsed in class and ambulance services were called to provide assistance.

Fortunately, there were no lasting consequences from either of the emergency calls, but it was only a matter of time. Breathing deeply, Tom issued a memo declaring a four-step process to be followed after a 911 call that included notifying the head of school in the first minutes.

There are, as any school administrator knows, dozens of relatively common crises that can envelop a school and lead to genuine disaster if not managed properly. The consequences of an uncontrolled fire, for example, have been recognized in schools for decades, and drills twice a year were already part of the emergency repertoire at Florence Bruce. But that was the extent of emergency preparedness.

While virtually every school in the nation was coming to grips with the consequences of living in a supremely litigious, risk-adverse and tabloid-prone society, John tempted fate and relegated the matter to the collaborative, committee-driven process—a process ill-suited to tackle a subject of such consequence.

As a result, Florence Bruce was woefully lacking in preparations to withstand a threat from an intruder, a utility breakdown, a poisoning, a kidnapping, a death of a community member, a crippling storm, a health emergency, a scandal, a bomb scare, an environmental hazard spill, or any of the off-the-shelf crises that will sooner or later strike at any school and for which the requirement for a "crisis management plan" exists in the accreditation standards.

Despite six years passing since receiving notification of the need for a plan to manage crisis, the school's administrative structure was unable to deliver an acceptable solution. An accreditation team would arrive within the year and expect a plan to be already written and implemented. So far, it didn't even exist in concept—except to address the extreme end of the continuum.

The morning after returning from Albany, Ruth was first to arrive at the 8:00 AM bi-weekly meeting of Tom's "advisory team." In addition to Ruth, the team consisted of the controller, Nancy Wolf; the director of the Upper School, Peg Scott; and the director of the Lower and Middle Schools, Everett Laurie. These four people were invested with the responsibility for guiding Tom in administering the school. "Your charge," as Tom put it succinctly in their first meeting, "is to keep me out of trouble." They were all solid administrators. Tom felt genuine affection for each of them and deeply appreciated their dedication and commitment to the school. Ultimately, they would all fail in his charge to them.

"We have a problem, and I'm going to need your help in resolving it," declared Tom as he described his concern with the existing *Crisis Preparedness Plan*. "Ruth has agreed to chair the effort, but I need each of you to put your weight behind her to get it done. This needs to be a priority for all of us."

There was little enthusiasm for Tom's remarks aside from an inner sigh of relief from both Everett and Peg, who prayed silent "thank you's" for having avoided the assignment for another year. Chairing the safety committee was a dreaded task, known by all to resist the best efforts of those who were tapped to lead it. In truth, Ruth resisted the assignment when Tom approached her earlier, but he was insistent. "I'll work right along with you. Besides the National Association of Independent Schools has a sample plan we can use to get us started."

Ruth agreed, reluctantly, and set to work. By January, a "plan" emerged, built around the sample. It elicited a few well-founded recommendations, and Tom was ready to declare the mission accomplished. It wasn't a great plan to be sure, but it would certainly meet the requirements for accreditation.

By this time, however, Ruth was a captive of the assignment—her tendency toward perfection having surfaced—and was reluctant to let it go. Tom stepped away and let momentum take its course.

By the time March came around, the completed plan found its way onto Tom's desk. It was an exceptional piece of work, detailed and thorough—the most comprehensive plan Tom had ever seen. The academic year was already well along, too late to attempt implementation, but a block of time was set aside prior to the opening of the next school year for training and execution of the plan—a mere thirty days before the accreditation team's anticipated arrival.

Two episodes reminded Tom of the importance of the work he and Ruth were about. Reaction to the sudden passing of a beloved member of the faculty snowballed into near hysteria when the news was carried by distraught students to their classmates rather than communicated in a manner that was sensitive but managed. In another instance, Tom was alerted to a death threat made against a high-profile family with a student in the school. Could he guarantee protection? Despite confident assurances to the family, Tom worried privately. How would the school handle an intruder? With no plan for crisis management, they were sitting on a bomb that sooner or later would explode. So far, his luck, as did John's before him, held.

Tom early on scrapped the management style used by John—not that he was against collaboration. In fact, collaboration was an integral part of Tom's style, but with no supportive culture at Florence Bruce, John's model was a monument to inefficiency and an excuse to do nothing. Instead, Tom set about wrestling into place a more traditional hierarchical structure. John's preference, despite his aforementioned nod to collaboration, had also been toward a hierarchical structure, albeit an extraordinarily flat one. Any decision he considered important flowed directly to the top, where he sat virtually alone. Unimportant decisions—the designation of "unimportant" being a factor of John's subjective whims more than anything else—were thrown into the abyssal depths of the committee process or, as was usually the case, judiciously expedited by a handful of capable but supremely cautious administrators.

"With the absence of both John Sanford and Roland Guyotte," Tom told his advisory team early in the year, "I have needed to invest greater authority and responsibility with Everett and Peg than was previously the case. I feel they have both risen to the challenge and are now performing at a level considerably above that of their current assignment as division directors."

Roland, the former assistant school head at Florence Bruce, had been brought in at the insistence of Phyllis Killam to take some of the burden off John when his wife became ill. John used Roland badly, and when it became clear that he was to be passed over as John's successor, Roland sought and received appointment as the head of a school in Virginia. The combined assignments of both administrators, which had now fallen on Tom's shoulders, were too much. His solution was to empower the two division directors and to count on them to rise to the occasion.

Tom continued explaining other administrative changes. "As you know, I've received the board's permission to have each of you sit in on its meetings from now on. There's a lot happening all at once at these meetings, and I'll need your insights to accurately decipher the board's intent."

Nancy was quick to acknowledge her support. "I've been called in to give reports, but then I'm expected to leave. I've always thought it strange that I wasn't included on a regular basis. Any significant item of business will have financial implications. I would think they'd want my input."

"Of course," said Tom. "I'm accustomed to having my CFO sitting right next to me during board meetings. I don't know how John did it."

Ruth, too, agreed with this sentiment. She was accustomed to attending meetings of the board in her previous employment, raising money to support a shelter for abused women. Development, like finance, usually impacted and was impacted by the policy decisions that occupy most boards.

Peg was more sanguine. "I certainly appreciate the invitation, but I'm not sure what I can contribute to the meetings."

"It isn't that you'll be expected to contribute during the meetings," assured Tom. "Your contribution will come afterwards when I'll need your help interpreting what happened."

"Can't you just read the minutes?"

"I will certainly do that, but what I need to know is a lot more subtle than can be captured in a set of minutes. Every item that comes before a board has supporters and detractors to varying degrees. Keeping track of the nuances that are expressed at these meetings is vital to maintaining support for initiatives in the future. Besides, I don't want the board's intentions to be filtered through me to your ears. I want you to hear it directly from them. That way, there's less opportunity for mistakes to be made."

Peg seemed satisfied, but her discomfort lingered. She was a bold leader and not easily intimidated. She had been at Florence Bruce for several years, however, and knew enough to keep her head down. She was wary of getting too close to the nucleus where the powerful played out the decisions affecting the school.

Everett was apathetic. Although he didn't say anything, his instincts told him to stay clear of the board. These were unpredictable people. He wanted to do his job and stay off their radar. When the December board meeting rolled around, he would find a reason to be excused.

* * *

Nancy's report at a mid-winter meeting of the advisory group concerned faculty compensation—one of the topics addressed by the trustees when they set goals for the year. "I've begun asking around for volunteers to form a committee to work with me. So far, I've got a half-dozen faculty members and two department heads interested in joining the discussion."

"How's the representation?" asked Everett. "Do you have someone from each of the divisions?" A common perception—so far unproven—was that faculty members with similar assignments in different divisions were compensated unequally. Lower-school faculty were convinced they were paid less than middle- and upper-school faculty.

"You bet. I've already reviewed the recommendations turned over by the board compensation committee. There are eleven. I think our first task will be to prioritize and select just a couple to address first."

"That sounds sensible," said Tom. "Fairness is the fundamental issue. It seems everyone around here watches everyone else, and everyone is convinced that someone else is making more or getting more than they are. It's a debilitating atmosphere. If we can put some of that to rest, we will have accomplished a lot for this year and addressed one of the five goals the board has given us."

"You'd better be prepared for what you might uncover," Nancy warned. "I've run a couple of scattergrams already, and I'm seeing a distinct difference between compensation levels for male versus female faculty members."

"You mean male teachers are getting paid more than female teachers?" Peg's question was more of a statement, as this was another common perception among the faculty.

"Well, I'm not sure yet, but it would seem that way. I've got some more data to drop into the mix, and I want to be sure I'm comparing apples to apples. John had some odd ways of equaling things out with special little deals he cut with individual faculty members."

"What do you mean?" asked Tom.

"He might exempt someone from special duties in return for a lower salary or give them additional time off. I know he agreed to pay the legal fees for Ms. Anakwa to get her green card renewed." Winifred Anakwa was a math teacher from Ghana. Math teachers were hard to find, and black female math teachers were much harder to find.

"None of this was ever written down, and I don't know if some of these things were a *quid pro quo* for accepting a lower salary."

"That would certainly make for an interesting headline," snorted Peg. "'All-girls school pays female teachers less than male teachers.' We'd take it in the shorts for that."

"Stay on it," added Tom, "and let us know as soon as you get more confidence in your results. Whatever you find, we'll need to address in contracts for next year. Well, if no one has anything else to bring up, we'll adjourn and get on with our day."

"I have one other item," said Everett. "We need to set our school calendar for next year so it can be distributed during Parent's Night next week."

Tom sighed in mock exasperation. "Jeez, it seems like I've just gotten started and already we're thinking of next year."

"I usually set it up, and Roland would approve it. There really isn't much for you to do. I'll get it ready and run it by you for approval."

"Okay, that's a relief," said Tom. "By the way, does anyone know how many days Florence Bruce is in session? When I worked with public schools, it was mandated they be in session for 184 days. I know independent schools are less, but how much less?"

"We're in session more hours in the day," Everett explained, "so we have fewer days in the school year."

"I realize that, but how many fewer? I'm just curious to know."

"I don't know offhand, but I'll find out and let you know."

A few days later, during a professional luncheon with heads of other New England private schools, Tom posed the question. The answers ranged from 174 to 176 days in session.

CHAPTER XVI

Foundations

♠

One needs to be accountable, and the accountability needs to be connected to the needs of the organization.[1]

"I'm off to the game," declared Tom, as much to himself as to Jackie. While jamming papers into his briefcase, Tom was, at the same time, extricating his mind from the day's business and hoping Jackie would fend off the next inevitable incoming phone call. His statement to her mingled a hope as well as a declaration of intent. It was, in effect, a "period" to the day, allowing a transition to the tumult of the gymnasium where already the buzzer had sounded to begin a volleyball game between Florence Bruce Seminary and Brentwood Academy.

As soon as the sports schedules were released, Tom entered every home game on his calendar and instructed Jackie to preserve them as best she could against the onslaught of meetings and other official duties to which he was subjected. For the most part, she was successful, and, about twice a week, Tom took his leave as close to 3:30 PM as possible to join the school's teams in their pursuit of

[1] Drucker, Peter F. *Managing the Non-Profit Organization: Principles and Practices*. New York: HarperCollins Publishers, 1992, p. 39.

athletic glory. All three divisions took part in soccer. Fall sports also included cross-country running and volleyball for the middle and upper divisions and sailing for the upper-school girls.

Tom viewed his participation at these events as having dual purpose—not only was it an opportunity to show the flag, as it were, in support of his charges, but the games also served as therapy for the mind-numbing pressures of his workday. An hour or so of animated cheering for the Seminarians was about as therapeutic as a fifteen-mile pedal on his bicycle.

Stopping by the front office to pick up his mail, Tom thumbed through the accumulation, glancing briefly at a fat envelope from Deanne Bakker. "Those must be the proofs from the *Seminary Log*," he mused before stuffing the envelope along with a dozen other miscellaneous communications into his briefcase, now crammed so full he had to force it before the locks snapped closed.

"Whazzup, Devon?" he said, picking out the one person he could positively identify from the group of students loitering in the lobby. He recognized two of the others but couldn't bring the names readily to mind. One was Geoffrey Bellingham's daughter, but her name still eluded him. "Hello, Dr. Whitman," said Devon. "I like your tie today." She was an attractive young woman, and her greeting shyly flirtatious.

"Thanks, it's one of my favorites, too," he said, a momentary flush rising in his neck. He turned to the others. "Come on. There's a volleyball game down in the gym. We can't win without you there cheering on the team."

They looked at him sheepishly. "We can't, Dr. Whitman," said one. "We're waiting for rides."

"Okay, I'll let you off the hook this time, but next time tell your moms to come *after* the game. See you tomorrow." Tom waved and pushed through the panic bar to the outside. It was already growing dark; the brick walkway was slick with ice and mirrored the streetlights buzzing awake on the street. Tom could feel tiny snow crystals striking his cheeks, but he was already acclimatized and barely gave them a thought as he drew a deep breath of the refreshingly cold early December air. Bareheaded and with his coat over his arm, his rapid strides carried him across the street to the Ahlborn House.

"Allison, game's started. Are you ready?" he shouted, closing the door behind him.

"In a minute," she called from the bedroom. He bounded up the stairs, taking them two at a time, and stepped into the doorway of the room he used as an office to deposit his briefcase and grab a digital camera off his desk. He kissed Allison on the cheek at the bedroom door as she hurried to meet him. No words were necessary, and they turned and moved toward the stairs together, adjusting various articles of clothing in preparation for leaving. Tom fumbled with the camera while trying to don the overcoat he carried on his arm. Allison, already wearing her coat, carried an umbrella—her preparations always a step more thorough than Tom's own.

They entered the gym together where a sparse crowd was gathered to watch the action. Tom noted that Brentwood Academy, which was a good hour's drive away, seemed to have generated as large a turnout as Florence Bruce. The score was 12-8 in the opponent's favor, and they added another point with an unblocked slam through a porous defense as Tom and Allison threaded through players and coaches to their seats behind the Florence Bruce bench. The gym accommodated perhaps two hundred spectators, but it was less than half full.

"So how are we doing?" he asked Everett Laurie, who, with his wife Clare, was seated in front of him. Everett turned to acknowledge Tom's presence while Clare and Allison fell immediately into conversation.

"Okay, I guess. The JV team won their match, but this game has just started. They look pretty strong," said Everett, turning back to the action.

Tom took his camera out of its case and set the zoom to bring the action in a bit closer. He surveyed the team, looking for students he could identify. The photos he captured would be e-mailed to the yearbook editor in the morning.

There were only two players whose names he knew. He snapped a photo of a tall African-American girl poised high above the net, blocking a shot. "That should be a good one," he mused, and asked Everett who she was.

"Sarah Jackson. She's new this year—only a freshman, but showing star qualities. I hope we can keep her."

"What do you mean? Why shouldn't we keep her?"

"We're only a single-A school. Really good players want better competition. They think it will make them more attractive when it comes time to apply to colleges."

"Does it?"

"Yeah, it probably does, provided they're as good as they think they are. We've had a couple of girls who were stars here. They transferred and ended up warming the bench."

"What! What! What! What! What we got? We got spirit!" Three Florence Bruce students tried to get a cheer going to compete with their boisterous visitors, but it died in a spasm of giggles. There were barely two dozen students in the stands anyway, and a quarter of them were Asian boarders who were too shy to express themselves so openly. Spirit—it was a difficult issue. Day students, who made up half of the upper-school student body, often commuted from some distance and were reluctant to remain after classes for sporting events. There was little affinity between the divisions, so an upper-school event seldom attracted middle- or lower-school students or vice-versa. With the Florence Bruce emphasis on academics, athletic participation, either as observer or player, came in a distant second in the competition for time. Most of the spectators at any athletic event were parents of the players.

Tom mulled over the problem, snatching an occasional photo among robust shouts of encouragement and stifled groans. With his feet on the bench in front of him and his elbows propped on his knees, he could watch for interesting shots on the LCD viewer while taking in the whole game, cheering and acknowledging the occasional greeting from a passing student or parent.

"Maybe a costumed mascot to visit classrooms and drum up a little enthusiasm before games would help," he reflected. He knew cheerleaders were out of the question. Despite the fact that local summer cheerleading camps attracted a following among younger students, Florence Bruce was staunchly, arrogantly feminist, and cheerleaders were degraded as virtual prostitutes-in-training by much of the faculty. Still, the school could use a good dose of spirit, and a winning team would coax it out, Tom decided. Unfortunately, the Seminarians lost the first game 21-13.

"Good afternoon, Dr. Whitman."

Tom turned to greet a well-dressed woman in a tailored business suit. "Hello, Mrs. Lair," said Tom. "Susan's doing well out there." Susan Lair was the flautist he first had met the previous year during his interviews. Her mother had been in his office on a number of occasions with some complaint or another. Peg and Everett, who were visited by Mrs. Lair with equal frequency, considered her a pest, but Tom found her business-like and generally reasonable. She just wanted to know what was going on and was driven by a cat-like compulsion to investigate whenever things weren't as she expected they should be.

"Did you hear what Mr. Barrera did?" Mrs. Lair did not engage in small talk but went straight to the point.

"No, I didn't," said Tom, moving closer. Anticipating where the conversation was headed, he bent toward her to create a semblance of privacy. According to Mrs. Lair, Miguel had been involved in some prank and barricaded another faculty member, along with some students, in a classroom. Mrs. Lair's middle-school daughter Trina, one of the imprisoned, had crawled through a window and gone around from the outside to remove the barricade.

"The windows in that part of the building are old and rusted," said Mrs. Lair. "Trina could have been cut, or she could have fallen. She said they were alone and she was scared. Suppose someone became ill, how would they have gotten help? I don't know why this kind of thing is going on anyway, when students should be in class learning. I've told you before that Miguel Barrera is a troublemaker."

Mrs. Lair was one of several parents who had come to Tom over the summer complaining about Miguel. This time, her narrative was secondhand, communicated to her by Trina, and she didn't have much to add to the basic story line. "Did you speak to Mr. Barrera about your concern?" Tom asked. Of course, she hadn't.

Go to the source! It was a mantra Tom was to repeat over and over when parents or faculty came to him with complaints. If you want to fix something, go to the person in the best position to fix it. People were habituated to go to John when they had a concern. John was a master at demonstrating empathy and soothing ruffled feathers, but he had done little to actually address the concerns—especially when they were relatively trivial as this one most probably was.

Tom admitted that Miguel's actions, on the surface, seemed to display a certain lack of discretion, but whatever had happened didn't appear to be all that serious. He also suspected many facts were still missing. As the volleyball game ended, he encouraged Mrs. Lair to follow up with Miguel and promised he would also investigate. The next day, despite a hectic schedule, Tom managed a quick meeting with Everett and Miguel. In addition to the facts as Mrs. Lair had described them, Tom learned that Trina's teacher was also in on the joke and another faculty member was monitoring the situation from outside the door. The whole incident was part of a custom started among some faculty years ago, whereupon players pulled practical jokes on one another.

Both Everett and Miguel immediately became defensive upon hearing the story. "This is ridiculous," insisted Miguel. "She's just out to get me. How come you're not supporting me on this?"

"I am supporting you. You know these parents are out there. I didn't create that situation; I'm trying to fix it. For the most part, they operate on rumors that go out of control when no one counters them with the facts."

"You're not going to change those parents," insisted Everett. "You've just got to let them know they're not running the school. If they don't like it, they can take their kid out."

"I disagree," countered Tom. "It's true that parents often overplay their role, but we want them to be active in their child's education. That means being critical as well as being supportive. Isn't it possible there is some validity to Mrs. Lair's comments? Maybe we need to be a little more circumspect about these practical jokes. Is it disruptive to classes? Is it okay to involve students, especially middle-school students, who sometimes lack the maturity to realize it's only a joke?"

Miguel was unwilling to concede there might be a downside. "These kids are at a formative stage in their lives. They're testing and probing boundaries. Middle school is like that. They need to be shaken up occasionally instead of being locked up and overprotected. It's part of their education. Tom, I need your support here."

Miguel did shake them up, and that was part of what made him an exceptional middle-school teacher. "Miguel, I truly want to be supportive of you, and I'm doing it in the best way I know how," said Tom. "Mrs. Lair will probably call on you in the next couple of days. Explain to her what you explained to me: that it was not an unmonitored, out-of-control situation, and that precautions were taken to ensure the safety of the students. When she makes her points, try to acknowledge her concerns, and let her know you'll consider them."

Neither Everett nor Miguel was convinced, but they had adapted to John's leadership style. Collaboration and teamwork were not developed skill sets. Confrontation was risky and self-defeating. The only safe form of resistance was passive-aggressive, and so they said nothing and did nothing.

"I'll write a note to Mrs. Lair letting her know we've spoken," Tom continued, "and I'll copy you so you will know exactly what I've said."

As the meeting ended, Tom moved toward Miguel. Cupping his hand behind Miguel's elbow, he gently steered him toward the door. "Miguel, John was very supportive of you because he believed you were a great teacher. I'm supportive of you because I believe he was right—you are a great teacher. These problems your style generates with parents, however, will not go away because we want them to. We need to communicate. We need to explain. And, we need to listen. Please bear with me on this, and give it a chance to work."

Miguel remained firm in his belief that the whole incident was inconsequential and simply blown out of proportion by a parent looking to get him fired. Tom's e-mail to Mrs. Lair added the additional facts as related by Everett and Miguel. He acknowledged the validity of her concerns and thanked her for coming to him while, at the same time, confirming his belief in the professionalism of Mr. Barrera and the Florence Bruce faculty. Mrs. Lair didn't go to see either Everett or Miguel, but, significantly, she also didn't choose to mention the incident the next week when she had coffee with the mother of one of Trina's friends.

After the volleyball match, Tom and Allison exited the gym and walked across the street to the Ahlborn House. Tom changed into comfortable sweats for a quick workout on a set of weights he kept in the bedroom while Allison started dinner. An Atlantic salmon fillet, marinating for the past two hours in a concoction of brown sugar, butter, garlic and soy sauce, went into the broiler while she turned her attention to lemon-mint orzo and sliced maple-glazed carrots. After the tumult of the game, they ate together in welcomed silence and watched the evening news on TV. Tom relished the sweet-scented, slightly crisp coating on the salmon, with its succulent pink outer meat giving way to the more translucent, nearly raw inner meat. The exotic mixture of tastes and textures was in startling contrast to his meat-and-potatoes upbringing. "This is absolutely delicious, hon," he commented during a commercial break. "We sure are eating better since you became a career hostess."

She laughed. She knew Tom was an appreciative, if indiscriminate, eater. "You get all my experiments. This is what I'm serving the Copelands on Saturday." Joanne Copeland was one of the capital-campaign co-chairs. She was also a trustee and, together with her husband Teddy, a major donor to the school. She and Tom had collaborated on a recent "ask" that resulted in a $150,000 contribution to the campaign. The dinner on Saturday was a celebration and, as both parties knew, an opportunity to nurture the budding relationship between them.

Following dinner, Tom retired to his office to sort through the accumulation in his briefcase. In due course, he came to the manila envelope left by Deanne Bakker. Opening it, he expected to find a proof copy of the November-December issue of the *Seminary Log*. To his surprise, he extracted instead a fresh-from-the-printer copy of the publication itself. For a long moment, he struggled to make sense of it. To be sure, it was already December, and the publication was way past deadline. On the other hand, he had been clear that he wanted to see a proof before going to press.

Tom was not one to stand on ceremony. If the job was well done, that was all that really mattered. He encouraged and rewarded initiative among subordinates. He respected creativity and was sufficiently open-minded to recognize the advantage of an approach different from his own. Perhaps there was no harm done.

Tom leaned back in his chair, lifted his feet onto his desk and read the headline for the lead article—a glowing piece on Archie's new appointment as president of the board. Tom smiled to himself. *Certainly an appropriate subject for the lead article, if a little self-serving in Deanne's case.*

He continued reading. "At the June board meeting, Florence Bruce Trustees appointed Dr. Archie Devlin as president for the school yaer." The typographical misspelling made Tom's skin crawl. *Not a particularly auspicious start*, he thought and reread the sentence. A good journalist, he knew, would not start the topic sentence of a leadoff paragraph with a prepositional clause. "Dr. Archie Devlin was appointed . . ." or "The Florence Bruce board of trustees appointed . . ." would have been better. "President of what?" the reader might ask. "President of the board" would have clarified the question.

Tom took a deep breath and read on. Another few sentences, and he reached in his desk drawer, choosing a red marking pen to keep track of the errors and other corrections apparent to his examination—his heart sinking deeper and deeper with each passing line. "Phyllis Killam was thanked for her leadership as board president for the past two years and her commitment to the board for the past eight years." Tom circled "the past" used twice in that sentence and circled the phrase four more times before he finished the paragraph. By the time he completed reading the eight-page publication, it was a mass of red marks: circled words, underlines, question marks and margin notes.

It was, he realized with chagrin, the worst publication he had ever attached his name to. How had this happened? Didn't anyone proof it? Was Deanne truly incompetent, or was this an aberration? Why hadn't she given it to him to proof when he specifically asked her to? Behind the questions was a profound embarrassment: *how would it reflect on him when the issue appeared in mailboxes?* He showed the publication to Allison, who had edited a newsletter for a country club. She agreed; it was terrible.

That night he lay in bed mulling over what he knew about Deanne Bakker. She had pretty much kept to herself since their close interaction on the website during the summer, although he had met with her twice to talk about the school's publications and share ideas. They were not comfortable meetings. She had often disagreed with his suggestions. Perhaps they were impractical, too costly or too time consuming. "Okay," he had countered, "what would you suggest?" But there was little forthcoming.

Recently, Deanne had been involved in a nasty incident that spilled over into a vitriolic e-mail repartee with Ruth Gladstone over some missing mailing labels. After the fourth exchange between them, Tom received a blind copy of the e-mail record from Ruth with her plea, "I can't bear to deal with this anymore."

Tom's first reaction was frustration with both parties. Their offices were separated by less than fifty feet. Why the impersonal e-mail between these two employees when a friendly face-to-face conversation could straighten everything out? Then he read this portion of the e-mail record:

[Deanne] I gave you all the mailing labels I had.

[Ruth] When you were in my office on Friday, you specifically said that I was not the only one who received labels. Was that true or not?

[Deanne] No, Ruth, you were not the only one to receive labels. I took care of the rest.

Deanne had directly contradicted herself. The e-mail exchange continued for several pages, with Deanne frequently contravening herself or avoiding responsibility with evasive and misleading statements. Colleagues who interacted with Deanne often described her behavior as "irrational." "We went round and round," was a common refrain. Tom recalled John Sanford's remark about Deanne's drinking problem. *Is that the explanation?*

The next morning, Tom called Deanne's office at 8:15 AM, but there was no answer. He called thirty minutes later, and she picked up the phone. "Oh, you're in. Can I stop by to see you for a minute?" His decision to meet on her turf assumed she might be more amenable than if he summoned her to come to him.

He greeted her pleasantly. "Good morning, how's Lexi doing today?" Tom asked, referring to Deanne's daughter. "Wasn't she out sick last week?"

"Yes, she's okay," Deanne replied, somewhat defensively. Her double vodka and orange juice earlier that morning had left her languid and slow to react.

"I read through the new issue of *Seminary Log* you put in my mailbox last night. To tell the truth, I expected to see a draft."

"You were out the day the proofs came back, so I went ahead and approved them myself." It was an excuse made up on the spot. Deanne only vaguely recalled anything at all about proofs.

"I thought I made myself clear. I wanted to see the proofs."

"We were past deadline, and you said you wanted to get it out." The retort was angry, and the eyes flashed ever so briefly with the venom of a disturbed rattlesnake.

Tom was stunned by her response to what he thought was a mild reprimand. His eyes narrowed slightly, and his lips thinned, but he didn't reply. This debate would not produce any winners. She could have shown him an earlier draft before it went to the printer. She could have warned him the proof was due. Even when away from the office, he was available by cell phone and might have been consulted. None of this would change anything, however, so he moved on.

"Okay, be that as it may, I'd like to schedule some time with you so we can review the publication together."

"When would you like to do that?"

"How about tomorrow in my office so we can spread out on the conference table—say ten in the morning, when we're both fresh?" Deanne nodded her assent, and they parted—Tom flushed and bristling and far removed from an accurate understanding of the underlying dynamics of the encounter; Deanne relieved she'd avoided a lengthy scolding and sure she could head off tomorrow's reproach.

Tom mulled over the exchange. Deanne was certainly quick to anger, and there would be no easy recovery if tempers flared. That evening he reviewed the newsletter with greater care, organizing his thoughts carefully on paper to present to her. As he worked, he decided to turn the next day's meeting into a formal evaluation to encompass his other concerns.

Previously, Tom had assumed the situation with Deanne John had warned him about could be salvaged. Now, he began preparing for a termination of Deanne's employment with the school—should it come to that. He carefully inscribed her name on a manila folder and slipped it in among his personal files, adding a note on the encounter earlier in the day and a copy of her e-mail exchange with Ruth. From this day forward, every communication relating to Deanne Bakker was carefully recorded and added to the file, along with every document that crossed his desk pertaining to her work. The path on which they were now embarked was an extremely difficult one with all the earmarks of a nasty journey ahead. At the very least, he would protect himself and the school from a legal challenge. That night, Tom took a sleeping pill to induce a needed night's rest and wondered, as he snuggled next to Allison, how he would inform Archie.

The next day at 10:00 AM the old floorboards in the hallway announced a visitor. Tom steeled himself for Deanne's arrival, but instead of knocking on his door, she stopped at Jackie's desk with an effusive greeting. The two women exhibited a genuine liking for each other. After five minutes of their chitchat as backdrop to his anxious thoughts, Tom intervened. Jackie's penchant for circuitous banter drove him crazy, but this time she probably didn't know he had a meeting scheduled with Deanne, who was delighting in taking advantage of the situation to keep him waiting.

"I hate to break this up, ladies," said Tom, not so subtly poking his head into Jackie's office, "but Deanne and I have a meeting scheduled, and I need to get started if we're going to finish in time for my next appointment."

"Oh, I'm sorry. I didn't know you were meeting." Jackie was crestfallen. Tom seemed always to be impatient with her. She scratched absently at her psoriasis, which was acting up again.

Deanne came into his office and immediately sat down in one of the two chairs opposite his desk. Ordinarily, Tom would have suggested they sit in more friendly confines around the coffee table in the other corner of the room, but thought better of it this time. The separation provided by the desk was welcome.

She was dressed in a conservative, black business suit. Her jewelry—a bracelet, watch, broach and earrings all in gold—had been assembled with a minimalist's eye toward achieving a discreet modesty. She was attractive and looked every bit the part of the professional public-relations expert she purported to be. A haughty arrogance to her bearing came from the certain knowledge that she still held the edge in this encounter.

Tom picked up the contentious newsletter. "I said yesterday that I wanted to review this issue of the *Log* with you. I do want to do that, but we haven't had a conversation in some time. I thought this might be a good opportunity to talk more generally about what I need from public relations this year."

Deanne looked at him, but didn't say anything. She affected a look of mild amusement, which Tom took to be an attempt at reconciling their differences from the previous day. He was wrong. She had fortified herself with a different medicine. Besides, Deanne and Archie had spent the evening with a group of powerful Florence Bruce parents, including Trish Calvert, president of the Parents' Association. They had treated her like one of them, and her relationship with Archie was strengthening by the day. Deanne decided her position was unassailable and, thus assured, was determined to control her temper and not let Tom get the best of her.

"You know that public relations plays a key role in the agenda I bring to Florence Bruce and a key role in the agenda the board of trustees has set for the school in the coming year. While there have been some positive steps forward, I have some serious concerns that make me question the ability of the department to meet the continuing demands being placed on it." Tom used the generic "department" to avoid accusing Deanne directly; although aside from a part-time assistant, Deanne was it.

Deanne was silent, letting his words flow over and around her.

"This latest issue of *Seminary Log*, represents a starting point," said Tom, trying to spin it in the most positive way he could, "but it still is a long way from where I need it to be." He went on to dissect the publication page by page, pointing out the items he had circled.

From time to time, Deanne took exception to his stylistic suggestions, but her defense was meager and suffered from a dual lack of conviction and background in the subject. Tom said he liked to see abundant photos and detailed captions. "In my experience," Deanne argued, "captions are kept to a minimum so as not to detract from the photo."

"In a publication emphasizing photography, that is certainly true, but in this case we are trying to tell a story, and we need to use whatever tools are at hand. Oftentimes our readers are only going to look at the photos and read the captions, so ideally, those two elements should tell the story by themselves."

Tom thought his point was made, but Deanne was unmoved. Cogent, well-reasoned argument did not impress her as much as he assumed it would. He took a deep breath. This was going better than anticipated. Tension weighed heavily in the room, but both of them were staying calm.

Deanne glanced at her watch. A half hour had passed. "Is this going to last much longer? I have a meeting scheduled with Craig Gowdy down in admissions," she lied.

"Not much longer," said Tom, backing off his earlier optimistic assessment of the meeting. "You need to improve your working relationships with colleagues, particularly with the business department. Nancy has brought some necessary procedural changes to Florence Bruce that have required everyone to adapt. You need to get onboard, get your vendors paid on time and follow procedures to get checks cut when you need them. Your relations with the development department are no better. Those folks should be your closest allies. Their careers rise and fall with the publication of the annual report and *Voyager*. They have a lot at stake, and you need to be sensitive to their deeply felt concerns."

Tom paused again. He knew his litany of complaints must be overwhelming, but this was the time to get them all on the table. If push came to shove, the consequences of a mistake now would be difficult to correct later on.

The meeting ended, and Deanne, having capitulated to denial, did not comprehend the seriousness of her situation. As Tom stepped around his desk to shake her hand, she proffered, "When you first came to interview, I frankly didn't think you were the best candidate, Tom, but in the last few months, I've decided I like you, and I think you have some good ideas."

Tom was flustered by her candor and surprised by the timing of her comments. "Well, I'm certainly pleased that you approve," he said. "I like you, too, and I've always been impressed with your confidence and the way you carry yourself. Let's hope we can get past these issues and on track for a great future together."

He took her comments at the end of the meeting as a positive sign that Deanne at least wanted to meet his expectations. Deanne, however, had no plans to change anything. When Tom's detailed memo with notes from their meeting arrived in her e-mail the next day, she printed off a copy and put it aside to read later. But, in fact, she never did.

On Thursday morning at 8:00 AM, Archie and Tom were seated around the conference table for their biweekly meeting, enjoying a cup of coffee and Mrs. Clayworth's oversized cinnamon buns. Outside the window, a sun break dispelled the ever-present mantle of winter grayness. The campus emerged briefly as if from a cocoon, colorful and brightly alive; sunlight danced off a million icy crystals.

As if taking their cues from the scene outside, the two men were animated and charged by an awareness of progress and impending accomplishment. A project manager had been hired and plans for the new building were generating a momentum of their own for the first time in several years. A million-dollar donation to the capital campaign had just been secured—an amount exceeded only once before in the school's history. Expenses were at or below budget. School enrollments had been creeping up since the September opening of school, with new students arriving mid-year, and were now at projected levels. The various board committees were up and running under good leadership and clear agendas. And, to Tom's relief, tension between the two men over the disputed date of his installation seemed to have dissipated.

The focus of their conversation was the agenda for the next meeting of the board of trustees scheduled in two weeks. Archie was determined to avoid a repeat of the last meeting when time ran out and many items were left hanging. "Tom, I really need your help here. Can you provide me with an agenda—this time with the projected times for each item so I don't lose track of the meeting?"

"Sure, that's easy, but you'll need to remember that your job is to run the meeting and manage everyone else. You can't let yourself get caught up in the discussion of each item." Tom continued coaching him in the basic protocols of meeting management while Archie listened, intently leaning forward, nodding from time to time in agreement and commenting appropriately. Tom enjoyed the role. He was good at it, and Archie was an apt pupil.

"Let's spend a few moments going over the agenda now," said Tom, "to see if we can anticipate where there might be some problems."

"Sounds good to me."

"After introductions and approval of the minutes, the first item is the president's report. At the last meeting, the report ran on for almost twenty minutes. We'll need to find a way to keep it to about half that." Tom hoped his criticism of Archie's verbosity was sufficiently oblique.

"I understand," said Archie, taking no offense. "I'd like to talk about the conference you and I attended last month. I thought there were some excellent pointers on board responsibilities that I'd like to share with the group."[2]

"That's a great idea. How about preparing a handout enumerating the specific points?" If Archie tried to freeform his ideas on the spot, it would double the time he needed; fortunately Archie agreed with Tom's suggestion and made a note to himself.

"Another item you might consider including in your comments is the Nunlist Report."

---

[2] Tom and Archie spent two days together at a conference organized by the National Association of Independent Schools specifically for heads and their board presidents. Most of us assumed this was the only assistance or training the two men would need to cement their relationship.

The Nunlist Report was an outsider's evaluation of Tom's first one hundred days. Markham Nunlist, who led the search process that resulted in Tom's selection, had prepared it after visiting the school in early November and interviewing faculty and trustees. Tom was proud of the five-page report. "Celebrate your success!" Markham had written. Aside from its positive admonition, the carefully articulated document repeatedly cautioned against expecting too much too soon—an important point, in Tom's opinion, that could not be stated often enough.[3]

"That's a wonderful idea," Archie agreed. The report had already been distributed to the entire board, so his comments could be limited to a few summarizing points.

As the end of the meeting neared, Tom broached the subject that had been occupying his mind and disturbing his sleep since the meeting with Deanne. "Archie, there's something we've talked about before that I just have to bring up again. The subject is so delicate and fraught with peril I don't know quite how to talk to you about it." Stumbling over his words, Tom described the meeting he had had with Deanne. Archie's demeanor was one of deep concern. He tilted his head with his right ear slightly forward in an expression Tom had observed before. Everything about him communicated, "I hear you, I empathize with your position, I understand."

Tom asked if Archie had seen the latest issue of *Seminary Log*. Of course he had seen it, but he had not noticed anything amiss. Tom went to his desk to find a clean copy, brought it back and showed Archie a number of the misspellings and typos. "This is simply not something I can tolerate," said Tom as firmly as he dared, "especially when two of the goals you and the board have set for me focus on improving public relations. I'm trying to work with Deanne and to

---

[3] Markham Nunlist couched his warning rather obliquely. "The insights and understanding expressed by the new head are astute and his ability to analyze, understand and draw some informed conclusions are superb. The difficulty comes when others are not at the same level or on the same timetable, and it is important to be aware of those discrepancies and be sensitive to them." This passage would later be interpreted by some as a critique of the changes Tom was making rather than as a critique of a board that had pushed for those changes.

mentor her as best I can, but, frankly, I'm not an expert, and there is only so much I can do."

Tom paused. He was getting his legs under him now. "I've decided to let things be until after the holidays. Deanne and I met recently, and I provided a detailed outline of the things I need her to work on. We've got another publication coming out, and I'm truly hoping there will be a substantial improvement. If not, I'm going to have to make a . . . change."

Tom let the last word hang in the air, but Archie didn't catch the intended meaning nor react to it. It was the second time a critical communication between the two men had been missed.

Archie knew Tom was having some problems with Deanne because he had spoken of it several times in their previous conversations together, and, despite his oath of confidentiality, Archie was not above testing the waters. "So what do you think of our new headmaster?" he inquired one evening while he and Deanne were enjoying dinner out.

"He's too serious, and he's always complaining about something or other."

"Do you get along with him?"

"About as well as anyone. He's not easy to get to know."

This comment, and others like it from Deanne, set Archie to thinking. He still chafed over the Veterans Day fiasco, but Tom's installation didn't seem to have been much of a big deal. No parent or trustee he'd spoken to had attended. On the whole, Archie was confident that whatever Tom's problem with Deanne might be, they would work it out.

That morning in the head's office, all he said in response to Tom's reference to a "change" was, "You can trust that I fully understand the sensitivity of my position. I'm very careful. Here at school when you and I are talking, I wear one hat. When I'm at home with my family and with Deanne, I wear another hat. Whatever is between the two of you will remain confidential."

Tom wanted to shout, "Give it up on the hats, buddy! If I fire Deanne, you won't be able to keep those hats separated." But instead he said quietly, "Archie, I only hope you're right. I'm confident that we both want what is best for the school, and that's the main thing. If we keep that thought uppermost, we'll be all right."

CHAPTER XVII

Malefaction

The [effective] board tolerates ambiguity, pursues information and encourages debate.[1]

"Tom, I've got the information you wanted on the school calendar." Everett was calling on the intercom line. Tom was deep into composing a letter to a former trustee who had just removed his daughter from the school and wanted an exemption to the rules on tuition reimbursement.

He shook his head, trying to refocus. Swiveling his chair away from the computer screen, he said in mild exasperation, "What's that Everett? Can you refresh my memory?"

"You remember the meeting about next year's calendar? You asked how many days Florence Bruce was in session."

"Yeah, okay, I remember. What did you come up with?"

"Well, it varies a bit. The upper division is in session for 168 days while the lower and middle divisions are in session 167 days. The variance is due to parent conferences."

---

[1] Chait, Richard P., Thomas P. Holland and Barbara E. Taylor. *The Effective Board of Trustees.* New York: MacMillan Publishing Company, 1991, p. 66.

Tom was silent for a moment running the numbers through his head. Finally, he said slowly, "I attended a conference recently with heads from all the New England schools. None of them reported being in session less than 174 days."

"Well, you know our days are longer than the public schools', so in the end it works out."

"But Everett, every one of these was an independent school. They all reported more days in the school year. It appears they are in session at least a week longer than Florence Bruce. How could that be? Imagine what would happen if that information were published."

Everett was silent, not fully comprehending Tom's concern.

"Let me talk to Peg and Nancy," said Tom. "Would you call a couple of the local independent schools and verify that what they told me is true?"

Everett said he would and confirmed Tom's fears the next day when they met.

"If this information becomes generally known, we'll have a revolt on our hands," Tom brooded. "The tuition here is about the highest in the area. What do you think parents will say if they find out that our competitors are all in session a week longer than we are?" Tom was deeply worried, but the others were more sanguine. The concept of schools being competitors with one another was somewhat foreign to them. What difference did it make what other schools did? Florence Bruce was special, and the assumption was that everyone who mattered knew that. Nancy, whose career was built around numerical comparisons, was sympathetic, but Peg and Everett were not convinced that parents evaluated the education the school provided on such quantitative measures as the number of days the school was in session. Nor did they feel Tom's urgency. This was a condition that had existed for some time without consequence; what harm would another year make?

When Tom stated flatly, "Everett, I think we have to add a week to the school calendar next year," Peg fished for a delay. "The faculty is not going to like this, and I'm having enough trouble with morale as it is. Shouldn't we take this question to them?"

"That's a good idea. You're right, of course. We really should take this to the faculty. We'll be meeting with them right after the holiday break." Like the others, Tom recognized the merits of including the major stakeholders, despite a personal conviction there could be no other responsible conclusion than to lengthen the calendar.

"We need to get the calendar out before the break," Everett demurred. Tom pressed for time, but Everett was adamant. There could be no putting it off.

Tom acquiesced. "All right. The consequences of this hitting the media are just too dangerous to ignore. You go ahead and work the extra week into the calendar. I'll send a memo to everyone putting it in the best light I can and hope we can make amends later for acting without faculty input."

As soon as the meeting was over, Tom called Archie to ask his advice. Archie listened without comment. At the end of Tom's explanation, he said simply, "You need to do what you need to do."

"Should I call anyone else on the executive committee?"

"I don't think that's necessary. The board meeting is only three days away. We can inform the trustees then. I mean, it isn't as if we have a choice."

A more experienced president might have advised Tom that he did, in fact, have a choice—that the likelihood of the discrepancy becoming public knowledge was very low given the secrecy surrounding the internal workings of the school. A more experienced president might have counseled Tom to leave the length of the school year as it was—at least for the time being.

Archie was not an experienced president, and Tom's attention was directed to the goals with which the board had charged him. Tying the anticipated increase in next year's tuition to an increase in the length of the school year was an obvious benefit to offset cost. His memo to the faculty was apologetic. He explained the impending deadline. He explored the consequences if Florence Bruce was found to have fewer days in session than other independent schools in the area. No one knew or could remember how the year had become shortened, but the fact that it was at least five days shorter than any other independent school in the area was not disputed.

The announcement of a lengthened calendar for the following year was, as expected, not well received. Around the faculty lunch table, over cups of coffee in the teacher's lounge, and among those gathered at the copy machine, voices grumbled and griped in protest. "Is this the Christmas present we get from our new head?" "Doesn't our input mean anything? When it comes down to it, we always get left out of the important decisions." "Doesn't he understand how hard we work and how little we get paid?" Some used the occasion to recall the installation ceremony as a self-aggrandizing display by a head too full of himself. Others, rankled over a recent review of department budgets, felt anew the resentment over the challenge to their professionalism.

For the most part, the talk was the kind of everyday grumbling that is ubiquitous in all organizations. It was something to talk about, something to occupy the time while charging batteries to renew the fray. And the faculty was, of course, genuinely surprised at the revelation.

In any case, the holiday season loomed, and there was little time to dwell on the inevitable. Every class had its own special activities. Each division was preparing a holiday production for parents. School projects were being rushed to completion. Exams were in progress. Grades were due. The griping passed quickly, but some of the more seasoned faculty—people like Corny Jolley—were alarmed. Corny knew the culture of Florence Bruce as well as anyone. She knew some were already keeping score, and this decision to lengthen the school year would someday become a weapon to achieve ends of their own invention.

A few days later, Jackie flitted through Tom's door with an armload of letters and bulletins directed to his office. "You sure are a popular guy," she smiled jovially. "You know I try to weed out some of this for you, but I'm not sure what you want to see and what you don't. I took care of everything for John except personal letters . . ."

Tom knew Jackie was at the beginning of a recitation that would wind a circuitous pathway through John's office protocols and into an entangled web of examples. He listened, not having the energy to interrupt, until the phone rang. On the third ring, Tom broke in with "Excuse me, the phone's ringing," and reached to answer it.

"Oh, no, I'll get that," said Jackie quickly, and hurried off.

Tom sighed and picked up the mail Jackie had brought. A large manila envelope with the words "Personal and Confidential" scrawled across its face caught his attention. Inside was a children's book, *The Emperor's New Clothes*—the story about a king with a penchant for showing off. According to the story, swindlers make him a wonderful suit of new clothes with the distinction of not being visible to those unfit for their office or too stupid. All who view the new suit, including the king, are too embarrassed to say anything until a child speaks up to point out, "But he has nothing on at all."

On a sticky note attached to the cover of the book was handwritten, "Dr. Whitman, the emperor has no clothes!"

What in the world is this? A joke? Tom turned the book over and opened it, thumbing through the pages. There were no other clues. He felt mildly violated. Over the next couple of days, his thoughts returned to the anonymous message. What did it mean? An ominous cloud loomed before him, but he could fathom no answer to the question. Finally, he extracted a modicum of revenge by giving the book to the school library with his name typed boldly in the donor's faceplate.

The December meeting of the board of trustees came in the waning days of the old year. Florence Bruce was already gaily decorated for the coming holiday and Mrs. Clayworth's creative vision overwhelmed the arriving trustees, imbuing them with an aura of anticipation. A magnificent, twenty-foot-tall Christmas tree occupied a position of honor in Kittery Hall. Wreaths and garlands festooned doorways and railings. Bulletin boards were decorated with all manner of student constructions, and the bright, smiling faces of their creators capering about the hallways put the season's joyousness in the hearts of these volunteer governors.

All except Phyllis Killam. Phyllis was in foul temper as she stomped into the lobby. Her full-length, unbuttoned coat flapped about, and her tendency to occupy space filled the hallway as she made her way to the library for the board meeting. For months, Phyllis had expected a call, expected a request for consultation, expected her status as president emeritus to propel her into the inner sanctum. That the sanctum no longer existed had not occurred to her.

She found her seat at the head of the table, where, in her day, the powerful held counsel. She was at Archie's right hand to be sure, but, to her dismay, Tom sat at the opposite end of the table. She watched with growing disdain as the two of them exchanged comments that traveled the length of the table, open to all, and basked in the light of a relationship that visibly strengthened as the meeting progressed. She noted with displeasure the presence of Nancy, Peg and Ruth at the meeting. Though she had concurred with the majority when permission was granted for the staff to attend, they now seemed like an intrusion inhibiting the convivial, tête-à-tête repartee of trusted colleagues.

Phyllis herself was no longer a member of the board of trustees, having reached the limit of her allowable service in June.[2] Her attendance at the meeting was, in point of fact, a courtesy extended to her—a courtesy albeit no one would have thought to challenge. As the former president, she was, however, an ex-officio member of the executive committee. There she was, positioned to guide the new board president and appointed head as they began their journey together. Instead, she had been overlooked. Neither Archie nor Tom had yet thought to call upon her expertise for guidance—an unpardonable oversight by the two preoccupied neophytes.

Archie's opening comments were upbeat as he summarized key points made in the Nunlist report. The business included preparations for a vote on the new wing, approval of a new investment policy, and permission to contract for a branding study to help guide marketing and admissions decisions. Committee reports followed, and Archie's handling of them was laudable. All the board committees were productively engaged. Reports were exciting and delivered with a degree of enthusiasm. Archie's knowledge of committee activities—by virtue of the fact that he attended every meeting—allowed him to comment cogently and tie disparate pieces together.

The meeting ended in three hours, precisely on time, concluding with the head's report. Tom shared with them the newspaper story of the student whose great-grandfather had died working on the roof of the school. He distributed the following year's calendar and pointed out the extra week the school would be in session. Archie brought down the gavel ending the meeting, and the two exchanged a congratulatory handshake as the trustees exited to a holiday reception with the faculty.

Phyllis was still disgruntled when she walked in the door of her home with take-out pasta from Luciano's. She felt like an outsider. Things were happening she had not even been aware of. Of course, no one had been rude to her, but the deference and respect customarily

---

[2] A trustee served a term of three years and could serve two terms in succession before having to go off the board for at least a year. Terms of office and term limits, in general, assure a gradual turnover and the infusion of new ideas while, at the same time, providing the opportunity to rotate unproductive trustees off the board.

accorded her was missing; the wielding of power was now absent from her portfolio. Jennifer entered the kitchen and began setting the table. "Jenn, does Dr. Whitman know who you are?" she asked spontaneously.

"I don't know, I guess so."

"I mean, does he ever say 'hi' to you or call you by name?"

"No, not really." Jennifer hardly ever saw the school's head, except in chapel or assemblies. Tom had been in her class once to observe, and they had passed each other occasionally in the hallway. She looked away when their eyes met, and nothing was said. In truth, Tom recognized her as he did many of the students, but couldn't immediately place her as being Phyllis' daughter.

"He's not at all like Mr. Sanford, is he?" said Phyllis, and Jennifer agreed. John knew the younger Killam well. Their relationship extended back through the first grade, and although she didn't often see him, he never passed her by without a hearty greeting and a comment of encouragement to brighten her day.

"I miss him, Mom."

The holiday season built to a climax with "Lessons and Carols" on the last day of school before vacation. A buzz of excitement and anticipation filled the hallways and bounced off the ceilings of the old building. Everywhere, last minute preparations for the traditional presentation of the season were underway.

Tom was on a walkabout in the Lower School when he happened upon a gang of tots wearing little elf hats on a mission to somewhere. "Mr. Whitman!" they squealed in unison, and like hounds with a treed bear they scampered around him, baying for his attention. One moppet with a jumble of cascading red curls that nearly engulfed her hat grabbed his leg in a full embrace and lifted her own legs so her weight pulled him off balance.

These youngsters were from a Kindergarten class Tom had visited several times in the fall. He knew most of them by name. "Molly," he said, catching his balance with a hand against the wall, "where are all of you going with such pretty hats?"

His question was ignored, but the others, quick to recognize Molly's effectiveness at capturing Tom's attention, grabbed on. The combined weight of three or four of the youngsters sent him down on one knee to keep from falling over. Their exuberance and disregard of decorum surprised him, but he couldn't help laughing. Getting into the spirit, Tom started tipping their hats off their heads as a distraction so he could regain his feet. The youngsters squealed with glee. Suddenly, he became aware of the compromised position he was now in. No other adult was in view. The sight of him virtually on the floor with a gaggle of little girls in his arms could easily be misconstrued, with resulting disastrous headlines. It was a crisis in the making, he thought, regretting for an instant the lack of a plan to cover his circumstances. Instinct told him to hold his arms out to avoid touching them, but that only provided handholds for more to clamor on.

Tom's demeanor changed suddenly from one of relaxed playfulness to that of stern headmaster. He willed himself to stand and one by one peeled off little hands as the youngster's feet left the ground and gravity could claim them again. Within a few seconds, he was on his feet. "It's time to get ready," he said gruffly. "You all need to get back to class." The hurt that crept into the little eyes melted his heart and made him curse the litigious bastards whose fondness for the courts had intruded into his life that day.

An hour later, he was seated in the balcony of Hanley Chapel with those lower-school parents who had been able to extricate themselves from work and holiday planning to attend the popular presentation of "Lessons and Carols." The youngest of the seminarians were seated in the pews by class below them. The faint aroma of incense wafted in the air. Poinsettias and garlands of greenery decorated the altar.

While pairs of fifth-grade students rose to pick their way through a reading of the Christmas story, a crèche slowly filled with Mary and Joseph, the Baby Jesus and other biblical characters of the familiar narrative. From time to time, a class singing a carol interrupted the scene or played out a short vignette imbued with the spirit of the season. Not a dry eye could be found among the assembled parents as the presentation drew to a close and the entire body of students stood. The organ swelled, and with their clear soprano voices blending as one, they sang, "O come, all ye faithful, joyful and triumphant . . ." At the end of the first verse, on signal from the music director, every child turned to face the rear of the chapel and the assembled adults. Trusting, innocent faces searched for a parent, and they sang, "Sing, choirs of angels, sing in exultation . . ."

Tears cascaded down adult cheeks, and sobs of happiness and joy mingled with the singing of the children. Tom glanced at Allison, who was seated next to him. Her face glistened as she dabbed at her eyes with a tissue, and he motioned for her to hand him one.

That afternoon, Tom slumped in his office limp with the accumulated exhaustion of his first months as head of school. Most of the students had already left and the boarders were packing up, waiting for parents to arrive or for rides to the airport. It was like listening to the air slowly leave a balloon, the pitch lowering by degrees as the pressure inside was released.

"Merry Christmas!" called out Jackie as she turned to lock her door. "You and the girls have a wonderful holiday."

"And you have a merry Christmas yourself and get some rest. We've still got a long way to go."

A half-hour later he gathered himself and packed up to go home. Only the maintenance staff sweeping out the corridors and the kitchen help cleaning up from the day's tempest were left going about their work in the old building. Tom crossed the street to the Ahlborn House to a prolonged and welcome embrace from Allison. That evening they enjoyed dinner at a favorite restaurant. Tom downed his customary Chivas Regal on the rocks and then uncustomarily ordered another, handing the car keys to Allison as he did so.

CHAPTER XVIII

Into the Abyss

♠

All boards should have conflict-of-interest polices that cover likely conflict situations such as business dealings and nepotism.[1]

The engine rpms slowed and the whine in the cabin pitched lower as the seatbelt signs aboard the American Airlines DC-10 chimed once and blinked out. The aisles immediately filled with passengers anxious to disembark from the long holiday and begin the inevitable return to daily routines. The excited chatter of children could be heard above the general din. Here and there a flowered shirt or palm-frond hat marked a procrastinating vacationer in subliminal denial.

"You be sure Bud takes care of that sunburn," said Archie, cheerfully directing his comment across the aisle to Trish Calvert, whose husband Bud was fumbling in the overhead bins, his pained expression the result of a brush with a fellow passenger. "It looks like it'll be tender for a couple more days."

---

[1] Lakey, Berit M. *Nonprofit Governance: Steering Your Organization with Authority and Accountability*. Washington, DC: BoardSource, 2000, p. 25.

About forty of the plane's passengers were Florence Bruce families joined together by the presence of a daughter in the fifth grade. Most of them had met for the first time during registration for Kindergarten, and the bonds forged in the commonality of that act had grown and strengthened over the years through constant reinforcement.

It is not unusual for families to build relationships around children of similar ages. This group of fifth-grade parents, however, was extreme in the exclusivity of their connection to one another. Year after year, membership remained intact. Stable family circumstances, as luck would have it, meant that no child had left the school. With the class full to capacity, no room remained for newcomers to enroll.

In the early, formative years, the children and parents of these families were seemingly interchangeable. The adult members rotated through myriad roles of mentor, coach, tutor, and scout leader year to year and season to season. Birthday parties saw the same collection of children; summer-camp sessions were coordinated; vacations often included multiple families from the same pool.

In due course, three families vacationed together over the Christmas holidays in the Grand Caymans. The next year, joined by two other families, Bermuda was the destination. Even more families were brought into the fold as the years passed.

This year, with the children getting older, Disney's Polynesian Resort in Orlando was the stage for a long, glorious, sun-drenched Christmas holiday together. With day trips to Epcot, Disney-MGM Studios and other feature attractions, it was a vacation that none would soon forget.

Archie, the Calverts and the other fifth-grade Florence Bruce families galloped through bright, tropical days and balmy nights, replenishing depleted stores of vitamin D and sipping mai tais while the kids frolicked in a gigantic outdoor pool with its own white-sand beach. An unsurpassed feeling of well-being suffused the gathering. So overwhelming was the sensation that each parent attributed its presence to the others in the group, and a profound sense of gratitude—one for the other—took hold.

It was a dream come true for Deanne and Lexi, who accompanied Archie and his two daughters on the trip. Among mostly older girls, the younger Lexi was fawned over and protected by the various cliques that spontaneously erupted and dissolved around her through the long, languid days. For her part, Deanne felt perfectly at home among the moneyed classes of Portsmouth's Heights district. And, overcome with feelings of good will, they in turn embraced the reserved woman and her charming little girl, because she was with Archie and he was with them.

To be sure, they were all—except Deanne—people of means. About half the families were at least partially supported by trust accounts established by a previous generation. Although one young man basked in his unearned leisure, the others dabbled at careers—architecture, law, public relations—but whether their enterprises succeeded or failed, financially speaking, it didn't really seem to matter. At least two were retired from the halcyon days of the dot-com boom, men in their late forties with younger second wives and families. There were also among them couples whose wealth was self-made and still being made; hard-driving, dual-career, type-A professionals who valued their worth in power, status and the accumulation of assets.

In truth, aside from their affluence the group had little in common—except that their children were enrolled together in the fifth grade at Florence Bruce Seminary. But that was more than enough. On this trip, the almost communal living arrangements had connected them as never before. Shared meals, de rigueur evening cocktails, joint sightseeing excursions, and games of all kinds that were underway simultaneously at all times of day had established unbreakable bonds of friendship and loyalty.

It was also worth noting that the fifth-grade parents were at the height of their influence in the school. Trish Calvert, of course, was president of the Parents' Association. Two-thirds of her dozen or more committees were chaired by parents from this group. In experience, they were unsurpassed. In commitment and dedication, they were unequaled, and their presence was a dominant influence on the school.

Tom bounded up the stairs to his office. He had spent the last weekend of vacation catching up on correspondence and reviewing the goals set by the trustees for his administration, and was eager to pick up progress from where it had been left prior to the holidays. Before Jackie had booted up her computer or Craig Gowdy had poured his first cup of coffee, Tom and Nancy were tête-à-tête in his office. Nancy worked at the same pace as Tom, but it would be at least an hour before the rest of the school was up to speed and ready to receive his inquiries.

The topic was next year's budget, and Nancy was explaining the school's endowment policies. "Florence Bruce has traditionally taken 6.5 percent from its endowment annually for operations, but at that rate, with the decline in the financial markets over the last two years, we'll begin cutting into principal pretty soon."

Tom was surprised. Most institutions were more conservative with their endowments. When financial markets were booming, 6.5 percent did not pose a risk, but a succession of bad years could quickly turn things sour. Nancy agreed and proposed a drop to 5.5 percent.[2]

"How much money does a drop of one percent translate to?" Tom asked.

"About $125,000."

"Geez, that's a lot. How can we compensate for a drop in revenue of that magnitude?"

"Don't quote me on this just yet," said Nancy, lowering her tone, "but I think we'll end this year with a $200,000 surplus or thereabouts. If that carries over into next year, we should still be fine."

The conversation moved on to faculty salaries. Nancy's research had produced the expected result that male teachers were getting paid more than female teachers. She handed Tom a scattergram displaying salary plotted against years of teaching. For the most part, as predicted, the longer a person had been teaching, the more they were getting paid.

"I see," said Tom, studying the graph. "But what's going on here?" He pointed to a half-dozen dots positioned well below the main grouping.

"You guessed it. We've got teachers who have been here a long time and who are barely getting paid what a beginning teacher makes. A disproportionate number of these, it turns out, are female."

"Have you addressed this with your compensation committee?"

"Up to a point. The committee saw this scattergram just before the holidays. They could see, as you did, that some of our faculty are

---

[2] Savvy managers of endowments do not draw on the actual interest earned from the portfolio but instead take a percentage of the portfolio's total earnings averaged over several years. This allows the portfolio to grow over time and provides a relatively stable and predictable source of revenue.

paid well below the norm. But I didn't tell them who these people are, so they don't know they're mostly female. I'd rather focus on getting *everyone* up to a minimum standard. If we succeed, it will correct the worst of the gender and divisional imbalances."

"You're probably right;" said Tom. "But we don't want to take all the subjectivity out of the system either. That's what gives independent schools their advantage. If we define compensation solely in terms of number of years in the classroom, it will limit our ability to reward the better-performing teachers or those willing to take on more assignments. How do you suppose it got this way?"

"I don't know," sighed Nancy. "I think if John liked you, you got paid more. If you were a good negotiator or complained a lot, you got paid more. If he thought he could get away with sweet-talking you or making you feel guilty by bemoaning the state of the school's finances, you got paid less. I really don't think fairness had much to do with it at all."

"You're doing a great job, Nancy. If you and the compensation committee can bring some order to this mess, it will be one of the great accomplishments of this year—and fulfill one of the major goals we've been charged with."

A few days later, a mixed group of interested faculty and staff members were gathered in Tom's office to pursue another of the goals set by the board. Termed a "focus group," this was one of five such groups organized by Tom to reexamine and update the building plan, which had been conceived more than five years prior to his arrival. In those intervening years, changes inside Florence Bruce specifically, and in the independent-school community in general, had rendered assumptions in the plan suspect and needful of review before being solidified in concrete and brick.

Tom addressed the group: "Planning documents from the mid-1990s assert that one of the goals driving construction of the new wing was to permit an increase in students enrolled in the Middle School. Some of you recall when the Middle School was filled to capacity with a waiting list. Now we have openings in every grade. What happened?"

"Back then there was a lot of demand. Florence Bruce had the best Middle School around and a well-established reputation. Since then, three new middle schools have opened in the area." The speaker was Monique Fontembleau.

"What are the chances we can capture enough new students in the future to fill our existing vacancies *and* fulfill the expectations of the building plan?" said Tom, throwing the question to the whole group.

No one was willing to venture a response.

"Another problem is the condition of the middle-school building. The classrooms are small; half are in the basement with no natural light, and they leak in the winter." Everett Laurie spoke this time.

"Tell it like it really is, Everett. They flood," said another.

"Seriously, no matter how good we are as a middle school," said Monique, "we'll never attract new students with the building we have now."

"I believe you," said Tom. "But here's the rub. All the new construction is focused on the Upper School: new classrooms, a new science lab, a new music room, etcetera. According to the plan, the Middle School will mostly inherit the leftovers." Heads nodded around the room in agreement. The discussion continued for over an hour. In the end, two recommendations emerged:

- Concentrate efforts for the immediate future on increasing enrollment in the Upper School.
- Provide the Middle School with some fresh, new facilities, including a science lab, student lounge and bigger classrooms.

The recommendations were reasonable. They added no cost to the building project, and, by converting to middle-school use some spaces designed for the Upper School, a cost savings might even be realized. Of even greater consequence, however, was the fact that the recommendations accurately reflected changes in conditions brought about by the passing of time.

Other focus groups organized around different questions relating to the building plan produced similar results. Diagrams and blueprints of the suggestions were posted in the faculty lounge, and Tom e-mailed summaries of the notes taken at the various meetings to the entire faculty.

The building committee, chaired by Keegan O'Connor, was now getting together almost weekly and devoted part of each meeting to a consideration of these questions and reports emanating from the various focus groups.

* * *

"Tom, can I come see you?" Nancy was on the phone. Her tone sounded more exasperated than urgent; Tom was not involved in anything of great import, so he agreed to see her.

"It's Deanne," she said, closing the door behind her and plopping into a chair. "She's driving my staff nuts. I've never seen anyone so rude. Today, they're refusing to have anything to do with her, and Debbie is threatening to quit."

"Okay, you've got my attention," said Tom, putting aside the building blueprints he was reviewing. "Now, what's the problem?"

"Well, to begin with, we can't get her to approve invoices for her department. She's three months behind on some of them, and we're getting hit with late charges. If we don't get them paid, the vendors will begin canceling services."

"What are you talking about? All you need for approval is her initial on the invoice, isn't it?"

"Not quite, but almost. We need her to indicate what the invoices are for so we can charge them to the proper account, but it's really simple. She just refuses to follow procedures. Look at this." Nancy spread four pages of sequential e-mail messages in front of Tom. Not waiting for them to be read, she continued, "She'd rather argue for an hour than spend the five minutes it would take to fix it."

"Have *you* spoken with her about it?"

"Yes, of course, but you know she always has an excuse. If I address one problem, she finds another. These things could be handled so easily, if she was just willing to work with us. She makes the routine things so difficult. Here's another example."

Nancy rooted around in her notebook and pulled out a sheaf of invoices clipped together. "Look at these credit-card receipts. I've indicated a number of the charges that are obviously personal. See, here's one for a hair-styling salon. Deanne is charging personal expenses on the school credit card. I asked her when she would be giving us a check for those expenses, and look what she wrote back."

Tom read from the e-mail Nancy showed him. "You guys owe me a reimbursement check for $30 or so, just let me know the difference. Deanne."

"Tom, you know we can't just subtract one from the other. First of all, charging personal expenses on the school credit card is a no-no.

Secondly, the auditors want to see a paper trail. We have to pay her on her request for reimbursement, and she has to cut us a separate check for her personal expenses."

Tom's shoulders sagged. "You're absolutely right. I can't believe practices like this were ever allowed before I got here." He paused, searching for an appropriate response. "Look," he said finally, "I'm trying to deal with this on another level. Do what you have to with Deanne, and I'll back you up."

Nancy looked at him cautiously. "Okay, but this could get pretty unpleasant. I'll probably start by cutting off her credit-card privileges."

"Do what you have to do, and I will back you up. You can count on it."

Nancy left, but not before leaving copies of her notes, e-mails and suspect invoices. Tom attached his own record of what Nancy had said and dropped the lot into the private file he kept of interactions with Deanne.

Tom had already reached the conclusion that he would have to let Deanne go—fire her. It was certainly not the first time he had fired someone. Indeed, there had been two firings at Florence Bruce since his arrival. But this one was different, because no egregious act precipitated it, and there were the extenuating circumstances of Deanne's relationship with Archie.

The reality that Deanne was in a romantic relationship with the president of the board did not alter the fundamental nature of what Tom felt he needed to do, but the potential impact of the act—of the firing—on the psyche of the individuals involved and of the institution that employed her was very much on his mind.

Separating a person from his or her work is an act of violence. For many Americans, work is synonymous with their personal identity. What they do is very much a part of who they are. When a person is fired, no matter how flagrant the transgression, a piece of them dies, too, and the institution—the cause of that death—also mourns the loss while absorbing part of the blame. Tom was sensitive to this and had made it his mission in times past to ease the trauma of these separations by whatever means at hand.

A few days after Nancy's visit, Tom found another manila envelope from Deanne in his mailbox. This time it contained a draft of *Voyager*, the Florence Bruce magazine. *Voyager* was published twice a year.

Its four-color cover and glossy pages were intended to evoke fond memories among the alumnae and to encourage their continuing loyalty to their alma mater. It was also directed at parents and donors to underscore the wisdom of their investment in the school and its future. *Voyager* was an important publication, and Tom had spared no effort to ensure the ultimate quality of the issue he now held in his hands. Two of the articles he had written himself, and a half-dozen of the photos were from his own camera. He had carefully guided Deanne through the process of article selection and lent his weight to encourage staff to complete research and writing assignments.

Once again, his expectations were no match for what lay before him. This time Deanne had delivered a draft—but just barely. It was a designer's first rough layout of the material. Article submissions were not edited, so errors and inconsistencies abounded. There were gaps—white space that needed to be filled. Photos were missing; captions incomplete. To thoroughly review the draft would cost him a full day. *Dammit*! He expected to see Deanne's best work and help her improve it, not do her work for her.

He took the draft home and that night struggled to concentrate on the larger picture. Admittedly, the basics were in place; the publication held promise. In his memo to Deanne, Tom tried to accentuate the positive, opting to target only two specific issues for comment. First, he reiterated his desire for more extensive captions to help tell the story.

His second comment was more obscure. The cover photo was of Tom with Bishop Moseley at the installation. Tom looked carefully at the black-and-white draft cover. The bishop photographed well, but his own face was tentative and unflattering. He grimaced, recalling the proof sheet and thinking the photo he had selected was better. On a sticky note attached to the cover, he wrote, "Deanne, please bring me the proof sheets for the cover photo again. Thanks. Tom."

In his covering memo to Deanne, Tom thanked her for the draft and asked to see it again when it was further along. He ended with this request: "Please schedule some time to meet with me next week. I need to talk to you about the future of public relations at Florence Bruce."

The executive committee had a lot of catching up to do when it met in Tom's office for the first time after the holidays. Following handshakes and hugs, Bermuda, Florida, a skiing trip to Stowe and family visits were all fodder for convivial exchanges. Mrs. Clayworth's lunch was a perennial favorite: split-pea soup, croissants stuffed with chicken salad and, for dessert, a plate of fresh-baked cookies with coffee and tea.

Bodie Bickerstaff arrived fifteen minutes early and plopped herself down in Jackie's office to chat. Tom heard Bodie arrive but didn't go out to meet her. The two women would enjoy each other's company better without him around, and their superficial gossip didn't interest him.

Jackie was lamenting John's absence when Archie arrived on the hour and extracted Bodie from Jackie's grip. Geoffrey Bellingham sauntered into the room exuding professorial self-importance. Behind him came Keegan O'Connor. Keegan often used his black skin and Irish surname to supply an opening. "Geoffrey, m'boy, you're lookin' mighty glum this marnin'. Has the weather gotcha, now?" he said, in perfect brogue.

Geoffrey, unable to fully reconcile the sound coming from the face, merely said, "No, as a matter of fact, I'm feeling just fine."

Saugus Wetherby cleared the doorway and, clasping Tom's hand in one of his huge maws, said, "Tom, I'm jealous. I'd love to be able to spend my whole day down here at the school like you. These short visits just—well, they end too soon. That's all." He laughed and clapped Tom on the back.

After several minutes of banter, Tom glanced at his watch and caught Archie's eye, signaling him to get the meeting started. Several more minutes passed before people served themselves and were seated around the large conference table. The Piscataqua was now largely visible through the bare branches of the trees edging the campus, and the *USS Maine*, an Ohio-class Trident submarine, could be seen moving slowly across the water to a berth at the Portsmouth Naval Shipyard.

"Welcome! I trust everyone had a wonderful holiday, and I'm pleased to see you all back safe and sound," declared Archie from his seat at the head of the table. "This is our first meeting of the new year, and we have much work ahead of us. So let's get started. Phyllis won't be able to join us today, but we have more than enough for a quorum. Tom, do you have today's agenda?"

The agenda was passed around. "To begin on a high note," Archie continued, "I think you are all aware that we obtained a million-dollar contribution to the Campaign for Florence Bruce just before the holidays. It came from the Alexander family. They already had pledged $500,000 and have doubled it to bring the total to $1 million."

"Don't I recall them making another pledge of $300,000 to a new art room?" said Saugus, staring out the window at the disappearing submarine and trying to disengage his mind from the workload that would face him when he returned to his office.

"That was the rumor," Tom responded. "Apparently, there was a conversation with John Sanford to that effect. The current plan doesn't include a new art room, and the family wanted to help us add one. Nothing was written down or signed, so it was never actually recorded. When we talked to them about upping their pledge to $1 million, I asked about the art room. They were pretty flexible. I think their main interest is helping us to achieve our goals, whatever they may be."

"So what you're really saying is we got another $200,000 gift; not $1 million," said Bodie.

"That's not it at all," said Tom. "It's $500,000 in new money for a total gift of $1 million. It's a real plus in a campaign like this if you can say you have a million-dollar gift; and now we can say that."

"Well, if you had $500,000 already, and I've heard reports before about the $300,000, too, then it sounds like only $200,000 to me."

"Tom's right," said Warren Hudson, as Tom sighed a silent thank you for the rescue. "We never had the $300,000. It's the difference between your kids saying they're going to clean their room and actually doing it."

"Well, I just think this campaign's gone on too long. We'll never finish it if we keep fudging the money. You didn't get a million dollars, and I think it's wrong to say you did."

Archie ignored her. "Keegan, I know your committee has updated numbers for the construction costs. Are you ready to share them?"

"Sure, but you may not like what I have to say." Keegan passed around a three-page handout breaking down the estimates for various elements of the new building wing. His speech, devoid of the usual jokes, showed no hint of a brogue now. Fifteen minutes later, he concluded his analysis, "The net result, as you can see, is that the project will cost about $8.7 million—that's $1.5 million more than we thought it would."

Tom wasn't the least bit surprised, but the others obviously were. Construction costs are bound to escalate, due to inflation and other factors, whenever they are allowed to languish for more than a year.

Aside from Bodie, who seemed to take a perverse pleasure in the news, the others showed deep concern. "Where are we going to find the extra money?" "Can we do the project in phases?" "How could the estimates be so far off?" The questions came at Keegan at rapid-fire speed. A lengthy explanation of value engineering followed a suggestion the project be cut back. Tom shared results of the focus-group meetings he was holding with faculty and staff, implying there might be some small savings to be realized. In the end, Keegan and his committee had done their work well. The numbers were solid—a major improvement, as Tom pointed out optimistically, from the meaningless estimates they had started with.

In the ten minutes remaining before the meeting adjourned, Tom reported he had just received notice from the director of technology that he would be leaving at the end of the year to pursue a private business venture. The director's entrepreneurial skills had given Florence Bruce a stellar technology program, but Tom knew he was ready to move on.

"How will you replace him?" asked a worried Saugus Wetherby.

"This is not necessarily a bad thing," said Tom, trying to convey something of his philosophy of the relationship between employer and employee. "This is good for him. He's learned what he can learn here, and progressed as far as he can. It's time for him to move on. This business venture is a great opportunity for him. It's also good for us. He's shared his talents with us, and Florence Bruce has gained immensely. We have stretched the technology program to the very edge. Now we need someone who can manage what we already have, bring in some cost controls and improve efficiencies."

"I don't think we should be talking about limits," said Saugus. "There shouldn't be limits on what we can do. Have you tried to convince him to stay?" Saugus didn't see things in shades of gray. The idea that there might be a mutually beneficial time for an excellent employee to leave his employer was beyond him. If a little bit was good, then a lot must be better. Tom realized there was nothing he could say to convince Saugus otherwise.

Archie adjourned the meeting. As the gathering broke up, Tom touched Archie on the arm, indicating he wanted him to stay behind. When the others had left, he closed the door to his office and, gathering his courage, said as firmly as he could, "Archie, the time has come for me to do something about Deanne."

With the mention of Deanne, Archie shut down. *Why, when things are going so well, does Tom have to keep harping on Deanne?* It had been more than a month since their last conversation about her, and Archie had forgotten about it during the long holiday that followed. As Tom spoke, Archie barely listened, and fierce, protective feelings welled up from within that he couldn't explain.

Tom, for his part, was embarrassed by his intrusion into the intimacy of this couple's private relationship. He stumbled over his words, searching for ways to mitigate their impact. Archie saw in Tom's furrowed brow and pained expression a stern headmaster issuing a report card, and he felt personally chastened.

"I've done everything I can think of to mentor Deanne, but the work is just not getting done to the standards we need here. We've talked about this before. Unfortunately, it's not getting any better, and I need to make a decision. I've asked Deanne to meet with me next Tuesday. I'm going to . . . to make a change." Tom couldn't bring himself to say that he was going to terminate her employment with Florence Bruce. "I have a proposal that I think provides a fair settlement. Do you want me to go over it with you?"

"Ah, no, I don't think that's necessary," said Archie, eager to extricate himself and not comprehending what it was Tom wanted to go over. The various hats Archie claimed to wear were beginning to blend together, and he was having difficulty determining which one he had on at the moment. "You're the head of the school. You need to do what you think is right."

The two men shook hands and an uneasy Archie departed, leaving behind an equally uneasy Tom.

That weekend, Tom joined a group of upper-school girls for a downhill ski trip to the local slopes. Peg Scott was leading the trip and asked if he'd like to join them. Tom had skied off and on for most of his life and had readily agreed. It would be a great opportunity to get to know a few more of his students. Besides, Allison was planning to attend the opening of an exhibit of Chihuly glass in Boston, so the opportunity to beg off a city trip for a day in the outdoors was welcomed.

Saturday morning at 6:30 AM, a dozen students and their two adult custodians boarded a Florence Bruce minibus for the two-hour trip to the mountains. Peg drove. Tom sat in the seat behind her, and the rest of the students scattered themselves to the rear of the vehicle. The excitement of departure and astonishment at the headmaster's presence among them faded quickly in the predawn gloom. Within minutes, the bus quieted as the early hour, the warmth of the heaters and the gentle bouncing made eyelids too heavy to keep open.

About an hour later, Peg pulled into a minimart, and the girls piled out to assemble a breakfast for themselves. As Tom chatted among them, he was surprised to learn there were only two experienced skiers; most were beginners, and four had never been on skis before. His expectations of a day spent in joyful abandon on the slopes faded as images surfaced from his past of ski trips with his daughters that were spent laboring with rental equipment, lost outerwear and the intricacies of ski school. *Okay, we'll just take things as they come.*

In an immense parking lot, red-jacketed attendants guided the bus to a reserved spot. The day was overcast and minute snowflakes swirled around them. Tom had become accustomed to skiing in California's Sierra Nevada mountains, where as often as not the weather was crystal clear and sunny. This, he was to discover, was the New England equivalent. Any day without rain or whiteout snow conditions was considered excellent skiing.

After a warning to meet at the mid-mountain chalet for lunch, the better skiers and those with their own equipment were dismissed to their own devices. Peg and Tom hauled the rest over to be fitted at the rental shop. With that task complete, they divided between them the four girls with no experience. Tom's charges for the day were Carlye Nelson and Chia-Ying Pei. Carlye was an eye-catching junior whose outgoing personality made her popular among her peers. Chia-Ying was from mainland China, a shy, withdrawn girl like many of the Asian boarders.

Tom marched the two girls to the beginning of the lift line and helped them into their skis. Within two shuffling steps, both were on the ground. *Okay, it's coming back to me now. The first thing we teach them is how to get up.*

Tom's initial disappointment at having to forsake his own enjoyment of the sport was forgotten as the turn of events awakened the innate teacher in him. The trio managed to board the quad lift to the top of the mountain without incident. They disembarked unsteadily with Tom firmly holding each student by the upper arm, his own poles tucked under an elbow, heart thumping in his chest with the exertion.

Once on the slope, he provided more instruction on the critical skill of getting up. "Skis go on the downhill side. No, where's downhill? Point. Show me where downhill is. Okay, that's great. Now make your skis perpendicular to the slope." Chia-Ying was more difficult to teach because of the language barrier. "Perpendicular, do you remember *perpendicular* from your geometry class? That's right, it's like a cross. Downhill is part of the cross; now make your skis the other part."

"Dr. Whitman, watch me!" screamed Carlye as she careened down the slope, flopping in the snow to stop when a tree loomed ahead. She rolled over, laughing in exhilaration, her face covered with snow.

"That was awesome. Now let's learn how to turn, okay?"

Both girls progressed well. At the agreed-upon hour, they reluctantly headed for the chalet. Amid the hubbub of bodies coming and going, piles of temporarily discarded clothing, and trays of half-eaten cafeteria food, Peg glanced at Tom. "So, how's it going, boss?"

"Hey, I'm having a great time. These kids are quick learners, and they're willing to take a few lumps in the process."

"Well, I'm glad you're having fun. I must admit I was a little worried about you—more so than I was about them."

Back on the slopes, Tom alternated between cajoling his two charges to attempt new heights and extolling their progress. "Dr. Whitman, you are my best teacher," exclaimed Chia-Ying breathlessly, as she managed an arms-akimbo stop at the edge of a steep plunge into the woods. Her eyes glistened with excitement as she took off again. Tom's eyes glistened, too, but not for the same reason. It wasn't often his work allowed him to witness so directly the *raison d'etre* of his administrative toil.

Monday morning an e-mail arrived from Deanne: "Re: Captions, I was trained—through working with advertising agencies, including a couple on Madison Ave.—that the rule of thumb for captions is one line. The photo should tell the story; the caption should identify the photo."

Tom grit his teeth. Whether Deanne was right or wrong was beside the point. He had repeatedly indicated what he expected—explained it in detail more than once, only to be ignored. Deanne had no intention of complying with his wishes. *Well, it'll be water under the bridge tomorrow*. On impulse, he got up and walked to Deanne's office. Careful not to betray his emotions or his intent, he said, "Have you got the proofs of the cover shot for *Voyager*? Something bothered me about the draft I saw, and I want to check the proofs."

Deanne produced the proofs, and he scanned them quickly, looking for the cover shot he had selected. There it was—four shots, all similar, with the one he had chosen marked with his initials. "Deanne, here's the one I chose," he said evenly. "It's a lot more flattering than the one in the draft."

"We already paid for the other one. It will cost another $75 to change," she replied just as evenly, and glanced at the partially open drawer to her desk to see if it revealed the bottle she had tucked away just before he arrived.

Tom seethed. If she had chosen the less-flattering photo deliberately, she was not about to admit any complicity. "Do it!" was all he said, and, turning on his heels, walked out. Deanne shrugged. *That man is such a nag.* She put away the files on her desk, closed the drawer and prepared to join Archie for lunch.

That evening, all Tom could think about was his meeting with Deanne the next day. Over the weekend, he had prepared two pages of notes outlining what he wanted to say. Like an amateur chess player, he scrutinized each move carefully for hidden pitfalls. *If I say this, and she responds thusly, what will I do?* He played out the scenarios again and again in his head. As a precautionary measure, he considered asking Nancy to join them so there would be a third person in the room, but the animosity between the two women would set the wrong tone, he decided. It was a decision he would come to regret.

"Do you think Deanne knows why I want to meet with her tomorrow?" Tom asked his wife as they undressed for bed.

"I can't imagine she doesn't suspect something. You've catered to her incompetence more than any boss I've ever seen. In my experience, if a supervisor does an evaluation at all, it's only one, and then if nothing changes—'boom,' they're gone. No one would be as patient as you have before getting rid of her."

To be sure, as she sat in her office the next day hurriedly typing out a list of the projects in her portfolio for Tom, Deanne was not looking forward to their meeting. His carping irritated her, and the thought of spending an hour alone in his presence was depressing. Getting wearily to her feet, she grabbed the sheet of paper off the printer and trudged to his office.

Tom had spent the previous fifteen minutes pacing the floor, reviewing once again what he would say when she arrived. At the sound of Deanne's footsteps in the hallway, he sat down at his desk awaiting her knock. When it came, he jumped to his feet and hurried to greet her. "Come in, come in," he encouraged, and waved her toward the conference table—not as formal as the chair at his desk nor as informal as the easy chairs around the coffee table. The conference table would provide just the right amount of separation between them. It was something to hold on to, but it wouldn't obstruct any revealing body language.

"So how is Lexi? Did she enjoy her holiday? You went to Florida, didn't you?" Tom moved from the personal into a discussion of the upcoming issues of the *Seminary Log* and *Voyager*. "Did you get the article from Ruth on the new technology grant? When can I expect another draft of *Voyager*?" Deanne's responses were short, lethargic—she simply wanted to get through this interview as quickly as possible.

Validated for what he needed to do next, Tom pressed ahead. "I've said before that public relations plays a key role in the agenda I bring to Florence Bruce and a key role in the agenda the board of trustees has set for the year." Tom reiterated the need to build a network of relationships with media representatives and collaborative relationships with colleagues in admissions and development. He spoke again of the importance of publications and his desire for public relations to take a lead role in marketing the school.

Tom acknowledged her accomplishments before saying, "But they are not enough, and improvement has been too slow in coming." He paused, looking at her carefully. "Deanne, I'm frustrated, and I assume you must be, too."

Deanne nodded, sensing what was at stake and just now beginning to pay attention.

"You've told me this position was a stretch for you, and I've mentored you about as far as I can go. Public relations is not my specialty, and I need someone with a lot more expertise than I have. My plan is to create a senior-level position, something like a 'director of institutional advancement,' to oversee marketing and admissions and to coordinate closely with development."

Tom paused again. Deanne was confused and stared at him fixedly trying to clear her head. Was she getting a new title and a promotion?

"Now, you know as well as I do this isn't a position you are ready to assume. I want you to listen carefully because I'm going to offer you a proposal." He looked directly into Deanne's eyes. Slowly, his voice carefully modulated, he said, "I want you to resign . . . so I can begin building the team I need to move the school forward."

Deanne went rigid. Her eyes smoldered. The only word she heard clearly was "resign," but it was enough.

"My intent, of course, is that you be treated fairly with the dignity and respect you deserve. You have been with Florence Bruce for over three years, and your contributions to the school will be recognized and acknowledged. Furthermore, as you transition your skills to another job, you will have my full support to make that as painless as possible."

Deanne choked on a vile-tasting acid that rose in the back of her throat and fought to control the impulse to reach across the table and strangle this little wretch of a man. She envisioned his eyes bugged wide with astonishment as he fought for air. "Are you through?" she asked slowly, quietly, the words dripping with malice.

"No," said Tom, taken somewhat aback by her reaction. "You need to hear what I'm proposing."

He had given a great deal of thought to the terms he would offer in return for Deanne's resignation. Her contract with the school extended through the end of June, but with the file he had accumulated, Tom could fire her outright for incompetence, inability to get along with colleagues and insubordination, any one of which he thought was sufficient grounds for termination.

In a worst-case scenario, she could sue. However, Tom had reviewed Deanne's file with a lawyer who specialized in school law, and had been assured that legitimate grounds did exist to prevent a lawsuit from being successful, although, as Tom well knew, nothing could prevent a suit from being brought.

The standard procedure would be to ask Deanne to clean out her desk and offer two weeks' severance pay, but that was out of the question. Tom had never treated an employee so harshly unless he or she had done something egregious. Although he was prepared to pay out her contract, he had decided to offer less. This journey, he knew, was likely to end in a negotiated settlement, and to leave a little give in his position was only prudent. *Deanne's ego is going to take a hit, and if she thinks she's extracted another couple of month's pay, this whole thing will go down easier.*

In the end, Tom had decided he would offer to pay Deanne through April, but request her resignation effective at the end of February. He knew her presence around the school would be problematic. The sooner she was gone, the better, but a precipitous exit would be awkward for all concerned.

Tom carefully enumerated the key points of his proposal while Deanne continued to glare malevolently from the other side of the table. Her mind was racing, planning her steps: how she would tell Archie and the appeal she would make to her coterie of Florence Bruce parents and faculty. Deanne was a fearless fighter and incapable of recognizing any wrongdoing on her part. Surrender was not an option.

When he was finished, she asked again, "Are you through now?"

Tom looked at her, trying to gauge the mettle of the adversary across the table from him. He underestimated what he saw. In fact, Tom was surprised at her reaction—not that he expected tears, although that reaction was common enough in his experience. He had fully expected an exchange of sorts. "Why are you doing this?" "Can we work this out?" "What do I tell my friends?" Tom had prepared answers to every question he could think of, but Deanne wasn't going to ask any.

Finally, he said, "Yes, I'm through, but we should meet again when you've had time to think this over." Before he finished the sentence, Deanne was already on her feet, her back to him on her way out the door.

Tom sat where he was for a long time. "Well, it's done," he said finally, heaving himself out of the chair to pack his briefcase to go home.

Deanne walked straight to Archie's house where Lexi was playing upstairs with Archie's two girls. She opened the door. Tears brimmed in her eyes and glistened on her cheeks. Her face was twisted in anguish and sporadic, controlled sobs racked her frame. Her arms hung limply at her sides and her shoulders drooped in abject misery. Archie was preparing dinner. She walked to the kitchen and glimpsed him cutting vegetables at the sink.

She whimpered. Archie turned and saw her. "Honey, what's the matter? What happened to you?"

"Oh, Archie, it was terrible. Dr. Whitman fired me. He was out of control, yelling and screaming at me, calling me names." Her body shook as Archie held her in his arms, unable to process what she was telling him.

CHAPTER XIX

Hostilities

♠

The head has complete authority for faculty, staff and student selection, evaluation and dismissal.[1]

Deanne didn't come to work for two days, and Tom's surreptitious inquiries into her whereabouts went unanswered. She wasn't hiding and licking her wounds as he supposed. Retreat into despair and self-pity was not part of Deanne's make up. Life had hardened her to much worse than this, and the prospect of conflict only fed her desire for revenge. For a while, she even stopped drinking to better focus her attention.

With her influential social contacts, Deanne was not without weapons, and she pressed her case. She and Tom were alone when they met. No one would contradict her version of what happened.

Archie was dumbfounded by the loathsome image that Deanne conveyed to him of Tom berating her, yelling, banging the table, abusing his authority. Tom didn't seem like someone who would lose his temper, and yet, what reason did Deanne have to lie to him? Her

---

[1] DeKuyper, Mary Hundley. *Trustee Handbook: A Guide to Effective Governance for Independent School Boards*. Washington, DC: National Association of Independent Schools, 1998, p. 116.

vivid, teary-eyed recollections, followed by a small sob or catch in her throat, gradually erased any conviction Archie may have possessed regarding Tom's natural inclinations.

Posturing as a defenseless, single mother turned out by a cruel overseer, Deanne played havoc with Archie's protective instincts. She accentuated her vulnerability, long a staple of their relationship. Appearing forlorn and exposed, she portrayed her situation as hopeless: a mother and her little girl casually tossed out to face the world alone. "How am I going to support Lexi? What will we do? Where will we live?"

Deanne cast Tom's settlement proposal in mostly fabricated and damaging terms. Conveniently, she did not recall much of what he had said to her and was able to honestly limit the information she conveyed to the simple fact that Tom expected her to resign effective the end of February—a scant forty-five days away. She did not mention an additional payout because, in truth, she did not remember that Tom had offered one—the heat of the moment having obscured her memory as to what had actually taken place.

"I thought I had a contract," she lamented. "Doesn't Florence Bruce honor its contracts?"

"Didn't Tom talk to you before you met?" Archie asked, recalling snatches of the conversations he and Tom had shared.

"No. Oh, no. I had no idea he was upset with me."

"You mean he didn't give you an evaluation of your work?"

"No, I don't remember anything," replied Deanne, without lying.

To say that Archie was bewildered was a gross understatement. It is hard to imagine anyone more ill-prepared for the feelings and emotions that now gripped him. Cosseted as a single child, sheltered through adolescence by doting parents, protected financially by a trust account from the vagaries of life's marketplace, and still in a semi-traumatized state from the loss of his wife eight years earlier, Archie lacked the experience or the reserves to control the turmoil that now engulfed his life.

After waiting for two days to hear from Deanne, Tom sent her a gently worded e-mail requesting a meeting to review the terms of his proposal. Later that day, as he prepared for his weekly meeting with Archie, her reply came back: "I have been advised not to meet with you without a third party present.—Deanne."

"Oh, great!" said Tom under his breath, as he typed a message back. "Okay, who do you want to be the third party? I'm sure Nancy would be willing to sit in with us. She might be a good choice, since she will be responsible for carrying out whatever we resolve.—Tom."

"Deanne is not going to like that," he mused, knowing the feelings of enmity each of the women shared for the other. "She'll have someone in mind anyway, or she wouldn't have proposed it."

Tom was genuinely looking forward to his get-together with Archie. There was an executive committee meeting scheduled for the following week, budget preparations and a decision to be made on tuition increases for the following year, and construction planning for the new wing. These issues and more were all pending, and Tom was coming to depend on regular collaboration with his board president to keep things moving along. He was pleased with Archie's steady improvements in leadership and their growing friendship.

However, he couldn't shake the sense of foreboding that had gripped him since the confrontation with Deanne. His last two conversations with Archie about her had been less than satisfactory. Archie had been uncommunicative, brushing off Tom's concerns with his "two hats" analogy. Now the deed was done. Although Tom didn't necessarily believe Archie's cavalier treatment of the situation had been truly reflective of his feelings, he was totally unprepared for what happened next.

The meeting was scheduled at a local coffee shop. Tom was already seated when, from across the room, he glimpsed Archie enter the restaurant. He stood up and waved to attract his attention, and even from that distance, noticed a change in Archie's demeanor—more somber, darker than he remembered. A premonition of the difficulties ahead gripped Tom when Archie nodded a greeting and sat down without shaking hands, as was their custom.

"So, you planning on taking advantage of some of the new snow in the mountains?" asked Tom, opening the conversation with a familiar topic, since they both enjoyed skiing.

"Yeah, maybe," replied Archie in a distracted manner.

Tom struggled to keep the conversation lighthearted until the waitress arrived to take their order.

"I'd like one egg over easy on an English muffin, and coffee," said Tom.

"Just coffee for me," said Archie. The coffee shop had been his idea. "They have great hash browns," he had told Tom, who now expected Archie to order breakfast. Tom didn't want to eat alone. It seemed impolite, but that was now the least of his worries. A scowl of dramatic proportions had crept across Archie's face. Gone absolutely were his empathy, his sense of compassion, and the deep connection with a companion that was Archie's trademark.

"Shall we talk about the agenda for next week?" said Tom hopefully, referring to the pending executive committee meeting.

"I want to know what happened to Deanne," said Archie, broaching the only topic that was currently on his mind.

"Well, I let her go, as I said I was going to do."

"What do you mean? You never said you were going to fire her."

"Actually, I did," said Tom evenly, unsure of what was coming next. "Four months ago, I started talking to you about the problems we were having. I told you I was evaluating her performance and shared with you some of her work. Not once, but several times. Just last week, I told you we were meeting, and that I was going to let her go."

"You *never* said you were going to fire her."

"Okay, I never said I was going to 'fire' her, but I gave every indication of what was going to happen."

"Not to me you didn't. And she says you never provided her with an evaluation either."

"Of course I did. That's ridiculous. I would never do anything like this without a thorough review and evaluation."

"She says you never gave her any warning."

Tom tried to mount a defense without really knowing what he was defending. Already, the brief conversation had so blurred the boundary between Archie's personal interests and his school responsibilities that reclaiming it was impossible. There would be no more talk of "two hats." Of that, Tom was certain.

He reminded Archie of the times he had mentored Deanne. He recalled sharing a substandard publication of *Seminary Log* with him and reiterated their conversation of the recent past regarding Deanne's performance.

None of it had a discernable impact on Archie. "I just hope you're right," he said at last. I just hope you haven't exposed the school to a lawsuit. You know she's talking to a lawyer?"

Tom said he expected as much, and added, "Archie, I have an extensive file—more extensive than any I have ever collected in a case of this nature. I've consulted with an attorney, an acknowledged expert in school law. I can't prevent Deanne from bringing a lawsuit, but I can assure you it won't be successful."

"For your sake, I hope you're right," said Archie, the hint of a threat in his voice. "You know, Tom, this is not the Florence Bruce way. This school is like family. We take care of our own. You don't just throw people out."

"What do you mean? I'm not throwing her out. She gets to stay on the job until the end of February, and I've told her she'll get paid for at least two additional months after that. That's not throwing her out, for heaven's sake."

"She has a contract that runs until the end of the year."

"The contract is 'at-will,' Archie. That means we can each break it with appropriate notice without cause.[2] When you throw in all her other problems, Deanne is lucky to be getting as much as she is."

Tom had gone too far. Archie gave him a look of pure, unmitigated loathing. "I can only conclude," said Archie, his words slow and emphatic, "that you are pulling a power play and using Deanne to get at me."

Tom was shocked into silence by the accusation and by the look he had just witnessed.

"I sensed it when you refused to change the date of the installation. That was the first indication. Now this. There is no other explanation for your actions."

"That's preposterous," said Tom, glancing quickly around to see who was listening. "Why in the world would I want to get into a

---

[2] Tom was wrong. Deanne had a one-year contract that precluded her from being fired without just cause. According to labor laws, an employee with an "at-will" contract may be fired or the terms of contract changed at the employer's will, i.e., without any reason (so long as the reason does not involve illegal discrimination). If there is no express agreement regarding the length of time of the contract, it is generally presumed to be at-will.

power play with you? You're the president of the board. Why would I want to pick a fight with you?"

"I don't know, but you just have. If you want a power struggle, you've got one, and you should know I don't intend to lose."

For the next twenty minutes, Tom tried to break through Archie's emotional barricades, but to no avail. Archie didn't budge, and they parted without ever discussing the agenda for the executive committee meeting or any of the other pending issues affecting the school.

Tom returned to his office shaken to the core. There was an e-mail reply from Deanne waiting for him when he arrived. It was short and to the point. "I've asked Bud Calvert to represent me. When do you want to meet?—Deanne."

There was also a voice message waiting for him from Bud Calvert, a lawyer and Florence Bruce parent who was married to the president of the Parents' Association. "Tom, I want to assure you, this is not the start of a legal action," Bud said quickly when Tom called him. "Deanne is feeling vulnerable and doesn't want to face you alone. My intent is to act as a mediator to help you both get through this."

Tom was relieved, especially after his recent conversation with Archie. The last thing he wanted was a confrontation with Deanne. "Bud, thank you so much for doing this. You have no idea how difficult this has become."

"You should know that we're going to ask that you pay out her contract through June."

Tom didn't hesitate. After his conversation with Archie, there was no point playing games. He told Bud he would meet the terms,[3] adding, "I do have one concern. I told Deanne she could stay on the job until the end of February. Based upon what I've seen, I don't think there's any point to her staying on. She's obviously very angry with me, and I don't think any further purpose would be served by her remaining here."

Bud assured Tom he would see if that was acceptable to Deanne.

---

[3] By Tom agreeing to pay out Deanne's contract to the end of its term, the question of whether it was an 'at-will' contract became moot and rendered any legal action over breach of contract problematic.

They agreed to meet the next day. Tom had developed an appreciative respect for the work Trish Calvert was doing with the Parents' Association, and he and Allison had enjoyed several interactions with the couple. Bud was an acceptable choice for mediator, and Tom welcomed his involvement.

At the appointed time, Bud arrived without Deanne. "I just want to spend a few minutes with you before Deanne gets here," he said. Tom asked if he wanted to sit down, but Bud demurred. "This will only take a minute. I know this must be a very difficult time for you. My goal is to help you, Deanne, and the school get through what is obviously an awkward situation."

Tom's heartfelt reply and expression of gratitude were genuine.

"I think we're fine with the settlement you've proposed and with the change I mentioned yesterday. We will, of course, expect Deanne's medical and vacation benefits to also run through the end of June."

Tom acquiesced to the demand.

"I should also tell you that Deanne wants to stay on until the end of February, as you originally proposed."

"I'd be a lot more comfortable with that if Deanne showed any indication of wanting to work with me," said Tom. "So far she's been intractable. Now she's also very angry, and I don't see that her presence here for the next six weeks will serve any purpose. Why doesn't she just take the time to get her life in order and begin the search for a new position? We're paying her anyway."

"I think it's a little too abrupt for her. Her support system is here at school, and right now that's important."

Against his better judgment, Tom relented. What's more, he didn't want to do anything to further antagonize Archie. "Okay, but I'll need to see some indication that she's prepared to work with me."

Bud left, and five minutes later returned with Deanne. With the specifics already determined, the meeting was mostly a formality. Deanne sat quietly while Tom and Bud reviewed the various points of the settlement proposal. When the subject of her staying on through February was raised, Bud asked Deanne directly if she would be cooperative and diligent in completing her assignments. Deanne's face was devoid of all emotion. "Yes, I will," she said in a flat monotone.

As the formal meeting ended, Tom stood and walked around the long table to see his guests to the door. Woodenly, Deanne approached him. Tom stuck out his hand to accept hers, but she brushed past it to catch him in a stiff, awkward embrace. They were the same height, so her hair brushed against his face, her cheek touched his—but there was no scent, no softness, nothing feminine about her that he would later recall. Caught off guard, Tom's face flushed, and his mouth contorted into a self-conscious half-smile.

Tom's surprise did not mean that Deanne's gesture was unappreciated. For a brief time, he hoped the chaos slowly engulfing him might be temporary. Deanne would begin a new life without Florence Bruce, Archie would get over his anger, and they could get on with the business of running the school for the benefit of its young charges. Eventually, however, he would come to realize that Deanne's act of reconciliation had been carefully coached. It contained not an iota of spontaneity; rather, every bit of Bud's considerable powers of persuasion had gone into its staging.

The next day, drama teacher Corny Jolley opened her e-mail to read a message to the faculty from Tom: "Please join with me in extending our best wishes to Deanne Bakker for her future success. Deanne has announced that she will be leaving FBS at the end of February after 3½ years of loyal service to pursue another challenge. Deanne will not be truly gone, however, as her daughter Lexi will continue as a student in the second grade."

Corny sighed. It was only 10:00 AM, and she knew the rumor mill, already grinding away over Deanne's recent absences, would be in full gear. Deanne didn't have many supporters among the faculty, but she had a few who would certainly rise to defend her. And, even if the feelings weren't moved for Deanne, there was enough grist here to fortify the private agenda of any of the disgruntled and dispirited souls walking the halls of Florence Bruce. And as Corny well knew, there were more than enough of those.

Her concern for the committed, passionate new head in the office upstairs deepened anew. He spoke to them of excellence, but did he really know the price? She wanted desperately to believe in him, but with more than half a lifetime spent in these selfsame halls, Corny had learned to keep her head down. Her goofy demeanor, which served her well as a drama coach, also kept her off the radar.

She heard things and saw things because she was always close by and no one took her seriously. It was an act. She had learned that Florence Bruce, even when challenged to a higher purpose, did not tolerate well those who would impose their will. Mediocrity was far preferable to change.

That evening, Tom clicked off an e-mail to his sister who had spoken so eloquently at his installation. "Hi Kiddo, It's been one heck of a long week, and I'm exhausted. I finally fired the girlfriend of the president of the board. Unfortunately, the process spun out of control early on, and I'll be dealing with the repercussions for some time.—Tom"

A hesitant Mrs. Clayworth stood at the doorway to Tom's office, a hand poised to knock. Sensing her presence, Tom looked up, surprised. Despite her size, she had managed to make her way down the hall without the old floorboards announcing her arrival. Tom leapt up to welcome her.

"Mrs. Clayworth, how are you today? I'm just delighted to see you. You know you don't come to visit me nearly often enough." Tom was charmed by Mrs. Clayworth, as nearly everyone was. She was matronly in appearance with a military officer's erect bearing—shoulders squared, back straight, standing evenly on both legs rather than shifting from one to the other as most people did.

There was, however, nothing at all aloof or overbearing about her. In fact, a slight forward tilt to her head gave her a deferential aura, as if the entire reason for her presence was to provide service to anyone in her proximity. Proper to the extreme, Mrs. Clayworth wanted everything "just so." She was perpetually on duty day and night, weekends and holidays, hovering over a devoted house staff in search of perfection.

"Dr. Whitman," she began. In spite of Tom's request to call him by his first name, Mrs. Clayworth had told him it just didn't feel right. "I've asked to speak to you in person, because I'm afraid I have some rather sad news."

"Oh, I'm sorry to hear that. Please, come sit down." Tom motioned to the comfortable armchairs in the corner of his office opposite his desk.

"Thank you," she said, sitting down on the edge of a chair. She didn't lean back but crossed her legs at the ankle, positioning her hands carefully in her lap. "As you know, my mother passed away last year."

Tom nodded to indicate he was aware of what she was saying. A look of concern crossed his face.

"She left me a small inheritance." Mrs. Clayworth paused, searching for the right words, took a deep breath and continued. "I've been thinking of retiring for some time. You know this will be my twenty-sixth year at Florence Bruce. In the beginning, my husband Clyde was employed here in Portsmouth. But more and more his work took him away, until now I hardly ever see him. He lives most of the time in Los Angeles. I've been wanting to join him, but we just couldn't afford it until we finished paying off the loans we took out for the children's education."

A glimmer of understanding crept across Tom's face. "My God! How long have you two lived apart?"

"About twelve years. Now, with my inheritance, we can pay off the loans, and I can move to Los Angeles to be with him."

"Twelve years . . ." said Tom incredulously. "Why that's fantastic," he added, genuinely happy for her, although he immediately knew what it meant for Florence Bruce. Mrs. Clayworth went on to confirm that she intended to retire at the end of the year. There was no one, absolutely no one, in the entire school who would be more difficult to replace than Mrs. Clayworth. She was extremely competent at what she did. But more than that, she was a legend. She was "Mrs. Clayworth," and there would never be another like her.

Days after Tom and Archie faced off over Deanne's termination, the finance committee gathered in Tom's office to adopt a budget for the following year and to offer recommendations for the carefully watched increases in tuition. Saugus Wetherby chaired the committee.

Twice Tom had e-mailed Archie following their confrontation without receiving a reply. Now he watched the clock's hands approach the meeting hour with growing trepidation. The players began to drift in. The display of camaraderie was remarkable, as it always was at these meetings of the various board committees. Snatches of conversation, mostly revolving around recent travels and family news, careened around the room as new arrivals were greeted and absorbed.

Tom was talking with Saugus about kids and college when Archie entered. Brusque and businesslike, Archie paused for a quick hello with two other committee members and then moved toward them. He met Saugus with words of greeting, a hand on the arm, and a warm familiarity—but it was as if Tom were invisible. No acknowledgment, no eye contact, nothing indicated he was aware of Tom's presence.

Archie moved on, setting down his appointment book at the head of the conference table, and joined the others who were filling their plates from another of Mrs. Clayworth's delectable lunch buffets. Tom and Saugus took seats around the table where they could find them.

Saugus opened the meeting by asking Nancy, who had prepared the budget draft, to provide them with an overview. She spoke forcefully with the aid of charts and graphs of the need to trim the amount taken from the endowment to 5.5 percent. She recommended a four percent increase in the allocation for faculty salaries to allow for a moderate correction in the inequities that were being uncovered. She suggested a five percent increase in tuition, approximately what she estimated would be representative of other private schools in the area, to balance the impacts of reducing the draw on endowment, salary increases and inflation.

"Well done, Nancy. That was the best budget presentation I've heard since I joined the board," Saugus enthused when she was through. "You've obviously put a lot of thought into the preparation. So, let's open the discussion and see what you all think."

"I'm confused about the money we're spending on the new building," said Paul Alexander, whose $1 million dollar gift to the building fund had not yet been formally announced. Paul was being groomed by Tom for board membership and was one of only two non-trustees serving on board committees.

"You don't see that money in here," explained Nancy. "This is an operating budget, and the money we're currently spending on architects and a project manager for the new building is part of a capital-projects budget. It doesn't work on an annual cycle like the operations budget, but on a project basis. I'll be bringing that to you as we get the costs better articulated."

The questions continued around the table for several minutes until Archie's turn came to speak. "I'm concerned about this tuition increase. Our parents got hit with a huge tuition increase last year, and there were many complaints. People feel like we're charging whatever the market will bear, and some families are beyond their limit. I feel it's important to respond to their concerns. Every year, we've seen large increases in tuition. This year, I'd like to see us not raise tuitions at all."

Tom waited for Nancy—anyone—to respond. The silence was uncomfortable, but no one seemed inclined to break it. Impatience got the better of him, and Tom filled the void to explain the fundamental problem. "Archie, lowering the amount we take from the endowment by one percent will cost us about $120,000 in lost operational revenues. Each percent increase in combined faculty salaries is about $40,000. We can't pay for this without increasing tuition or taking the money from somewhere else."

It was a mistake. Archie looked at Tom for the first time. His eyes were cold and hard as the winter skies outside the window; an ominous shadow crossed his tanned features. "Our parents are rebelling, and I for one am not going to stand by and see them squeezed to the wall with ever-increasing tuition."

Nancy found her voice, explaining that funding at the current levels without a tuition increase would require tapping the school's reserves. Furthermore, every year forward would be impacted, requiring even larger tuition increases in the future if it became necessary to make up the difference.

Her argument was lost on Archie, who seemed uninterested in the financial consequences. By now, he had taken charge of the meeting, calling on people and directing the discussion. The engineer Saugus was unaccustomed to business-meeting dynamics and seemed oblivious to the capitulation of his chairmanship.

The rest of the committee, while empathizing with Archie's conviction, struggled to find common ground while staying true to their responsibility to bring in a balanced budget. In the final tally, Nancy was directed to rework the numbers and trim the tuition increase back to three percent. Archie left the room credited with the reduction while continuing to champion a zero percent increase. It would become a popular stand among parents.

The next day, Tom called Warren Hudson at the university. "Warren, I've got a serious problem with Archie Devlin. Can we talk?" A lunch meeting was arranged for the following day at a campus watering hole. Tom outlined the course of events leading to his termination of Deanne while Warren sat quietly eating a Cobb salad, interjecting a question from time to time for clarification.

When Tom finished, Warren said, "Okay now, you eat while I reflect on what I've heard." Tom smiled sheepishly, realizing he had been so caught up in the narrative that his lunch had sat untouched while the efficient wait staff had already removed Warren's plate.

"It's been clear to me for some time that Archie's relationship with Deanne presented the school with a potential conflict of interest. Now, it's no longer just a potential. The conflict exists. The question is what to do about it. Trustees need to constantly guard against conflicts of interest, whether business-related or personal. It would be convenient to believe that Archie will address this himself."

"You mean by resigning?"

"Yes, that would be one way. He could also break off the relationship with Deanne, but I suppose it's too late for that now."

The two men continued to discuss the options without making much headway. Finally, Warren asked if Tom thought it would be worthwhile for him to meet with Archie. "Absolutely!" said a relieved Tom. Warren was well regarded and the only board member with relevant management experience, the university being under a board of governors much like Florence Bruce. Maybe he could help Archie make some sense of the increasingly tense situation.

Two days later, Archie and Warren met in the same restaurant and, as it turned out, sat in the same corner booth. Warren ordered the Cobb salad. When they had been served and pleasantries done away with, Warren said he wanted to keep their dialogue open and above board—no secrets. "You need to know that I met with Tom Whitman a couple of days ago," he said. Archie, clearly agitated by the news, did not immediately reply. "I understand this must be a deeply disturbing time for you. It isn't easy when someone close to you is hurting. At the same time, you need to remember your responsibilities to the school. Trustees need to stay clear of specific management and personnel issues."

"Tom is the one being irresponsible here. He's treating the employees unprofessionally. He has no regard for their feelings. He's utterly insensitive. Did he tell you he was planning to dismiss Deanne with only a month's pay? This isn't the culture of Florence Bruce. Where is the compassion? Where is the caring that has always been a hallmark of this school?"

"Whether that's true or not, Archie, you need to stay out of it. You're too close to this to be objective, and that makes it a clear conflict of interest. You can't afford to get involved. Tom's doing what he thinks is best for the school. We pay him to make difficult decisions, and we need to support him when he makes them."

Archie was not listening and continued to press his case until Warren, his temperature rising, demanded, "Archie, listen to yourself. You're basing your entire argument on what happened to Deanne. She's very important to you, I know, but you can't judge Tom based on his decision to let her go and still be effective as president of the board. If this is the way it's going to be, you need to think about resigning."

At the mention of resigning, Archie's passion quickly quieted. "He's not right for this school," was all he said in response.

"Your responsibility is to support Tom and demonstrate that support within the community. Keep your disagreements private. In this business, the president is the head's number-one public advocate. You will succeed or fail together."

"But he's undercutting my authority as president. It started when he insisted on holding his installation on Veterans Day against my express wishes. Now this." Archie stood abruptly to leave. Taking a twenty-dollar bill from his wallet, he threw it on the table and strode out. Warren hurried to catch him, but Archie was younger and faster.

"Dammit," said Warren under his breath as he returned to the restaurant to take care of the rest of the bill.

"I'm sorry, but I don't think I had much of an impact on Archie," Warren told Tom two hours later on the phone. But he was wrong. Warren's words had had a profound impact, although not the one desired. Archie now realized that he could not depend on Deanne's dismissal and interactions with Tom to carry his crusade. He needed more ammunition, and was with Nancy in her cramped office at that very moment with a goal of collecting it.

"I just stopped by to see how you're coming along with that budget," Archie said cheerfully, poking his head in the door.

"I think I've got it," replied Nancy. "I managed to cut some expenses and we're going to defer a couple of maintenance projects. But I've got it balanced—of course, it's going to be tight, and we can't expect any surpluses at the end of the year."

Archie didn't care about the budget, but he covered nicely. "That's great, I'm glad to hear it. Maybe, if I leave you alone, you can get that tuition increase down to zero. Tell me," he continued, changing subjects, "how is Tom Whitman treating you these days? Are you two getting along okay?"

"Oh, Tom's great. He really understands this budget stuff."

That wasn't what Archie wanted to hear. He tried a couple more feints without extracting anything useful and then excused himself. With Peg, he tried a more direct approach. "I'm deeply concerned about some of the things I see Tom doing," he told the director of the Upper School. "He's spending too much time in the office. I never see him out in the halls with the kids."

Peg was accustomed to the shenanigans of slip-sliding young ladies and was sufficiently astute to pick up on Archie's intentions. Her disagreements with Tom were frequent, and she was not afraid to share them, but she also knew airing them now was out of place. "Archie, I realize you're the president of the board, but I report to Tom. It's awkward for me to discuss Tom's behavior with you. Why don't you talk to him directly?"

"I . . . I just thought I'd get your opinion."

"Well, I hope you understand my position; I have to remain loyal to the person I report to."

Archie had better luck with Everett. Everett interacted constantly with parents as head of the Middle and Lower schools and was known for a brusque, no-nonsense demeanor—especially if you were a parent with a child in difficulty, academic or otherwise. When these parents were also trustees, however, his tactics changed. Everett knew trustees were trouble. More than once, John had called him on the carpet for something he had said to a parent who also sat on the board. As far as Everett could determine, there was no rhyme or reason to it. Policies that applied to other parents often didn't apply equally to trustee parents. The board was a different breed altogether, and a low profile with them was the best strategy.

Everett didn't disagree with Archie, but he didn't agree with him either. Instead, he allowed himself to be led. Didn't he think Tom was spending too much time in the office? "We don't see him down here very much, it's true. But we're pretty far from his office," Everett replied carefully, seeking the middle ground.

Shouldn't Tom be visiting classrooms and having more interaction with faculty? "That would be nice. The faculty always appreciates it when the headmaster drops by," hedged Everett.

Tom didn't really seem to enjoy being around the students, did he? "No, I suppose that's right, he's usually focused on business." It wasn't much, but Archie would later bolster his case against Tom by attributing these quotes to Everett without the context of his leading questions.

Archie hit a home run on his next stop. Ellen Stein was chair of the history department and a resident advisor. Gregarious and social by nature, Ellen was well liked by students and an icon to parents, many of whom had placed more than one child into her care. Ellen was an institution at Florence Bruce and enjoyed an elevated status. More than once she had chafed at Tom's intrusions into her territory—something John had never done.

First, there was the incident with her ex-husband Gene, who she accused of harassing her after their breakup. To be sure, Tom eventually fired him, but it had not been quick enough to suit her. She resented the grilling Tom had put her through and his apparent willingness at times to side with Gene.

Then there was the budget incident. Ellen exercised considerable leeway over her departmental budget, as did all department heads at Florence Bruce. She was more fortunate, however, to have an admiring alum supplement her budget from time to time with contributions earmarked specifically for the history department.[4] That left Ellen with more discretionary funding than other departments enjoyed, and she was prone to hand out favors to her faculty, such as upgrades in accommodations at conferences or a pitcher of beer and pizza after exams.

After spending several hours with Nancy sorting out the intricacies of a practice that brought some departments more funding than others irrespective of any intrinsic need, Tom had questioned Ellen. "You have to be careful of how this looks. Other department chairs who don't have access to these extra funds are complaining that the

---

[4] Contributions earmarked for departments should be identified with specific departmental needs. Accepting a contribution for the discretionary use of a department creates a situation ripe for abuse and misunderstanding.

history department is getting special treatment." That comment came after Tom dissected her spending practices going back three years, while she had to sit and listen. It had been insulting. Ellen didn't pay much attention to budgets, and Tom had made her feel ignorant. As long as the money was there, she felt she should be able to spend it as she pleased.

Archie found a ready audience in Ellen, who was more than eager to add to his arsenal. "Tom just doesn't understand that this is a school and not a business," she told him with little prompting. "The people here are more important than money."

"Of course they are. Doesn't Tom recognize the important contributions you make to the school?"

"He micromanages everything. It's like he's looking over our shoulders all the time, as if he doesn't trust us to do our jobs." Ellen's use of the first-person plural was not missed on Archie. He assumed Ellen was speaking for others as well as for herself.

More than a week had gone by since the announcement following Deanne's termination, and she was back in her office halfheartedly scratching away at the assignments left in her portfolio. She and Tom had not met, conversed or even spoken by telephone, preferring instead to maintain distance and communicate via e-mail. A month remained until Deanne was to vacate her office, and despite a lack of enthusiasm for the work, she would use the time to good effect.

Shortly after 11:00 AM every school day, Kittery Hall came alive with the lunch crowd. Students were dismissed in three waves so as not to overburden Mrs. Clayworth's serving staff, and for the next hour and a half, the dining hall was in continuous commotion as students and faculty hurried to complete their meals and still have time for a trip to restrooms or lockers before afternoon classes commenced. Deanne came early and stayed late.

She occupied a seat at one of the two staff lunch tables. A few administrators and faculty who had crossed swords with her deliberately looked for alternate seating, but most plunked themselves down without regard to Deanne's presence. (Being too choosy often meant sitting alone . . . or with students.) Deanne was a member of the Florence Bruce community, and for the most part the community was unbiased in its acceptance of her.

Seated glumly at the table, Deanne looked as if the weight of the world were on her shoulders. No one had been fooled by Tom's announcement, and Deanne had no interest in fostering an illusion of normalcy. Within hours, the basic facts of her termination were common knowledge. Being let go from a job is always painful, and Deanne's anguish could not fail to evoke feelings of empathy from those around her. She didn't need to play a role at these times; her pain was real enough. But she was also cognizant of its impact on those around her and not indisposed to play it to advantage at her dining hall vigils.

At times she blamed the process. "This is just so unnecessary; if only I had been warned."

Sometimes she was petulant. "This school has changed; there's just no compassion for people anymore."

Or she let her anger show. "That man was so rude to me. John would never have done what he did."

When one group of faculty left for afternoon assignments, another took its place, and Deanne stayed. Exposure to her once or twice might have left a minimal impression, but the cumulative impact of her misery and gloom began to profoundly affect those around her. Gradually, Deanne's story, as she had shared it with Archie, was revealed sound bite by sound bite until Tom's cruelty and willful capriciousness were subliminally established in many of the faculty, who lacked the means to counter Deanne's account of her meeting with Tom.

Jackie was a frequent figure around the lunch table and recognized in Deanne a confidant for her own feelings of inadequacy. No one had been more distressed by Tom's arrival than Jackie. To John, she had been indispensable. His existence revolved around her dictation skills and the organization she brought to his chaotic life. Tom eschewed dictation and organized his own life. He valued her knowledge of the school and its history, but now he was catching up and occasionally surpassed her. Under John's leadership, she had been a valued, indispensable member of the inner circle, but her time now was given over to receiving phone calls, composing meeting minutes and doing odd jobs.

Tom recognized the problem, too. His previous assistant Penny had seemed able to read his mind and was usually a step ahead of whatever he wanted her to do. Publicly, he credited his past success to her skills, and her loyalty to him had been unshakeable. Jackie, on the other hand, appeared lost. Her chatty, gossipy ways annoyed Tom. His fast-paced style quickly outdistanced her, and, although he tried his best to include her, she was often left out of important deliberations, unaware they were taking place and unable to be of assistance to him in resolving them.

Tom's efforts to include her were not helped by her frequent absences. Jackie was not lazy by nature, and when the workload fell off, as it often did, she left Tom's outer office in search of someone to help or just to talk to. Recently, stress from the changes engulfing her work assignment had created a new crisis. Her psoriasis had flared up, and digestive problems left her contorted in pain after meals. An ulcer was suspected but could not be proved despite numerous tests and trips to the doctor. Between her absences for recovery and doctor visits, Jackie was not around the office very much.

Tom understood and empathized. He tried not to begrudge her the time she needed to heal herself, but he also couldn't help the fact that the two of them were growing apart—or that his need for her skills was diminishing, while his need for a different set of skills was increasing. He craved an efficient, trustworthy confidant with a discriminating intellectual sharpness. Jackie would never be that person.

Jackie confided her fears to Deanne. She had been at Florence Bruce for more than two decades and served under three headmasters. She was well paid, and the thought of finding another job was terrifying beyond words. In her fragile psychological condition, Jackie required a cause—somewhere to place the blame—for the despair overtaking her life and was highly receptive to the power of suggestion.

Deanne sensed Jackie's vulnerability and took advantage of it to advance her own agenda. "Don't you feel Tom lacks John's kindness and compassion for the staff?"

"Oh yes. Florence Bruce just isn't the friendly place it was when John was here. Tom doesn't seem to care that I'm in pain all the time. He just sits in his office at that silly computer of his."

"I certainly never see very much of him."

"Of course not. He's working at that computer when I arrive in the morning, and he's usually there when I leave in the afternoon.

You know, he doesn't have many visitors either—not like John used to have."

"I wonder," said Deanne, "if he was really a good fit for this school?" Jackie, sunk in her own misery, nodded her agreement, and felt the better for it.

CHAPTER XX

Arbitration

♠

The board's relationship with the CEO must be formed around the accountability of the position, not its responsibilities.[1]

Tom's apprehension deepened. He and Archie had not met face-to-face in three weeks, and the executive committee was gathering at noon. Archie's unconstrained anger and Tom's fear of provoking him created an impasse that neither man seemed able or willing to penetrate. Archie's self-generated agenda for the executive committee meeting held enough items to keep them in session until midnight; when Tom e-mailed him a suggestion or two for shortening it, Archie responded with imperial disdain—and ignored him.

To compound Tom's problems, Admission Director Craig Gowdy informed him that he would be resigning at the end of the year to move closer to family in the Midwest, his wife having recently had a baby. On the one hand, Tom welcomed the news, for it carried with it the opportunity to reconstitute the admissions department to

---

[1] Carver, John. *Boards That Make a Difference: a New Design for Leadership in Nonprofit and Public Organizations.* San Francisco: Jossey-Bass Publishers, 1990, p. 114.

his own design. Craig's lack of energy and increasing unwillingness to travel was stagnating the department. On the other hand, this was the fourth administrative departure to be announced this year, which could easily be interpreted by someone so inclined as a vote of no-confidence in his leadership.

Tom's apprehension was well founded. Despite a number of positive initiatives to report, the executive committee meeting was miserable from start to finish. Phyllis was absent for the second time, but more importantly, so was Warren Hudson, along with his stabilizing influence.

Archie opened the meeting pontificating on the necessity for open, honest communications, indicating that a breakdown had occurred in his communications with Tom. There was no quarrel there. Although this was the first time the group had met since Deanne's dismissal, all were familiar with the facts. Archie had already briefed them by phone, and most had several sources, including their own children, to keep them on top of events at school.

Tom opened his report with progress on the school's new crisis-preparedness plan. No one expressed concern that Florence Bruce was currently without such a plan, nor did anyone seem particularly impressed with the work that had been done—just impatient with having to deal with it again.

"When can we expect implementation?" Bodie Bickerstaff demanded as soon as Tom finished.

"We're planning a full day at the start of the next school year to get everyone up to speed."

"If this is important, shouldn't we be doing it now?

"Yes, of course," said Tom. "I would like to start implementation as soon as possible, but all our release days this year have been scheduled. The plan will be completed next month, board-approved in the spring and implemented next fall."

"Can we be implementing the part of the plan we've already approved?" Bodie continued to press in ever more strident tones. She seemed to Tom forever on the verge of coming unglued.

"Cut loose, girl, and chill out," Keegan O'Connor interjected, laughing and chiding Bodie's relentless pursuit. "We need to walk before we can run."

"You know me. I'm going to ask the difficult questions; that's what you pay me for."

"You go right ahead and ask them," said Archie, relishing Tom's discomfort. "We need someone to keep us honest."

Archie, preempting Saugus Wetherby, next presented the budget for approval and again moved that the school adopt a zero increase in tuition. The executive committee officially approved budgets, and within a few days, tuitions for the following year were to be announced to parents. The importance of this was not lost on anyone present.

Tom held his breath, but Saugus, the rightful chair of the finance committee, had found his voice. "I must object, Archie. There is no one who would like to see tuitions stay where they are more than I would . . ."

"What's the matter, Saugus, old boy? When you breed like a rabbit, you have to pay the consequences," laughed Keegan, referring to the four little Wetherbys who were currently students at Florence Bruce.

"Be that as it may," said Saugus, ignoring Keegan's humor, "we have to balance this budget. If we reduce tuitions any more, we'll have to cut expenses somewhere."

Archie protested: "Parents are being squeezed;" " . . . lose some students next year;" " . . . soon no one left but rich kids . . ."

"Let me see if I understand you," said Saugus, after waiting for Archie to finish. "You want to keep tuitions where they are. According to what was said at our finance committee meeting, that will put us about $150,000 in the hole. Where is the money going to come from? What expenses would you cut to balance the budget?"

Archie didn't have an answer. A number of suggestions were made that Nancy, who had been called in for the discussion, deftly handled. Cuts of the magnitude required were deemed just too drastic. Archie's motion was ignored, and the budget approved as submitted.

As the voting began, Keegan interjected, almost as an afterthought, "Archie, shouldn't we ask the head what he thinks? After all, he's the one who will have to live by whatever we approve."

Archie didn't object, and Tom was thankful for the opportunity. "I think this is a good budget. I agree with the three percent tuition increase." He lied, realizing his goal of a five percent increase was clearly out of reach.[2] "I'd like to see more, but three percent is reasonable and will give our parents some relief from the larger increases they've experienced in the past. Furthermore, one of the goals the board has set for this year is to match tuition increases with a demonstrable increase in benefits."

"That's right," Archie interrupted, suddenly seeing the opening Tom had created. "We can't increase tuitions because we don't have an increase in benefits to show for it."

"Actually, we do," said Tom. "You recall I reported last month that we were adding another week to the school year to bring Florence Bruce up to par with other private schools. It turns out that five days more of school is an increase of about three percent. We have a direct one-for-one increase in tuition equal to an increased benefit."

Archie seethed, but had no ready rebuttal.

The meeting dragged on until they reached the one item Tom was dreading. One after another he named the people who would be resigning at the end of the year and their reasons for leaving: the director of technology, Mrs. Clayworth, Craig Gowdy and Deanne Bakker.

Archie waited for Tom to finish. "I feel the list of resignations at Florence Bruce for this year is alarming. I want to know what the rest of you think. I believe it is something we need to look into, and perhaps, take action—"

Archie's antipathy toward Tom had become too blatant to ignore any longer. The tension in the room was palpable. Before Tom or anyone else could respond, Geoffrey Bellingham broke in. "It is becoming increasingly clear that our president and our head of school are at an impasse. Perhaps Dr. Whitman should have consulted more widely before certain actions were taken. Be that as it may, I suggest we ask the National Association of Independent Schools to help direct us as we resolve this situation."

---

[2] Private school and college tuitions often appear to increase at an inordinate rate, even surpassing the inflation rate or cost of living (COLA) increase. Part of this is explained by the fact that schools have few tools available to them to increase productivity short of increasing class size, which happens to be one of the few proven variables affecting student achievement. With no ability to increase productivity and with labor outweighing all other costs, schools often have no option but to lay the burden on tuition.

"I couldn't agree more," said Tom, immediately praising the suggestion. Archie followed suit, and Geoffrey volunteered to contact NAIS to make the necessary arrangements. *At least we have one positive outcome from this meeting,* Tom said to himself as the group adjourned.

Archie and Saugus were the last to leave. As they passed through the door, Archie turned around and came back, closing the door behind him. His face was a mask of fury as he approached Tom, not stopping until their noses almost touched. "You went to see Warren Hudson behind my back."

Tom flinched. "I met with him, as I do with all board members from time to time."

"You won't do it again. If you have anything to talk to the board about, you see me first." With that, he turned on his heels and left the office.

That evening, Archie called Phyllis. She had skipped the last two meetings of the executive committee largely because she was feeling overlooked and unimportant. The new administration did not sit well with her, and she was not feeling particularly charitable toward the school. "Hello, Phyllis. I'm just calling to let you know how much I've missed you."

They talked for some time, as there was much catching up. With five daughters between them attending Florence Bruce, the two parents shared much in common. As they talked, Phyllis recalled how fond she had been of Archie and how much she admired the noble young doctor who had left a successful career to care for his family after the passing of his wife. It was difficult, Archie had told her at the time. Young girls need a mother's influence, but he was doing what he could to make up for it. As she listened to Archie now, a tear came to her eye at the memory.

"I have some real concerns about what is going on at Florence Bruce," said Archie finally, "and I wonder if I can ask your advice."

"Of course, Archie. I'll be glad to help you in any way I can. You can always count on that."

Archie said he felt that decisions were being made by the head of school without proper oversight. He said money and the bottom line were overshadowing the compassion and caring that made Florence Bruce such a special place. Phyllis was surprised to hear that four administrators had already announced they were not returning when school opened in the fall.

"Deanne Bakker is one of them. She had a falling out with Dr. Whitman, and he fired her," said Archie. "You know I've been dating her—we have a relationship, sort of. It's been really good for my girls to have her around. Now I'm worried that my involvement with her might be coloring how I see things. That's why I need your help."

Phyllis understood immediately. "Of course, I'll help. Let me ask around and see what I can find out. I'll make plans to come to the next executive committee meeting. You can count on me."[3]

After his call to Phyllis, Archie sat at his computer to jot down his reflections on the meeting from that afternoon.

> Dear Phyllis and Warren, Sorry you weren't able to attend the executive committee meeting today. This is an account of what transpired. A copy is being forwarded to the rest of the executive committee for their review.

Before he was finished, Archie enumerated nineteen points, constituting a damning indictment of Tom's management of the school.

> . . . major deficiency . . . will not take 'no' for an answer . . . serious concerns . . . faculty were not involved . . . board not consulted . . . no one in favor of moving ahead . . . I hope this gives you a sense of the meeting. Let me know if you have any questions. With best regards, Archie.

A few clicks and the message went speeding through cyberspace.

Tom opened the e-mail that evening after dinner, and a cold anger engulfed him. Ignoring Archie's warning, he composed a message to Geoffrey and Keegan as the only two members of the executive committee besides Warren who seemed to have an open perspective on what was happening:

---

[3] I wonder what would have happened had Tom called Phyllis before Archie did. I suspect the reason Tom did not was his tendency to handle problems by himself and his hopeful optimism that things would work themselves out. Whatever the case may be, his failure to enlist Phyllis' assistance early on was, in my opinion, the major omission of his tenure at Florence Bruce.

> I find Archie's note offensive and riddled with mistaken ideas about his role and the conduct of a proper executive committee meeting. I am choosing not to respond to him in the interest of getting us back on track, but Archie is way out of line and for the good of the school, he cannot continue in this vein or I will have no choice but to return the fire.

A reply from Keegan came the next day:

> Archie was way out of line with his memo. I just want you to know that you have my full support, as well as my thanks for your self-control considering the circumstances.

Tom breathed a sigh of relief. *He does understand. I've just got to be patient. This will all work out.*

His reply to Keegan read:

> Thanks for your support. I feel like things are starting to come back together and I appreciate the real effort everyone is making to maintain a good working relationship.

Geoffrey was as good as his word, and within a week two gentlemen arrived from NAIS to arbitrate. One was the longtime head of a well-regarded school in Massachusetts, the other a respected trustee of several private-school boards, including a term some years back on the Florence Bruce board of trustees.

The arbitrators first met with the two combatants together. Barely waiting for introductions, Archie grabbed the opportunity to launch into a condemnation of Tom's management, or "mismanagement," as he termed it.

Tom sat listening to Archie's rant, interrupting only occasionally to correct a factual error—much to Archie's annoyance. Deanne was never mentioned as a reason for Archie's bias against Tom, but that bias came across loud and clear.

When Tom's turn came to meet alone with the two mediators, he used the opportunity to unburden himself, describing in detail his interaction with Deanne and Archie's response following her termination. Although the two gentlemen were careful to maintain a professional distance, he was sufficiently astute at reading body language to sense a strong empathy for his predicament and left the meeting confident of vindication.

It arrived four days later in a large envelope marked CONFIDENTIAL.

> This report is intended for the sole use of the Florence Bruce board of trustees. The comments herein should establish a foundation for reflection and, ultimately, action.

The first part of the report consisted of notes and impressions observing Tom's minimal experience with running a school but adding that this was well known when he was chosen for the position. The report acknowledged his known strengths—including fundraising, an important need for the school—and quoted verbatim the five goals approved by the board of trustees, concluding:

> The head has been in place for less than a year and, when he arrived was handed a substantial agenda. While some heads would have been given a honeymoon period, it is clear from the agenda set by the board in September that the new head was expected to get to work quickly. Active verbs and timelines set high expectations.

The report went on to acknowledge Archie's longtime membership in the school community while citing his lack of experience in nonprofit governance and his "social relationship" with the director of public relations. The timeline of the breakdown was described—a positive and productive relationship until after the holidays and then a turning point, which, coincidentally, matched Deanne's termination.

Tom read the report trying to gauge the reaction of the trustees to whom it had been directed. It was fair and unbiased in its treatment of the head-president communications breakdown, with an unstated but unmistakable empathy for the difficult conditions under which Tom had assumed leadership. Of Archie, it was a damning indictment:

> It is clear that Archie does not trust Tom. He speaks of his relationship with him in the past tense. His closeness to the school and his ample time to be involved in the daily

> operations suggest that he has not been able to separate policy responsibilities—the business of the board—from daily operations. He does not appear to have a clear understanding of the difference between being informed and making the decision.

Tom's spirits climbed as he continued reading:

> We cannot overemphasize the awkwardness and conflict of interest based on Archie's relationship with the terminated director of public relations. The school's legal liability must be considered in how this is managed.

And:

> In the event the differences cannot be resolved, one or the other of them should be asked to resign. We encourage the board to refer to the *Trustee Handbook* for guidance on this matter: 'Because the head and the president are partners, the premature resignation of a head is usually a sad reflection on the performance of the board president. If president and head differ too greatly in style to be able to work together, the president should consider resigning.'

Tom let out a whistle and leaned back in his chair. The problem and the solution were described in unmistakably explicit language. If Archie did not immediately change his stance, resignation was the considered outcome. Two days later, Tom received an e-mail from Geoffrey Bellingham directed to the executive committee:

> Here appended find the complete text of the NAIS report. It is largely fact-finding and self-explanatory but contains the following direct observation: if the president of the board and the head of school cannot mend their relationship, they should end it for the good of the school, and when a head of school and a board president have irreconcilable differences, the board president should consider resigning. I should be glad to have, in absolute

> confidence, your comments, suggestions and reactions.
> Sincerely, Geoffrey Bellingham

Beyond a doubt, or so it seemed to Tom, the executive committee was taking control of the situation, and so he turned his entire attention to the task of running the school. Job announcements for the four soon-to-be-vacant administrative positions had been distributed, and applications were pouring in. Another board meeting and a parent luncheon loomed, along with innumerable committee meetings. The self-study in preparation for a review of the school's accreditation was well underway, and basketball season was nearing a climactic conclusion with an undefeated varsity team.

CHAPTER XXI

Day-to-day

♠

The executive committee is powerful by definition and poses a danger if it usurps the board of directors.[1]

Winter was nearing its end, but precious little of that fact revealed itself. Dirt-speckled snow blanketed the ground. Twenty-five days without a sun break, and gray, overcast day piled upon gray, overcast day while the collective populace gritted its teeth and hung on. Tempers were at their shortest, and a meanness of spirit, detached and pitiless, hung in the air, infecting the affairs of those in its grip.

In the evenings, Tom found himself prone to napping in a lounge chair, his face upturned toward the light from a nearby reading lamp—a far cry from the four-season sunshine of Southern California. Perhaps the light-induced naps helped, for he remained remarkably upbeat despite Archie's dogged pursuit. Trudging from the Ahlborn House to school in the predawn hours, ice crunching under his feet, he savored the challenges before him. A great deal had been accomplished, but much more remained. Far out on the

---

[1] Duca, Diane. *Nonprofit Boards: A Practical Guide to Roles, Responsibilities, and Performance.* Phoenix, AZ: Oryx Press, 1986, p. 26.

horizon, he envisioned Florence Bruce Seminary taking its rightful place among top-tier private schools and fulfilling the promise of its auspicious heritage. Obstacles remained, but the school was going in the right direction. Of that, he was certain.

Phyllis Killam sat in her kitchen, sipping from a cup of chamomile tea, morosely contemplating the featureless gray landscape outside her window and listening to the drip of a cold, steady rain running from the gutters. The family had planned a Saturday skiing trip, but a warm spell had turned the forecast from snow to rain. After being rousted out of bed at 6:00 AM to begin preparations for the trip, the rest of the family had now gone back to sleep, but Phyllis was wide awake and alone, except for the cat nuzzling against her leg. She clenched her teeth and gave it a shove with her foot, but it was too small and too defenseless to relieve the indefinable rage that welled up and threatened to overwhelm her.

Her mind fell to pondering Archie's request for help. She had done her homework and found more than a few on the faculty eager to complain about the changes overtaking them and her beloved Florence Bruce Seminary. Phyllis deeply resented being ignored by Tom and took it as a personal affront that even now contorted her face at the insolence of it. At the same time, Archie's overture played to her dealer's instincts to broker an outcome. She was irresistibly drawn to the center of influence; she loved authority and delighted in the feeling of power it gave her.

She was determined to help her successor. Phyllis could not but realize the difficulties presented by the report from the NAIS intervention. Archie and Tom could not both remain at Florence Bruce, of that she was certain. The problem was how to tip the balance in favor of Archie. While contemplating the options, she felt herself warming to the task.

"Hello, Geoffrey? This is Phyllis—Phyllis Killam. How are you?" A few days had passed, and the outline of a strategy had formed itself in her mind. Geoffrey Bellingham, as board vice-president, was critical to her plan. Geoffrey was the archetypal college professor. He smoked a pipe, wore tweed jackets with leather elbow patches, and spoke in the slow, deliberate pontifications of a self-enamored academic. Greatly admired among the trustees for his pedantic discourse, Geoffrey's opinion would sway others to the cause.

"I've been extremely busy these last few months," Phyllis informed Geoffrey, "and haven't been able to attend executive committee meetings. Tell me, how do you think things are going?"

"Oh, well, let's see . . . There are a number of matters grinding away in the mill. As you probably know, we're preparing to break ground this summer on the new wing. Fundraising is a bit depressed, but we're making progress and just received a substantial gift to the campaign from the Alexander family. You know, the usual stuff." Geoffrey reached for his pipe.

"What's going on between Tom and Archie? I hear it's pretty ugly."

"It couldn't be worse," said Geoffrey, slurring the words as he attempted to light his pipe while holding the receiver to his ear with his left shoulder. "I'm sure you read the report from the NAIS mediators. It's a fair summary of the divergence between them. Archie's relationship with that girl on the staff is positively unfortunate, and Tom was downright brainless to let her go."

"Have you sent the NAIS report to the rest of the board?"

"No, I thought I'd wait to consult with the executive committee. We're meeting in a couple of weeks, and I've asked Archie to include the report on the agenda."

"Well, I, for one, don't think it should be sent to the board. It doesn't reflect very well on Florence Bruce and the more we can keep this unseemly mess in-house, the better off we'll be."

"You've got a point," replied Geoffrey, sucking deeply on the stem of his pipe. His lack of experience with the protocols of governance left him with inadequate tools to respond to Phyllis on informing the school's trustees on a matter of this importance.[2]

"You know, Geoffrey, as vice-president, you're going to need to assume a stronger role for the good of the school if this thing

[2] Nonprofit organizations frequently empower an executive committee to make decisions between board meetings on behalf of the full board or in an emergency or other special circumstances. Every source on nonprofit governance, however, makes it clear that the executive committee acts responsively to the board, not in place of the board. Geoffrey's eventual decision to keep the board uninformed of so important a matter was a clear error.

between Archie and Tom is going to be resolved. I suppose it's okay for Archie to continue to chair meetings, but he can't have anything to do with Tom's evaluation."

"I couldn't agree with you more; the evaluation must be conducted in an atmosphere of objective, unbiased inquiry," asserted Geoffrey. "I'm chairing the transition committee, which will be overseeing the evaluation anyway. I'll make sure Archie stays at arm's length."

"When does it take place?"

"We have the survey instrument in place. The plan is to distribute it to the board and a few faculty members next month. Then we'll compile the results, and the transition committee will issue a report."

"Don't you think," said Phyllis, choosing her words carefully, "that it would be a good idea to include all the faculty and staff in the evaluation, rather than just a handpicked few? I mean, how would you choose them?" Phyllis listened for a reply. Hearing none, she continued. "Geoffrey, you've done research. You're experienced in these things. Statistically speaking, you know the bigger your sample, the more accurate the results."[3]

Geoffrey was an anthropology professor. His specialty was anecdotal research into the oral histories of the Abenaki peoples of northern New England. Geoffrey didn't know the difference between correlation, cause and effect and a chi-square test, so Phyllis' flawed assertion went uncontested.

"I think you're the only person who can get us out of this mess," Phyllis confided as they concluded their conversation. "You've got to focus on the process and not let any bias for or against Tom interfere with the conduct of the evaluation."

Geoffrey felt a flush of importance at Phyllis' endorsement and vowed to exercise due diligence in watching over the process that was about to unfold.

* * *

> This Parents' Association has been very active. I think they are as enthusiastic as anyone in the school about

[3] Increasing sample size, when it favors one group over another, introduces a bias, thereby *decreasing* accuracy.

> having a new head—and new opportunities to pursue avenues closed off in the past. I have a feeling, however, that some parents are coming to this luncheon loaded for bear—they don't want any BS answers, and they want to be really listened to.—Peg

Tom mulled over the communication from Upper School Director Peg Scott while preparing for his luncheon with the Florence Bruce parents—an annual affair providing an opportunity for parents to meet with the head of school, ask questions, and learn about plans for the future. He took Peg's warning seriously and prepared for the meeting by shopping a half-dozen questions to Peg, Everett and a few others to help sharpen his responses to whatever the parents were loaded for.

The parent's luncheon was a lively affair held in Kittery Hall while the student body was confined elsewhere with box lunches. A fine buffet served up by Mrs. Clayworth's minions set a convivial tone for the discussion and questions that began as soon as Parents' Association President Trish Calvert opened with a few lines of introduction and this question:

"My daughter is a junior this year. I want to know if we are competitive with other private schools with respect to the number of graduates we enroll in prestigious universities?"

"Our main goal in college placement is to help find the right school for your child," Tom said, thankful for Peg's coaching on the subject. "The right school is not necessarily the most prestigious school. Having said that, last year we graduated twenty-one seniors. One went to Yale, one to Amherst, and one to Colgate. One in seven went to what most people would call 'prestigious' colleges. Florence Bruce is a small school, so while our total number of students going to elite schools may be low, the proportion of students going to these schools is high."

"Florence Bruce has a strong reading program, but mathematics is weak. We have a reading specialist for our Lower School. Why can't we get a math specialist, too?"

"You know, I . . . I'm not sure. That's certainly a possibility we can investigate. I wasn't aware the math program was considered weak."

Tom's faltering response hung in the air for an instant before another parent picked up the beat. "The math program here isn't weak. My older daughter transferred to Brentwood last year in the ninth grade, and she says she's way ahead of her classmates."

Another parent weighed in. "It *is* weak! Have you seen the results from the Iowa Tests? We're only about twelve percent ahead of the public schools on our math scores. Is that what we pay nine thousand dollars-plus in tuition for?"

And another, "Twelve percent isn't bad. I heard it was closer to eight percent. I would certainly support hiring a math specialist."

The temperature of the room began to rise, and Tom gingerly stepped in. "Let me do some research, please. I want to satisfy myself as to how Florence Bruce stacks up against the norms for other schools on the Iowa Tests. I'll report back to you next week. If it seems we need to improve math instruction, enrichment for existing teachers might be more effective than adding another specialist."

The questions now came at a rapid-fire pace, and Tom fielded them for over an hour on topics ranging from faculty evaluations to the new building construction to school uniforms.

Finally, Trish broke in. "It's getting late, and I know some of you have to go. We'll take one more."

"I don't understand why we teach Russian in the Lower School. Will Florence Bruce explore offering French, Spanish or other Romance languages?"

"The theory behind teaching Russian in the Lower School is that the Russian language structure, with its rules for verb tenses, feminine/masculine forms, and so forth, provides a strong foundation for studying other languages. Students are also able to study the Russian culture. In sixth grade, our students begin Latin, taking their understanding of language structure and applying it to the building blocks of the Romance languages. Beginning in seventh grade, we offer Spanish or French along with Russian."

Tom was exhausted, but he stayed on until only Trish and the cleanup crew remained. "That was a very nice affair, Trish. I really appreciate the opportunity to talk frankly with a group of parents. Usually, it's just one or two who buttonhole me in the hallway."

The following day, Tom received a note from a couple who had attended the event:

> We appreciate your explanation for the study of Russian in the lower grades. We think what FBS is doing makes great sense. Prior to the 'shoot the director' luncheon, we would have guessed that FBS made a bet on Russia

> having a larger influence in world economic affairs than it does and found it hard to overcome inertia.

* * *

Tom charged ahead on his board-assigned, five-point agenda. Deanne's last day had come and gone, so he no longer rounded corners fearing a chance encounter with her. Archie was as obstinate and critical of him as ever and continued to attend every meeting of every committee, always on the lookout to cast the head in as negative a light as he could.

Archie was an irritant, but Tom was patient and carefully maneuvered around him as best he could. The NAIS mediators had placed the onus on Archie to at least meet him halfway, but there was no sign of that happening. Certainly, Tom assumed that other trustees were cognizant of the NAIS report and were monitoring Archie's behavior.

The varsity basketball team was carrying a 12-0 record into the final game of the season with its crosstown rival, Brentwood Academy. Tom arrived early to a gymnasium already packed with cheering, foot-stomping fans. Florence Bruce had been abuzz all week with anticipation, and Tom noticed even some of the lower-school and a significant number of the middle-school girls in attendance with their parents. *That spirit thing,* he thought. *It's amazing the difference a winning athletic team can make in a school's perception of itself.*

"Hi, Dr. Whitman," shouted Sarah Johnson, a tall, African-American freshman who was one of the primary reasons for the team's success. "I'm so glad you came tonight. Your support means a lot to us."

He acknowledged her greeting with a broad smile and held up two fingers in a V. "We're gonna win this one, right?"

"You bet we are," Sarah laughed, and hurried off to join her teammates.

The Seminarians jumped off to an early lead but were down by five points at the half when Tom spotted Phyllis Killam in the stands. He got up and maneuvered his way through the bleachers, acknowledging well-wishers as he went, until he reached her bench and sat down beside her. "Phyllis, long time, no see," he said, his voice a bit raspy from cheering. "Jennifer is looking really good out there tonight. You should be proud of her."

"Hello, Tom," replied Phyllis, looking up a bit surprised. "Yes, she is playing well."

"How have you been? I've missed you at the executive committee meetings. There's a lot going on this year, as I'm sure you've heard." Tom searched for a subject to engage Phyllis, but found it difficult to keep the conversation going. He told her the new wing was on track for a groundbreaking in the summer and then asked her what she thought of the three percent tuition increase recently approved. Phyllis was cordial and seemed pleased to see him, but at the same time, cold and a little bit removed. She answered his questions, but there was a reticence about her responses and an unwillingness to fully engage him that Tom thought unlike her.

Putting aside his concerns, Tom raised the subject that had brought him over to her side in the first place. "You know, Phyllis, I've given a great deal of thought to what you said about Everett Laurie back at the beginning of the year, and I think I have a solution. I want to make him director of just the Lower School and appoint someone else to head the Middle School. Everett's strength lies in his lower-school relationships; it's always been the Middle School that has given him problems."

For a moment, Phyllis seemed taken aback. "That's an interesting solution. You know, it just might work." She seemed about to say something else, but thought better of it and stopped. She was not going to encourage Tom at this point; her loyalties lay too far from him now.

Just then the Seminarians emerged from the locker room to a cacophony of noise that made conversation impossible. Tom bid Phyllis goodbye, taking her hand in both of his: one in handshake position and the other resting on her arm. "I hope you're able to attend the next meeting. We need your wisdom and common sense," he shouted over the din.

That night, Tom downloaded an action-filled photo from his digital camera of Sarah Johnson hitting a jumper behind a pick set by Jennifer Killam. He e-mailed a copy to Phyllis with a short note of congratulations. The same photo would fill a half-page in the yearbook under the heading, "Varsity Basketball Team Goes Undefeated 13-0."

Filling four administrative vacancies was no small chore. Despite many inquiries and multiple file searches by Jackie, job descriptions for the positions appeared nonexistent and needed to be created from scratch. Convinced the burgeoning local food industry would yield a replacement for Mrs. Clayworth, Tom placed an ad in the *Portsmouth Tribune*. When a flood of applications began rolling in, Nancy took on the task of winnowing them down to three finalists.

A professional educators' conference in New York yielded multiple candidates to lead the admissions and technology departments. Abandoning his hope of attending any of the conference meetings, Tom devoted himself full-time to interviewing. He was anxious to find the right person to replace Craig Gowdy in admissions, convinced that his own legacy at Florence Bruce would hang on the selection. Two candidates emerged from the pool: one was a man in his late thirties from a school in the Southwest with sixteen years of admissions experience; the other was a young woman, an assistant director at a large school in New York.

Tom liked them both. The male candidate had proven ability, but he would cost half again as much to lure to Florence Bruce. The female candidate, about fifteen years younger, demonstrated a youthful zeal and many leadership skills that Florence Bruce badly needed—and, of course, she would be relatively cheap to obtain. He decided to bring them both to campus, and asked Jackie to make the necessary arrangements and schedule a round of interviews for them.

A local candidate was emerging for the technology position. She had held up well in initial interviews, but Tom decided to interview another candidate from a Pennsylvania school before making a decision.

The early spring months were a time of furious activity. Tom, unaccustomed as he was to the annual cycle of any school, much less this one, was amazed at the opportunities to enrich the regular curriculum in the latter half of the year. Field trips to symphony concerts, science museums and historical sites were a daily occurrence. Speakers costing multiple thousands of dollars were brought to campus to claim the attention of students. The entire Upper School even recessed for four days to engage in mini-courses that sent some students to Nova Scotia on a marine-science research project.

Allison immersed herself in trying to understand the extent of the school's myriad community-service activities. The subject was of inherent interest to her, and Tom had been unable to find anyone to explain to him the "scope and sequence" across all three divisions. A plethora of service activities benefiting the community appeared on the daily schedule posted in the lobby: food and clothing drives, fundraising activities, and off-campus visits to nursing homes, food banks, and shelters of various kinds. What was driving it? Why was one project chosen over another? What made a project suitable for first-grade students and another appropriate for juniors and seniors?

Allison described her discoveries one evening as she and Tom sat enjoying their regular evening repast. Gradually, the remarkable contribution Florence Bruce was collectively making to the Portsmouth community dawned on both of them.

"You must write this up," Tom told her. "It's a noteworthy story. I don't think anyone is aware of its full extent, even the faculty who participate with their students on a regular basis."

With Tom's encouragement, Allison continued gathering information and assembling it into a report. In the end, she discovered Florence Bruce was contributing to thirty-six separate charities. In cash alone, the annual total came to more than twelve thousand dollars. Tom planted the story with a reporter, and in May, a full-page spread appeared in the *Portsmouth Tribune* under the headline "Seminarians take community service a step beyond." For the second time, Tom had directed a frontal media attack on the parsimonious attitudes of the locals toward the all-girls private school he had been chosen to lead.

"Dr. Whitman, thank you so much for allowing us to meet with you this morning." The speaker was Carlye Nelson, one of the girls Tom had taught to ski six weeks earlier. She and another member of the junior class—representatives of the prom committee—were ushered to a comfortable couch and cozy armchairs arranged around a low coffee table where Mrs. Clayworth's staff had carefully arranged a tea service with small pastries.

"Of course. I'm always delighted when students take the time to pay me a visit. Now, what can I do for you girls?"

"We want to make this year's junior prom the best one in the history of Florence Bruce," exclaimed Carlye with a determined pout.

"Now that's an admirable goal I can get behind. How can I help?"

Carlye, who did all the talking, explained that the prom fund was too small to achieve the committee's vision. They spent a half-hour reviewing plans for the prom and discussing fundraising ideas before Tom said, "You girls have done a fine job. I'll approve a contribution of $1,500 to the fund, on one condition."

"What's that?" asked Carlye.

"I'm concerned that many of our boarding students don't know any boys to invite to the dance. I want the prom committee to help find dates for the girls who would like them."

"That's a good idea, but how are we going to find them dates?" asked Carlye, who had obviously never encountered such a problem herself.

"By sending invitations."

Carlye was perplexed, so Tom agreed to meet with the prom committee to outline his idea. Soon, an attractive invitation filled with all the wit, charm and dignity that a half-dozen creative teenage women could muster was mailed to a select portion of the male population of Brentwood Academy and two other nearby schools. As the day of the prom approached, the matchmaking took hold with a passion, and by hook or by crook a date was made for any young lady offering the slightest interest in an escort.

The junior prom proved to be, as Corny Jolley pronounced, "the best in the history of Florence Bruce"—and with almost thirty proms to her credit, there was no one more qualified to dispute the claim.

Every Friday, for Tom's edification, Jackie produced a calendar of the following week's activities, which was forever chock-full of surprises for the neophyte head. "What's Grandparent's Day?" he asked, coat in hand as he headed out early to help Allison prepare for a reception that evening at the Ahlborn House.

"Oh, it's when we invite all the grandparents of Lower School students to spend the day with us."

"And what am I expected to do?"

"You give a little speech in chapel welcoming them. That's all."

"Little speeches" are a constant in the life of a head of school, but Tom was not yet in a position to take them lightly. Every one presented an opportunity for him to communicate a message, often to an audience that had not heard from him and would be listening carefully. They were also rare "teachable moments" he was not prone to pass up.

"You are some of the luckiest people in the world," said Tom, adjusting his glasses and peering out across the sea of elderly faces in front of him. The turnout filled the front half of Hanley Chapel.

"You get to have all the fun of having children without any of the burdens. No diapers, no fevers or runny noses, no disciplining, no curfew enforcement, no nagging to get homework or chores done. You are indeed lucky. As grandparents, you enjoy all the innocence and sweetness, all the excitement and wild-eyed enthusiasm of your grandchildren. And it comes with very few drawbacks."

Now Tom removed his glasses and paused. Leaning out over his prepared text, he continued in a more serious tone.

"There is, however, a responsibility that comes with being a grandparent. We are, all of us, part of an unbroken chain that stretches back through generations into prehistory. Your generation and mine have supported the chain for quite some time. Now we are beginning to let go. And we are seeing the next links of the chain being forged right in front of us. While others do the supporting, we get to let go at our end and hold these new links while they are still hot and malleable, before they have any weight to support.

"In the time of *our* ancestors, our generation had an important job to do. It was up to us to convey the essence of this unbroken chain to the next generation. We told stories. We told the stories our grandparents told to us, and we told the myths that had passed from one generation to the next from somewhere beyond knowing. By doing this, we passed on the things we deeply cherished, the things that were important to us, the things we valued. And, in telling our stories, we passed on these same values to the next generation.

"Now this job is being taken from us. History books give us the facts. Science has taken the myths. Radio, TV and the Internet now compete to tell the stories. But the stories they tell lack heart and warmth, and they lack the values that are so important to us as a people.

"In welcoming you to Florence Bruce Seminary this morning, I give you this admonition. Resist the temptation to let TV and radio and the computer do your work. Find the time to communicate with your grandchildren. Tell them the stories from your childhood.

Tell them the stories your grandparents told to you. Within those stories lie the clues to the things that are important to you—the values that will guide your grandchildren to be good and responsible people."

Tom stepped down from the lectern to polite applause, and Everett Laurie took the microphone. In matter-of-fact, administrator tones he reviewed the planned schedule and answered questions. As the pews slowly began to empty, Tom moved down among the milling grandparents to return to his office. A man, frail but very erect, stopped him and said haltingly, "I appreciated your comments, Dr. Whitman. I will have to think about what you said."

The March executive committee meeting was rapidly approaching, and, as before, its organization was left very much in doubt. The agenda Archie passed around the table was substantially different from the one e-mailed earlier, and Tom lamented the circumstances that prevented him from being able to prepare adequately for the best use of their time.

It was almost a full house. With the exception of Warren, absent again to Tom's dismay, all the players were present. Archie opened the meeting and turned to Geoffrey, asking him for an update on the NAIS report.

"I've sent you all the report as I received it from the mediators, and I trust you have taken the time to read it through carefully." Geoffrey paused, looking from person to person around the table.

"Are you planning to forward it to the full board?" asked Keegan.

Geoffrey, abandoning his original intentions to put the very same question to the group, said instead, "My recommendation is that we not do that. By and large, the board is not up to date on the circumstances." Geoffrey emphasized "circumstances," and everyone knew what he meant. "They would lack the background to adequately process such sensitive information. Therefore, I recommend we keep the report within the executive committee for the time being."

"I just thought since the board is the official governing body of the school, they should be apprised of things like this."

Keegan's comment was right on the mark and Tom was about to second it, but Bodie chimed in at that moment with, "No sense getting everyone riled," and cut off further discussion.

The conversation moved on, and Phyllis smiled inwardly. She knew Geoffrey would play along with her plan and not even be aware he was doing it. Tom was stunned into silence by this turn of events, and was still processing the revelation that not only had the full board yet to see the NAIS report, but now they might not see it at all.

"As long as I have the floor," Geoffrey continued, "allow me to enlighten all of you on the process for Dr. Whitman's evaluation. As you know, the survey instrument we will use was prepared by Warren Hudson, Kay Johnson and by Dr. Whitman himself." He looked at Tom, who smiled back weakly in agreement.

"I have requested that Jackie prepare labels for the trustees, along with the staff and faculty. The survey, which will be mailed out the first week in April, will include a stamped envelope addressed to my office at the university. I will open each one personally and collate the responses for the transition committee to review. To guarantee confidentiality, all surveys will then be destroyed."

Tom cleared his throat to speak. "I just want to remind everyone that the survey is not the only evaluative instrument we crafted. You recall we spent considerable time defining a number of goals for this year—goals against which the school and my leadership are to be judged. I trust that while we are discussing my evaluation, sufficient time will be allocated for a discussion of progress toward meeting those goals."

"Of course," said Geoffrey. "That will also be part of the process."

"We'll put it on the agenda for the board meeting next week," Archie added quickly.

"Are you sending it out to the entire faculty?" asked Keegan.

"Why, yes," replied Geoffrey. "We want to be sure to give everyone a chance to respond and provide input."

Tom felt a lump rising in his throat. "I recall the original plan for the survey was for it to be sent to trustees and a select group of the faculty—not to all of them."

"The more people we hear from, the better. Naturally, we want our results to be as complete as possible."

"I understand your thinking," said Tom, "but you need to consider what you want from the results. There are twenty-eight trustees and about a hundred and thirty employees. From such a sampling, the views of the trustees will be overwhelmed by the views of the faculty."

"Tom has a point," said Saugus Wetherby in his customary booming baritone, "As Keegan said, the board is the governing body. Shouldn't our views be given primary consideration?"

Tom needed the point reinforced. The board had challenged him with an active agenda. He knew his vigorous pursuit of the goals laid out for him was making more than a few faculty members uncomfortable. It was entirely likely the trustees would provide him with a vote of confidence that would be overshadowed by a more tentative faculty. Before he could speak, however, Keegan interjected. "Saugus, no one would be so foolhardy as to not give your views full consideration."

Keegan's penchant for humor had broken the train of the conversation. Before Tom could gather his thoughts, Phyllis added with finality, "It would be difficult to decide which of the faculty to include. We need to include them all, or it wouldn't be fair." That ended the discussion, much to Tom's growing dismay.

Keegan's report on the building plan included a recommendation to send the project out to bid. He described a few alterations in the original plans to accommodate changes in conditions with the passage of time. They included renovation of a science laboratory and a student lounge for the Middle School, conversion of two classrooms to a music studio, and several room reassignments in recognition of expanding enrollments in the Upper School. The recommendations were the result of weeks of focus-group sessions with faculty and staff; they had been vetted through the building committee, which Keegan chaired, and the executive committee had received briefings in previous meetings.

Phyllis, who had not attended any meetings since December, became visibly more and more agitated as Keegan proceeded with his report. Finally, before he could conclude his remarks, she challenged, "Have these changes been approved?"

Keegan looked perplexed. "What do you mean 'approved'?"

"Something like this needs to be approved by the board. You can't just go making changes without board approval. This is the first time I've heard anything about changes to the plans, and I'm not sure I can agree with what you are doing." In fact, Phyllis was incensed. She and John had worked together for years crafting the original plans for the expansion. The thought that their work was now being disputed infuriated her.

"Actually," said Tom, breaking the silence that followed Phyllis' outburst, "these changes were the outgrowth of a number of faculty meetings, and they have been reviewed by the building committee. The basic plan is still the same. These changes affect less than ten percent of the project."

Phyllis was not mollified. She shot him a glance meant to silence any further comment and said, "Ten percent or not, these changes need to be approved by the board. I move we stick with the original plan as written. If the building committee wants to make changes, they need to bring them to the board first."

"I'll second that," said Bodie, pleased to support Phyllis and anything that appeared regressive. Archie also threw his weight behind the motion.

The stupidity of what had just taken place and Phyllis' ability to flummox the executive committee astounded Tom. An item of this importance would normally be taken up by the executive committee and carried on a recommendation to the board. Keegan's report was simply a precursor to just such an action. Keegan also knew this, but he was too unsettled by Phyllis' outburst and the vociferous support from Bodie and Archie to object. Phyllis had killed months of work on an apparent whim. He shook his head. The project would proceed and be out of date before it was even built.

The meeting continued, moving from topic to topic more or less at random. Whatever the subject, Archie quickly became fully engaged, forgetting that his charge was to manage the proceedings.

Tom reported that contracts for the following year would be released to the faculty during the first week in April, recollecting as he said the words that this was also the week the evaluation survey would be mailed. "I am very pleased," he said, "that we've been able to mitigate much of the perceived unfairness in the way faculty is being compensated."

"Can you enlighten me as to what was unfair about the system?" asked Saugus.

"Contracts have always been shrouded in mystery. There never has been a general understanding of why one faculty member might be compensated differently than another. That has created perceptions that lower-school faculty are paid less than upper-school faculty and that female teachers are paid less than male teachers."

"Is it true?"

"In fact, it appears it might be. Nancy ran some scattergrams that seem to show male teachers are paid more than female teachers."

Bodie erupted from her seat. "Are you accusing the school of a gender bias?"

"I'm not accusing anyone of anything. But there is a risk here, and I'm pleased—we should all be pleased—that it is being addressed."

"Well, all I can say is that if you're going to go around accusing people, you'd better have the documentation to prove it." Bodie fell back into her seat, letting her forearms bang the table to break her fall.

Oh, please. Tom looked at the faces around the table. Bodie and Phyllis would be termed out in June and would be leaving both the executive committee and the board. Tom wondered if he could wait that long and prayed for release as the meeting slowly ran out of steam. One discussion item marked "administrative departures" remained on Archie's agenda.

"I have been deeply concerned," Archie intoned, "at the number of administrative departures announced so far this year." He looked at Tom, brow furrowed. "Perhaps Dr. Whitman would be willing to enlighten us as to what he suspects is the cause."[4]

"I have already briefed you on the reasons for the departures," said Tom. "With the exception of Deanne Bakker, the other three are leaving for personal reasons. Mrs. Clayworth recently received an inheritance and is retiring to live with her husband in Los Angeles; our tech director is leaving to pursue a business venture; and with a new baby, Craig Gowdy and his wife want to move closer to their family in Michigan."

"But four in one year?" pressed Archie. "Don't you think that is a bit excessive?"

---

[4] It is not particularly noteworthy to have resignations announced early in the year. Recruitment for positions in independent schools, especially if the search is done in an orderly manner, routinely takes about six months. In consideration of their school, responsible employees who intend to give notice of retirement, or who plan to leave for other reasons, often announce in January or February.

"No, I don't. We have one hundred and thirty employees. If each of them stayed with us for an average of ten years, we'd expect a yearly turnover of about thirteen. The fact that we have four administrators leaving may be a little high but certainly not excessive." Tom wanted to say there would probably be more departures the following year as he sought to build and strengthen his team—but kept silent. Better not to open that can of worms.

"These are all sterling employees," said Archie, unwilling to let go. "How do you anticipate replacing them?"

"We have been interviewing extensively," said Tom, ignoring the fact that Deanne certainly did not fit Archie's description. "I am pleased to report that Margaret Jones has been appointed director of admissions. Margaret comes to us from the Dalton School in New York, where she is associate director of admissions and director of financial aid. Next week we'll complete interviews with the two finalists for the position of director of technology and the three finalists for the director of house."

Tom didn't mention the public relations position recently vacated by Deanne and no one thought to bring it up. Tom was already doing much of her work himself with help from Ruth and the development department; they would finish the year without a replacement.

Archie had had enough and didn't pursue his point. Seeds of doubt, however, were taking root in at least one of those present. Saugus Wetherby, whose exacting profession dealt in thousandths of a millimeter, sat deep in thought. His endorsement of Tom's leadership had been heretofore unwavering, but now: why would Craig and Mrs. Clayworth leave unless they were unhappy? It was a simple question with a simple answer, but Saugus, unfortunately, attributed the correlation between Tom's arrival and their leaving to cause and effect.

"I would like your input on one other matter," said Tom. "As you know, Everett Laurie is director of both the Lower School and the Middle School. Since I am new to Florence Bruce this year and covering the duties of both John Sanford and Roland Guyotte, I've had to invest Everett and Peg with a great deal more responsibility than they were accustomed to under John. Everett has always struggled with his middle-school assignment. His strength lies in the Lower School. I'm thinking of making him responsive to the Lower School exclusively and seeking someone else to oversee Middle School."

"How much would you pay a new middle-school director?" asked Archie, instantly alert and sensing an opening that would not have been present had the two men been conversing on a regular basis.

"That depends," said Tom, looking to parry but not sure of the direction of the attack. "I think about sixty thousand dollars per year is the going rate."

Archie pounced. "Sixty thousand is more than a one percent drop in tuition is worth," he snarled. "If you've got sixty thousand dollars hidden somewhere, you should have told us before this!" Archie was shaking with anger.

"It's not a *new* sixty thousand," replied Tom. "Everett will take on other duties; he may even teach. A new middle-school director would also be expected to teach and perhaps coach a sport. These are roles we would otherwise have to pay for. When all is said and done, a reassignment would likely cost no more than ten to fifteen thousand dollars."

"Sixty thousand is sixty thousand. I can't be supportive of this change until you can show me where the money is coming from. Show me the money, show me the money," repeated Archie, echoing Jerry McGuire.

"I understand Archie's concern," added Saugus. "I think we need more information."

Come on, Phyllis. You said this was a good idea; now give me some support. But Phyllis remained silent. She had bigger things on her mind and was not at all interested in bailing Tom out of trouble, even if she happened to agree with him.

Seeing no one step forward to shore up his position, Tom said he would continue his review and return to the executive committee when he had more information. That evening he said to Allison, "My hands are tied as long as Archie remains on the executive committee. No matter what I do, he will find something to protest. I've tried to connect privately with Geoffrey and with Keegan, but Archie finds out about it and raises a stink. I sure hope they do something about him soon; this simply can't go on."

She kissed him reassuringly.

The next morning, he asked Jackie who was on the list to receive the evaluation survey. "Did Deanne receive a copy?"

"Yes, I was told to include everyone who had worked with you this year."

"How about the maintenance and kitchen staff?"

"No."

"Why not?"

"Well, they don't have mailboxes."

They don't have mailboxes! Tom left Jackie's office shaking his head in disgust. Certainly, here was the clearest indication yet of whose input was considered valuable and whose wasn't.

CHAPTER XXII

Duplicity

The bottom line is that head evaluation . . . is ultimately the responsibility for the board and the board alone.[1]

Spirits were on the upswing as the faculty and staff of Florence Bruce Seminary made their way into Kittery Hall. It was late March. For the second day in a row, skies were clear, sunlight streamed through the tall windows overlooking the campus, and the shouts and excited laughter of children wafted through the halls. Classes for the afternoon had just been dismissed to make way for the faculty gathering, and boarders and day students alike were eager to be outside soaking up the sunshine.

Amid the pronouncements, kudos and repartee from those gathered in Kittery Hall, Tom's opening announcement that contracts would be distributed the following week subdued, for a moment, the extant clamor. The distribution of contracts at Florence Bruce had long been accompanied by considerable anxiety. With no provision for faculty tenure, no teacher was ever completely assured of being

---

[1] DeKuyper, Mary Hundley. *Trustee Handbook: A Guide to Effective Governance for Independent School Boards*. Washington, DC: National Association of Independent Schools, 1998, p. 118.

rehired the following year, and without a published salary scale, annual raises—or the lack thereof—were a subject that employees at Florence Bruce approached with trepidation.

John, in his day, was a wheeler and dealer, extracting favors and meting out punishment to supplicants. Extra duties, budget perks, room assignments and special deals in addition to salary enhancements were all tools he used to keep his faculty in line. His basic strategy was simple: reward loyal friends but avoid giving away any more than necessary. The lower-school faculty, who were mostly young and female, often received short shrift. "They are absolutely the worst negotiators," he once confided to Tom. "You can offer them anything, and they'll go away happy you didn't fire them."

Unlike John, Tom divided the responsibility for faculty contracts between himself, Everett and Peg. Together, they devised specific objectives to review with the faculty. Furthermore, with guidance from Nancy, they followed a strategy for eliminating the worst of the discrepancies in the salary range by capping the upper levels and directing available monies toward the most egregious examples of John's discriminatory handiwork.

At this gathering, Nancy distributed a pair of scattergrams to show the effectiveness of the strategy. Those teachers once farthest removed from the norm now fit within the general pattern, while sufficient variability remained to provide extra compensation for those exceptional teachers whose skills and willingness to extend themselves warranted special attention. Murmurs of understanding laced with appreciation flickered around the room as Nancy explained the scattergrams and answered questions.

After the meeting, a biology teacher, someone so close to the top of the scattergram plot that he had discerned his own placement, approached Tom and said, "I see that my raise this year will be a small one. I just want you to know, I appreciate what you are trying to do. If this will help fix the unfairness we all know is there, I will support it." In the scheme of things, it was a small gesture, but that evening, lying in bed, Tom decided it was enough to make the troubles with his recalcitrant executive committee worth it.

Before the faculty meeting adjourned, Tom advised the group that a survey would be distributed next week. It was an opportunity, he said, for them to reflect on their relationship with him personally and to comment on his leadership. Their comments would be used in a formative manner by the board to help him improve next year. They would also be used summatively, he cautioned, to determine his future at Florence Bruce Seminary. No one understood the significance of the distinction. "I sincerely hope," he said, "that you will treat this evaluation seriously and give it the time it deserves."

Jackie's head popped around the corner of the door to his office. "Tom, I need to make an appointment to see you, if that's okay."

"You don't need to make an appointment. What's the problem?"

"It's my vacation time. I've earned eight weeks, but Nancy says I can only carry over four." Jackie explained the problem had first come to light back in the fall. Nancy had instituted a policy change well before Tom arrived in an attempt to gain control of an out-of-control system for reporting sick leave and vacation time. Claims could not be verified since no records had been kept. Nancy had granted a year for all employees to use undocumented vacation time and bring themselves into compliance. The final deadline for taking the time had been the beginning of school seven months prior. Whatever was not used would be forfeited. Jackie had not used her extra vacation time last summer, as required, being so busy with the transition between John and Tom.

"You mean this issue has been hanging around all this time and you're just now trying to get it resolved?"

"Well, I never did understand Nancy's memos and just thought things would take care of themselves." In actuality, Jackie never bothered to read Nancy's memos, although she *had* assumed things would take care of themselves, and if they didn't, Tom would fix it for her like John had always done.

The more she talked, the more confused Tom became. Finally, he asked her to leave the paperwork and took it to Nancy's office for clarification. A few days later he responded, "Jackie, this should have been dealt with long ago. There are no records of all this time you are claiming. I tell you what; I'm going to split the difference with you. I'll authorize an additional two weeks, so long as you make arrangements to take them sometime this summer."

Jackie's eyes brimmed. She couldn't believe what she was hearing. "You mean you're not going to give me the vacation time I've earned?"

"I'm not going to give you all the time you're *claiming*. I'm very sorry, but frankly, I can't understand why you're bringing this to me now when it should have been taken care of when John was here."

As her ulcer kicked in, a bitter bile rose in Jackie's throat. Disappointment, fear, insecurity and anger rolled over her in wave after wave all that day. The pain was intense, and she left the office early after taking medication to sooth the convulsions in her stomach.

A week later, Jackie went down to the mailroom midmorning to place Tom's evaluation survey in faculty mailboxes; Nancy distributed contracts before she left the office at the end of the same day. Most of the faculty picked up both of them together when they arrived for work the following morning. Deanne, of course, did not receive a contract, but her survey arrived at her home, and she immediately set to work composing her thoughts on a separate piece of paper so the handwritten response would be free of errors and her meaning as clear as she could make it. When space for writing was filled, she turned the paper over and used the backside. When that was used up, she grabbed another sheet of paper. She had a lot to say about her relationship with Tom Whitman.

Contracts generated, by far, the greater interest among faculty. Some tore open the envelope in the mailroom, grunting under their breath as eyes found the sought-after figure announcing their salary for the coming year. A few did the math on the spot, computing the percent gain. Most hurriedly retreated to the privacy of classrooms or offices to peruse the two-page document. A small number, mostly female and mostly removed from the faculty mainstream, were elated at what they found. Finally, a substantial raise and recognition for the dedication and hard work they gave to the job.

The predominant response was one of resignation—another year with barely enough to live on; another year with a teacher's salary far below the mean for their education and experience; another year with too much work and too little recognition. There was little to cheer about. For many of these people, the survey was added to a stack of paper in the get-to-later pile. If time permitted, and often it did not, they filled it out by checking the boxes: mostly "good" or "fair" with a few marked "excellent," a few checked "poor," and maybe a comment or two added by way of explanation.

For a small group of people, however, the contract envelope did not meet expectations. An unanticipated change in assignment or a raise not quite up to par was cause for consternation or irritating to delicate sensitivities. For these teachers, the survey provided an opportunity for release, and they made sure to give it the attention it deserved.

A board meeting came and went. Archie lost control of the meeting almost as soon as it began, and the assembly found it impossible to stay on one topic for very long. Discussions on all manner of subjects erupted and fell back like boils on a pool of lava. Tom watched in dismay as the hours ticked away with nothing of much substance being accomplished. He contributed as best he could, but under the circumstances, thought better of trying to bring order to the chaos of the proceedings.

The building project was approved for bid—exactly as it had been defined six years previously—but no date for groundbreaking was set, leaving prospective contractors to wonder when they were expected to begin work. The budget, which had already been approved by the executive committee, was again approved by the board—a redundancy that didn't seem to bother anyone. Archie, pontificating on tuition excesses, led the discussion astray for twenty minutes while Tom drummed his fingers on the side of his chair wishing for it to be over.

By 5:30 PM, so many trustees had left that a quorum was lost. Archie's call to begin the next board meeting an hour earlier than usual to avoid running out of time was tabled—until the next meeting. As the dysfunctional meeting dissolved, Tom was left holding his report entitled *Year-to-Date Progress on Board-Approved Goals*. He was disappointed at not being given the opportunity to share with the board the major achievements of his administration. It was probably just as well. Tom concluded there would be another opportunity at the annual meeting in June to give the complete report when some of the problems with Archie might be resolved.

Tom e-mailed the next day:

> Hello Geoffrey, I've left a couple of voice messages and would like to speak with you. After yesterday's board meeting, I feel it is imperative for Archie and me to be able

> to sit down together. There is simply no communication between us. Can't we find a third person from the executive committee to sit in on a planning session so we can make these board meetings more productive?

Geoffrey opened the e-mail. He had a stack of midterm exams in front of him and a growing pile of surveys to contend with; the last thing he wanted was a conversation with Tom Whitman. He wrote back:

> I guess the third person will have to be me, but I'm up to my eyeballs in alligators right now, so we'll have to put off a meeting for at least a week or two.

Tom shook his head when he read Geoffrey's reply and went back to work.

Now well into April, the weather was steadily improving. The forsythia had already dropped its bright yellow blooms. Daffodils, tulips, rhododendron, dogwood and a menagerie of other plant life had burst from the earth in glorious color around the seminary. The end of the school year was on the horizon, and spirits were high. In between the occasional committee meetings that Archie never failed to attend, it was easy to forget the problems that accompanied his presence.

A week passed following distribution of the surveys, and those who intended to return them had done so. "Geoffrey, have you had a chance to look at those surveys yet?" It was Phyllis calling. Enough time had passed, and it was time to check in.

"No, I'm sorry, but I've been bogged down with midterms. I'll get to them tomorrow."

"Okay, well, there's no real hurry. I just thought I'd see how it was going. Actually, I'm kind of curious to see what we got. If you need any help, just let me know."

"Thanks for the offer, Phyllis, but it's a matter of confidentiality, you know. I promised no eyes would see these surveys but mine."

Eighty-one envelopes lay before him, which represented about two-thirds of the total surveys distributed. As Geoffrey opened and scanned the contents, he sorted them into separate groups, combining some and separating others, until a pattern emerged. When he was finished, one group, smaller than the others, contained fifteen surveys in which most of the items were marked "undecided" or "no opportunity to observe." A second group, thirty-five in number and the largest of the three, contained mostly positive responses and relatively few comments. It was to the third group, containing thirty-one surveys, that Geoffrey next directed his attention. These were generally negative with extensive comments, and in some cases, the comments went on for several pages. The surveys themselves, having been submitted anonymously, gave no clue as to the respondents.

As Geoffrey began to read, the blood drained slowly from his face. He was shocked at what he saw: page after page reproachful and critical, disparaging Tom's leadership of the school. Blunt, forceful and often repetitive, the comments were overwhelming, as much from sheer volume as from the sharpness of their attacks.

Geoffrey continued to read, trying to comprehend what he held in his hands. "Tom listens but seems to have his mind made up before he asks;" " . . . doesn't always comprehend what he is told;" " . . . appears to listen but does not." Geoffrey leaned back in his chair recalling a recent conversation with the academic dean at the university concerning his own research. The dean had seemed closed to his ideas from the very beginning of their meeting.

"The head is very focused on business as opposed to education and thinking about people. Money comes first—end of story;" "His decisions are based more on financial, business and management criteria than on program and educational policy." Again, a recollection flickered into Geoffrey's consciousness: My university's administrators don't understand the human dimension of education either and are constantly reducing the work we do to dollars and cents. Geoffrey chafed at the thought, his indignation driving objectivity before it.

Geoffrey disdained his university's overseers, whom he viewed as effete bureaucrats. They had, he asserted to anyone who would listen, fled the challenge and rigors of the classroom for the safe and sequestered cocoon of an office, a pronouncement that, in truth, masked a deep-rooted jealously at the elevated status shared by the university's top administrators and a covetous view of the perks they enjoyed.

Slowly, imperceptibly, a transformation began, and Geoffrey found himself identifying with the writers. "Tom seems much more skilled, comfortable, and interested with exterior constituencies—trustees, donors, and parents—than he appears to be with faculty and students." Geoffrey frowned at the memory of his university president, surrounded by "suits" at the recent alumni dinner, oblivious to the faculty at the next table and to the students serving the meal. The superficiality and snobbery of these administrators were an affront, and the whole affair had grated on him.

Geoffrey took a deep breath and, leaning back in his chair, propped his feet on the desk. He took his pipe from a shirt pocket and filled it from the tobacco pouch he kept in a drawer. Taking an old Zippo lighter from another drawer, he lit the pipe, sucking gently to draw the flame down into the bowl. Watching the smoke curl slowly toward the ceiling, Geoffrey reflected on what he knew about Tom Whitman. His only contact came at executive committee and board meetings, which, he admitted, had not been a showcase for anyone's talent of late. Archie's messing around with that girl had certainly thrown a wrench into the works, but he couldn't remember that Tom had been especially coherent or articulate during these recent meetings either, nor did he "lead" the proceedings, as one might expect from his position as head of the school.

He remembered seeing Tom in the brand new Volvo the school had purchased—a pretentious choice, if ever there was one. Geoffrey's image of Tom with neatly pressed shirt and tie was mentally juxtaposed with that of the university administrators with whom he often found fault. *Did we ever approve the purchase of that car?* The more he thought about it—comparing what he read to his own observations and circumstances—the more he found himself able to relate to the more vitriolic comments. By this time his pipe had gone out. He tapped out the ashes and reached for the phone.

"Phyllis, this is Geoffrey. I've just finished going over the surveys. There's some pretty interesting stuff here."

"What do you mean?"

"Some of these comments are highly critical of Tom, and there are a lot of them. I think we've got a serious problem on our hands."

"Perhaps we should get the executive committee together. Do you want me to help?"

"No," said Geoffrey. "I just wanted to get your advice, but I think you're right. I'll call around and see what can be arranged."

* * *

The executive committee, or at least part of it, gathered in Geoffrey's office to review the results. Archie was, of course, recused from the meeting because of his open conflict with Tom, and Warren Hudson had said he was not available until the week following. "We can't afford to wait any longer," Phyllis maintained, relieved not to have to contend with Warren, who she thought might present an obstacle to the conclusion that was playing itself out in her mind.

And so it was that Phyllis Killam, Saugus Wetherby, Keegan O'Connor and Bodie Bickerstaff assembled around a long conference table in a classroom adjacent to Geoffrey Bellingham's office on the campus of Concord and Franklin University to determine the fate of Florence Bruce Seminary and the new leader that had been installed a scant six months earlier.

Geoffrey opened the meeting with the quantitative results of his analysis: the number of surveys returned, the groupings, and then his surprise at reading the contents of the third group. Those negative surveys were then passed around, more or less at random, to the four recruits gathered at the table. For a while the only sound was of papers being shuffled and an occasional cough or clearing of the throat as the contents were digested.

Finally, Phyllis broke the silence. "Well, this is quite a shock. I guess it's time we ask ourselves if we made the right choice."

The question was too much to take in all at once, and for a while, no one spoke. "It seems pretty clear to me," said Bodie at last. "Whitman has to go." A shiver of anticipation went up her spine as it always did when she joined in a frontal attack.

"Are we really in a position to make that decision?" said Keegan. "Isn't this something that should properly be brought before the board?"

"That's a fair question," Phyllis responded, "but the board has delegated full powers to the executive committee to act in its behalf."

"That may be so, but this is pretty serious. Somehow, I think we need to get the full board involved."

"Keegan, you know this school. There is no possibility we could keep this contained. As soon as we get the board involved, we might as well send out a press release."

Keegan wasn't satisfied, but before he could respond, Saugus, who had thus far remained silent, spoke up. "I must tell you all I am truly shocked. Tom is a friend of mine. I like him a lot, and personally, he's never done anything for me to complain about—but this is too much." He picked up a stack of the surveys and set them down again. "If this is the way the faculty feels about him, in my mind, we have no choice."

Although he was unaware of the fact, Saugus had just perused Deanne's survey response, the fifteenth in his group. As he finished each one, a running tally had formed in his engineer's mind. Over ninety percent of what he had just read was critical of Tom.[2]

The conversation continued for over an hour. It was soon clear to everyone that all were in agreement—Tom needed to be removed for the good of the school. Although Keegan did not dispute the fact, he still argued that the board needed to be part of the decision.

"This is not going to be an easy thing to accomplish," said Phyllis, "and there may be some legal repercussions before we're through. It will be a lot easier if we have a unanimous vote. Keegan, it's your decision as to how you vote on this, but I will ask you once—only once, as a friend—can you go along with us here and make it unanimous?"

All eyes turned to Keegan. "As you can tell, I'm not in agreement with this committee going it alone without the support of the board. But, I can also see I'm outvoted. For the good of the school, I'll make it unanimous."

As chairman, with Archie recused, Geoffrey agreed to convey the committee's decision to Tom. Although it would be difficult to regard Geoffrey as enthusiastic about his mission, there was about him a sense of satisfaction at having reached a reasonable conclusion through the dutiful oversight of the process of evaluation. Later that evening, Geoffrey asked his daughter what she thought of Tom Whitman. "I don't think about him much; I really hardly ever see him," she answered.

---

[2] Mathematically speaking, Saugus was far more accomplished than anyone at the table. He was, however, unfamiliar with the uncertainties of surveys and social science research. He didn't, for example, account for the one-third of non-respondents, nor did he consider the large group of essentially positive respondents who simply checked off the boxes.

"Does he know who you are?"

"Maybe, I dunno. We've never spoken to each other that I can remember."

Geoffrey nodded, satisfied they had made the right decision.

"I left the results of the faculty survey in your mailbox last night. If possible, I'd like to meet tomorrow afternoon after school in your office to discuss the results. If this does not work for you, please call my secretary." Tom picked up Geoffrey's voice mail when he arrived at his office in the morning; a fat envelope marked CONFIDENTIAL was still under his arm in the stack of mail he had just retrieved.

Another envelope, black and silver in the colors of the junior prom, caught his attention. It was from Carlye. In the envelope was a beautifully hand-decorated card with the word "Thanks" written boldly across the front. Inside was a note.

> You were there for us more than any other faculty member. You are one of the reasons why this year's prom went so well. Thank you. PS: Enclosed is the prom committee's picture.

Tom smiled, deeply touched by the gesture.

Next he turned his attention to the contents of the fat envelope. Geoffrey had compiled the report, almost seven pages in all after the executive committee meeting. It was a fair representation of the results of the survey and, while tough to read, was not unexpected in its findings. Tom examined it carefully, viewing each paragraph through the analytical lens of his graduate training. The information would be useful. There were certainly changes to make, misperceptions to correct, and needs to address, but he noted the majority of the respondents were still with him after almost a year of significant change.

One sentence in Geoffrey's conclusion caught his eye: "These comments taken together are a cause for the most profound concern about the ability of the current head to continue on and succeed at Florence Bruce Seminary."

Whew, it was closer than I thought. Opening up the survey to the whole faculty was a mistake, but Tom didn't really have a choice in that. A head of school is fundamentally responsive to the board of trustees, not the faculty. Unfortunately, the opinions of the trustees were buried in the sheer number of responses. The process for his evaluation, sound at the beginning, was flawed in its execution. Fortunately, that process was only half over. Tom was confident his presentation of the year's achievements at the next board meeting would shift the balance back.

Still, in all, Geoffrey's concluding comment continued to bother him. He didn't share the report with Allison, saying only that he had received the survey results and would be meeting the following afternoon with Geoffrey Bellingham to review them. The comments were a harsh commentary on how his performance was being viewed in some circles, and he didn't want to unduly upset her.

Geoffrey knocked at Tom's office door and let himself in. He was stiff and formal, more so than usual. There was a foreboding sense of the inevitable about him. The two men shook hands and Geoffrey walked quickly to the conference table, moving around the end so that the table separated them. He handed Tom an envelope he was carrying and said, "I'd like you to read this before we begin."

Tom opened the envelope and extracted a single sheet of paper.

> I am writing to inform you that the executive committee of the board of trustees has decided not to renew your contract as head of school.

The world became suddenly quiet as Tom slowly contracted like a moon snail exposed on the tidal flats. He showed no outward emotion, save for a slight chewing at the corner of his lip, as he continued to read. He was glad he was sitting down. He learned that all salary and benefits would end June 30, as would his use of the Volvo, and by which time he and Allison were expected to vacate the Ahlborn House.

From somewhere in the eternal recesses of his soul, Tom found the strength to look up and meet Geoffrey's eyes. "I understood we were meeting to discuss the results of the survey. I guess there isn't any point to that now, is there?"

Geoffrey ignored him and nervously stood up to go. "I am authorized to extend to you the option of resigning your position, and would appreciate being informed of your decision on that point within a reasonable length of time."

Tom stayed seated. "I'll consider your offer and let you know."

Geoffrey left the office, closing the door behind him. Tom stayed where he was without moving, the letter still in his hand, slowly emerging from the place where he had retreated. Almost an hour passed before he got up to go, his body still numb from the shock of the encounter. Jackie had long since departed, and the building was nearly empty as he closed his briefcase, grasping the handle to lift it off the credenza. With floorboards creaking sharply underfoot, he walked the long hall to the stairway and descended into the lobby.

The sun was still well up in the sky and birds were singing in the sugar maple by the street as he crossed to the Ahlborn House. Allison heard the door open and shouted down from the upstairs bedroom, "I'm up here."

She smiled as he emerged on the landing, "So, do we still have a job?"

"I'm afraid not, honey." Tom bent down to place his briefcase on the floor and stood wearily again to face her.

Allison's face distorted in disbelief. She looked stricken, as if a lightening bolt had shot through her heart. He gathered her in his arms and the tears rolled down both their faces.

CHAPTER XXIII

Battle Engaged

♠

Unplanned departures can be disruptive to school enrollment, faculty morale, community perceptions, and fund-raising.[1]

Tom and Allison fidgeted nervously in the anteroom of the firm of Ruggeri, Cummings and Walder. Allison's eyes were puffy and rimmed red. She had spent two sleepless nights unwilling to believe the impossible had happened and reworking the few facts available to her, convinced they would eventually lead to a different outcome. So preemptory was the decision made by so few that it didn't seem real to either of them. At school and in the Florence Bruce community, things went on as before, so no evidence manifested itself to lead them to believe anything had changed.

Tom held a small, leather-bound folder carrying his employment contract and a few notes from the previous day's consultations with Roger Davenport, a colleague and head of Brentwood Academy, as well as Edmund Round, executive director of the New England Association of Independent Schools. Adrift after Geoffrey's surprise

[1] DeKuyper, Mary Hundley. *Trustee Handbook: A Guide to Effective Governance for Independent School Boards*. Washington, DC: National Association of Independent Schools, 1998, p. 120.

announcement, Tom was desperate for guidance, but who could he talk to? A message for Warren Hudson, the one executive committee member whose counsel and advice he could trust, had gone unanswered. Presumably, no one else in the Florence Bruce community was aware of the executive committee's action, and Tom didn't want to break the news until he was sure of his bearings.

"The hiring and firing of the head is the most important function a board undertakes," Edmund Round had told him. "In my experience, it is highly unusual and should be considered derelict for a board to delegate this authority to the executive committee."

"Unfortunately, that appears to be the case," said Tom. "The executive committee at Florence Bruce certainly thinks it has the authority. Do you know of other cases where a first-year head was dismissed in so abrupt a fashion?"

"It's certainly rare. I am aware, however, of one unplanned departure. There was an underlying factor of inexperienced trustees who urged the head's termination when parents grumbled too loudly. Her precipitate departure was a disaster for the school."

"How so?"

"Several of the better faculty left. Enrollment plummeted. It took the school many years to recover."

Roger Davenport had told him that a school will generally offer a multi-year contract to indicate that it is committed to the head's leadership for at least that period of time. "Continuity of leadership is a valuable commodity. The expectation is that the head will honor the commitment and stay focused on the school's priorities for that term."

"That's what I understood," said Tom. "The term on my contract is for three years."

"It is?" Roger was clearly surprised.

"Yes, I have a copy right here."

"Well then, you need to find yourself a good lawyer."

A young woman of about thirty, slender and dressed in a loose-fitting, gray pants suit, entered the anteroom at Ruggeri, Cummings and Walder and introduced herself as Elena Ruggeri. She was not unattractive, although her close-cropped chestnut hair, no makeup or jewelry—not even a watch—and reticent manner showed only the raw material. Tom wondered if they had made a mistake.

They shook hands all around and were escorted into a small conference room. "I've reviewed the contract you faxed to me pretty carefully, and your position seems sound." Elena had a calming effect on Allison, which, under the circumstance, overrode Tom's initial apprehension respecting the young lawyer's toughness. Besides, Elena's being female might play to advantage at the all-girls seminary.

"While there are some ambiguities in the language, it's pretty clear that you have a three-year contract. The school cannot simply *not* renew it. They can, of course, terminate you, but that isn't what they appear to have done."

"If the executive committee did terminate me, they'd have to show cause, and the contract says it cannot be done 'arbitrarily or capriciously.' This sure feels arbitrary and capricious to me."

"I know it does," said Elena, "but that's a very difficult thing to prove in court. The school wouldn't have to show much in the way of evidence."

"And here," said Tom, pointing to a paragraph in the contract, "it also says I have the right to a hearing before the board of trustees. Except for the five or six people on the executive committee, I'm sure no one else on the board is even aware of what's happened. I have a lot of support there. I feel that if I can get this before the board, it would be reversed."

"Is that possible?" asked Allison.

"I can't answer you with any assurance," said Elena. "The board is, however, the ultimate arbiter. If it wants to reverse this decision, it can."

Allison sat up taller. "We should fight. How can such a small group make such an important decision affecting so many?"

The executive committee's letter offered nothing in the way of a settlement simply saying that all salary and benefits would stop at the end of June—less than two months away—and that Tom and Allison were expected to be out of the Ahlborn House by then. "That isn't going to happen," Elena assured them. "You have a solid case here, and we can make things very difficult if they try to force the issue."

Aware that positions would quickly harden and fence-sitters would rally to defend the school as soon as a lawyer was brought into the fray, Tom elected to keep Elena in the background for the time being.

The next day, Geoffrey Bellingham called. "Tom, it's been two days. We need your answer."

"There are a lot of complex factors here. I thought I had a three-year contract. I don't understand how you can 'not renew' it after only one year. It also appears I have the right to a hearing before the board . . ."

"The question I need answered is whether you want to accept our offer and submit your resignation."

"I just don't know at this point," said Tom, stalling. "Frankly, I don't understand why I should resign. I just don't see any advantage in it."

"We just thought it would be . . . shall I say, *easier* for you to find another job if you resigned."

"Can you give me another day? I need to check on a couple more things before I can give you an answer." Tom was already sure resigning was not an option, especially without a settlement offer on the table.

"All right, I can give you one more day, but we can't sit on this any longer. We need to get the word out to the community before the rumor mill goes to work."

"If it's acceptable to you, I'd like to be the one to tell my faculty," said Tom, suddenly realizing the time had come to establish some control over his future while he still could. "I will meet with them on Friday, so they'll have the weekend to deal with it. Tomorrow, I will fax you a letter with my answer."

Geoffrey agreed, and the conversation ended. He dialed Phyllis Killam without hanging up. "I just got off the phone with Tom Whitman. He's talking to a lawyer."

"Is that what he said?"

"Not in so many words, but I could tell. He's brought up the fact that his contract is for three years, and he's talking about a board hearing."

"Okay, don't panic," said Phyllis. Geoffrey filled her in on the rest of the conversation, and they decided to wait for Tom's letter.

"John? This is Phyllis. I'm afraid this thing with Tom Whitman may turn nasty. Can you get me the phone number of that school lawyer we had draw up his contract?"

Phyllis and John Sanford had spoken several times about the executive committee's decision to get rid of Tom. It was John who had assured Phyllis in advance that the group had the authority to take the action they did. John had even contacted the female candidate who had been passed over when Tom was selected to succeed him. "She's interested if you need a replacement quickly," he told Phyllis. Retirement had not been kind to John. He felt lost and was floundering away from the familiar halls of Florence Bruce. It was good to be back in action, and he looked forward to more frequent encounters with his old friend.

Late that afternoon, Geoffrey heard his fax machine come to life. He picked up the single sheet of paper addressed to the executive committee and skimmed Tom's letter:

> Your letter stating that my contract would not be renewed was entirely unexpected. Since beginning my assignment, the welfare and education of Florence Bruce students have been foremost on my mind. They are still foremost. I am respectfully requesting that you rescind your decision and put the matter before the board. If the decision is irrevocable, then I request the opportunity to present my perspective to the board. I believe this right of appeal is within the terms of my contract. Whatever your response, I want you to know that I will continue to represent Florence Bruce Seminary throughout the remainder of my term to the very best of my ability.

"It doesn't look like he's going to resign," said Geoffrey to himself as he began calling executive committee members to bring them together for another "closed session" meeting. This time John Sanford would join their ranks at Phyllis' request.

When Geoffrey checked his computer, there was an e-mail waiting from Warren Hudson addressed to Archie and copied to the board:

> Dr. Devlin, please accept this as my official resignation from the executive committee and from the board of trustees of Florence Bruce Seminary. I am forwarding a

hard copy to Dr. Whitman for the school files. Sincerely,
Warren Hudson

Geoffrey expected Warren might be upset at being excluded from the last executive committee meeting, but resignation? That was not part of the equation. Hadn't Warren seen the results of the faculty survey Geoffrey had sent him? Clearly, the committee was only doing its job.

When Tom read the same e-mail, he immediately placed a call to Warren. To his surprise, Warren answered the phone himself. "What's going on, Warren? You must be aware of the executive committee's decision. Why did you resign?"

"I've been away on a business trip," said Warren, "and just read a copy of the letter you received. I wasn't able to attend the meetings of the executive committee when the vote was taken, and as you might imagine, I'm none too happy about it."

"You and me both, but I can't understand why you resigned. The executive committee has made all sorts of mistakes, not the least of which is derailing the evaluation process you and I created."

"I know that, and I'm truly sorry."

"I'm casting about for advice right now, and I don't know what direction things will take, but I may need your support. If this ultimately goes to the board, your vote would be important."

"Tom, you know I support you," said Warren. "But I think you'll find my resignation will have a greater impact than my vote would have."

Tom wasn't of the same opinion, but he thought too highly of Warren to disagree with him. As time went on, he came to understand the validity of Warren's words. No matter how many lies were told or how the evidence might seem stacked against Tom, Warren's resignation forced a residual of doubt into even the most hardened view.

Tom left the office early on Friday to fetch Allison before the faculty meeting began. They had begun the adventure at Florence Bruce together as a team, and they were determined to face the future together as a team. Allison was dressed in a navy-blue print skirt with a light-blue matching sweater set accessorized with pearl choker and earrings—modest, yet feminine. Her eyes were still puffy, but she was composed and determined to maintain her dignity. They had done nothing wrong, he had repeatedly told her. All their actions had been taken with the best interests of the students in mind. They had nothing to be ashamed of.

Together they crossed the street, hand in hand. The early May sun shone brightly, and the green of the lawn was as brilliant as when they had first laid eyes on it. Steeling their resolve, they crossed into the portico beneath the large granite lintel engraved, "Florence Bruce Seminary, 1784" and the smaller granite blocks on which was chiseled, "TRUTH WITHOUT FEAR." Tom opened the door and followed Allison into the lobby and straight into Kittery Hall, where the faculty was already assembling.

Allison sat in a comfortable armchair beneath a tall window while Tom stood at her side, a copy of the survey report in his hand. Sunlight, filtering through the canopy of the old elm tree outside the window, bathed them in its soft light as they watched people arrive for the meeting. It had been five days since his meeting with Geoffrey Bellingham—perhaps the most trying of his life. It would prove to be, however, only the initial skirmish in the battle for his job, his reputation and his dignity—a battle that was now fully joined.

Anticipation in the room was high when Tom started to speak. It was rare for a special meeting of the faculty to be called on such short notice. Something was afoot. "I appreciate your taking time out of a busy schedule to join Allison and me here this afternoon," said Tom, laying a hand on the shoulder of his wife.

Choosing his words carefully, he continued, "I have been informed that the executive committee has chosen not to renew my contract next year." A shocked silence settled over the room. No one moved. Here and there a gasp of astonishment escaped from an open mouth. "It is not clear to me exactly why the executive committee is taking this action, or whether it is legally defensible. I assume, however, that it is a result of the survey that was distributed to all of you a few weeks ago."

"I have a copy of the results with me, and, from reading it, I understand many of you feel that I have not been all that you expected." Here and there a head, still shocked by the revelation, nodded in unconscious affirmation while most of the faculty simply struggled to grasp the reality of what they had just heard. "If you would indulge me, I'd like to share with you my take on what you have said about me."

He looked up. There was no response. "Well, to begin with, many of you had some pretty bad things to say about me . . . but many of you didn't." Tom explained the distribution of responses, concluding that three-fourths of those receiving the survey didn't bother to return it, didn't have an opinion or were generally favorable toward his work. It was the one-fourth of the respondents with generally negative views that he would address next. "My expectation was that the survey was to have been used in a formative way to guide me in improving what I've been doing and to open important communications between us. It may be too late for that now, but I still think it is valuable for me to reflect back on what I've heard from your remarks."

"Some of what you have accused me of is, I think, accurate, and points to areas that need improvement. For example, you have said I don't listen." Tom read a few of the faculty quotes from the survey results to illustrate. "You're right. Sometimes I don't listen closely enough. I've been called a quick study, but sometimes I'm too quick. I've come to realize that many of the issues here at Florence Bruce are not as simple as they seem. I need to learn to listen longer and to try harder to understand. If I were to be here next year, that is something I would work on."

"Some of what you have accused me of is, I think, based on misunderstanding. For example, many of you think I micromanage, but that's simply not accurate. I'm new to Florence Bruce, and there is a lot I don't understand. The way I learn is to ask a lot of questions. I admit that I have probed and prodded many of you, but my intent has not been to micromanage you. It has been to better understand what it is you do. If I question you, it's not because I doubt you; it's because I don't understand." The tenor in the room relaxed as the shock dissipated from Tom's announcement. His reassuring remarks brought a few knowing smiles.

"There is, however, one criticism that some of you have leveled that strikes me to the core." The room again grew quiet as Tom continued in a lower voice. "A number of you, it seems, feel that I don't enjoy the company of children. You say I don't know the children's names and that I don't take an interest in their accomplishments."

Tom took a deep breath that caught in his throat. Laboring to maintain control, he continued, "As a career educator and teacher—having lived a life committed to the nurturing of children—there is nothing so painful as to be told that you 'don't enjoy their company.' I have, I admit, struggled to learn the names of our students—all four hundred and thirty of them—with only a modicum of success. That's because I was also struggling to learn all of your names, all of the parents' names and all the names of the alumnae. Most of you are faced each year with learning a couple of dozen new names. I was faced with learning about two thousand new ones."

Tom's confidence had fully returned by now, and his voice was firm and reflected a determination to stand and fight. A tear had formed at the corner of Allison's eye that would not go away. She dabbed at it with a handkerchief. "I visited each of your classrooms at least once this year. Allison and I attended many home sporting events, dramatic performances and the special events for which Florence Bruce is famous. Perhaps we should have done more, but the fact is that I was busy. My job is different than yours. I lie awake at night thinking about how to keep everyone safe, about how to provide all of you with modern teaching tools, about compensating you fairly, about how to find the very best teachers I can when one of you leaves . . ." His voice trailed off.

"My job is different than yours. It doesn't allow me the kind of everyday contact with children that yours does. *But that doesn't mean I care any less or enjoy the company of our students any less than you do.*"

Tom let his eye wander over the faces of the faculty. "I'm sorry that our relationship will likely end when this year is over. I can truly say Allison and I have enjoyed being here, and we count many of you as close personal friends. We have accomplished a lot together, and I hope you feel as proud of those accomplishments as I do. But, despite the turn of events, we're not done yet."

Tom hesitated and wisely decided against issuing a call for support. Stability in the ranks would best serve his cause now. "I expect my tenure to extend through the end of the school year, and we still have four weeks to go. Help me to put aside what's happened, and let's make this year as special and memorable for our students as we can."

Tom concluded his remarks and bowed his head, a hand resting on Allison's shoulder. The emotion of the moment threatened to overwhelm him and he fought for control, biting his tongue, focusing on the pain to keep his lip from quivering. Someone blew their nose and then the clapping started, restrained and respectful. It filled Kittery Hall and continued for some moments. As it receded, Ruth and then Nancy stepped forward, their eyes brimming with tears. Each woman took his hand in turn and fell into an embrace. Allison stood beside Tom as more members of the faculty and staff came forward in twos and threes to embrace them and to espouse astonishment at the turn of events.

The effect on Allison was powerful. For the first time she actually understood that only five people had made the decision to remove her husband—only five. Of course, there were others who wished to see them gone, but the greater majority still supported them. She steeled herself. "We'll fight them. We won't let this evil win."

Over the weekend, letters from Geoffrey Bellingham, vice-president of the Florence Bruce board of trustees, arrived in the mailboxes of the school's constituents. By Monday every faculty member, parent and school alumna had read: "I am writing to inform you that Dr. Tom Whitman will be leaving his post as head of school at Florence Bruce on June 30 of this year." Two short, throwaway paragraphs followed, one expressing appreciation to Dr. Whitman for his efforts and the other thanking the reader for continuing support. It was a bewildered community that began a tentative assessment. Why did the vice-president and not the president write the letter? Why was Dr. Whitman leaving? Had he resigned or had something else happened?

Tom, of course, was not consulted in the drafting of this letter. He faxed a copy of the missive to Elena, expressing his dismay that the news had been formally dispatched beyond the school walls. He still had not heard a reply to his request for a hearing with the board of trustees, and it seemed premature to announce his departure in this unambiguous manner.

On Monday, Tom played in the annual Seminary Shamble Golf Tournament, giving Archie as wide a berth as possible. Ordinarily a focus of curiosity anyway, Tom was now the subject of conversation on all eighteen fairways as golfers queried one another and eyes surreptitiously followed him around the course. Most were already aware of the animosity between Tom and Archie over Deanne's termination, and many made the linkage with Tom's dismissal. Parents who appreciated Tom's efforts on behalf of the school expressed dismay and helplessness over the situation. What can we do to help? Who can we talk to? Tom felt awkward and uncertain—at first declining comment and then suggesting that a call to Trish Calvert, the parent representative on the board, might be valuable.

On Tuesday, Deanne returned to hang out in Kittery Hall and gloat—she had won. The brazen audacity of her sudden reappearance was repugnant and most kept their distance. There were, however, those who saw a gain for themselves in the recent turn of events and encouraged Deanne and one another in a thinly veiled celebration of Tom's impending departure. It was a deeply divided faculty that struggled toward the end of the school year.

When Geoffrey heard Deanne was back in school, he called Archie. "Get her out of there. She only exacerbates the appearance of your conflict of interest. With Whitman on his way out, you need to keep your hands clean." Archie was puzzled by Geoffrey's intensity and, genuinely, did not feel that he had done anything wrong. He did as he was told, however, and three days after she reappeared, Deanne vanished from the lunchroom.

By Wednesday, the calls and e-mails from an indignant and concerned faculty overwhelmed the executive committee. A middle-school math teacher whose survey still sat in her "to do" pile wrote:

> Many of us believed the purpose of the Head of School Survey was to provide feedback for continued dialogue and growth. There was, in fact, virtually nothing to indicate the intent of the survey was to determine if Dr. Whitman's contract would be renewed. Knowing that such a pivotal outcome was entailed in this evaluation might well have inspired many of us who did not take part in the evaluation process to have done so.

Corny Jolley, who had seen more than a few heads come and go, cried in secret for the new head and his wife. Fearful of the sinister forces now at work, she warned of dire consequences, hoping to restrain her husband Buster as he replied to Geoffrey's letter in righteous indignation:

> For Dr. Whitman to be summarily dismissed without a process involving a sequence of corrective steps puts each

> of us employed at Florence Bruce in an equally vulnerable, and, ultimately, untenable position.

Geoffrey was worried. "Phyllis, this is getting out of hand. Whitman is making us look bad with the faculty. I don't know what he told them, but we're the ones getting blamed now for his incompetence. What did he say to them?"

"I know, I'm getting some of those calls myself. I don't know what he said, but we need to get our story out before this starts to snowball. I'll ask Jackie to set up another meeting of the faculty and we can address them ourselves."

"Good idea, the sooner the better. Let's see if we can't get some of the others on the committee to join us. We need to show solidarity."

"I'll call them myself," replied Phyllis between clenched teeth. She was angry. She wasn't used to having her judgment questioned, and the inquiries following Tom's dialogue with the faculty had been unexpected and unappreciated.

Less than a week had passed after Tom and Allison met with the faculty to announce the executive committee's decision when Phyllis, Geoffrey and Saugus stood before the same people to respond to widespread concern. "We are not at liberty to divulge the reasons behind our nonrenewal of Dr. Whitman's contract, for reasons of confidentiality," said Geoffrey. "Of course, this makes it difficult, because that's how rumors get started."

"It just seems so drastic," said Buster from his seat near the back of the room. "He just arrived. What are we going to do now?"

With studied nonchalance, Geoffrey said, "We had one headmaster; we'll get another one. The head of school is simply not that important." Even Phyllis couldn't contain her surprise as Geoffrey continued, "At Concord and Franklin, the president is gone for months at a time raising money, and it doesn't change what happens at the university." The absurdity of Geoffrey's statement was not lost on Peg and Ruth, who looked at each other with raised eyebrows.

"Is there any chance this decision will be reversed?"

"Absolutely not! There is simply no chance. If we had known that Dr. Whitman's meeting with you was going to go like it did, we never would have let it happen." The question had come from Ellen Stein. Emboldened now with such powerful allies, Ellen was to become a rallying point for any snippet that could be twisted or spun to Tom's detriment.

Miguel Barrera, who, despite sporadic disapproval, had come to an appreciation of Tom's contribution to the school, asked what—besides the survey—had led to the decision. Like many faculty, he was concerned that his comments critical of Tom might have been misinterpreted.

"The nonrenewal of Tom's contract does not rest solely on the survey," said Saugus Wetherby, entering the discussion for the first time and doing his best to support the others. "There were other . . ." And here he paused while Phyllis and the others wondered what he would say next. "There were other 'data points' from which the decision was made." His engineer's vocabulary had come to the rescue.

There were several requests by the assembled faculty for further explanation of the "data points," but Phyllis was quick to cut them off. The need to preserve confidentiality prevented it, she said. In actuality, there was no "story" the executive committee was willing to share. No explanation would ever come forth, and if pushed, those responsible would be hard-pressed to come up with any documented omission or failure on Tom's part.[2]

---

[2] Tom was discouraged from attending this meeting, but I saw it as a missed opportunity to face his accusers. Tom had a timid side to him, however, that I saw turn passive in the face of direct confrontation. I often wondered what would have happened had he been more aggressive in his own defense. At this meeting, he might have disputed Saugus' "data points" and forced the hand of the executive committee—although any public confrontation of the executive committee would likely have resulted in Tom being banned from the school for the remainder of the term.

CHAPTER XXIV

Dissolution

♠

It's up to the board to maintain control.[1]

A week passed without a reply to Tom's letter requesting a hearing with the board of trustees. Concluding that no response was to be forthcoming, Tom reluctantly directed Elena to formally enter the conflict with a letter to Geoffrey Bellingham:

> This firm has been retained by Dr. Thomas Whitman to represent him regarding his employment with Florence Bruce Seminary . . . . I am writing on Dr. Whitman's behalf to demand a hearing before the full board of trustees. Dr. Whitman's contract provides in pertinent part: "The head *shall* have the right of notice of any changes and the right to a hearing before the board of trustees" (emphasis added).
>
> Dr. Whitman's employment contract expressly provides that it is for a term of three years . . . . The executive committee's decision to terminate Dr. Whitman is, therefore,

[1] Duca, Diane. *Nonprofit Boards: A Practical Guide to Roles, Responsibilities, and Performance*. Phoenix, AZ: Oryx Press, 1986, p. 26.

> not a "nonrenewal" of the contract. Instead it is a material breach . . . . Please cease and desist immediately from making any further public statements representing that Dr. Whitman is leaving his post, pending the outcome of the hearing.

Twenty-eight copies were mailed, one to each trustee.

Three voice messages from various Florence Bruce trustees awaited Geoffrey when he returned from instructing his morning classes. He listened to the first one. "Geoffrey, what the dickens is going on here? Have you seen the letter from Dr. Whitman's attorney?" He quickly rifled through his mail while listening to two more messages with essentially the same content. The return address to Ruggeri, Cummings and Walder must be the letter he was looking for. He tore open the envelope and scanned the contents.

Within twenty-four hours the executive committee, all present except for Archie Devlin and the recently-resigned Warren Hudson, gathered to caucus in "closed session" with the school's attorney. Lyle Fain addressed the group. "I wish you had come to me earlier when you began this course of action.[2] Dr. Whitman's attorney is essentially correct. He does have a three-year contract, so nonrenewal is not an option unless you're talking beyond the three-year period."

"A nonrenewal seemed less harsh than a termination," said Keegan. "The guy tried hard, and none of us wants to kick him in the teeth."

"Be that as it may, you can't do it."

"Well, that settles it," Phyllis said with finality. "We'll just have to terminate him."

"There is also the matter of the hearing. You need to be aware that he has that option, and it looks as though he intends to exercise it."

---

[2] Mr. Fain said he would have advised the executive committee against unilaterally taking action in the first place. While the committee was granted broad authority to conduct the board's business, he noted that actions taken "shall not conflict with the policies and express wishes of the board of trustees." Although legally acting within its mandate, the executive committee abridged its "good faith" relationship with the board. The bylaws of most nonprofits and all tenets of good governance expressly prohibit an executive committee from firing the chief executive.

This was the opportunity for reconsideration that Tom was hoping for, but Phyllis, Geoffrey, Keegan, Saugus and Bodie looked at one another and decided that Florence Bruce would be best served by terminating Tom. They assumed that other trustees would see the wisdom of their action when the time came for a hearing. The committee directed Lyle Fain of Pierrel, Keeney, and Fishman to carefully backtrack when writing to Elena Ruggeri of Ruggeri, Cummings and Walder:

> The executive committee readily acknowledges that some of what was said in your letter regarding procedures to be followed is accurate . . . . The executive committee thought it might be in Dr. Whitman's best interest if the termination were characterized as a nonrenewal rather than a discharge . . . . Accordingly, the executive committee is rescinding the letter delivered by Geoffrey Bellingham to Dr. Whitman and will issue a new letter communicating a decision to terminate . . . . I have also been authorized to inform you that the executive committee—at least for the time being—plans to make no further public announcements or statements regarding Dr. Whitman's employment status until after Dr. Whitman has been given an opportunity for a hearing before the board of trustees.

"I have their answer, and I think you're going to like what you see," said Elena to Allison in a phone call. "I'll fax you what I have. Tom can call me when he has had a chance to read it."

"Does this mean what I think it does?" asked Allison, after Tom read Lyle's letter.

"It appears so. The executive committee has admitted they were wrong and that I have the right to take this to the board on appeal."

"And they'll support you, won't they?"

"I think so. It's not a slam dunk, but right now, I think I have the votes."

Three weeks had passed since Geoffrey had informed Tom of the executive committee's decision, and two weeks since Geoffrey's letter communicated the decision to parents and alumnae. Conversations throughout the community buzzed with speculation as new rumors circulated daily. Only the students of Florence Bruce, tumbling toward graduation and summer vacation, appeared oblivious to the swirl of innuendo and gossip around them.

Although Archie was not included in the executive committee's deliberations, he was among the first to learn of each new development. His expectation—that Tom would slink quietly away—was not fulfilled. Instead, Tom was very much alive and his leadership seemingly undiminished. Aware that his relationship with Deanne was a part of the speculation, Archie sought to deflect the focus to Tom's defects.

While Tom's attention was otherwise directed towards the press of school responsibilities and dealing with communications from the executive committee, Archie mounted a campaign of disinformation in the hallways of Florence Bruce and around the backyard barbeque circuit.

"Arch, when are we going to get that new wing started?"

"I don't know. The changes Tom wanted in the building plan pushed up costs . . ."

"What's this I hear about a survey?"

"The faculty is in revolt. They're all against him . . ."

"Did you guys fire him?"

"Tom's lied to us repeatedly. The board just doesn't trust him . . ."

"I heard he dumped Deanne?"

"He fired her all right—without justification, I might add. He doesn't care about people . . ."

"What's going on with our new headmaster?"

"He's making too many mistakes. He tried to change things too quickly . . ."

Archie's persistent barrage of criticism, in the absence of countering arguments, had the desired effect.

It was common knowledge that Archie's association with Deanne was a conflict of interest. But for many, Archie was also a good friend, and no one begrudged him the joy of a loving relationship—no one more than Trish Calvert, whose fondness for Archie went back many years to the untimely death of his wife. Trish was the parent of a fifth-grade student. She had vacationed with Archie and Deanne in Florida and watched their interaction with affectionate approval.

Trish also admired Tom and appreciated the energy he brought to the school. Constantly sought out by other parents seeking answers because of her leadership in the Parent's Association, Trish struggled with her conflicted feelings, but loyalty—loyalty to Archie and loyalty to her beloved Florence Bruce—gradually won out. "Tom had to go," she reluctantly told parents who questioned her. If asked to elaborate, she said that the faculty didn't support him and he had even lied to her personally.

"How so?"

"He assured me the changes he wanted in the new building would not increase the cost; now the new cost estimates are almost two million dollars over budget." She felt badly saying this, but with Archie's insistence that it was Tom's fault and without the enlightened perspective that the increase was actually the result of inaccurate estimates from long before Tom's arrival, what could she do?

Trish invited Allison to accompany her to a home-and-garden show to assuage her guilt. To Tom, she empathized, "I know this must be terrible for the two of you. If there is anything Bud and I can do, please don't hesitate to ask."

"We're doing okay," said Tom in reply, grateful for her empathy. "I know there's a lot of disinformation circulating out there. Just promise me you'll keep an open mind."

"Oh, I will, Tom. I promise."

"I'm so angry I could spit nails," Kay Johnson, who represented the Alumnae Association, told Tom over the phone. "The board is as much in the dark over this as anyone else. The executive committee isn't talking. I've called Geoffrey. He only says it's a confidential matter and the executive committee is perfectly within its authority. Now, he won't even return my calls."

"Have you spoken to anyone else?"

Kay named a half-dozen other trustees, and Tom wanted to know what each one thought. "Most are taking a wait-and-see attitude. They assume the executive committee must have its reasons. I told them, reasons or not, it's our responsibility to make decisions regarding the hiring and firing of the head."

"Kay, I'm in a difficult position. I've got a good lawyer who tells me we have a case. I'm being advised to go for a settlement, but Allison and I have invested a year of our lives in this school, and I think we've done some good here. I want to stay the course. I also don't believe the school is being well served by an executive committee—run by a president in an obvious conflict of interest—that shuts itself off from the rest of the board to make epic decisions affecting the entire organization."

"You know I've always supported you, Tom. I can't accept that you did anything so egregious as to deserve firing, but, simply put, I don't know that for sure. Nevertheless, I agree with you wholeheartedly that this is a matter for the full board to decide."

"If you believe that," said Tom, "there is a way, according to the school's bylaws, to get this in front of the board sooner rather than later. Five current trustees have to request a special meeting . . ."

"Do you think we can get five?"

"I know we can."

Kay agreed to provide leadership, and together they probed the list of trustees for candidates, dividing up between them the names of those who might be favorable to their cause. Tom agreed to approach Steve Harrison and Caroline Odum while Kay took the others. It was not a difficult sell, and all five agreed to sign a letter requesting a meeting:

> Pursuant to Article IV, Section 2(c) of the Florence Bruce Seminary bylaws, we are requesting that you call a special meeting of the board of trustees . . . to provide the full board the opportunity to consider Dr. Tom Whitman's future employment with Florence Bruce Seminary.

Steve Harrison was livid when Tom came to collect his signature on the letter. "But for that idiot banging his bimbo, this never would have happened," he blurted out in language more appropriate for the construction sites he frequented. On his own volition, Steve took it upon himself to prepare Archie to receive the letter. In a two-hour conversation, in which he alternated between stern, fatherly reprimands and overt chastising, he told Archie the Florence Bruce community would forever tie his relationship with Deanne to Tom's dismissal. "Is this the way you want your legacy here to be viewed?" asked Steve. "Archie Devlin, president of the board, and *scandal* linked together forever?"

Archie pouted. "It's not my fault. Tom was a disaster for Florence Bruce."

"It doesn't matter, Archie. The perception in the community is that you and the executive committee are conspiring to get rid of Tom because he fired Deanne."

"But I wasn't part of Tom's evaluation."

"It doesn't matter. The perception will become the reality unless . . ."

"Unless what?"

"Unless you bring this before the full board in the light of day. If the board votes to terminate Tom, then you will be acquitted in the eyes of the community."

In the end, a reluctant Archie agreed to schedule a meeting of the board to address the issue of Tom's termination.

"So, Tom, how're things going for you?" John Sanford had accepted Tom's invitation to join him for lunch at the Gables on Market Square.

Tom had asked for a table with some privacy, and they were seated at the edge of the main dining room by a window with a view of the old North Church across the street. George Washington had worshiped in the original church built in 1712, according to John—and Daniel Webster had preached there. Tom had acknowledged John's history lesson without enthusiasm. Their orders were placed.

"Not so good, I'm afraid, John. You're aware, of course, that the executive committee is terminating my contract."

"Uh . . . I . . ." John's poorly disguised attempt at surprise wasn't going to be persuasive, and he changed tactics. "Yes, I did hear that happened. I . . . I'm sorry, Tom."

"Yeah, well, I'm sorry, too. I thought things were going pretty well."

"What are you going to do?"

"The decision was made by only five members of the executive committee, and the board is pretty upset about it. No one can imagine why they thought a decision like this was within their purview. Have you ever heard of an executive committee taking it upon themselves to fire a head?"

"Uh . . . no, I don't think I have."

"John, the reason I asked you to have lunch with me today is to share some pretty ugly rumors going around about you. I don't have any reason to suspect they're true, of course, but I just thought you ought to know."

"Rumors? What rumors?" John was taken off guard by the unvarnished candor of Tom's statement.

"Well, to begin with, people are saying that you've been meeting with the executive committee—advising them, as it were." John's face took on a look of feigned astonishment. "They say you've even contacted one of the former candidates for my position—asking about her willingness to take over once I'm gone. People are saying these things. Of course, there's no evidence. But even so, actions like that would be considered highly unprofessional, and you know perceptions are so important."

"I . . . I just don't know what to say . . . I had no idea . . ."

John did not sleep well that night, and the next morning he begged off Phyllis' invitation to attend an executive committee meeting planned for later in the week.

Knowledge of Tom's termination by the executive committee spread outward from Portsmouth. As it circulated among the heads of private schools around the country, an outpouring of empathy bolstered Tom in his isolation, including this one from the former assistant head of Florence Bruce:

> Please know there are many of us who know both how and why these deplorable events happen. The first thing we know is that you, the head, are not at fault here. The board, in its entirety, has failed miserably in its single greatest charge and responsibility. You are a victim of the board's incompetence. Where was the partnership, the guidance, the counseling and support for a new head in any real way as he transitioned to FBS? Who were his confidants on the board? Where was his support group? You deserve better.
>
> Roland Guyotte, Bennington Academy

And another from an acquaintance of Tom's:

> How foolish and destructive to use a school survey to condemn the head. This was a blatant maneuver by some on the board to avoid responsibility for making the decision themselves. The responsibility for evaluation is the board's alone. No one in this business recommends a faculty survey as part of the evaluation process. John Littleford, the recognized national expert on head's compensation and evaluation issues, states, "Only the most naïve of schools would involve faculty or other representatives outside the board in the evaluation of a head of school." I am outraged.
>
> Josh Ortum, Cedar Break School

A former trustee wrote to Geoffrey and copied Tom:

> The apparently secretive and partisan nature of your letter has cast a damper of concern and suspense over Florence Bruce Seminary. Why did only you, the vice-president, sign this communication from the board? For what reasons did other members of the board—including the board president—apparently not concur with this announcement? Why is an issue of such community-wide import declared in such a nonprofessional, casual communiqué over your signature alone?

Paul Alexander, picked to serve on the board of trustees for the coming year, was incensed when informed of the executive committee's actions and defiantly declared his allegiance to Tom:

> I request that this letter be offered in support of a formal review by the board of trustees of the decision not to renew his [Tom's] contract. First, I believe the decision was not based on objective, measurable criteria, nor was it subject to fair process. The board of trustees set very general goals for the head of school to achieve during his first year. Among those goals were increased equity in faculty compensation, value for tuition paid, and progress toward achieving the fundraising goals of the

> capital campaign. From an outsider's point of view, I see evidence that he has made progress toward achieving each of these goals.

Daily, Tom and Allison received support from every quarter. Allison, especially, was overcome with well-wishers as she made her rounds. Parents approached her at the grocery store. Faculty stopped her in the hallways. Acquaintances unrelated to the school contacted her by phone. All this reinforcement left her upbeat. "Tom, the whole community is being supportive. Only five people made this decision. How can they win?"

Tom was more circumspect. Aware that things were not always as they seemed, he was affected by more sinister elements in the culture of Florence Bruce Seminary and urged caution.

"You are such a 'boy scout,' Tom," Allison responded. "Stop being so considerate. These are wicked people, and they deserve to be punished. Let's take off the gloves."

Arriving at school early, as was his custom, Tom found a manila envelope in his mailbox. "Personal and Confidential" was scrawled across its front. He turned the envelope over. Something about it seemed familiar, but he couldn't place it and headed off to his office.

Opening the envelope, Tom extracted a children's book, *Marvin K. Mooney Will You Please Go Now!*, a story about an obtuse Dr. Seuss character who refuses to leave despite considerable encouragement to do so. Tom was startled by a recollection. Whoever sent this was the same person who anonymously delivered *The Emperor's New Clothes* in December, he was sure of it. As before, there was a note. It read, "Change Marvin to Thomas and it's quite a read! Enjoy." Mildly offended when the first book arrived, this time Tom was genuinely frightened. There is a very sick person among us, he thought to himself as he tucked the book away out of sight where Allison wouldn't see it.

Despite a preponderance of support from the larger community, Tom was acutely aware that it would make very little difference in the eventual outcome. The power to change the executive committee's decision rested entirely with the board of trustees. First, he had to get in front of the board to present his side of the story. Secondly, his presentation needed to be sufficiently persuasive to carry a majority of the trustees, which could be even more problematic than getting in front of the trustees in the first place.

While Tom was convinced his position was strong and he could back up his case with documentation in the form of meeting minutes, e-mails and memos, he knew an element of unpredictability existed in the interplay of alliances among the trustees. He was well aware of the powerful protective forces that would come to the fore when some of them were challenged. He was, after all, an outsider, and these people had been together for a long time. This board had no familiarity grappling with conflict and no recent history of having been divided—even by one vote. Could enough trustees be rallied to his side? Could he overcome the prevailing culture with its old-boy network and behind-the-scenes decision making? So far he thought he had the votes, but would they hold when push came to shove?

For the third time in less than a month, the executive committee met in secret session on the campus of Concord and Franklin University. This time Archie was present and he held in his hand a letter with five signatures delivered to him personally by Kay Johnson. "I don't feel I have a choice. According to the bylaws, I've got to schedule a meeting of the board to discuss Tom's contract."

"The son of a bitch already has half the community up in arms. If we let him get in front of the board, we could lose this entire thing," said Bodie Bickerstaff with uncharacteristic insight.

Phyllis gave Bodie a look of resigned reproach. "We're not going to let him get in front of the board. Here, take a look at this section of the bylaws." She passed out a single sheet of paper. "I talked to Lyle this morning. There's nothing in the bylaws that says how soon the meeting has to be scheduled. It could be six months from now."

Keegan examined the paper in front of him "That may be true, but we can't postpone it that long without contradicting the spirit of what's written here. I just couldn't support that."

"I'm not going to argue your point. We don't have to postpone it that long anyway—just long enough to hold a meeting of our own where we get to present our side."

"What do you mean?" asked Saugus.

"It was Lyle's idea. We schedule our own special meeting ten days from now. The announcement will carry only one item: a *discussion* of the decision to terminate Whitman. It will be for discussion only; no vote will be taken. That way we can maintain control."

"How will we keep someone from making a motion to take a vote?" asked Keegan.

"Read the next section in the bylaws," said Phyllis, obviously enjoying herself. "It says, 'No business other than that stated in the notice shall be transacted at special meetings.' If we word the announcement correctly, they can't vote on the termination. The bylaws won't allow it."

Keegan was obviously disturbed. "This seems like trickery to me. I've always said this was something that the board needed to decide."

"Do you want to look like a fool?" hissed Phyllis. "You let Whitman get in front of the board like Bodie says, and he just might carry it. How do you think that will make us look?"

The others nodded in agreement.

Archie, who suffered no qualms at all over Phyllis' suggestion, said, "I, for one, like the idea. Tom is simply unqualified to head this school, and I welcome the opportunity to talk to the board about what we've uncovered."

"There's a problem with that," said Phyllis softly. She hated what she was about to do, but there was no help for it. Her original objective to protect Archie had been superseded by the need to prevail at all costs. "Lyle also says we can't go into that meeting with you as president. Whitman's claiming a conflict of interest on your part, and, if this goes to court, I'm afraid you're going to be at the center of it."

"Well, if it's for the good of the school, I'm more than willing to step aside for this meeting."

"No, Archie, I'm afraid you don't understand. You have to resign as president of the board altogether."[3]

---

[3] Lyle told Phyllis that Archie needed to resign from the board, too, not just as president of the board; she had pleaded with him to reconsider. "It your choice," Lyle told her, "but you'd better make sure this doesn't get to court. You folks have dug yourselves in pretty deep. Even if you win in the end, every sordid detail of that fellow's peccadilloes is going to be exposed to the whole world."

"I . . . I have to resign?"

"I'm sorry."

Archie was stunned by the betrayal. His handsome face went slack. Without another word, he got up and left the building. Those remaining behind heard the squeal of his tires as he exited the parking lot."

The five others moved on to the next item on the informal agenda. Already stung from criticism over their cavalier treatment of Tom and aware of the need for an incentive to keep him from litigating, the committee considered a settlement offer. Bodie was for holding firm and damn the consequences. "He doesn't deserve a nickel," she said, ready for a fight, but the others knew the situation called for a pragmatic solution.

What was the minimum amount they could offer to insure Tom wouldn't take them to court? It was determined that one year's salary should be sufficient incentive in turn for his resignation. "I think I know Tom pretty well," said Keegan. "He's stubborn and idealistic. I know he means to have his say. Can we give him an opportunity to address the board, say whatever he wants, after he resigns?"

Reluctantly Phyllis agreed that he was probably right. "The annual meeting in June is a good time. Provided we already have his resignation, we'll give him a chance to speak then."

A special meeting of the board of trustees was scheduled ten days out, and announcements were sent. Despite a flurry of calls between Tom and his trustee support group, there was nothing they could do to change the agenda to allow a vote. Phyllis had been right.

Phyllis and Geoffrey opened the meeting with nineteen trustees in attendance—plus the five executive committee proselytes. Issues of trust and the sharing of information, they said, coupled with the survey results, led to their decision to terminate Tom. A few anecdotal examples were offered alluding to larger issues too complex to review in detail. Archie's contribution to the debacle was not once mentioned. The presentation was, however, persuasive in the absence of a counter-argument, and before it was over, a half-dozen undecideds had begun to wonder if Tom had, in fact, been a good choice for Florence Bruce.

Next, Lyle Fain, attired in pinstripe business suit with vest and pocket watch, took the floor. His analysis of Tom's employment contract, the school's bylaws and the executive committee's decision to terminate Tom was exhaustive. Yes, the legal authority of the executive committee to act as it did was firm. The message hidden in the analysis, however, was that the situation was tenuous. Lyle was splitting hairs that might just as easily be split the other way by a sympathetic jury. The consequences to the school and its reputation were profound if resolution did not come quickly. Several of those who remained committed to Tom were visibly moved by what they heard. Despite a desire to correct an injustice, it was the school they held in trust, and protecting Florence Bruce was their primary responsibility.

Finally, Keegan and Saugus revealed that the committee was prepared to offer Tom a settlement. Although no official vote was allowed, a show of hands, indicating a consensus, determined that it was fair.

As agreed, Archie did not attend the special meeting. Instead, he sat in the privacy of his study overcome with the emotion of his resignation. Gone now were the days when empathetic friends surrounded him, showering him with their affection and admiration for his commitment to Florence Bruce, his stalwart parenting and his devotion to his dead wife's memory. Anger welled up over the unfairness of it. Hadn't he only done what was best to protect the school? Couldn't people see that?

The phone rang. "I'm . . . I'm sorry, Deanne, but not tonight. I've got to work late on a report for the school."

"It's that damn Tom Whitman, isn't it?" she demanded, in a rare display of anger.

"Yes, I'm afraid so. We fired him, but he isn't leaving, and now they've asked me to resign as president."

"Poor baby, can't I come over? I'll cook you and the girls a nice dinner. After they go to bed, maybe we can have some time to ourselves and have a little . . . fun."

"Not tonight. Maybe tomorrow. I've just got too much work," Archie lied. In truth, he didn't want to be seen with her. He was taking the girls to a movie tonight and other parents would be there, too. Archie's feelings for Deanne were cooling. When they were together, acquaintances subtly avoided them, but he could feel their eyes—eyes that showed not softness and admiration but that gawked in reproach.

Deanne hung up the phone, cursing under her breath. Archie had not fooled her. She took a glass from the cupboard, slammed the door, and rummaged around in the freezer for a handful of ice.

Tom and Allison again found themselves seated in Elena's office. "This is a decent offer. If you decide to litigate, it will take three or more years and cost you about sixty thousand dollars even before the case comes to trial."

Tom knew she was right. He was also keenly aware that acceptance meant the opportunity to make a timely statement before the board of trustees, while declining the offer meant the opportunity would surely be lost in a drawn-out legal contest.

For Allison, it was too bitter a pill to swallow all at once. In the tumult, her lasting contribution to Florence Bruce—renovation of the Ahlborn House—had been ignored, and there was the matter of her investment. "I spent sixteen thousand dollars to make that house what it is," she lamented, unable to hold back the tears flowing down her cheeks. "Does that mean it's all lost? How can they do that? This isn't what Florence Bruce is all about."

Her grief was too great to be overlooked, and, despite its futility, Elena was directed to craft a counter-offer requesting reimbursement for Allison's expenses. It was refused.

The annual board meeting was less than ten days away; graduation ceremonies were in four days. The executive committee demanded an answer to its settlement offer. Steve Harrison told Tom, "No one supports you or believes in you more than I do, but the tide is turning, Tom. Too much time has passed, and there is an urgency to get this resolved."

Tom had not seen the Rt. Rev. William P. Moseley, bishop of the Diocese of Boston, since his installation seven months earlier. The two men had bonded immediately when they met, and, instinctively, Tom knew the bishop would be an ally. Therefore, along with his other trusted confidants, Tom had kept the bishop informed of recent developments with a steady stream of correspondence.

Now he and Allison were in Boston to keep an appointment with the bishop. They arrived early and were ushered into an ornate residence of polished wood, musty drapery and old books. Bishop

Moseley emerged and, after a warm greeting, escorted them to his study. He was a tall man of about sixty with just enough bulk about him to soften the outline. He wore a clerical collar underneath a cardigan sweater with worn khaki slacks and comfortable-looking shoes.

"These are difficult times for the both of you," he said once inside the privacy of his office. He embraced each of them in turn with the familiarity of an old friend. "In your correspondence, I have felt the pain you must be going through."

Tom and Allison poured out their story, with the bishop asking questions now and then to fill in gaps in his knowledge—Tom's difficulties with Archie over his firing of Deanne, his isolation from the executive committee, the co-opting of the survey, and his cavalier, awkward dismissal. "Throughout this ordeal," said Tom, "I have tried to keep the best interests of Florence Bruce foremost in my thoughts, always aware there might be a time when the interests of my family would need to take priority. I'm afraid that time may be here."

"Nobody will blame you, Tom."

"I am still the head of the school, and everything I've done—even to opposing the will of the executive committee—has been with the best interests of the school at heart. The board needs to confront the executive committee and purge itself of the secrecy and backdoor manipulations that currently pass for governance. Part of me wants to engage the battle, but the sensible part of me says that doing so would put my family and future at considerable risk."

The bishop leaned forward and looked Tom straight in the eye. "You have done your part. A new head often runs into opposition following the departure of a long-term leader. In the Church, we insist on installing an interim cleric for a year or two before appointing a permanent pastor. You are what we, in the Church, call an 'involuntary interim.'"

"An involuntary interim?"

"Yes. Unfortunate though it may be, there is a certain inevitability to what happened to you. It's just too bad the school didn't recognize it and provide you with some protection." The bishop sighed, then smiled to reassure Tom. "You have opened the door wide and shown the school the path to its future; now it is up to the board to walk through it. You don't need to feel you are letting the school or yourself down."

As they stood to leave, the bishop called them to prayer. Tom assumed a prayerful stance out of respect for the decorum of the occasion, but in listening to the words, he found himself touched by how deeply this man of God understood what he did not. Conjuring imagery from recent conflicts in the Middle East, the bishop spoke of the brutality and horror that men inflict upon other men and prayed for healing. "The atrocity of words violates the soul as bullets violate the flesh. An unspeakable cruelty has been inflicted upon these two people, Tom and Allison, by brutal and unfeeling adversaries. A grave harm has been done them through no fault of their own. They are Your children. They are in Your arms. Bless them. Watch over them. In the name of Our Father . . . Amen."

Two other voices struggled unsuccessfully to join in the ratification. Tom bit his lip, pinched his eyes closed and struggled to control the convulsions that gripped his shoulders. Allison had no such compulsion, and huge sobs emanating from the soles of her feet racked her body.

Struggling to maintain a semblance of normalcy, Tom went about the routines of his office. For over a month now, the fact that the executive committee had fired him had been common knowledge. Now, Tom's uncertainty as to the temper of the people who surrounded him made interactions awkward. Aware that opinions ranged from profound empathy and sadness to gleeful celebration over his departure, Tom blundered about gripped by an inability to distinguish friend from foe.

"We've done nothing wrong," he told Allison. "We're going to hold our heads up with dignity and see this through to the end."

"Yes. I refuse to give the executive committee the pleasure of thinking they defeated us." Her response was delivered with an uncharacteristic ferocity.

The end of the year at Florence Bruce Seminary was a flurry of celebrations and awards ceremonies, culminating in commencement exercises for the senior class. Tom officiated at every one, often with Allison by his side. Each event was approached with great trepidation despite the kindness and expressions of sympathy from attending parents that often followed. The last and most demanding of these was commencement itself. With most of the trustees in attendance, it would be a definitive test of his mettle.

"We'll show them what they're going to lose," he told Allison. His speech, in draft form, had been on his desk for months undergoing revision after revision. He planned an unusual closing—an old sea chantey, culled from his work at the maritime institute. The chantey was traditionally sung after a ship was tied up in port by sailors preparing to go ashore after a long voyage, its melancholy mood reflecting the conflicting feelings of departure from a ship and shipmates that had been a home and family for months—sometimes years. It was to be a metaphor for the senior class as its members prepared to leave the "ship" that had so long been their home—an allusion, as well, to his own departure as their "captain."

"Allison, help me with the melody. I can't seem to get it right." Tom's vocal abilities did not include carrying a tune, and, despite Allison's coaching, he could not master it. Finally he said, "I'm going to call you up on the stage to sing with me. We came in together; we'll go out together."

A few hours later, Tom stood at the lectern in Bowers Theater and surveyed the senior class: thirty-two girls crowned with mortarboards and dressed in white, floor-length gowns, each carrying a bouquet of flowers. He could name every one, although, ruefully, he admitted real familiarity with fewer than half. *Another year is all it would have taken*, he thought grimly.

The faculty was seated on the sides of the auditorium while family and friends were arrayed in darkness to the rear. Tom adjusted the folds of his tunic, with its three stripes signifying his Ph.D. and the rich blue colors of his Ivy League alma mater, and cleared his throat. "I met the senior class for the first time this year when we opened school in September. They will recall that I used a tall sailing ship as a metaphor and asked Ms. Scott if she would dedicate herself to turning them all into a fine, capable crew. She said she would, and it appears she has done a most credible job of it."

Tom paused again and directed his comments to the seniors, striving to address each one individually.

"You are my first graduating class and while I've come to know some of you pretty well, there are others I hardly know at all. I did not have the good fortune of seeing you arrive at Florence Bruce as gangly, awkward, freshmen. I did not have the good fortune of seeing you struggle into maturity through your sophomore and junior years. I have, however, been a part of your senior year and have enjoyed the opportunity of seeing you lead this school as confident, mature young women.

"Allow me to share with you what I have also seen. You are a class, in my opinion, that is distinctly and boldly counterculture—at once rebellious and defiant of that which is popularly accepted as the norm. Now, I doubt this is the way you see yourselves, so let me explain."

Tom said these words as sternly as he could, with just a hint of menace. A ripple of nervous laughter went through the auditorium. Geoffrey Bellingham, seated near the back, was afraid for what might come next. Phyllis Killam gritted her teeth and glared.

"You are surrounded by a popular culture that rationalizes dishonesty. 'Truth in advertising' is a hollow phrase for the millions of people taken in by TV hucksters and junk-mail advertising. 'Is it legal?' or 'Can I get away with it?' are more often the questions asked, rather than 'Is it right?'

"Here at Florence Bruce Seminary, you have made honorable behavior the norm. The honor code here is real and respected—not that it hasn't been occasionally broken, but there are consequences accepted and meted out by an honor board. This behavior, you must realize, is counter to the culture that surrounds you.

"You inhabit a popular culture that values winning above all else. Breaking the rules or cheating on the playing field is only wrong if the perpetrator is caught. Trash-talking athletes are feted as heroes.

"At Florence Bruce, you belong to an athletic league that was specifically established to promote the values of good sportsmanship and fair play. Not only do you belong to a league which values sportsmanship, but you also won the sportsmanship of the year award from that league. Your behavior on the playing field is defiantly counter to the culture that surrounds you.

"You inhabit a culture that values conspicuous consumption. Status markers of success are designer clothes, high-priced cars, and exclusive addresses where the motto is, 'She who dies with the most toys wins.'

"You inhabit a popular culture where vulgarity, coarse behavior and crude language are the norm. Walk the halls of a public school and one hears barely a sentence without a four-letter word. Road rage and the breakdown of civility create an ongoing dialogue in the media.

"At Florence Bruce Seminary, I have attended formal dinners where manners and decorum are very much in evidence. I am not so naïve as to think there isn't an occasional four-letter word spoken in these halls, but it is certainly not the norm. You are fundamentally kind, and you take care of one another. This is clearly counter to the culture that surrounds you.

"In the popular culture, we lionize the individual—witness star worship in sports and movies. We have individual rights, but we forget communal obligations and responsibilities. Spill a cup of hot coffee and sue the company for making it too hot.

"At Florence Bruce, you have embraced President John F. Kennedy's admonition to 'Ask not what your country can do for you, but what you can do for your country.' You have answered the current president's call to raise funds for Afghan children. You have volunteered at the Lutheran Home, Three Oaks Retirement Community, St Luke's Episcopal Church and My Sister's Pantry Food Bank. This list goes on and on and on. My gosh, what rebels you are!

"Cultural tribalism, or the assertion and celebration of one's differences, is the norm, but you have said that inclusivity is more important than differences.

"Promiscuity and sexual profligacy are the cultural norms, but at Florence Bruce Seminary abstinence is expected, and even public displays of affection are rare.

"You are rebellious. You are distinctly and defiantly counterculture, and you should be proud of it!

"As Pat Bassett, president of the National Association of Independent Schools,[4] says, 'What is unusual about our times is that the American culture projected in the popular media and popular imagination has become so distorted and grotesque—so reflective of only the more sordid aspects of our collective values and aspirations—that counterculture is something we long for.' You have responded to his call, and I applaud you for that."

Tom paused at the end of his litany and was surprised to hear a smattering of applause start in the back of the auditorium and

[4] Many of the ideas incorporated into Tom's speech he attributed to Pat Bassett, president of the National Association of Independent Schools. See his article, "Why Good Schools Are Countercultural." *Education Week*, Volume 21, Number 21 (Feb. 6, 2002), pp 35.

sweep forward. He stood silent and let the sound swell until even his hard-core detractors were forced to join in.

"Soon, in a matter of hours, you will be leaving the halls of Florence Bruce to find your way in a larger world," he said, smiling back at them.

"Throughout this year, I have often used sailing ships as metaphors, and I'd like to use one now. Just as you have spent your high-school years in the close embrace of Florence Bruce Seminary, crews of nineteenth-century tall ships often lived close together within the hulls of their ships for one, two—even three or more years. Like you, looking forward to graduation, they looked forward to the time when they would return to port, to home, to family and friends. As that time approached, however, they often grew melancholy with feelings they could barely express.

"Whenever I sailed, it was only for a week or so. But even in that short time, my fellow shipmates and I bonded as a crew, and coming into port, we knew things would never again be the same. After the docking and before leaving the ship, we sang a traditional sailor's tune. Most sailor's tunes, or chanteys as they are called, are heavy with the rhythm of the work, but this one is different. It's about the sadness of leaving one's shipmates and saying goodbye to a life that for all its difficulties, held the rewards of close companionship and teamwork.

"There are verses in the song about the bad food, the captain, the mates and the difficulty of the work, but it is the short, haunting chorus that has always touched me. As you prepare to leave Florence Bruce, I'd like to sing it for you."

Tom motioned to Allison, waiting in the wings, to join him on stage. Taking her hand, Tom stepped out from behind the lectern, and with Allison's high soprano backed by Tom's tentative baritone, they sang:

> Leave her, Johnny, leave her.
> Oh, leave her, Johnny, leave her.
> For the voyage is done and the winds don't blow,
> And it's time for us to leave her.

As the sorrowfully evocative melody trailed off, the applause began—lightly at first, then loud and robust. It flowed over Tom and Allison and continued unbroken while they bowed, embarrassed, and exited the stage. Peg Scott then stepped forward with the diplomas and began to call out the names.

Afterwards in the lobby, amid the throng of now graduated seniors, Geoffrey Bellingham approached Tom. "That was . . . ah . . . . that was a fine speech, Tom. You did well."

"Why thank you, Geoffrey. That's the first of my speeches you've heard, isn't it?"

The next morning, Tom called Elena and directed her to fax the signed settlement agreement to the executive committee.

CHAPTER XXV

The Meeting

♠

The board's decisions and actions reflect and reinforce institutional values.[1]

At 2:00 AM, Tom stumbled out of bed and felt his way to the bathroom. Fumbling for the vial of sleeping pills in the medicine cabinet, he removed a small white pill and threw it back with a half-swallow of water. Even in his partially numbed state, he knew that to allow the neurons to start firing would mean no more sleep for the rest of the night.

At 6:00 AM, he was aroused again by the faint bonging of the grandfather clock downstairs in the living room. For days he had dreaded this night and the long sleepless hours of anticipation it presaged. But that had not been the case, and he felt relaxed, well rested and ready for whatever the day would bring.

He picked up his reading glasses from the study, turned left at the top of the stairs, descended, opened the front door for the morning paper and padded off to the kitchen. Banana, bowl, cereal, spoon,

---

[1] Chait, Richard P., Thomas P. Holland and Barbara E. Taylor. *The Effective Board of Trustees*. New York: MacMillan Publishing Company, 1991, p. 17.

milk—sort the paper into easily readable chunks, pour the milk and settle in with the comics. He ate slowly, deliberately, not really aware of what he was doing, focusing instead on the little squares of humor and political satire before him.

Later, freshly showered and dressed, he retired to his study and arrayed his notes on the old music stand he used to practice his speeches. He took off his watch and set the timer. In six hours, the board of trustees of Florence Bruce Seminary would gather to hear him defend his leadership of the school against the decision of the executive committee to terminate it. Before he could begin his practice, however, the phone rang. It was Caroline Odum.

"Tom, did you see the e-mails from Steve and Joanne?" She seemed excited, out of breath—as if she hadn't expected anyone to pick up the phone.

They all think they're alone. Tom mentally kicked himself for not doing more to organize the opposition.

"Yeah, I saw them. It looks like you've got the support you need and a second to your motion."

"I think you're right. Tell me again how that 'point of order' thing is supposed to work."

Tom grimaced. *We've been over this before.* "A point of order involves a procedural question. If you bring up a point of order and someone seconds it, the president must address it before any other business is conducted."

"Okay, I think I understand. See you at the meeting this afternoon."

Tom had stopped his watch when the phone rang. Now he stood a moment to clear his head and restarted the timer.

When he finished his rehearsal, the accumulated time was one hour and thirty-two seconds, and he made a mental note of places where he could carve a half-minute or so from his presentation. He'd been told he was to be allowed exactly one hour. He knew they would cut him off in midsentence if he strayed over.

At 12:55 PM, Tom walked into the kitchen where Allison was puttering. Without looking up, she announced, "It's showtime." He grunted his assent and kissed her on the cheek, embraced her and felt the reassuring curves of her body through her cotton dress. She wished him luck, and they kissed again.

Tom pulled away, choosing not to linger as he normally might. His demeanor became even more serious as he headed for the door, collecting the box containing his notes and the reference materials for his presentation—twenty-eight briefing books, one for each trustee, each containing thirty-eight pages. He used a knee to balance the heavy carton and free up a hand to open the door.

He walked quickly across the street, used his knee again to open the front door, and stepped briskly up the steps into the lobby. The slightly musty smell of old wood and tradition, by now familiar, greeted him as he entered. In the center of the lobby was a table with a large bouquet of flowers, their sweet scent mingling with other aromas in the room.

As he turned the corner into the hall leading to the library, Tom caught sight of the portrait of Florence Bruce at the head of the landing on the grand staircase. She smiled down demurely with an expression that today seemed vacuous, uncomprehending. Was the look the result of the painter's brilliance or his incompetence? Tom had wondered about that more than once. Her look struck him differently depending upon his own mood. It was clear to him this time that she was as baffled by the turn of events as he was.

He strode quickly toward the library. Rounding the corner, he encountered Paul Alexander and Trish Calvert. They were to be voted in as new members of the board at this annual meeting and would be excluded from the proceedings at first to permit the board to elect them. He opened the conversation innocuously. "All set for the meeting?"

They turned and greeted him. "I guess we're supposed to wait out here for the first ten minutes," said Trish.

Knowing that it would be more than ten minutes, Tom offered to find them chairs. "We'll be fine," said Trish, with Paul echoing the sentiment. He didn't press the issue and continued on into the library.

There were less than a dozen people in the room. He glanced quickly around the group, trying not to make eye contact. He needn't have worried. Archie was at the far end with Keegan and Geoffrey; Phyllis was in consultation with Saugus. No friendly faces were immediately evident, so he continued over to his customary place at the table, turning into the low stacks nearby to deposit his carton of briefing books.

He ambled toward a nook by the window where refreshments were neatly arranged: grapes, cheeses, crackers, a dessert tray of sweets—the usual. He took a bottle of water and picked up a plate—killing time now—absently filling it with whatever came to hand. Walking back to his seat, he deposited the plate, opened the bottle of water and filled his glass, just as he caught sight of Steve Harrison.

A friend. Steve asked how he was doing, a common greeting now whenever Tom met people who were aware of his termination.

"Okay, I guess. I'll be better when *this* meeting is over."

At that moment, Geoffrey Bellingham, acting president of the board since Archie's resignation, gaveled the meeting to order. Tom looked around. The room wasn't even half full. He glanced at the clock. It said 1:00 PM exactly. Why so early? It was customary to allow an extra five minutes or even ten for stragglers to arrive.

Glancing down at the papers before him, he noticed a fresh agenda had been placed on top. It was the agenda for what was termed the "Annual Meeting,"[2] now about to get underway. He saw the names being placed in nomination for officers of the board. Geoffrey was asking for approval of the minutes as Tom read them: Phyllis Killam for president; Saugus Wetherby, vice-president; Keegan O'Connor, secretary; and Reveta Bowler, treasurer; with two other members at large.

Well, they brought in a little new blood, he noted cynically, perceiving that Reveta and the two members at large were fresh faces. *But the executive committee obviously plans to remain in charge. We'll see about that!* He didn't have time to dwell on that thought, because the minutes had been approved, and Geoffrey was calling on the nominating committee to give its report.

Reveta Bowler stood. She was chair of the committee that drafted new board members and nominated a slate of officers for election by the board. Reveta announced her report would be in three parts and would conclude with one motion to approve all three parts. She

[2] An annual meeting, at which new directors are elected and officers chosen, is often distinguished from regular meetings where the ordinary business of the organization is conducted. Most nonprofit organizations choose simply to designate one regular meeting a year as the "annual meeting."

used words like "customary" and "normal" to describe the procedure. *My God,* Tom thought, *Reveta is in on it with them, too. They're going to try to ram this through and keep themselves in power before enough trustees get here to stop them.* The room was still largely empty except for the executive committee and a handful of others.

Reveta read the names of the trustees returning for second terms, the names of the new members, and finally, the names of the officers, ending her report with a motion to approve. Keegan O'Connor quickly offered a second. The air seemed to thicken as Geoffrey asked if there was any discussion and barely paused before declaring that he would call for the vote. Tom held his breath. Only Caroline Odum, seated across from him, and Joanne Copeland had the information to halt the proceedings. Joanne had not yet arrived, and Caroline had taken her seat only moments earlier.

Tom looked straight at Caroline, begging with his eyes for her to intervene. This was what they had talked about, although this wasn't the way it was supposed to happen—without backup.

Caroline looked back, gathered strength and half-raised her hand, speaking in a halting, trembling voice. "I . . . I think maybe we should look at a fresh slate of officers. I . . . I just think . . . Well, there's a lack of trust right now. People are concerned. Maybe we need to . . . Perhaps a new slate of officers would help rebuild confidence."

It was tentative. It was crude. Was it enough? Keegan O'Connor, invoking all the authority he could muster, interceded with a rebuttal. *Wow, they must have rehearsed for this.*

"Caroline, I understand your concerns," he began. If they had been closer, Tom was sure Keegan would have patted her on the head. "There have been some misunderstandings to be sure, but now, more than ever, we need the experience and the depth this slate brings to the table."

Keegan continued, trying to marginalize Caroline's concern. He focused on Phyllis—her experience, the high regard in which she was held by the community, and especially her service as board president while John Sanford and the school were going through so many changes.

When he finished, someone asked if Phyllis agreed to accept the nomination.

"I had planned on taking a vacation this year," said Phyllis, speaking in the words of a reluctant commander-in-chief, "but these are difficult times, and if called on, I will serve for the good of Florence Bruce."

The future of Florence Bruce Seminary hung in the balance. Tom felt the hairs on his neck prickle. Caroline had opened the door, but it had been quickly closed. *Is it too late now?* Geoffrey again made preparations for the vote.

As if on cue, Steve Harrison spoke up. "How can Phyllis be president? Doesn't her term end? Doesn't she need to be off the board for a year?"

Yes! Tom fairly shouted it aloud.[3]

Geoffrey was taken off guard, but grasped the situation and valiantly tried to cover before the hole gaped any wider. "Phyllis has been off the board this last year," he improvised. "She was . . . uh . . . she was just ex-officio because she served the year before as president."

"Well, she's not on the board now. How can she be elected president when she's not even on the board?"[4]

Geoffrey staggered, struggling to maintain composure. The meeting had moved into unanticipated territory. It was now 1:10 PM; seats had begun to fill with late-arriving trustees. Bishop Moseley arrived; then Jo Copeland. The tension was palpable as the new arrivals sensed what was going on and struggled to catch up with the discussion.

Geoffrey acknowledged the "oversight" and offered that Reveta, as head of the nominating committee, could amend her motion to include Phyllis on the slate of new trustees.

Reveta, now clearly out of her element and working without a script, stumbled, saying she was just following directions from the

---

[3] Tom immediately sensed the contradiction raised by Steve: Phyllis could not be president or even a trustee for the coming year. The bylaws required a one-year hiatus after serving six years (two three-year terms) before an individual could return to the board. Phyllis, as outgoing president the previous year, had earned an additional year on the board, but now she had to leave for a minimum of one year before she could return.

[4] Steve was right again. The executive committee dictating to the nominating committee had neglected to include Phyllis in the list of nominations for new board members. Even if the argument had been made that she was eligible for another term, she had not been nominated for one.

executive committee—giving lie to the next exchange with Caroline, who questioned the independence of her nominating committee.

Reveta didn't know how to amend her motion, and Geoffrey couldn't help her without giving up his cherished "objectivity." Phyllis, annoyed and unable to hold back any longer, announced, "All you have to do, Reveta, is nominate me for membership on the board." Phyllis was not accustomed to operating out in the open. When Steve again pointed out that the bylaws seemed to prevent it, her comment seemed self-serving. The aura of the executive committee was pierced.

Jo Copeland, now fully engaged, weighed in. "I recommend we break the motion into two parts. I move we vote on the trustees nominated for the board. We can consider the officers and other actions in another motion." There was nodding consensus around the table. It was a brilliant move, although Tom doubted that Jo knew exactly what she had done.[5]

Reveta and Keegan withdrew their motions—Keegan with a quip and a flourish to demonstrate an eagerness to bend to the common will. A new motion was made limiting the action to the election of new trustees. It was quickly seconded and passed.

Geoffrey, however, wasn't ready to give up. He tried to elicit a motion for nominations from the floor, but his request was awkwardly phrased: "Is there anyone else we should vote on right now?" Tom realized he wanted someone else to place Phyllis' name in nomination, but the tide had ebbed as far as it would go and was already on the rise.

No one responded before Jo spoke again. She articulated how disturbed she was over the recent turn of events. She told of the numbers of people who had communicated with her who were also deeply disturbed. She spoke of the damage that had been done to the capital campaign and to the trust that must exist between a school's various constituencies and the board of trustees. She spoke of the need for healing and the necessity for people untainted by the past to lead the healing.

---

[5] Once new members were elected, Phyllis' name could no longer be inserted into an existing slate. She would have to be nominated and stand on her own—an unlikely scenario, under the circumstances.

As she concluded, there were nods of assent; Bishop Moseley interceded next and the momentum grew. His experience, he said, was with congregations. When serious conflicts arose, the regaining of trust between the parties was of paramount importance, and this could only be done if the emerging leadership was untouched by the conflict. Others picked up on the theme to restate or add their own nuance. The executive committee was quiet. Phyllis knew their cause was lost.

The conversation turned to other choices for president. If not Phyllis, then who? No one else had been approached. Caroline asked, "Can we elect the slate of officers as presented except for the president, and save that for another time?" Her suggestion was made into a motion and approved. Saugus and Reveta were left in place, so the slate was not quite clean—but clean enough provided the right president was selected to lead the others.

The Annual Meeting adjourned. It was now 1:30 PM.

Geoffrey stood to welcome the two newly elected members who had been waiting in the hall. Paul and Trish filed in, looking somewhat anxious, and took their assigned places. Geoffrey extended an exaggerated welcome extolling their credentials for membership in "this august body" and then made a grand presentation in passing the gavel to Saugus.

Saugus Wetherby, newly elected vice-president and now in charge of the proceedings, stood to perform his first official function. "Due to irreconcilable differences, Dr. Whitman has tendered his resignation," he read from a prepared script. Part of the settlement arrangement, Saugus explained, his booming voice laced with the authority of his new-found position, provided Dr. Whitman with the opportunity to speak directly to the board. He reminded the assembly that this would not be a question-and-answer session, that no motions or resolutions would be made, and that no discussion would occur. It was simply an opportunity for Dr. Whitman to address the board without additional comment.

"Dr. Whitman, are you ready?"

Tom indicated that he was and stood to arrange his presentation. He picked up the carton of briefing books, which had already been divided into two piles, passing them to his right and to his left. He positioned the small lectern provided for him and arranged his notes. Saugus was saying in his clipped baritone that Tom would have exactly one hour. "It is now 1:32 PM," he proclaimed dramatically. Tom glanced at the clock. "At 2:27 PM," Saugus continued, "I will issue a five-minute warning." After repeating his admonition that there would be no questions and no comments following the presentation, Saugus sat down.

Tom refilled his glass and left the bottle within easy reach. He spread his legs slightly apart, distributed his weight over both feet, squared up his shoulders and was ready. He took a deep breath and forced his body to relax; then, taking in the room beginning to his left, he made eye contact with those who were willing. Most weren't. Caroline Odum, seated on the other side of the table, gave him a look of encouragement that provided a momentary lift. Bishop Moseley, looking directly back at him, conveyed a confidence that easily traveled the distance between them. The former members of the executive committee at the far end of the room held their heads down, studiously examining the briefing books. Kay Johnson acknowledged his look with a wan smile. Steve Harrison nodded. Tom took a sip of water and began.

"Members of the board of trustees of Florence Bruce Seminary, thank you for this opportunity to appear before you. I want to spend my time this afternoon talking about my termination and sharing with you my perspective, as your former head of school. My goal is that some good—some learning—may come out of this."

Tom got right to the point. One hour was enough time, but only if he stayed focused in his presentation. "I will do this by examining the written record—the documentation. When this chapter of the history of Florence Bruce is written, these are the files, the memos, the e-mails, the reports and the notes that will be used to tell the story."[6]

There were two contributing factors that resulted in his termination, Tom told the assembled trustees. One was an evaluation process gone awry. Initially well conceived and entered into with the best of intentions, the process had been misguided and derailed, resulting in mistaken conclusions and errors in judgment.

The second factor was a near total breakdown in communications between himself—the head—and the members of the executive

[6] Tom was right. Without that record, this book could not have been written.

committee. "It was a breakdown," he said, "that came about because the executive committee permitted the board president to remain in office with an untenable conflict of interest." The president was in a romantic relationship with an employee of the school, which, Tom pointed out, was *de facto* a conflict of interest. Termination of the employee created an inevitable clash with the president. It should have and did—raise a red flag, he said. But nothing was done, and a barrier came between himself and the executive committee that neither party was ever able to cross.

Tom drew their attention to the briefing book. Pages were numbered consecutively, and he referred to them as his presentation progressed.

Page one was the first page of his employment contract. He reminded them that everyone now agreed—including lawyers from both sides—that the action taken by the executive committee was a "termination" rather than a "nonrenewal"—a termination that required a cause and could be neither "arbitrary nor capricious."

He moved on to a memo written by Geoffrey Bellingham one week after Tom officially began his tenure. The memo initiated a process that resulted in the approval of five goals against which his leadership was to be measured. From the minutes of the executive committee meeting two months later, Tom read, "Professor Bellingham reported the committee met in late July to identify the goals to be used to evaluate the school's achievements and Dr. Whitman's leadership through his first year."

"All summer," Tom said, "we worked on those goals. Ultimately, you approved them. Clearly, these goals were designed to become the primary instruments of my evaluation."

Tom continued reading from the minutes. "Dr. Hudson reported that he met with Dr. Whitman and Ms. Johnson to develop an instrument for evaluating the head and gathering feedback on a more personal level."

"This mention," said Tom, "is the first indication that my evaluation would also include a survey. But the survey is of secondary importance, and the major thrust of the evaluation was to be the goals—as it should have been."

The minutes also identified the intended participants: "Dr. Bellingham reported the transition committee determined the survey should be used to gather feedback from the full board and from a select group of faculty."

Tom was tight-lipped and angry as he read. It was the failure to adhere to these conditions to keep to a *select* group of faculty, he believed, that had given the executive committee the ammunition to unfairly terminate him. "The survey," he said, "did *not* go to a 'select group.' It went to the entire faculty, even *to the individual I fired.*

"You and I, together, established a fair and worthy process for my evaluation. Had it been followed, we would not be here today having this discussion. But it was not followed. It was derailed and then co-opted to achieve a specific, predetermined end."

Tom paused for effect and stepped back to take a drink of water. As he surveyed the room, he noticed that no one was looking at him. Embarrassment seemed to emanate from the assembled body like heat waves off the tarmac.

He steeled himself and drew their attention to a report presented to the board in November by Markham Nunlist, the consultant who had guided the search process a year and a half earlier. Tom summarized the consultant's four-page report with this quote from the introduction:

> In general terms, the transition seems to be going well, with a few minor exceptions, and those are noted in the report. They have to do mainly with the difficulties that some have in adjusting to a change of the magnitude experienced by any school following the long and successful tenure of a previous head. Comparisons are inevitable even if sometimes unfair and inappropriate.

Tom pounced on the last sentence. "We were told there would be comparisons between my style and John's, and we were told they would be 'unfair and inappropriate.' You were warned that this would be the case. The fact that the survey attracted criticism and negative comments was expected, and yet, many of you seem surprised that it had." Tom looked up from his notes. There was scattered eye contact around the table.

"In January, two months later, something else was to occur that would change everything." Tom described how he and Archie

Devlin had met weekly throughout the fall and into the winter. His briefings to the president had included major items worthy of board consideration as well as the routine minutiae that consume the days of a school head. Among the items included in these briefings were personnel reports—which were the people rising to the challenges of new leadership, which ones were slipping; who showed promise, who was failing. Archie was an eager listener and learner, and things were going well, Tom said.

"However, I then fired the director of public relations—having briefed Archie several times on her failing performance. From that day forward, my relationship with Archie changed. In the seven days following the firing, I met twice with Archie. I say 'met,' but they weren't meetings, they were confrontations. Archie accused me of making a power play that he intended to fight. Despite my protestations to the contrary and despite a review of samples of her work and her evaluations that I shared with him, Archie maintained that my actions regarding Deanne Bakker were a personal attack on him. And he still believes that to be true. From that day forward, our relationship became adversarial, and it remains so today."

It was the first time he had referred to Deanne by name. Tom glanced up from his notes. In his peripheral vision, he could see Archie staring at him—eyes wide, mouth agape like a cornered opossum.

"I know you are all aware that I terminated the director of public relations. Are you also aware that this was the third termination I made at Florence Bruce? I doubt it, and that is as it should be. But the termination of Deanne Bakker was different." It was different, said Tom—although no one needed reminding—because she was in a romantic relationship with the president of the board.

After a pause for a sip of water, Tom began again. His voice was quieter now as he tried to forge a bond with those trustees who still retained a semblance of objectivity, who were still capable of a dispassionate examination of the circumstances that had overwhelmed them a few short months earlier. "I know you have all heard about the firing of Deanne Bakker, because there has been a lot of talk about it. You've probably heard, for example, that she was let go without cause. I am telling you today that was not the case."

Tom said he had fired Deanne for three reasons. Those reasons were poor performance, inability to work with colleagues and insubordination. If any trustees wondered whether a corrective process had been followed, he assured them that it had. He had closely mentored Deanne through the construction of the new website. He had carefully reviewed her publications and provided written recommendations and requests for changes. Did they wonder whether he had protected the school from legal repercussions? Tom assured them that he had. The file of meetings, evaluations, and e-mails was thick and comprehensive. He told them that he had realized the circumstances of this termination were unusual and had consulted a legal expert. Absolutely, the school had not been put at risk.

"You may have also heard there was a 'lack of compassion' in the manner in which she was let go. That is not the case either." Tom asked the trustees to simply consider the final result. Deanne's one-year contract was paid out to its end with full salary and benefits—far more than had been offered him.

"I would now like to move to the minutes of a special meeting of the executive committee held in February." Tom directed the group to the appropriate page in the briefing book. "Everything changed after Deanne was let go. Archie's desire to exact revenge on me began to color every meeting, every exchange, and all communications between me and the members of the executive committee."

To help resolve the problem, on this date the executive committee voted to contact the National Association of Independent Schools—a wise move, said Tom. "At this suggestion, I breathed a sigh of relief. Things had gone from bad to worse. Archie's practice of attending every meeting of every committee and his pursuit of a separate, personal agenda at these meetings was very disruptive. Any private contact that I attempted with members of the executive committee was seen as a challenge to his authority and brought on a confrontation with him.

"The NAIS report was pivotal and most of you have never even seen it." Tom directed their attention to sections in the report he had marked with highlighter: "The head arrived with a substantial agenda," "active verbs and timelines set high expectations." Here was proof positive, Tom said, that change was part of his mandate.

Especially telling was this passage: "We cannot overemphasize the awkwardness and conflict of interest based on Archie's relationship with the terminated director of public relations."

Tom's voice began to rise. "Here it is, in black and white. Archie clearly had a conflict of interest. It existed before I got here when a romantic relationship was allowed to exist between an employee of the school and a trustee of that school. It was exacerbated when that employee was discharged. It continues today. It was only two weeks ago that Archie resigned his position as president of the board, but he remains as one of you still—in what any self-respecting board of trustees would certainly recognize as a clear and present conflict of interest."

Archie gasped and their eyes met. Tom was breathing hard. His eyes flashed back at Archie, and he scanned the room. No one dared look at him. Even Bishop Moseley used the occasion to fumble for something in his pocket. Trish Calvert was frantically scribbling notes. "Archie," he said, his voice growing husky with emotion, "should have resigned much earlier, or, failing that, you should have told him to do so."

Tom was getting close to the end now and he was feeling the fatigue of talking for forty minutes with intense concentration. No one got up to refresh by-now cold coffee or to snack from the nearby buffet. Light that was muted by the tall trees lining the grounds streamed into the room through the library windows. The sight and smell of books—books everywhere—lent the occasion an austere cast. He breathed, deeply fortifying himself for the next charge.

While Tom's conflict with Archie created a breakdown within the executive committee, the results from his evaluation were used to rationalize the committee's actions to the rest of the community. It pained Tom to think how carefully he had planned for his evaluation, how sound it was in concept, and how it had become so distorted in the implementation.

"On March 21, the executive committee met. The minutes record a report from Professor Bellingham that the head's evaluation survey was ready to be mailed. At this meeting," said Tom, "I learned for the first time that the survey would be sent to *all* administrative staff and faculty."

Tom said he also learned at this meeting that he would not be able to review the returned surveys, even though that had been promised earlier. He would not be meeting with the transition committee to review the results; he would not be preparing a report for the executive committee and the board of trustees—all of which had been part of the original plan. Instead, there would be a report drafted by the executive committee and sent to him while the NAIS report would be withheld from the full board. "It would appear," said Tom slowly, "that there was already a plan underway to manipulate the evaluation process to my detriment. At the conclusion of this meeting, the executive committee held a closed session. And so it began—a series of secret meetings that would lead to my termination. There were no records kept of these meetings. No records of attendance. No records of who voted or how they voted, and no records of the decisions reached.

"Two weeks ago, you met as a full board. Did anyone take minutes at that meeting? Did anyone keep a record of who attended? Saugus Wetherby was your secretary at that time. Article V, Section 5 of your bylaws states: 'The secretary shall be responsible for the keeping and reporting of adequate records for all transactions and of all minutes of the board of trustees.'" Turning toward Saugus, Tom asked, "Saugus, did you keep minutes of that meeting?"

Saugus looked thunderstruck. He had declared before Tom began that there would be no comment, no discussion. Even if he had a ready answer, he couldn't very well offer it. He did, however, make a mental note to put some minutes together when he got home that evening.

"Your mission statement says that this school guides students to be 'responsible citizens.' Is this the kind of example you want to set? Are decisions made at meetings held in secret with no records kept the hallmark of responsible citizens in a country that values democratic traditions?" He fairly thundered the accusations. It was at these meetings, Tom continued, that the decision to terminate his contract was made. That decision was never recorded nor was it known when the meeting took place at which it was made. It is not known who was present. Was there a quorum? Who voted? What exactly was the motion? The board, he said, would be hard pressed to even prove that a termination had occurred.

In May, Tom said, he had received the results of the survey in a report from Geoffrey Bellingham. The overwhelming preponderance of negative comments, he emphasized, was entirely consistent with survey instruments of this nature, which are recommended by experts for use in formative evaluations when the intent is to reveal problems and concerns that need to be addressed. Surveys expose these issues in their rawest form so that corrective measures can be brought to bear on them. In this case, such a survey was used not to help develop his leadership, but to justify his removal from Florence Bruce less than a year after he had arrived.

"By now," said Tom, weariness showing in his voice, "the enormity of the executive committee's failure should be abundantly evident. If this were a courtroom, the legal test that would be applied to their decision is that it not be 'arbitrary or capricious.' In your considered judgment . . ." Tom stopped to survey the room. "In your considered judgment, does it seem that my termination was arbitrary . . . or capricious?"

Tom stepped back from the lectern. It was 3:30 PM. Saugus had apparently decided against interrupting him with a warning. Not quite trusting his voice, he declared gruffly he would be outside in the hall if he was needed and, picking up his notes, walked toward the door.

Bishop Moseley rose from the other side of the table and moved with him. As they drew abreast, the bishop said, loud enough for everyone to hear, "Tom, I'd like to pray with you."

Tom was not inclined toward prayer in his personal habits, but with heart pounding, head spinning, and knees weakening, he was profoundly grateful for the offer. They pushed through the double doors of the library together while in the background Saugus declared a ten-minute recess.

Tom and the bishop walked down the short hall to an outside doorway and pressed through to Hanley Chapel. The ornately carved hardwood doors stood open, and they entered, stopping a short way inside. Turning so they faced each other, the bishop took Tom's hands in his own. "You didn't stand a chance, did you?"

"No, I guess not."

There was a roaring in Tom's head, but from somewhere within, there was a sharpness and clarity of sound and sensation that surprised him. Afterward, he would try to recall without success what Bishop Moseley had said. He did remember the calming effect of the cleric's voice and its soothing texture as the words washed over him. The words, too, were distinct and meaningful at the time. He just couldn't recollect what they were.

Later, Tom would remember that moment as the most powerful and profound in his life. Its power came from the impact of the bishop's prior actions in validating the sacrifice he and Allison had suffered on behalf of Florence Bruce Seminary—a sacrifice forced upon them, to be sure, but one that they willed themselves to endure for the sake of the school.

With his accomplishments for the year in question and his integrity and honor on the line, Tom had poured himself into the presentation. The bishop's bold statement of support in full view of the board was dramatic. Disenfranchised trustees were awakening and regaining control. He had given them the information and the confidence they would need to assert themselves.

When the bishop's prayer concluded, they embraced. Tom sagged. The roar in his head subsided, but he still felt weak and unsteady. His stumbling expressions of gratitude were feeble and inadequate, but they were all he could manage. He said he wished to remain in the chapel, and they parted. Bishop Moseley returned to the meeting and Tom walked up the aisle to a front pew and sat, collecting himself. Twenty minutes went by during which there were no sounds except the birds in the dogwood outside the chapel windows. His head finally clear, Tom stood. A feeling of deep relief turning to elation swept over him. It was over. He retraced his steps back down the aisle and emerged outside into the sunshine.

When Saugus declared a recess, Phyllis gathered up her things in silence and followed the other trustees out into the hall, deliberately making her way through the tiny knots of people without stopping. Archie, suddenly realizing that she wasn't coming back, hurried to catch up. "Phyllis, are . . . are you leaving?" he stammered.

She looked at him with bemused detachment, "Yes, Archie, I'm leaving."

"But, Phyllis, the meeting isn't over. We still have to pick a new president and vote on the building plan."

"No, Archie, it *is* over." She turned away from him toward the parking lot while Archie looked after her in bewilderment.

Back in the library once more, Saugus gaveled the meeting to order. "The next item on our agenda is the approval of a contractor for work on the new wing. We have received three bids for the project—"

"Point of order!" Caroline had no idea if what she wanted to say was a point of order or not, but her saying so stopped the meeting in its tracks. "You should all be ashamed of yourselves," she proclaimed, directing her remarks to Archie and the three remaining members of the former executive committee. "What you did was absolutely disgraceful—beyond words. I simply can't describe how violated I feel.

"I was the one responsible for bringing Tom to Florence Bruce. I was the one who championed him during the selection process. All of us on the search committee put in many long hours to find the right person to lead this school. Many thousands of dollars were invested in a consultant, and we found the right person. But your abrogation of the authority we placed in you and your corruption of the principles on which this school was founded undid all of our work.

"We—the board of trustees—must reclaim our rightful place as the governing authority of Florence Bruce Seminary. I move that we do this by electing Jo Copeland to lead us—as president of the board."

The room was silent. Saugus looked like a deer caught in the oncoming headlights. Caroline waited a moment and then asked, "Do I have a second?"

"I'll second it." Steve Harrison made sure there was no mistaking his words.

"Mr. Wetherby," said Caroline, turning toward Saugus, who still had not moved, "if there is no discussion, then I'd like to call the question to vote." Tom's briefing on *Robert's Rules*[7] was paying off.

Saugus cleared his throat. "Is there any discussion?" he asked weakly.

Again, no one spoke, so a vote was called. Caroline, Steve, Bishop Moseley and several others raised their hands immediately. Others more tentatively joined them until all hands were raised, even those of the ousted executive committee who were sufficiently astute to realize the pendulum was starting a swing back toward center. Keegan sat dejectedly with his chin in his free hand; Geoffrey tried to hide behind Saugus while Archie sat aghast with his arm weakly raised, scarcely comprehending what he was seeing. Bodie, whose term was officially over, had left with Phyllis at the break.

---

[7] In the nineteenth century, U.S. Army officer Henry Robert saw the need for a uniform set of rules to be used to manage the give-and-take of meetings. He published the first edition of *Robert's Rules of Order* in 1876.

CHAPTER XXVI

Consolation

♠

Effective boards respect the integrity of the governance process.[1]

Allison surveyed the entrance to the school from the bedroom inside the Ahlborn House, where she had been watching almost continually since her husband left earlier in the day. She had seen him cross the street and breathed a small sigh of relief when the friendly forms of Steve Harrison and Caroline Odum followed him into the school.

An hour passed. Dreamily, she marveled at the stately Tudor-style architecture of the Seminary and reveled in the vibrant contrast between the rich red brick and the brilliant green of the surrounding fresh-cut grass. The sheer beauty of that building had filled her heart when she first saw it. That it would no longer be a part of her life was now utterly impossible to accept—her forced abandonment felt like an abominable assault on an entitlement she had honorably earned.

---

[1] Chait, Richard P., Thomas P. Holland and Barbara E. Taylor. *The Effective Board of Trustees*. New York: MacMillan Publishing Company, 1991, p. 78.

Suddenly, her throat clenched as the image of Phyllis and Bodie leaving the building seared her consciousness. She pulled away from the window until they were gone, not realizing that distance and glare on the window shielded her from their view.

Twenty minutes she waited, gripped by the fear of uncertainty. Finally, the door opened again, and she saw Tom come into view. She watched him stride down the walkway out onto the sidewalk; she searched eagerly for clues and telltale signs in his step, in the way he scanned the street for traffic at the crosswalk, and in his face as he drew nearer. Somehow, she had expected to see him burst through the door and pump his fists into the air.

She greeted him as he entered the house, anxious for news. "Did you get your job back?" she questioned with hopeful optimism as soon as he was inside.

"No," said Tom wearily. He knew that wasn't in the cards, but Allison had been holding out the hope that some miracle would occur to reverse the awful reality. "But it went as well as could be expected. I'm afraid we lost the battle, sweetheart, but we may have won the war." Allison didn't know what he meant. To her, it seemed like they had lost both.

Later that afternoon after the meeting adjourned, Caroline called to tell Tom that Jo Copeland had been elected board president. "If it weren't for you," she said, "I don't know what would have happened."

Epilogue

Life, in real time, can't always be condensed into neat storylines wrapped up in comforting bows. Real life is much less tidy. Sometimes bad stuff happens, and that's the end of it. There's little or nothing about a situation that can be considered reassuring or redeeming. Sometimes justice doesn't prevail. Sometimes the agony doesn't end, as those around the edges of the maelstrom continue to be sucked in one by one, spiraling around a black hole that grows bigger and more powerful with each speck of matter it swallows up.

In a sense, Tom did win the war. He had been brought to Florence Bruce to affect a change, and that he had done. The conviction of mission accomplished sustained him through the long, dark days that followed his departure.

As soon as he and Allison had relocated out of the Ahlborn House, Tom mounted a nationwide quest to find another position of leadership in an independent school. Unfortunately, his candidacy for such positions now had two strikes against it. In addition to his nontraditional background, he had to confront the "questionable" circumstances of his departure from Florence Bruce. Joanne Copeland, Warren Hudson and others wrote excellent references, but the questions always lingered. A year passed, and while there were interviews and some hopeful signs, no offers came.

Allison's suffering was palpable. Rebuffed in her effort to seek repayment of the money she had put into refurbishing the Ahlborn House, she took it as a personal rejection of her work. Whereas

Tom had been able to forcefully confront his accusers and win some measure of solace from bringing them to bay, Allison was isolated and bewildered, for a long time unable to come to terms with what had happened to her life.

Ultimately, the couple decided to remain in Portsmouth. Both got jobs: Allison as a community relations coordinator in an elder-care community and Tom as director of a small wooden-boat museum. While their combined salary was less than two-thirds that of Tom's salary as head of school, they appropriately downsized and settled into the local community among supportive friends—very few of which had ties to Florence Bruce. Allison soon joined the board of a local food bank, and Tom hosted a gathering of tallships that made the Boston papers. They entertained frequently and spent many weekends touring the New England countryside together.

Florence Bruce Seminary fared poorly. The organizational culture in nonprofit organizations is far more potent than is generally recognized. In the best of times, the pull of culture binds people together in community and encourages the building of structures and institutions that are monuments to human achievement. When conditions change and the culture no longer serves, even the best intentioned are often swept along by the tide of events and circumstances, unable to shrug off an embrace that has turned destructive.

The mission of Florence Bruce Seminary—to put the education of students foremost—remained subjugated for a long time to adult fantasies playing themselves out in the governance of the school. Although Joanne Copeland served out her term as president of the board, she was unable to overcome the prevalent school culture or convert its many practitioners.

Archie, having forfeited his position of importance, grumbled as his image lost its luster and he became a bit player again. Life was different. Peers, familiar with his part in Tom's demise and aware that a connection existed between him and the convulsions overtaking the school, didn't want to stand too close. Archie was isolated. He and Deanne drifted apart—the impetus for the breakup coming mostly from Deanne, whose original attraction to Archie was based more on his position and power than anything else he had to offer her.[2]

A John Sanford protégé, the female candidate who had interviewed poorly during the process that selected Tom, was recommended as his replacement. The trustees were desperate for stability, and against the better judgment of several of them, acquiesced. Her appointment reinstated the benign neglect of business matters, the irregular but dictatorial oversight of power, and the behind-the-scenes manipulation of people that had characterized John's administration.

Anxious to show a positive face to their constituents, the trustees increased the capital campaign goal to $10 million to cover the increased costs of the new wing and ordered the contractor to break ground. Ruth Gladstone, the development director, wisely counseled against increasing the goal, saying, "We introduced Tom to all our major prospects, and many of them took to him. They are already upset at his departure. Increasing the goal will send the wrong message."

Ruth was ignored, and within two months of the opening of school the following fall, the new headmaster confronted her. "The campaign has stagnated. Your continuing negativity is dragging us down." Ruth was forced out by Thanksgiving.

Over the next year, the financial fortunes of Florence Bruce declined into the red as the capital campaign grew moribund and bills for new construction came due. Sanford Hall was dedicated in the fall, but financing the construction with bank loans only postponed the inevitable. Nancy, whose job it was to maintain solvency, tried aggressively to reign in costs. With little support, her assertive cost-cutting incurred the wrath of the same faculty members who had chafed at Tom's incursions into their domain. By the end of the year, Nancy, too, was asked to leave. The handwriting was on the wall, and two teachers of exceptional ability departed for cleaner chalkboards.

Another year passed and the trustees were appalled to discover enrollment at an all-time low, with only nine students entering the

[2] Archie and I were termed off the board at the same time, one year after Tom's departure. My work soon carried me to another state, although I remained in touch with many of my Florence Bruce colleagues while working on this book.

ninth grade. Still they shouldered on, dipping into the endowment to cover operating costs and making excuses to parents who expected more from an institution into which they paid so much.

Healing, when it eventually comes to Florence Bruce, will take place on two levels. One is personal. Those who were appalled by what happened will have to regain their trust in the institution that so unceremoniously ousted one of their own and come to an understanding that what was done to Tom and Allison is now a part of history rather than of the present. They will have to learn to carry themselves again with dignity and without fear and to make choices as people of conscience and good will, regardless of the possibility of retribution.

The other is systemic or institutional healing. There are people at Florence Bruce who have very different views as to what the process of Tom's dismissal meant. These differing views, which float just beneath the surface of the school's daily life, accompany an underlying tension as people chat with each other in the halls or sit together in deliberative meetings and chart a future course for the school. The elephant in the living room is huge and remains, so far, unacknowledged.

Perhaps this manuscript will help the healing at both levels. For those caught around the periphery of events at Florence Bruce, the truth remains elusive. Fitting the bits and pieces of that experience into a larger context may guide the willing explorer to that missing truth and might even illuminate the elephant *behind the hedge*.